DOCTOR WHO CLASSICS

Two timeless adventures featuring the third Doctor.

THE DAEMONS

When plans are revealed to open up the prehistoric barrow at Devil's End the Doctor (Jon Pertwee) and the local white witch become concerned. In fact the only person who wants the dig to go ahead is the new vicar – but is he really who he says he is?

First broadcast on BBC Television: 22 May – 19 June 1971
Director: Christopher Barry
Producer: Barry Letts

THE TIME MONSTER

To stop the Master harnessing the power of the Chronivore, the Doctor and Jo travel back in time to Atlantis to a terrifying confrontation with the Time Vortex...

First broadcast on BBC Television: 20 May – 24 June 1972
Director: Paul Bernard
Producer: Barry Letts

GW00503729

DOCTOR WHO
CLASSICS

The Daemons

The Time Monster

Based on the BBC television serials by Robert Bank Stewart and Robert Holmes by arrangement with BBC Books, a division of BBC Enterprises Ltd

---

Barry Letts

Terrance Dicks

A STAR BOOK
published by
the Paperback Division of
W.H. ALLEN & Co. Plc

A Star Book
Published in 1989
by the Paperback Division of
W.H. Allen & Co. Plc
Sekforde House, 175/9 St John Street,
London EC1V 4LL

The Daemons novelisation copyright © Barry Letts 1974
Original script copyright © Guy Leopold 1971

The Time Monster novelisation copyright © Terrance Dicks 1985
Original script copyright © Robert Sloman 1972

'Doctor Who' series copyright © British Broadcasting Corporation
1971, 1972, 1974, 1985

This dual edition published 1989

Printed in Great Britain

ISBN 0 352 32382 5

This book is sold subject to the condition that
it shall not, by way of trade or otherwise,
be lent, re-sold, hired out or otherwise circulated
without the publisher's prior consent in
any form of binding or cover other than that in
which it is published and without a similar
condition including this condition being imposed
on the subsequent purchaser.

CONTENTS

Prologue

Thunder rumbled ominously; fitful lightning mocked the darkness of the green with a sudden day; a few threatening drops of rain splashed heavily on the cobbled road . . .

'G'night, Josh.'

' 'Night, Pete. 'Night, Tom.'

Old Josh Wilkins turned reluctantly away from the friendly light of the pub and set off across the green.

'What's the matter with the dratted dog . . . ? pulling fit to choke hisself. Wants to get home, I reckon. Don't blame him; we're in for a soaker. Better cut through church-yard . . .'

Josh shivered, turned up the collar of his jacket and plodded on.

All at once, the sky split open with a crack that jolted Josh's old heart, and the rain came. In a moment he was wet to the skin.

'Hey! Come back, Dan, you great fool!'

The dog, yelping hysterically, had pulled the lead from his master's hand and dashed through the churchyard gate. Cursing under his breath, Josh stumbled after him.

Suddenly the barking became a howl like a scream of fear. A high-pitched chattering noise cut through the hiss of the rain.

Josh stopped, irrational terror clutching at his throat. But the dog was silent. He had to know.

Fearfully, he rounded the corner of the church and saw Dan, still and lifeless; and, crouching menacingly above the poor thin body, there was . . .

Josh struggled to run, to scream, to fight the roaring in his ears and the agony in his chest. He pitched forward on his face.

There was a rustling in the undergrowth. The 'thing'

was gone. But Josh just lay there, quietly, one arm lying protectively across the drenched fur of the dead animal . . .

    .   .   .   .   .

'He died of fright, Doctor. I don't care what you say . . . the man simply died of fright.'

Doctor Reeves sighed. 'My dear Miss Hawthorne, the medical diagnosis is quite clear. He died of a heart attack.'

The morning sunshine flashed on Miss Hawthorne's indignant *pince-nez*. 'But his face . . . !' she exclaimed.

'An expression like that is quite common in cases of heart failure. Now, if you'll excuse me . . .'

The doctor walked across to his car. Miss Hawthorne, clutching desperately at the folkweave cloak slipping from her shoulders, scuttled after him.

'The signs are there for all to see, Doctor. I cast the runes only this morning.'

The doctor frowned irritably. 'Superstitious nonsense!' he snapped. 'I'm sorry—I have my rounds to do.'

With an exasperated crunching of the gears the doctor's ancient car rumbled away. Miss Hawthorne took a few frustrated steps forward, raising her voice as the doctor receded . . .

'If Professor Horner opens that barrow, he'll bring disaster on us all. I'm warning you! This is just the beginning!'

I

The White Witch

Doctor Who was a happy man : the birds were singing a spring song, the sun was gleaming on Bessie's new coat of daffodil paint and there was a pleasant tang of engine oil in the air ...

'Doctor ! You haven't been listening !'

The Doctor looked up from the open bonnet of his beloved old car. 'Oh yes I have,' he said, smiling at the indignation in Jo Grant's face. 'You were talking about this new pop group who wear vine leaves in their hair.'

'That was ages ago ! I mean, simply *centuries*. I've been going on about that TV programme. What do you think'll happen?'

'Happen? When?' The Doctor wandered over to the bench and picked up a fearsome-looking monkey-wrench. Jo followed him.

'Tonight, of course . . . when Professor Horner opens up that burial mound. I mean, what with the ancient curse and all.'

'Oh, Jo,' sighed the Doctor patiently. 'You don't really believe in all that nonsense, do you?'

'Of course I do,' she replied. 'There's been a lot of it about lately.'

'You make it sound like the measles,' commented the Doctor, returning to his car.

'But it really *is* the dawning of the Age of Aquarius just about now. Astrologically, like in the song. And that means the occult . . . you know, the supernatural and all the magic bit.'

The Doctor smiled to himself somewhat ruefully. He was obviously wasting his time trying to turn Jo into a scientist. He gave the wrench a final tug and stood up. Jo frowned.

'But how do you *know* there's nothing in it?'

The Doctor started to fasten down Bessie's bonnet. 'How? I just know, that's all. Everything that happens must have a scientific explanation, if you only know where to look for it. Excuse me, my dear.'

Jo moved thoughtfully away from the bench. The Doctor picked up a little black box, looking like a transistor radio, and started to work on it.

'Yes, but ...'

The Doctor grinned at her. Jo never gave in easily!

'Suppose . . . suppose something happens and nobody *knows* the explanation . . . nobody in the world . . . in the *Universe*! That'd be magic wouldn't it?'

This time the Doctor laughed out loud. 'Really, Jo,' he said, 'for a reasonably intelligent young lady, you have the most absurd ideas. In the first place ...'

But Jo wasn't listening. Her eyebrows had shot up and she was gasping feebly, 'Doctor! Look!'

The Doctor looked up from his work. His old yellow car was quietly driving herself out of the open doors of the UNIT workshop into the car-park outside.

'There's nobody driving her!' said Jo.

Bessie continued serenely on her way. The Doctor eyed her sternly.

'Bessie! What are you up to? Come back here at once.'

The little car flashed her lights rebelliously and executed a tight clockwise circle.

'Do as I say, now. This minute!'

Bessie stopped. She revved her motor a couple of times, as if tempted to take off into the distant countryside.

'I shan't tell you again.'

Slowly, reluctantly, she rolled towards the workshop and stopped by the Doctor and Jo, whose eyes by now were popping out of her head. The Doctor wagged a finger at the errant Bessie.

'You're a very naughty girl. How dare you go gallivanting around like that?'

Bessie honked her horn a little aggresively.

'Are you sorry?'

'Honk, honk.'

'Very well then, I'll forgive you this time. Now, go back to your parking place, before I change my mind.'

Under the astonished gaze of poor Jo, Bessie backed away and sedately settled herself into her accustomed place, giving one last self-satisfied honk of her horn.

The silence was broken by a male voice.

'I know there's a good explanation for all this but I just can't think of it for the minute.'

The Doctor looked round. During Bessie's little dance, Captain Yates had appeared from the little office at the back of the workshop. The Doctor looked at him quizzically.

'Would you believe in magic?' Jo asked Captain Yates at the same time casting an infuriated glance at the Doctor.

'No, of course not,' said Mike.

'Jo would,' the Doctor said provocatively.

'That's not fair,' burst out Jo. 'It must have been you doing it. Some sort of remote control, I suppose.'

The Doctor solemnly held up his little black box and pressed a button on it.

'Honk honk,' said Bessie from the other side of the car-park.

'You see how easy it is to be a magician?' said the Doctor. 'Would you like to see some more?'

'No thanks. I've had enough of your childish tricks,' Jo said severely, 'I want to see that programme. Would you give me a lift back to H.Q., Mike?'

And off she marched. The Doctor looked at Mike and winked. Mike grinned and started to follow her. At the door, he turned back.

'Are you coming, Doctor?'

'Coming where?'

'To see that TV programme.'

The Doctor groaned. 'Not you, too, Captain Yates!'

'Wouldn't miss it for the world,' answered Mike cheerfully. 'Should be fascinating. Forecasts of doom and disaster and all that. After all, it has a funny reputation, Devil's End . . . you know, the village near the dig. I remember reading . . . I say, Doctor, are you feeling all right?'

The Doctor didn't even hear him. He was too concerned with the large disturbing bell sounding in his mind. Devil's End? Where *had* he heard the name before? Oh, this wretched memory of his! Devil's End . . . The Doctor shuddered. It had an evil ring to it.

'Doctor?'

The Doctor came to himself with a start. Mike Yates was peering at him anxiously.

'Are you sure you're all right?'

'Of course, of course,' replied the Doctor absently.

Suddenly he leaped into action, seizing his cloak and making for the door. 'Come on then,' he said urgently.

'Where to?'

'To see that TV programme, of course!'

.   .   .   .   .

High on the ridge known to the village of Devil's End as the Goat's Back is the strange mound that everyone calls the Devil's Hump. It is a bleak place. Even in the bright sunshine of a spring day a cutting wind slices through the silence. Apart from the thin cry of a lonely curlew, no birds sing there.

But today, the usual emptiness was alive with the bustling of some thirty human beings all intent on setting up a television Outside Broadcast. Thick electric cables leading from the cameras and the immense lights formed a web to trap the unwary foot. Little figures darted to and fro, dwarfed by the immensity of the Wiltshire sky, and trucks the size of removing vans littered the grass like abandoned toys.

The tension in the air, like the spiky heaviness of the atmosphere before a thunderstorm, was nowhere more evident than in the immediate neighbourhood of Alastair Fergus, the well-known Television Personality.

'Professor Horner! Professor Horner!' Fergus looked wildly round. Where had the old fool got to, for Pete's sake? 'Harry! Where's the Professor? He's up and vanished from the face of the earth. One minute he was here and . . .' Harry, the floor manager, moved into action with all the smoothness of the professional calmer of nerves.

'Not to worry, not to worry, Alastair. He's probably in make-up, unless he's had second thoughts and scarpered.'

'What?'

'Well, you know the local chat. Death and disaster if he opens the barrow.'

Fergus's voice grew shrill. 'There'll be a disaster if he doesn't get a shift on; he's supposed to be on the air in three-and-a-half minutes.'

'Not quite, old son,' replied the imperturbable Harry, 'we've the cavern bit to go out first.'

Alastair Fergus shuddered dramatically. 'Don't remind me. I'm trying to put that dreadful place out of my mind. But *right* out of it!'

That very morning he had recorded the opening of the programme right inside the notorious Witches' Cavern of Devil's End. According to local legend—and who would dare suggest the legend was a lie—this curious place, half natural, half hewn from the bedrock of England by pre-historic man, had been a centre of mystery and evil since the beginning of humanity.

Here pagan man performed his rites of human sacrifice, here the druids met to conjure up their secret power, here the covens of the seventeenth century hid from the fires of Matthew Hopkins, witch hunter; here the third Lord Aldbourne used to play at his eighteenth century parody of the more unspeakable rituals of black magic . . .

.   .   .   .   .   .

Jo Grant hurried into the Duty Office of UNIT H.Q. 'Am I in time?' she gasped.

Sergeant Benton didn't need to ask her what she meant. 'He's just showing us the Witches' Cavern, Miss,' he said.

'Ooh, isn't it creepy. I mean, like spooky!' she said. 'I went there once. In the summer you can actually go in. Through the vestry.'

Mike Yates had followed her in, accompanied by the Doctor. 'The vestry? What on earth are you talking about?' said Mike.

'The church of course. It's built right on top of the cavern. How about that?'

'A perfect symbol, Jo,' the Doctor said shortly. 'Now, be quiet, both of you. I want to listen. Look, there's the archaeological dig . . .'

Jo pulled a rueful face at the grinning Mike and turned towards the TV screen where Alastair Fergus, all traces of petulance quite hidden, charmingly wooed the affection of the Great British Public.

'. . . Professor Horner and his gallant little team have cut their way into the Devil's Hump as if it were a giant pie. But now the question is, can Professor Horner pull out his plum?'

Alastair Fergus's appropriately fruity laugh was abruptly interrupted by a loud Yorkshire voice—the voice of the, as yet unseen, Professor.

'Get on with it, man!' the voice said.

Fergus got on with it. He talked of the previous attempts to open the Devil's Hump: from the first in 1793, when Sir Percival Flint's miners ran back to Cornwall leaving him for dead—right through to the famous Cambridge University fiasco of 1959. Always, the Devil's Hump had remained an enigma.

'But tonight, the enigma will be solved! Tonight, at midnight, the witching hour, the viewers of the B.B.C. will have the privilege of being present when Professor Gilbert Horner, the noted archaeologist . . .'

Again he was interrupted. The burly figure of Professor Horner lumbered into the picture. 'Got round to me at last, have you? About time too! Hey, you there with the camera —bring it over here! Come on!' And off he stumped into the hole cut into the great mound behind him, followed by the camera and the feebly expostulating Alastair Fergus.

Professor Horner was always a great favourite with a television audience : guaranteed never to stick to the script, guaranteed to speak his mind and call a spade a spade, guaranteed to lose his temper with fools and generally make himself unpleasant—he was of course universally loved. To see him disconcert the other great favourite, the oh-so-smooth Alastair Fergus himself, was a treat rare in the annals of broadcasting.

Struggling gamely to regain the initiative, Alastair stumbled down the muddy tunnel, talking hard. 'I'm sure the viewers will be fascinated, Professor. What exactly are you going to . . .'

Professor Horner reached the end of the tunnels and pointed firmly at an unappetising clod of earth. 'There That's the spot. Six inches behind that lies the biggest archaeological find this country has known since Sutton Hoo.'

Alastair Fergus struggled into range of the camera, muddy and irritable. 'Sutton Hoo. Ah yes. Would you like to explain that reference, Professor.'

'No, I wouldn't.'

Alastair wouldn't give in. 'Sutton Hoo was, of course, the place where the greatest archaeological . . .'

'Never mind about Sutton Hoo, lad. This is what your precious viewers are interested in . . . the Devil's Hump and what's inside it. Right?'

Back in the Duty Office, the Doctor leaned forward intensely. Alastair Fergus rallied. 'And what *is* inside it?'

'Treasure, that's what. The tomb of a great warrior chieftain, 800 B.C.'

'No, no, no . . .' murmured the Doctor.

Jo glanced at him. His face was as desperately concerned as ever she had seen it. 'Doctor . . . what's wrong?'

The Doctor shook his head and nodded towards the screen.

Jo turned back to watch.

'And why tonight, Professor? I mean, why open the barrow this night in particular? And why at midnight?'

The Professor growled. Several million viewers sat up,

eager for the edged retort, the quick insult, the snap of teeth in poor Alastair's soft white hide. 'I should have thought that that would have been obvious to the meanest mind. Seems I was wrong.'

Several million sighs of satisfaction.

'April 30th,' the Professor continued, 'Beltane, isn't it?'

Alastair took a deep gulp of much-needed air. 'Beltane?'

'The good Lord preserve me from overpaid incompetent nincompoops! You ought to do your homework before you—'

Alastair Fergus's indignation was great. He dared to interrupt. 'I know, Professor Horner . . . and *you* know . . . but perhaps some of our viewers might like to know as well. What is Beltane? Please!'

For once in his lifetime the Professor was taken aback. 'Ah . . . yes . . . I see . . . Beltane,' he said, 'greatest occult festival of the year, bar Hallowe'en.'

The Doctor jumped to his feet. 'Beltane, of course!'

Jo looked at him, amazed. 'But, Doctor! I thought you said you don't believe in all that.'

Once again the Doctor hushed her.

A deep growling roar came from the TV set. The Professor was laughing. 'Ghosts? Witches? Demons? Of course I don't believe in 'em, lad. It's just that my new book comes out tomorrow!'

Alastair's tone was acid. 'So it's what you might call a publicity stunt?'

'Top of the class, lad!' said Professor Horner approvingly.

The Doctor growled. 'Most implausible,' he commented. 'His mind's being manipulated.'

'Whose mind?' asked Jo. 'That creep of an interviewer's?'

'No, no,' replied the Doctor. 'The Professor's mind. There's something dreadfully wrong.'

'What could be wrong?'

'I don't know.' The Doctor walked over to the window and stared at the blossom on the apple trees in the garden. 'Aquarius . . . Devil's End . . . Beltane . . .' he muttered to himself. 'Come on, come on. Think!'

His reveries were broken by Sergeant Benton. 'Hey look, Doctor. Something going on ...'

Something indeed *was* going on. In full view of the television cameras, a Fury in homeweave cloak, good strong brogues and *pince-nez* was beating Harry the floor manager about the head and body with an old green umbrella. Miss Hawthorne had arrived.

'Now come on, love,' he exclaimed, dodging a fresh onslaught, 'be a good girl and buzz off ... ouch!'

He was saved from further damage by the advent of Alastair Fergus from the barrow. 'It's okay, Harry,' called Alastair as the Professor also emerged.

Miss Hawthorne pulled her arm free and marched across to them. 'I have come here to protest!' she announced grimly. 'And protest I shall.' The Professor mumbled ominously.

Alastair turned and spoke into the camera. 'This is Miss Olive Hawthorne, a prominent local resident who is very much opposed to the dig. Professor Horner. I believe you two have already met?'

The Professor erupted. 'Met? I'll say we've met. The daft woman's been pestering me for weeks.'

Miss Hawthorne's *pince-nez* flashed dangerously in the cold sunlight. 'I've merely been trying to make you see reason. I was obviously wasting my time. You are a dunderhead, sir!'

Viewers with colour television were fascinated to see Professor Horner turn a novel shade of purple as he struggled to find a suitable reply. Hastily, Alastair intervened. 'Miss Hawthorne, will you tell the viewers *why* you are so against this excavation?'

Miss Hawthorne looked straight into the camera. 'Because this man is tampering with forces he does *not* understand.'

A movement made Jo look round. Without knowing it, the Doctor was nodding his head in vigorous agreement.

The Professor regained his speech. 'Poppycock!' he exploded.

Miss Hawthorne turned on him. 'You will bring disaster upon yourself and upon the whole area if you persist!'

'Balderdash!'

'Death and destruction await you. Believe me, I know.'

Once more Alastair Fergus jumped in. 'Ah, but that's just it, you see. Why should we believe you and how do you know?'

His charming smile froze as Miss Hawthorne turned a piercing eye on him. 'Because,' she said, 'I am a witch.'

The Professor's anger suddenly subsided. He grinned almost in triumph. 'You see?' he said, 'I told you she was daft.'

'I tell you, I'm a witch. A white witch, of course. And that's why you should listen to me. I *know*.'

With a sense of overwhelming relief, Alastair Fergus caught sight of Harry waving his arm in a circle, giving a 'wind-up' signal. 'Well, thank you very much, Miss Hawthorne, for a most interesting...'

But Miss Hawthorne was by no means ready to 'wind-up'. 'I have cast the runes,' she announced dramatically. 'I have consulted the talisman of Mercury; it is written in the stars : when Beltane is come, tread softly, for lo, the Prince himself is nigh.'

'You see,' said the Professor. 'Mad as a hatter!'

'The Prince?' enquired Alastair nervously.

'The Prince of Evil,' declaimed Miss Hawthorne. 'The Dark One; the Horned Beast...'

All at once, the Doctor tore his eyes from the screen as if forcing himself to awaken from a hideous nightmare. Turning on his heel, he strode to the door. 'Come on, Jo,' he said, urgently.

'Where to?' she asked, scrambling to her feet.

'Devil's End, of course. The woman's quite right. We must stop that lunatic before it's too late...'

2

The New Vicar

Montmorency Vere de Vere Winstanley—Monty to his friends in the 'county' and addressed as 'Squire' by Devil's End—leaned forward, turned off his television and chuckled. Good for Miss Hawthorne! She had kept her end up well. Wretched London chappies taking over the place. You'd think they owned it.

He tapped out his pipe and rose ponderously to his feet. Hastily averting his eyes from his too plump reflection in the doors of the Chippendale glass cabinet, he looked round for his favourite red setter.

'Hereward! Hereward!' The dog came bounding in, eager for his usual evening walk. Confound the creature! How did it manage to keep so thin? Always stuffin' itself, wasn't it?

The drive of End House, some half a mile long, was lined by rhododendron bushes. In the season people would come from hundreds of miles to see the Winstanley rhododendrons, and the Winstanley lawns, and the Winstanley roses and ... 'Evening, Squire.'

'Heavens above, never noticed you, Bates. Everything under control?'

'Yessir, apart from a touch of blackfly. Soon put paid to 'un, though.'

Bates, latest in the long line of Bateses, gardeners to the Winstanleys since the days of good Queen Anne, touched his hat as the Squire rolled away down the immaculate gravel of the drive. Feudalism died hard in Devil's End.

'Oh ... Squire, sir.'

The Squire turned back. Bates' mahogany face was troubled.

'The missus. She's worried, like. Asked me to speak to you ...'

'Well?'

'It's her hens, you see. Haven't laid a single egg for nigh on a fortnight.'

'Go on.'

Bates shuffled slightly, obviously embarrassed. 'That's it, sir.'

Winstanley looked at him in some perplexity. Not like Bates to be so roundabout in his manner. 'I don't understand, Bates. How can I help?'

Bates took off his hat and carefully brushed some invisible dust from its mud-caked crown. 'Well you see, sir . . . she says . . it's a lot of nonsense, and I . . . well, *she* says they've been bewitched, like!'

'Ah. I see. Bewitched, eh?'

'Yessir.'

The Squire puffed at his old briar for a few seconds. 'Be that as it may . . . what can I do about it?'

'Well, you see, Squire, we was thinking . . . that is, *she* was . . . well, you might have a word with Vicar, like. He'd listen to you, sir.'

The Squire grunted. 'Doubt it. Doubt it very much. Sensible fellow, this new chap. Can't see him worrying about a few fowls. Still, could mention it in passing, I suppose.'

'If you'd be so good, sir. Elsie, you see . . . she does carry on so. If I could say I'd spoken to you . . .'

'Of course, of course, leave it to me . . .'

Bates replaced his ancient hat and vanished into the shrubbery, lifting a respectful forefinger to Squire Winstanley's retreating back.

'Hereward! Heel, sir!' The Squire automatically fell into his accustomed routine as he stepped through his front gate. But his heart wasn't in it. Hens not laying, for Heaven's sake! Always happening. Fox about, probably. Must have a word with the hunt.

Still, Elsie Bates was no fool. If she thought they were bewitched . . . no, no, no, a lot of nonsense. Like those ridiculous rumours put about by Miss Hawthorne after poor old Josh dropped dead in the churchyard . . .

. . . And the rotund figure of the Squire of Devil's End

progressed in stately fashion down the hill to the village, the gun-dog at his heel. Nobody could have guessed that his heart had been gripped by a sudden fear that had almost stopped the breath in his throat.

.　　.　　.　　.　　.

Down the steep track leading from the Goat's Back flew a strange figure, cloak fluttering behind like the wings of a giant moth, and uttering occasional weird cries such as 'Ha!' or 'Fool, fool, fool!' Miss Hawthorne on her bicycle. Swooping through the spinney at the corner of Longbottom farm and out into Shady Lane, she narrowly avoided the Ransomes' ginger cat and never even noticed—this being most odd as Marmalade was a personal friend—so exhilarated was she still by her righteous anger at that idiot Horner.

'My giddy godfathers, but I told him!' she thought to herself, starting to pedal as the road turned itself upside down and she faced the long pull up Box Hill. 'He won't forget little Olive Hawthorne in a hurry . . .'

Slower and slower went the bicycle as Miss Hawthorne's spirit slowly sank back to earth. What good had she done after all? He was still going ahead. Devil's End still faced the ancient curse; the terrible curse which every child in the village could repeat and no adult would dare; the curse whose origin was lost in the morning of time.

As she reached the top of the rise and started to coast downhill past the high stone walls of the Winstanley grounds, Miss Hawthorne's face became grim and determined. Ha! He needn't think he'd won. There was a shot or two in the locker yet, by Jove.

Slowing down and jumping off with a hop-hop-hop— she really must get those brakes fixed—she arrived at her own front gate, wheeled her faithful steed into the front garden and leant it against the ivy-clad wall of her little cottage.

Resisting the temptation to escape into the cool haven behind the lilac front door, there to slake her dusty thirst with camomile tea, she walked out into the roadway again and turned firmly towards the Vicarage.

.   .   .   .   .

Surprised at the change in the usual pattern, Hereward sat down, his tongue lolling, as his master stopped at the edge of the village green.

'Hang on, old son,' said the Squire to himself. 'Better decide what you're going to do.' Straight across to the pub, as usual? Or was it his duty to seek out the Vicar and drop the promised word in his ear? The bar of 'The Cloven Hoof' was certainly very tempting. Ludicrous name for a public house; just cashing in on the superstitions of the locals and the curiosity of the trippers who crowded the village in the summer.

Better see the Vicar first. Only fair to old Bates. Pandering to Elsie's nonsense of course, but still . . .

With the puzzled Hereward at his heel, he set off across the green, past the painted Maypole standing in the middle. Mayday tomorrow! Good Lord, seemed only yesterday since last year's shenanigans. Good thing tradition, of course, but a fearful bore, what with those interminable Morris dancers and all that tripping around the Maypole.

'Have to show my face, I suppose,' he said to himself. '*Noblesse oblige* and all that tosh. Only happens once a year after all . . .'

Suddenly, the same cold fear gripped him once again and he stopped dead, white terror behind his eyes, as he remembered Professor Horner's words '. . . greatest occult festival of the year, bar Hallowe'en.'

With an effort, he pulled himself together and set off again, but now he made straight for the welcome of the bar door.

'Just one, then on to the Vicar. Medicinal purposes; that's what they say, isn't it? Can't think what's the matter with me. Must have been overdoing it . . .'

And in he went, trying not to notice the shaking of his hands or the cold sweat on his brow.

.　　　.　　　.　　　.　　　.

Miss Hawthorne didn't notice the door of 'The Cloven Hoof' closing behind the Squire as she came out onto the green. She was too busy rehearsing to herself the best way to approach the new Vicar, whom she had yet to meet. Unfortunately, he was something of an unknown quantity. If only dear Canon Smallwood were still here . . . strange that he didn't say good-bye to anyone, when he left. No doubt he couldn't face it. Must have been a terrible wrench to have to retire after all those years . . .

As Miss Hawthorne approached the churchyard gate, past the corner by the old smithy with its too bright poster announcing the availability of teas for tourists, Police Constable Groom appeared, his beaming face shining even redder than usual in the light of the setting sun. ' 'Evening, Miss Hawthorne,' he said. 'Saw you on the telly before I came out. Very good you were. Least, that's what I thought. Told them, didn't you?'

Miss Hawthorne's indignation was at once rekindled. 'Ha!' she exclaimed. 'They chopped me! Cut me off! But don't you worry, Constable. I'll get my chance tonight. You'll see.' And off she stalked, leaving the Constable smiling tolerantly after her.

Putting her hand on the gate, she started to push it open. Immediately, almost as if this were a signal, a sudden fierce wind sprang up; a gale; a hurricane; a typhoon—all in the space of a thirty-yard circle. An impossible wind.

Miss Hawthorne rallied at once. Leaning into the blast, her hair and her cloak blowing every which way, she raised her arms on high, and began to chant an Exorcism. 'Avaunt, all ye elementals! Avaunt, all ye powers of ad-adversity . . .'

In the meantime, Police Constable Groom was behaving in a very strange way. Moving as if he were in a trance, he picked up a large stone and started to move forward with the apparent intention of bashing in Miss Hawthorne's skull. She, all unawares, was desperately continuing with her incantation. 'In the name of the Great Mother, I charge thee,' she cried, 'be still and return to thy resting; be at peace in thy sleeping ...'

Police Constable Groom lifted the stone above his head ... a moment later Miss Hawthorne's worries would be over. For ever.

However, at this very moment, her words seemed to take effect, for the wind dropped as suddenly as it had sprung up. The evening air was still once more. The stone dropped from Groom's hand and he swayed on his feet.

'Mr. Groom!' exclaimed Miss Hawthorne as she turned and saw the pallor of his face. 'Mr. Groom! Are you all right?'

The Constable rubbed his forehead. 'I ... I think so ... I just felt a bit faint for the moment ...'

Miss Hawthorne nodded wisely. 'I'm not at all surprised. Not at all. It will pass, Mr. Groom. It will pass.'

Groom essayed a weak smile. 'I'm okay, now,' he said.

Olive Hawthorne looked at him: looked past him and through him. Her eyes were distant, as if she were seeing such things as cannot be spoken—things not of this world. 'We must be on our guard,' she said, 'all of us.' She turned and walked up the path, between the rows of gravestones, and disappeared round a buttress of the church.

. . . . .

In the bar Montmorency Winstanley downed his second Scotch and gratefully accepted the offer of a third. 'Just this one,' he thought, 'and then I'll go off and have a natter with the Vicar. Get him to have a chat with Elsie Bates. Soon set her right.'

All his fears were now forgotten.

. . . . .

Miss Hawthorne came round the back of the church and

was making for the Rectory gate when a sour-faced man appeared in front of her, as if from nowhere.

'What do you want?' he asked aggressively.

Miss Hawthorne, jolted rudely from her reverie, was very angry indeed. 'How dare you jump out at me like that, Garvin,' she said. 'Get out of my way.'

'I said, what do you want?'

'If you must know,' she answered acidly, 'I wish to see Mr. Magister.'

Garvin smiled. 'Well, you can't,' he said. 'What do you want to see him about?'

'I'm hardly likely to discuss my affairs with the verger. Kindly let me pass.' She made to continue on her way but Garvin stepped into her path again. Miss Hawthorne shook with anger. 'You wouldn't dare behave like this if the Vicar were here,' she said.

'Mr. Magister doesn't want to be disturbed. He said so.'

'Not him! The real Vicar!'

Garvin laughed. 'What'd you call Mr. Magister then?'

'I meant Canon Smallwood, our old Vicar, who left in such mysterious circumstances.'

'Nothing mysterious about it. Taken ill and had to retire, that's all.'

Miss Hawthorne was regaining her control. 'In the middle of the night? And where is he now? Why hasn't he been in touch with anyone? Tell me that.'

Garvin grunted. 'I've got no time to listen to your nonsense. I've got work to do.'

Miss Hawthorne stood her ground. 'I repeat. I wish to see Mr. Magister.'

'And I tell you again. He doesn't want to be disturbed.'

'Then he can say so himself. Let me pass, do you hear?' Saying this, she raised her old umbrella, the weapon which had routed Harry that afternoon. Garvin eyed it uncertainly.

'You're wasting your time.'

Miss Hawthorne flourished the brolly. 'If you don't stand aside, Garvin, I shall be forced to use violence!'

'Violence won't be necessary.'

25

The curiously gentle, yet firm voice at once dominated the situation. Miss Hawthorne swung round, momentarily quite discomfited, as if she were abruptly thirty years younger, an eight-year-old surprised in some naughtiness.

'Ah . . . Mr. Magister. Good evening.'

Slim and dapper in his dark suit of clerical grey, the new Vicar was a striking figure. His handsome, yet almost Mephistophelean, face was curiously ageless. True, the neat black beard had streaks of pure white in it, but these seemed merely to offset and emphasise the smooth skin and youthful eyes.

And yet, as Miss Hawthorne gazed, intrigued and fascinated, those eyes seemed to her to become deep pools of unfathomable knowledge; the knowledge of a thousand years or more.

'Good evening. Miss Hawthorne, isn't it? What a very real pleasure to meet at last.'

Olive Hawthorne pulled herself firmly together. This was no time for day-dreaming, nor indeed for social niceties. 'I have to see you most urgently, but this uncouth fellow of yours refuses to let me past him !' she complained.

At once the Reverend Mr. Magister was all apology. Taking her by the arm he led her out of the churchyard and up the path of the Rectory garden, talking, talking, talking, in a ceaseless flow of smooth platitude. Again and again, Miss Hawthorne tried to halt the torrent of words, only to have her interjections swept away downstream and lost in the swirls and eddies of the Vicar's expert small talk.

At length Miss Hawthorne found herself sitting uneasily on the edge of one of the worn leather armchairs in the Vicarage sitting-room, with the Vicar hovering solicitously at her elbow.

'. . . a cup of tea, perhaps?' he was saying, 'I always feel that a good cup of tea can go a long way to solving most of life's little problems . . .'

Suddenly Miss Hawthorne could stand it no longer. 'Stop it !' she cried.

'I beg your pardon?' Mr. Magister seemed genuinely taken aback

'Stop treating me as if I were a village ignoramus! We deal in the real things you and I—life and death; Heaven and Hell—you in your way and I in mine. The forces of evil are abroad tonight. We must be up and doing; we must prepare our defences; we must gird ourselves against the Enemy...'

The Vicar sat down opposite her and leaned forward, clasping his hands together as if about to say a quick prayer. 'I can see that you are most upset. But really, Miss Hawthorne! The forces of evil? What can you mean?'

'Haven't you heard of the Curse of the Devil's End, Mr. Magister? A man assuming such a responsibility as yours, must surely be aware of...'

The Vicar held up a hand.

'One moment,' he said. 'Perhaps I should make my position clear. Of course I've heard talk of these—forgive me—these foolish superstitions. How could I not? This area is plagued by them. But I consider it my responsibility, and indeed my duty, to combat the disease, not to spread it by giving credence to such irrational notions.'

Miss Hawthorne swallowed hard. She must not let herself become angry again. No matter how misguided this man might be, she needed his help and needed it badly.

'I beg you to help me, Mr. Magister,' she said intently. 'Help me to stop that foolhardy man.'

The Vicar looked bewildered. 'Er ... stop whom? From doing what? I don't understand, I'm afraid.'

'Professor Horner, of course. He must *not* enter the tomb, tonight of all nights!'

Mr. Magister's face cleared. 'Of course, of course. Stupid of me. Your battle royal with the worthy Professor. But you know, Miss Hawthorne, I still find it difficult to understand. Even allowing for your ... ah ...' Mr. Magister smiled placatingly, 'your somewhat quaint—dare I say eccentric—ideas, why are you so against this very ordinary archaeological excavation?'

With a great effort Miss Hawthorne held her temper. 'I tell you, Vicar, we're all in mortal danger. Have you no concern for the souls in your care?'

'The "soul" as such, is a very dated idea,' he answered. 'The modern view would tend to see the personality as . . .'

Miss Hawthorne could stand it no longer. Rising to her feet she looked down on the Vicar with the utmost contempt. 'The modern view! Sir, you are a blockhead! I can see that I am wasting my time here!' And she swept to the door, her cloak swirling around her.

'Miss Hawthorne! One moment!'

Even in her rage, Olive Hawthorne responded to the authority in his voice. She stopped and reluctantly turned to face him. 'Well?'

Mr. Magister moved with the smooth elegance of a cat across the threadbare carpet. He looked deep into Miss Hawthorne's troubled eyes. 'You're very distressed, I can see that. But I'm sure you're worrying yourself unduly. Everything will be all right. You must believe me . . . you must believe me . . .'

Once more, Miss Hawthorne found herself caught by his eyes. The extraordinary large pupils, the irises, so dark, so brown as almost to be black and yet flecked with lighter tones of . . . surely not gold?

'You must believe me . . .' the soft voice went on.

This seemed a very reasonable and desirable proposition. Of course she must believe this most excellent man, this man with the eyes of such incredible blue, a blue so dark, midnight blue . . . but weren't they brown just now?

'I . . . I must believe you,' she heard herself murmur—and came to herself with a shock of anger.

'Why should I believe you?' she gasped, her voice trembling. 'A "modern" man are you? A rational man? I'll tell you what you are, sir. You are a fool! If you won't help me to prevent the barrow from being opened tonight, I must find someone who will!'

She turned and left. A moment later came the slam of the front door.

Mr. Magister's face was livid with frustration and thwarted rage. He looked out of the window. Miss Hawthorne was letting herself into the churchyard. Mr. Magister's face twisted. Under his breath he swore in some strange alien tongue. He turned to the door. 'Garvin!' he shouted.

At once the verger was in the room. The Vicar raised his hand and pointed. Miss Hawthorne was on the point of going out of sight.

Garvin smiled, nodded and slipped noiselessly from the room. The Vicar took a deep shuddering breath and followed him out of the house, across the churchyard and around the north-east corner of the church.

.　　.　　.　　.　　.

Squire Winstanley was roaring with laughter.

Bert Walker, the landlord of 'The Cloven Hoof', really was a wag! He was keeping the whole bar in fits.

'Well, I'll tell you, sir,' he went on as he put a replenished glass in front of the Squire, 'when the hens start giving milk and the cows a-laying eggs, that's when I'll believe all this nonsense. Leave all that to the addle-pated tourists.'

A weaselly little man with smudges of oil on his face, looked up from his game of dominoes. 'You'll sing a different song tonight, Bert, if they open up the Hump and Old Nick walks out.'

'Maybe you're right, Tom Wilkins,' Bert replied, grinning. 'Tell you what, though. If the Old 'un does come along, I'll offer him my best room. My bread-and-butter, he is!'

As the bar exploded with laughter once more, Squire Winstanley wiped the tears of mirth from his eyes. His intention of visiting the Vicar had quite gone from his head.

.　　.　　.　　.　　.

Garvin finished tying the unconscious Miss Hawthorne's hands.

'Right,' said the Vicar. 'In here,' and he unlocked the lid of a large carved-oak chest in the corner of the vestry.

The verger picked her up. Her thin, wiry body was surprisingly light. He could feel her bones through the loose weave of her cloak, like the ribs of a dead squirrel.

And Mr. Magister stood back and watched with a smile of satisfaction as Miss Hawthorne was laid gently in the chest onto a fresh white bed of newly-ironed surplices . . .

3
The Opening of the Barrow

It was twilight in Devil's End. All over the village shutters were being fastened and doors, front and back, bolted against the perils of the night. A solitary child, hustled indoors, caught the unspoken terror from her frantic mother, and earned herself a smack by wailing a protest. A foolish old man, awakening from a senile day-dream, hammered on his daughter's door. A brief flash of light as she opened to his voice, then dusk again and the clank of bolts to seal the silence—a silence more intense for the distant howling of a hound, baying the pock-marked face of the full moon rising above the Goat's Back.

Across the churchyard flitted a shadow a little more dense than the shadows of the gravestones in the moonlight. Seeking the sanctuary of the church wall, it paused momentarily as if to make sure it was unobserved and then vanished through the vestry door.

Nervously crossing the darkness to the far side of the room, the figure halted by the low oaken door with the heavy wrought-iron hinges, which led to the steps down into the cavern beneath the church. Flashing a light to find the handle of the door, he revealed a bony unsatisfied face —the face of Wilkins, the player of dominoes in 'The Cloven Hoof'.

Cautiously, he opened the heavy door, its groans echoing round the high vaulted ceiling of the vestry. Step by step he descended to the cavern. At the bottom he paused, stared into the improbable blackness and hissed, 'You there, boy?'

A tremulous whisper came back at once. 'Is that you, Uncle?'

'And who the blazes would it be, you great fool?' said the man in slightly more normal tones, switching on his flashlight and turning it to find his nephew's face, hovering like a death's-head ghost in the gloom of the cavern. 'Why didn't you light the candles, then?' he went on, crossing to the boy.

'I was scared. I thought you'd never come.'

'Nothing to be scared of,' said Wilkins, suppressing the memory of his fearful scuttle across the churchyard. 'Better get on with it, hadn't we?'

Taking out a box of matches, he lit two tapers, handed one of them to the boy, and crossed to the nearest wall where a seven-branched candlestick stood ready in a niche. As he lit the first of the seven black candles, the boy let out a low shuddering moan of fear.

'What is it now?'

'Over there,' the boy breathed. 'Someone . . . some . . . something . . .'

Wilkins turned on his torch once more and approached the vague white shape the boy had indicated. 'Why, it's only old Bok!' he laughed in relief. 'Bok's our friend, ain't you, my beauty', and he affectionately patted on the head the hideous gargoyle-like figure which squatted balefully on its stone pedestal against the far wall.

'I thought . . . I thought I saw it move.' The boy's voice was still a-quiver.

'Yes, well, that'll be enough of your fancy, now, won't it, young Stan? We've come here to do a job. That right?'

Reluctantly, the boy started to light the hundreds of candles which were all round the cave, moving with the slowness of an imperfectly learned ritual. His uncle, more adept with his taper, hurried from alcove to alcove, impatiently urging each wick to take light.

As the flames took hold, the Cavern came alive in all its strange beauty. Flickering shadows animated the carvings on the rock walls, some dating back to Roman times, some more recent, but all depicting the secret ceremonies of the

31

old witch religion, literally thrust into the darkness of the underground by the light of Christianity.

Near the gargoyle figure, a large slab of marble let into the floor was carved and painted with an ancient Cabbalistic Seal of Magic, while in the very centre of the floor stood a large rock, rough hewn into the shape of an altar. On its smooth upper surface were several dark stains, long whispered to be the stains of blood . . .

The candles were all alight and Tom Wilkins stood by the steps and surveyed the result. 'Why it's . . . it's beautiful,' he murmured.

'I don't like it, Uncle,' whispered Stan. 'Let's get out of here.'

'I'll be wishing I hadn't suggested you to join us,' his uncle snapped. 'All right, get along home. But don't be late for the ceremony tonight.'

Stan gratefully slipped away. Wilkins took one last look. His eye lighted on the marks on the Stone of Sacrifice. A shiver ran down his spine, but whether it was a shiver of excitement, of anticipation, or a shiver of fear, he could not tell.

'I need a drink,' he said to himself and went, leaving the Cavern once more silent and still, contemplating its own evil beauty.

．　　　．　　　．　　　．

'I told you, love, I can't—I'm on duty . . . any other night . . . well, I know that . . . just because, that's all. Sergeant Feather had a sudden attack of . . . Mavis?'

Sergeant Benton carefully replaced the telephone on its cradle. He looked up glumly at Captain Yates who was sitting in the corner of the UNIT Duty Office with his feet on the desk, doing *The Times* crossword. 'Rung off,' said Sergeant Benton.

'Girl trouble?' asked Mike.

'Tonight's the knockout for the Southern Area Championship. Mavis and me, we'd entered together.'

Mike Yates looked up from his paper. 'What championships are those?'

'Ballroom dancing, sir.'

Yates hastily turned his attention back to the puzzle. The thought of the burly sergeant in white tie and tails doing an intricate twinkle-toe quickstep was nearly too much for him.

'She's been sewing those blooming sequins on her dress for over three months. Three thousand, four hundred and seventy-two of them.'

The door opened and Benton leaped to his feet.

'At ease, Sergeant,' said Brigadier Lethbridge Stewart, strolling in immaculate in full regimental Highland Dress. 'Everything in order, Captain Yates?'

Yates was also standing. 'Yes sir. No problems.'

'Right then, I'm off to this wretched dinner.'

'Reunion, is it, sir?'

'In a way. All the old codgers crawling back out of the woodwork and filling their bellies at the regiment's expense. A bore.'

'Good food though, sir?'

'Mm. Regiment rather prides itself on setting a good table . . .'

'Dancing, I suppose, sir,' said Benton.

'Heaven help us, yes,' replied the Brigadier. 'The wives expect it. Well, you know where to reach me if anything crops up.' The Brigadier turned and left. The unaccustomed aroma of an expensive after-shave lotion lingered in the air.

Mike Yates picked up his paper and sighed.

'All right for some, isn't it, sir?' grumbled Benton. 'The Brigadier tripping the light fantastic with the Colonel's lady. Doctor and Miss Grant swanning down to the country, and here we are, stuck with the telly and a plate of corned beef sandwiches . . .'

．　　　　．　　　　．　　　　．　　　　．

'Can't we have the hood up?' asked Jo Grant, shrinking into her anorak for protection against the drizzle.

'It's only a shower,' replied the Doctor. 'It'll stop in a minute.'

Jo huddled gloomily down into her seat. Bessie was definitely a fair weather car. 'Just think, Mike and Sergeant Benton are all cosy and warm in the Duty Office. Probably having a cup of coffee—and a sandwich.'

The Doctor ignored the hint.

'I never thought it would take so long,' she went on.

'We should be nearly there,' rejoined the Doctor, skilfully zig-zagging through a series of double bends at a speed which would have put any ordinary car into the ditch.

Jo switched on a minute torch and peered at the swaying map. 'We'll be coming to a crossroads soon and that's the turn to the village. I should slow down a bit, if I were you, Doctor.'

'No time to be lost,' he retorted, as Bessie hurtled round another bend in the road, with Jo hanging on for all she was worth, and inwardly congratulating herself for having put on her safety-belt.

About half a mile ahead lay the crossroads. On a grassy island in the middle stood a signpost. 'Devil's End' it announced, pointing dumbly to the right. The sound of the Doctor's approach disturbed the tranquillity of the twilight.

Suddenly there was a fierce gust of wind, a wind as uncanny as the one which had assaulted P.C. Groom's placid mind. It was almost as odd in its effect, too. The signpost shivered, almost as if it had begun to come alive, and slowly turned, until its lone finger was pointing in diametrically the opposite direction. Its purpose apparently achieved, the wind died, just as Bessie came into view.

'There it is,' cried Jo. The Doctor abruptly slowed down. 'To the left. That's funny. Looks on the map as if we ought to go to the right.'

'You probably had the map upside down,' said the Doctor, swinging the wheel and shooting the car up the side road.

'Cheek,' said Jo and disappeared inside her anorak hood.

.　　.　　.　　.　　.

'Here, at the Devil's Hump, the stage is set . . . no, no . . . here at the dig, the tension is intense. No, no, no. Can't say "the tension is intense". . . sounds dreadful.'

Alastair Fergus, systematically chewing the nail of his left middle finger down to the quick, was pacing up and down the springy turf outside the entrance to the barrow rehearsing his opening remarks in a low and agitated mutter. Some little way away, Professor Horner watched him cynically while noisily sipping tea from a large enamel mug.

'Good evening, ladies and gentlemen, here we are again . . . ! Huh ! Sounds like a circus . . .'

Harry, doing the rounds, checking on the cameras, the lights and the hundred and one other things that had to be ready, arrived at Alastair. 'You all right, then?' he asked briskly.

Alastair was exasperated. 'Of course I am ! Why shouldn't I be all right, for Pete's sake? Of all the stupid questions . . .'

Harry, well accustomed to the varied symptoms of pre-performance nerves, grinned amiably. 'Well, I only asked,' he said.

Fergus grunted and wandered off into the night, fever-ishly muttering to himself.

Harry moved on.

'Everything okay, Professor? Won't be long now.'

Professor Horner looked up from his mug. 'Any sign of that fool woman?'

'Not so far.'

'Well, keep her out of my hair. I tell you, lad, I'll do her a mischief.'

'I'll do my best,' replied Harry. 'Now, you've got every-thing straight? We start with the intro from Alastair, then I'll give you a cue to launch into your spiel.'

'Spiel?'

'You know, the chat bit. Momentous occasion and all. And then comes the big moment . . .'

'Oh aye,' growled the Professor.

'If you could manage to break into the burial chamber just as the first stroke of midnight sounds on the church clock, that would be absolutely super.'

The Professor regarded Harry for a moment from under his heavy eyelids. 'Righto, lad,' he said, 'I'll do my best to be absolutely super.'

Harry laughed and said, perhaps half-seriously, 'Look, Professor, what if something does happen?'

'Like?'

'Like a personal appearance of you know who.'

The Professor smiled maliciously. 'Use your initiative, lad. Get your chatty friend over there to interview him!'

*　　　*　　　*　　　*　　　*

Bessie's speed was now considerably less. The road had quickly become a lane and by now was little more than a cart track.

'This can't be right,' said the Doctor, changing gear yet again.

'You saw the sign. Oops!' said Jo as the car went over a particularly deep pot-hole.

'Maybe the sign was wrong.'

'And maybe I didn't have the map upside down. Oh well, at least it's stopped raining.'

Bessie ground to a sticky halt.

'What now?' groaned Jo.

'At a glance,' responded the Doctor. 'We appear to be stuck in the mud. Have a look at that map, Jo, and see if you can see a ploughed field. We're apparently in the middle of one . . . !'

*　　　*　　　*　　　*

The camera crew were quietly laying bets on the outcome

of the evening. Ted, on Number One Camera, was sceptical. 'Hundred to one on nothing being there at all,' he said, looking up into his viewfinder, where Alastair Fergus could be seen, a charming smile glazed onto his face, waiting for his cue to start the programme.

Suddenly a shout from Harry : 'Right, quiet please ! Lots of lovely hush. QU-I-ET !'

A moment of dead silence. Alastair glanced at his reflection in the camera lens, licked a finger, and smoothed his eyebrows into a yet more perfect shape.

'Stand by,' went on Harry, listening hard to the instructions coming through his earphones. 'On the Studio announcement now . . .' He raised his hand.

Alastair Fergus licked his lips, watching from the corner of his eye. The hand dropped and he slid smoothly into action. 'Here, at the Devil's Hump, the excitement is intense. The stage is set. What shall we see when the curtain rises?'

The momentous broadcast had begun.

.   .   .   .

Tom Wilkins was feeling a lot better with a couple of pints inside him. He glanced at his watch. Better get down there. Already he was cutting it a bit fine. Trouble was, an exit now might be a bit obvious with the bar so quiet, watching the TV programme.

At that moment a diversion was provided. The door crashed open and in came a tall man with a shock of near-white hair and a cloak, followed by a girl.

'Sorry, sir,' said Bert, 'it's long after time.' After all, though everyone knew that old Percy Groom was safely out of harm's way up the Goat's Back, a licence was a licence, and this was a stranger, a foreigner.

'We don't want a drink,' said the Doctor. 'Will you please direct us to the Devil's Hump?'

'Where the dig is,' explained Jo.

'No need to go all the way up there,' said Bert. 'You can see it on the telly,' and he gestured to the set on the bar, where Alastair could be seen in full flow telling yet again the history of the Devil's Hump.

'It's extremely urgent,' said the Doctor.

'Always in a hurry you townsfolk. All be the same in a hundred years, sir,' said Bert placidly.

'I can assure you, it will be no such thing,' replied the Doctor, becoming more and more irritated.

A round figure detached itself from the group around the bar and swayed over to the Doctor and Jo. It was Squire Winstanley.

'You one of these television chaps, then?' he asked.

'I am no sort of "chap", sir,' snapped the Doctor.

'Oh. Forgive me,' the Squire answered. 'I thought that . . . well . . . the costume, y'know . . . and the wig . . .'

Jo, seeing that the Doctor was about to explode, hastily stepped in. 'Now, Doctor . . . !'

But in her turn she was interrupted by Tom Wilkins. 'What do you want to go up to the Hump for, then?'

'There's no time for all these questions. I simply want to know the way.'

'All the time in the world, sir,' said Bert, leaning on the bar as if ready to listen all night.

'Oh, very well,' retorted the Doctor. 'I intend to stop that maniac Professor before he brings devastation upon you all.'

The statement was met by a general groan of disbelief. Wilkins turned on his heel and walked out of the bar.

The Doctor was by now very angry indeed. 'Is nobody here capable of answering a simple enquiry?' he said, fiercely. 'What on earth's the matter with you all?'

Jo again spoke up. 'Please can someone tell us the way? Please?'

Winstanley beamed at her. 'Of course, my dear. Turn right outside, past the church, over Box Hill, turn into Shady Lane about a half mile on and straight up the rise onto the Goat's Back. Can't miss it.'

'Oh. Thank you. Would you mind repeating that, I don't think . . .'

38

'Come on, Jo,' said the Doctor urgently, and swept her out of the bar.

'Extraordinary fellow,' said the Squire turning back to the interminable Alastair Fergus.

. . . . .

'And did he by any chance call himself "the Doctor"?'

'Yes, Mr. Magister, that's what the girl called him. Do you know him, then?'

The Vicar smiled. 'I believe I have made his acquaintance, yes. You have done well, Wilkins. But . . . why aren't you ready?'

'Well, I thought I ought to tell you. Said he was going to stop the dig.'

'Hurry now and prepare. We start the ceremony in only a few minutes.'

As Wilkins hurried across the vestry and disappeared through the door leading to the Cavern, the Vicar opened a cupboard and took out a robe, a robe of such magnificence that it would have made the congregation of Devil's End wince. But this was no High Church vestment : bright scarlet, of heavy silk, thickly embroidered in gold with curious esoteric signs, the robe spoke of decadence, of evil, of the secret arts.

Donning it quickly, Mr. Magister walked through the Cavern door and stood at the top of the steps. There, grouped in a circle around the Stone of Sacrifice, were twelve figures in hooded black gowns. As they caught sight of him, they raised their voices. 'Io Evohe' they chanted in unison.

The Vicar surveyed them. Garvin was there; Wilkins and his quaking nephew; Fenton, the caretaker from the village school; Ashby who kept the General Store; and so on and so on. A poor lot, he thought.

He swept down the stairs, his scarlet robe aflying and approached the Stone of Sacrifice on which were now seven black candles, a chalice and a thurible covered with runic signs. Taking some incense from one of the hooded figures,

Grouped around the Stone of Sacrifice were twelve figures in hooded black gowns

the Vicar threw it into the thurible. There was a flash, and a sweet cloying scent filled the air, as smoke drifted across the Cavern.

'As my will, so mote it be.' His rich powerful voice filled the cave.

'Nema,' responded the group.

Mr. Magister raised his arms high and spoke the words of conjuration :

> *'Hearken to my voice, oh Dark One;*
> *Ancient and awful; supreme in artifice;*
> *Bearer of power; I conjure thee!*
> *Be present here at my command*
> *And truly do my will!*
> *EVA, EVARA, EGABALA!*
> *GAD, GADOAL, GALDINA!'*

Young Stan Wilkins, pale and sweaty, stared up at the triumphant face of the great figure in the scarlet robe of silk and trembled . . .

     •   •   •   •   •

Professor Horner, having been kept waiting in a cramped and awkward position at the end of the tunnel, was in no mood to play games when, at last, Alastair Fergus stopped talking and Harry waved a cueing hand at him. 'Oh, my turn at last is it, young man,' he growled at Harry and turned to speak to the camera. 'Let's face it, you've had enough blether from t'other fellow. You want to see for yourself. Well, I'll tell you what you're going to see. A stone wall.' His trowel chinked on something hard. The professor began to scrape away the earth, to reveal some large stones, obviously set in place in the long distant past. 'What did I tell you? I'm not so daft . . .'

All showmanship forgotten, the Professor of Archaeology started to clear the edges of the largest stone as gently and as lovingly as a craftsman of old working on his masterpiece.

The Doctor's old car came racketing and bumping up the steep track at an impossible speed.

'What's the time?' he shouted above the din of the engine.

Jo struggled to focus her eyes on her wristwatch. 'About two minutes to midnight, I think.'

Bessie seemed to leap forward as the Doctor, abandoning all caution, put his foot hard down.

There was no need now to ask where the dig was. The enormous lamps lit the Devil's Hump as if it were a film set —and the trucks and the cameras made a barrier impossible to get through.

The car shuddered to a halt, the Doctor jumped out and ran at top speed towards the barrow, shouting, 'Stop him! You must stop him!' And as he ran the church clock started to chime . . .

In the Cavern, as the chanting grew louder and louder, the mighty figure in scarlet raised the smoking incense high in the air, and cried in a kind of ecstasy:

> *'By the power of earth,*
> *By the power of air,*
> *By the power of fire eternal,*
> *And the waters of the deep,*
> *I conjure thee and charge thee:*
> *ARISE, ARISE, AT MY COMMAND,*
> *AZAL, AZAL!'*

More by luck than design, the Professor finished clearing the wall, just as the clock finished its preliminary chimes, and as the first stroke of twelve echoed across the valley, he gripped the largest stone, quite oblivious of his audience and of the commotion behind him in the tunnel, and gave it a great wrench.

By sheer speed the Doctor had made his way past Harry and the cameras, foiling every attempt to stop him. But all in vain, for as he arrived at the end of the tunnel, the stone came out like a decayed tooth from its socket.

From the hole came a blast of icy wind. An unearthly screaming filled the air and the earth itself began to shake.

Outside the barrow, the sudden high wind and the quaking of the ground threw monster lights and cameras to the ground, tumbling them over and over like leaves in a gale. As Alastair Fergus and the technicians struggled to protect themselves from the terrible sound and the falling equipment, Jo fought her way against the freezing wind towards the barrow. 'Doctor! Doctor!' she sobbed.

As she reached the entrance to the tunnel, the wind suddenly stopped : the noise died away and all was still, the silence broken only by the low moaning of an injured man.

'Doctor, are you all right?' she desperately called out as she stumbled down the tunnel. But the Doctor could not reply. All that could be seen of him, emerging from a great pile of earth and rubble, was his hand, the hand with his beloved silver Roman ring.

4

The Appearance of the Beast

It had been a very dull evening at UNIT Headquarters : a rumour from Hampshire of a monster which turned out to be a Jersey cow on a spree; the usual crop of UFO sightings just after closing time; a report of little green men in Tooting ('Why are they always green?' said Benton. 'These hoaxers haven't got any imagination!') In fact the only item of any interest was the TV report of the Rugby International at Twickenham—England v Wales. Captain Yates and the Sergeant spent a jolly hour watching the cream of English manhood being beaten into the ground by their Celtic cousins.

'Thirteen nil!' grumbled Mike.

'Lucky it wasn't a hundred and thirteen nil,' said Sergeant Benton. 'Useless lot.'

Mike Yates yawned hugely and idly looked at his watch. 'Hey, it's just gone twelve. We've missed the dig!'

'Might just get the end of it,' said Benton, lazily wandering over to change channels, 'unless of course the Doctor managed to stop it.' He pressed the button. The picture which swam into view appeared to be upside down. There was somebody—a girl was it?—scrabbling feverishly in a big pile of earth. Suddenly, the sound cut in: 'Doctor! Doctor!'

'It's Jo!' Mike said, appalled.

At that moment, the screen went blank. The familiar B.B.C. 3 emblem came up and a smooth voice calmed the worried millions with well-bred aplomb. 'We seem to have lost contact with the barrow at Devil's End. We shall of course, resume the programme as soon as we can. In the meantime, here is some music.'

Mike snapped into action. 'Benton, get onto the B.B.C. and find out what's going on down there. I'll try to raise the Brigadier.'

The next few minutes were spent in a chaos of words, with Benton trying to get past the bland public face of the B.B.C. to those actually in charge of the broadcast from the Devil's Hump, while Mike Yates learned that he had just missed the Brigadier who had 'gone on somewhere' at the end of his regimental 'do'.

'This is stupid,' Mike burst out, 'I've a damn good mind to go down there and find out for myself!'

'The Brigadier'd go spare, sir,' said the Sergeant, 'I mean we might get news at any moment.'

'Oh yes, sure,' replied Mike, 'and in the meantime, what's happening to Jo and the Doctor?'

The Doctor, Professor Horner and Ted the cameraman lay in a neat row on the grass, stiff and cold.

Harry looked up. 'It's no good,' he said, 'he's gone too.'

Jo was frantic.

'No! No, he can't be! We must get a doctor.'

'Look, love, face it. They've had it.'

'There must be a doctor in the village, or somewhere.'

Harry looked at the turmoil around them. His eye lighted on Alastair Fergus, who seemed to be the only one of the whole unit without an urgent job to do. 'Hey, Alastair! Can you drive a truck?'

Alastair took in the scene at a glance. He forced himself to speak calmly. 'I'll try anything once,' he said.

The journey from the Goat's Back down to Devil's End was always to remain one of Jo's nightmares. Bouncing about in the front of a three-tonner driven by a man who had never driven anything larger than a sports car, knowing that the three men in the back were probably dead, knowing that the Doctor had for once failed and maybe had paid for his failure with his life, Jo clung desperately to the memory of another time when the Doctor had lain apparently lifeless, only to recover completely after a few hours' rest.

As it happened, Alastair Fergus's truck was merely the first of a convoy of vehicles carrying the injured and the shocked down to the village. Soon the long bar in 'The Cloven Hoof' looked like a casualty ward, with Doctor Reeves in his shirt sleeves trying to be in a dozen different places at once. He looked up from examining Gilbert Horner. 'It's impossible,' he said.

Winstanley, shaken into a sort of sobriety, looked down at the lifeless form of the Professor. 'Poor chap was suffocated, I suppose. Or was he crushed?'

'Neither,' said Reeves. 'Frozen to death.'

'Frozen? But that's impossible.'

'I said so, didn't I? That makes three of them. They're the same.' He gestured to Ted and the Doctor.

'But you haven't even examined the Doctor,' cried Jo, trying to hold back her tears.

'No need, I'm afraid,' said Doctor Reeves. 'He's very nearly a solid block of ice, just like the other two.' As he spoke he put a perfunctory finger on the Doctor's wrist. 'Can't perform miracles, you know.'

Jo turned away, blinded by silent tears.

'There, there, my dear,' said Winstanley, embarrassed.

Suddenly Reeves gave a start. 'Good grief! Here, bring some blankets over, will you? And get some hot water bottles. Lots of them.'

'Coming up, Doctor Reeves,' called Bert from the other end of the room, where he was dispensing hot sweet tea.

Jo could hardly dare to believe what she had heard. 'He's alive?'

'It's incredible, but I think I felt a pulse.'

'There's a chance then?'

'Maybe, maybe,' said Reeves cautiously. 'He must have the constitution of an ox to survive a temperature reduction like that.'

The Squire awkwardly patted Jo on the shoulder. 'Stiff upper lip, my dear. Where there's life, there's hope.'

As Jo gave him a watery smile, Bert arrived with a bundle of blankets and two or three hot water bottles.

'Good, good. More if you can spare them.'

'I'll have a look round,' and Bert turned to go.

'I say,' said Jo, stopping him, 'is there a 'phone I could use?'

'In the corner, Miss. Help yourself.'

'Oh yes. Thanks.'

Jo picked her way slowly through the B.B.C. team. She could see Alastair in the middle. Already the terror of his experience was fading and it was becoming just another tale for the club at lunchtime. Alastair Fergus was too tough a nut to crack easily.

Jo was quickly through to UNIT and had soon put Mike Yates in the picture.

'But is the Doctor all right now?' he asked.

'It's touch and go, I think,' replied Jo. 'Mike, can you get down here?'

'Yes, of course We'll come down in the chopper.'

46

'Well, get a move on, won't you. I can't take much more of this.' Mike could hear the quaver in her voice.

'I've never been so scared in my life,' she went on, 'there's something awful going on here. The whole place has a feeling about it, as if . . .' Abruptly her voice stopped, to be replaced by the dialling tone. At once, Mike rang the number of the pub, which Jo had given him.

'What's up, sir?' said Benton.

'Number unobtainable . . .'

'So what do we do?'

'Go down there, Sergeant. Both of us.'

'But . . . what about the Brigadier?'

'The Brigadier can . . .' Mike stopped himself just in time. Even though UNIT was somewhat informal, military etiquette must be preserved. 'He can follow us down later. Go and change into civvies, Sergeant, and get the Brig's helicopter fuelled up and ready for us to take off at first light . . .'

.   .   .   .   .

Harry leaned out of the window of his car. 'Well, that's the last of us,' he said thankfully to Police Constable Groom. 'You've been a great help!'

'Happy to oblige.'

'Can't wait to get away myself. I don't envy you, stuck up here.'

P.C. Groom grinned. 'Can't leave it all open, like. Just another night duty. I enjoy a bit of peace and quiet.'

'You're welcome to it, mate,' said Harry and drove away with a cheerful wave of his hand.

Thank the Lord, thought the Constable. Friendly lot, but still, look at all the trouble they'd caused.

He walked over to the entrance to the tunnel, now firmly sealed off with planks. He shone his torch on the large 'Danger' notice outside and grunted with satisfaction. Then, carefully spreading his waterproof cape on the turf he sat down, and opened a packet of sandwiches—apricot jam, his favourite—and a flask of tea.

His supper finished and tidied up, P.C. Groom settled down, his back against the warning notice, to wait for dawn. Already he could see the sky brightening in the east . . . within minutes he was asleep. It had been a long and busy day.

But the Constable's sleep was not a restful sleep. Almost at once he plunged deep into a dream; a dream with no story; a dream which was nothing but a jumble of disconcerting images. He saw the face of the new Vicar, Mr. Magister, apparently mouthing some strange incantation, while swirls of coloured smoke almost hid him from view. He saw the notorious gargoyle from the Cavern, Bok, the tourists' favourite, stretching his stone wings and hopping from his pedestal. He saw a pair of red eyes watching him steadily from the darkness of the tunnel in the barrow. And as he stirred uneasily in his sleep, he saw alien creatures, giant creatures with cruel faces, flying through space past uncountable suns. He could feel his heart thudding as he fell down, down, down, into the heart of the brightest sun of all . . .

Abruptly he awoke. The brightness was the brightness of the dawn. The thudding of his heart was the tread of heavy footsteps shaking the earth beneath him. He struggled to rise, but in vain. And as P.C. Groom drew his last breath, he recognised one of the giant beings from his dream as it indifferently crushed the life out of his body with one of its great hooves.

.   .   .   .   .

With the sun at their backs Captain Yates and Sergeant Benton, no longer in uniform, flew through the azure sky of the May Day morning.

'If only helicopters weren't so blooming noisy!' said the Sergeant. 'It's by far the best way to fly. Time to look around. Even better than gliding in a way.'

Mike Yates, concentrating on the map on his knee, was in no mood for small-talk. 'Well, you have a look round and see if you can see the village,' he said. 'We should be there by now.'

'Right ahead, sir,' Benton replied, in no way abashed. 'See the church?'

Mike looked for himself and soon made out the church tower nestling in the woods. But then something else caught his eye. 'Hello, what's that?'

'Must be the dig.'

'No, beyond that. Going across that big field, a line of ... they couldn't be hoofmarks?'

'Shall we go and look, sir?'

'Yes, better.'

The helicopter settled to the ground, noisily, softly, beating the grass flat with the force of its gentle descent. Mike and the Sergeant jumped out and ran over to the line of curious identations in the soft turf.

'They are, you know,' said Benton his voice tinged with awe. 'They're hoofmarks.'

'But they can't be. The animal that made these would have to be twenty or thirty feet tall.'

Benton followed the track with his eye. 'It's gone into that wood, sir.'

'Well, whatever it is, it'll have to wait. Come on. First thing's first,' and Mike turned and hurried back to the helicopter.

'Like—er—breakfast, you mean?' said the Sergeant following him.

'No I don't,' said Mike grimly. 'I mean Jo and the Doc.'

No sooner was the chopper in the air again than it started to descend once more and soon landed neatly in the very centre of the village green.

'Where's the red carpet then?' said Benton as they climbed out, 'and the brass-band?'

Yates looked round at the sleeping village. 'After last night I reckon they're entitled to a lie-in,' he said.

Out of the front door of 'The Cloven Hoof' came a small figure, flying across the grass so fast her legs almost became a blur. 'Mike! Sergeant Benton!' she gasped as she reached them. 'Boy, am I glad to see you two.'

'Are you all right, Jo?' said Mike, disentangling himself from her hug.

'Yeah, great.'

'And the Doc?'

'Come and have a look. He's in the pub. They got him to bed.'

'Is he any better?'

'I think so, a bit. But he's still out cold.'

'He'll pull through. You know what a tough old bird he is.'

'Anyway,' said Benton, 'you're both safe. That's the main thing.'

Jo stopped by the door of the pub. 'I don't *think* there's any danger here,' she said, 'but out there . . .' and she nodded in the rough direction of the distant barrow, her eyes filled with fear.

'Look, Jo, what is going on?' asked Yates.

'I . . . don't really know. Something really *bad*. You know, devilish . . .'

Mike caught the Sergeant's eye. 'Those tracks?'

'Look sir, if you don't need me here, I'd like to do a quick recce.' No need to alarm Miss Grant, his eyes said. 'Just fifteen minutes' shufti round,' he went on. 'Well . . . say twenty.'

Mike felt doubtful. Perhaps they ought to stick together. On the other hand, the sooner they got this lot sorted out, the better for everybody. 'Mm. . . right,' he agreed, 'but at the first sign of trouble, straight back here.'

'Oh, do be careful,' said Jo.

'Don't you worry, Miss,' said Benton cheerfully, 'I know how to look after myself.'

'Come on,' said Mike, 'let's go and see how the Doctor is —and you can tell me the whole story.' He put his arm round the reluctant and fearful Jo and gently took her inside.

Sergeant Benton looked round the green to get his bearings. They must have approached from the north-east; perhaps east-north-east. That would mean that the wood into which the tracks disappeared would be up there to the right of the church. Couldn't be far—a half-mile, perhaps. He set out, manfully ignoring the protests from his empty stomach, and made his way past the Maypole towards the churchyard. Thirty feet tall! That was some creature, whether devil or animal. The Sergeant cast his mind back to some of the curious beings he had encountered since he first met the Doctor, as a lowly Corporal. Nothing could be worse than the Cybermen, of course, though the Axons ran them a close second, and as for those plastic Daffodil Men with their great grinning heads . . ! Benton shuddered in spite of himself and brought his mind back to the job in hand. 'Just as well I don't believe in devils,' he thought wryly, 'or I'd be scared out of my wits.'

The path through the churchyard took him close to the wall of the church. How quiet it was. Surely in the early morning there should be a regular choir of birdsong. Suddenly he stopped. What was that?

Again it came, faintly; so faintly that if the birds had been singing he would surely have missed it.

'Help! Help!'

It could only have come from inside the building. Out of long habit and experience, Benton gave his surroundings a quick glance before making for the nearest door into the church.

Inside the vestry, he stopped. Silence. 'Hello!' he called.

'Help me! Oh, please help me.'

There was no mistaking the source. Benton hurried over to the old oak chest and tried the lid. Locked, of course.

'Hang on! Have you out of there in no time at all!' he said reassuringly, looking around for something to use as a jemmy. Seizing hold of the stand of a broken lectern which was leaning against the wall, he pulled off its wrought-iron base and using all his strength, managed to break open the lock.

Miss Hawthorne looked up at him. Her long ordeal had exhausted her, but her spirit was unbroken. 'And who are you,' she said, 'friend or foe?'

'Friend, I hope, ma'am,' answered Benton, helping her out of the chest.

'A true knight errant. Well, your damsel in distress may be a bit long in the tooth but she's very grateful.'

'Lucky I heard you,' said Benton, starting to untie her.

'It took me hours to work that gag loose—and oh ! what a relief it was ! Who are you?'

'My name's Benton, Sergeant Benton.'

'A police sergeant?'

'No, Army. And you're Miss Hawthorne, aren't you? I saw you on the telly with that Professor Horner.'

Olive Hawthorne took a deep breath and asked the question she hardly dared to ask. 'And what happened? At midnight, I mean.'

'Nobody seems to know exactly. But the Professor's dead,' and Benton told her everything he knew.

'Poor silly man . . .' Miss Hawthorne was obviously upset.

'But who shut you in that chest? Stupid thing to do. You might have suffocated.'

'Luckily the lid was by no means a close fit. I think it must have been Mr. Garvin, the verger.'

'But why?'

'I have a theory . . . but come, we mustn't dilly-dally here. It could be dangerous.'

The Sergeant shook his head. 'I wish I knew what was going on. All hell seems to be breaking loose in this place.'

Miss Hawthorne paused at the door. 'You know, Sergeant, you speak more truthfully than you perhaps realise. Come on.' She started to open the door, but immediately held up a warning hand. 'It's Garvin,' she hissed. 'The one who tied me up. He's coming this way . . !' Quickly she led the way to the Cavern door and down the steps into the Cavern. 'We can hide down here until he's gone,' she whispered, as she hurried to an alcove near the back of the Cavern. 'Great Heavens !'

'What is it, Miss?'

'The gargoyle. It's gone !'

'What gargoyle?'

'Sssh!!' The vestry door had slammed. 'We didn't close the chest,' Olive Hawthorne breathed into the Sergeant's ear.

They could hear Garvin's footsteps on the stone floor of the vestry. The door of the Cavern opened slowly and Garvin's head appeared. Apparently satisfied, he withdrew and the door closed. After a moment, again the slam of the outer door.

'Phew!' Benton started to move towards the exit.

'No, wait till he's clear.'

But Benton had stopped anyway, his eye caught by the strangely-marked stone let into the floor.

Miss Hawthorne joined him. 'The sign of the Evil One,' she said grimly. 'That proves it. You know who's at the bottom of all this?'

'Who?'

'The Reverend Mr. Magister. Our new Vicar. He's an impostor. I should have realised that at once. Magister is the name given to the leader of a black magic coven!' She crossed to the now empty Stone of Sacrifice and looked at the dark stains on its surface with disgust.

'Black magic?' said Benton incredulously. 'That stuff died out years ago.'

'Do you know when the last witchcraft law was repealed in the country? 1957 ... It's as alive today as ever it was. Come on. It should be safe to leave by now.' But as she put her hand on the handle of the heavy door, it was flung open and Miss Hawthorne was precipitated to the bottom of the steps. There stood Garvin with a shotgun in his hands.

Slowly he came down into the Cavern. He opened his mouth to speak, but before he could utter a word, Benton was in action. With a straight leg kick which would have done credit to a member of the Royal Ballet, he had the gun flying out of the verger's hands, and leaped upon him. All Benton's weight and skill were not enough to subdue the slight figure of the verger. Round and round the Cavern they stumbled as they struggled for mastery. Suddenly Miss Hawthorne screamed—'Look out!'

But it was too late. With a desperate heave, Garvin managed to push the Sergeant right onto the flagstone marked with the esoteric sign. At once, it seemed, he was assailed by a hundred invisible clubs. Vainly fighting the empty air he was forced to his knees, twisting and turning as he tried to evade the heavy blows. At last, all his strength sapped by the punishment he had taken, he collapsed to the ground, luckily falling clear of the diabolic stone.

Miss Hawthorne rushed to him and knelt by his side.

Garvin, who had retrieved his gun, laughed. 'Right, on your feet,' he ordered.

'Don't be stupid,' said Miss Hawthorne as though to a recalcitrant schoolboy. 'He's almost unconscious.'

Garvin flushed and moved closer. 'Somebody'll have to help then,' he said, putting the barrel of the gun up at her face. 'Come on, move.'

As Miss Hawthorne helped the stumbling Benton up the steps of the Cavern and across the vestry, she became conscious of a flutter of fear, a fear very different in quality from her natural apprehension at being threatened by a gun. Then she realised why : the ground was quivering beneath her feet.

'Wait! Can't you feel...'

'Quiet,' snapped Garvin, 'get him outside.'

She staggered out into the churchyard with the almost helpless Sergeant, followed by the verger. As they started to move down the path, the movement of the earth became too obvious to ignore. Garvin stopped the others and wildly looked around.

Out of the woods, its great hooves shaking the ground with each step, came a gigantic creature, some thirty feet tall, with the legs of an animal, the body of a man and the head of...

Miss Hawthorne struggled to see clearly, but the outlines of the face and head were strangely blurred, as if a red haze of heat were surrounding them. As the creature ap-

Out of the woods came a gigantic creature some thirty feet tall . . .

proached, the heat encompassed its whole being, and it became apparent that it was starting to grow smaller. The temperature of the air rose rapidly, and an oppressively hot wind started to bend the branches of the trees. Miss Hawthorne suddenly found deep down inside herself a reserve of courage and strength, and with seemingly no effort she dragged the still dazed Sergeant into the shelter of the ornate tomb of an early Winstanley.

Garvin, white with a primeval terror, raised his gun, and blindly let off one, two barrels, straight into the face of the advancing creature.

And Miss Hawthorne, cowering behind the protective marble, watched with horrified fascination as it lazily lifted a gargantuan arm and pointed at the paralysed Garvin. A thread of unearthly light streaked from the pointing finger and the verger vanished forever, vaporised by a flash of fire hotter than the heart of the sun.

5

The Heat Barrier

Mike Yates's usual optimism was severely tested by his first sight of the Doctor: the blueness of his face against the crisp whiteness of the old pillowcase was so different from his usual healthy glow that it was almost impossible to believe that he was not dead.

'Shouldn't he be in hospital?'

'Well, no, apparently not,' said Jo. 'Doctor Reeves said we shouldn't move him from here.'

'Then we'll just have to wait,' said Mike. 'Now, tell me all about it.'

Jo started to tremble. 'Oh, Mike,' she said, 'it was terrible . . .' She had in fact little more to recount than she had already told him on the 'phone, but Mike, sensitive Mike, knew that she must have been bottling up her emotions so fiercely that she was near to bursting. By the time she finished her story, she could hardly speak through her tears.

Mike waited quietly until she had finished and her sobs had subsided a little. 'Well done, Jo,' he said gently. She smiled and accepted the large clean handkerchief he offered her. 'Tell you what,' he said. 'You stay here with the Doctor and I'll go and rustle up a cuppa.'

'Okay,' she agreed and blew her nose loudly.

Mike soon found the kitchen and had the kettle on. While he rooted around amongst the pots and pans, he tried to make sense of Jo's story. He had already learnt from the B.B.C. before he left London that the extraordinary freak weather had been confined exclusively to Devil's End. Indeed, it had been a very mild, quiet night throughout the country; and it had certainly been a perfect morning for flying. In fact, the Brig's chopper had never behaved so well . . . Oh Lor', the Brigadier! He'd forgotten all about the Brigadier. According to Jo, all the telephone lines out of Devil's End were out of order. It took only a couple of minutes for Mike to run to the middle of the green and a further couple to contact UNIT Headquarters on the helicopter radio.

'Yessir,' reported the duty corporal, 'I managed to get in touch with him. Just getting into bed, he was. About half past four. No, sir, I wouldn't say he was overjoyed. I passed on your message. No, he wasn't very pleased to hear that you'd taken his helicopter. Still, it woke him up, sir. Said you were to stay put. He's on his way down to Devil's End. By car, sir . . .'

The kettle had nearly boiled dry when Mike got back to the kitchen and by the time he'd boiled another, made the tea, let it brew for four minutes exactly, poured it out and carried it upstairs, Jo was, of course, curled up in the cushioned basket chair by the Doctor's bed, fast off in the deep sleep of pure exhaustion. Mike smiled, sat down in the window seat and sipped his tea. It would do her no harm at all to have a bit of a rest until Sergeant Benton returned. He put down the cup and leaned back. Just the chance he needed to get his thoughts in order, he said firmly to himself. Those hoofmarks, for instance. Either there was a monster lurking in the woods, or a hoaxer was at work. If it were to turn out to be a monster it simply became a question of whether the anteater's tongue was longer than the jelly baby or, on the other hand, vice versa . . .

Mike Yates's eyes snapped open. For Pete's sake, he was on duty, wasn't he! This was no time to fall asleep.

Fifteen seconds later, he was snoring softly. All was still in the rosy twilight of the little curtained room . . .

Moments later, it seemed, he was struggling out of the blank depths of dreamlessness into a waking nightmare. It was hot, hotter than a tropical noontide, and the room was all ashake. The collection of little pot animals on the mantle fell, tinkle by tinkle, into the brick hearth and a picture of Edward the Seventh as an infant crashed irreparably to the floor. Jo, abruptly tipped out of her cosy chair, was scrambling to her feet screaming, while the Doctor's bed rolled hither and thither, its occupant still oblivious, his face streaming with sweat. Somewhere nearby a baby howled in fear.

The earthquake stopped. The temperature fell. All was still again; even the baby had stopped crying.

Mike and Jo rose shakily to their feet.

'What . . . what happened?' Jo gasped. Mike shook a bewildered head.

A sudden movement from the bed: the Doctor sat bolt upright, the flowered eiderdown falling away, and said, at the top of his voice, 'Eureka! I've got it!'

.   .   .   .   .

Bert surveyed his bar in some dismay. Okay, he was insured, but that didn't replace all the broken glasses right now. In any case, the insurance company would probably wriggle out of it; they'd say the earthquake was an Act of God. An Act of God! That was a laugh . . .

Down the stairs came a little procession. Hey! It was the girl and some other fellow with that Doctor! Supposed to be dying, wasn't he?

'Hullo, you better?' said Bert, 'I thought you'd had it.'

'Fortunately, no,' replied the Doctor.

'But are you sure you're okay?' fussed Jo. 'Better come and sit down.'

'She's right, you know,' agreed Mike. 'You ought to take it gently for a bit.'

'I tell you I've recovered completely,' said the Doctor. 'It was a bit parky there for a while, I'll admit, but it soon warmed up.'

'I'll say it did!' said Jo.

'The final confirmation of my theory, that wave of heat,' the Doctor went on.

'You mean, you know what caused it?'

'Yes, Jo, I think so.'

'Tell us then.'

'No, not just yet. I have to be sure. I'm going up to the dig.'

Jo shuddered. 'Oh, Doctor, haven't you had enough of that place?'

Before the Doctor could reply, the front door was flung open and Miss Hawthorne, hair awry, staggered in, supporting Sergeant Benton. For a long moment nobody moved.

'If I drop him,' said Miss Hawthorne, a trifle plaintively, 'he'll go a dreadful wallop.'

At once Mike Yates and the Doctor, all apologies, hastened to relieve her of her burden.

'He's out on his feet,' exclaimed Mike, as they helped him onto a bench.

'Whatever's happened to him?' asked Jo.

'He's been beaten up,' replied Mike. 'By an expert, I'd say.'

'You might indeed say that; you might indeed.' Miss Hawthorne sank exhausted into a chair. 'Oh dear, oh dear. He's a very heavy young man.'

Bert looked at the bruised Sergeant. 'He's in a bad way. I'd better fetch Doctor Reeves.'

'No need for that,' said the Doctor, looking up from his examination of Benton's injuries. 'I am medically qualified myself. Now then, let me see. No bones broken, thank goodness, and no open wounds. No internal ruptures . . . Mm. He's a lucky young man. Slight concussion, a few nasty bruises and, of course, shock.'

The Sergeant was shaking his head gently from side to side as if to find out whether it were still attached to his body. He looked round at the anxious group. His eye lighted on the Doctor.

'Doctor . . .'

'No, no, don't try to speak. Just sit quietly.'

Benton leaned back and closed his eyes. The Doctor looked over at Bert. 'You are our host, I take it?'

Bert grinned a little uncertainly. 'Could call me that, I suppose. I'm the landlord, yes.'

'The best medicine friend Benton could have would be some hot sweet tea. How about it?'

Bert nodded and made his way towards the kitchen.

'Thank you,' said the Doctor. 'And thank you, Miss Hawthorne, for looking after him.'

'You know who I am?'

'Indeed I do. If only they had listened to you.'

'If only they had. I shall be eternally grateful to this young man. It is thanks to him that I am alive to tell the world what I have seen.' Her manner was so intense that it compelled attention.

'And what have you seen, Miss Hawthorne?'

She paused, relishing the moment. 'Why, Doctor,' she said. 'I have seen the Devil.'

There was a moment of silence; a moment of disbelief, of amusement even—but also a moment tinged with cold horror, which touched everyone present, even the Doctor himself.

'I think you'd better tell us the whole story,' he said.

And so Miss Hawthorne told them of the attack upon her and her incarceration in the chest; of her rescue by Benton; of their being surprised by the villainous Garvin . . .

'And it was this verger fellow who worked over poor old Benton?' asked Mike.

'No, no, no. That was done by the elementals in the Cavern.'

'Elementals?' Mike was way out of his depth.

'Impersonal primitive spirits. One can learn to control them. These were controlled by evil . . .'

Jo took a long shuddering breath. 'And you say you actually saw . . . the Devil?'

'Yes, my dear. Satan, Lucifer, the Prince of Darkness, Beelzebub, the Horned Beast; call him what you will. He was there.'

The Doctor leaned forward urgently. 'What did he look like?'

'I only had a glimpse, you understand. He was twenty or thirty feet tall—the cloven hooves were there—and the horns—and that face !'

Jo seized Mike's hand.

'The Devil !' she murmured.

The Doctor frowned. 'Miss Hawthorne,' he said, 'I've agreed with you from the first about the danger. But now I think you are utterly mistaken. Whatever else you saw, it was not the Devil.'

Miss Hawthorne's manner became even more grave. 'Oh, but it was,' she said. 'You see, there's a Satanist cult in the village and last night they held a Sabbat.'

'A Sabbat? What's that?' asked Mike.

'An occult ceremony. To call up the Devil.'

'And it worked . . .' breathed Jo, completely carried away. 'The Devil came . . .'

'Nonsense,' said the Doctor, impatiently. 'It's all rubbish. Superstitious rubbish !'

Miss Hawthorne bristled. 'I assure you, sir, that every word I have uttered . . .'

'Oh, I'm not impugning your veracity, madam. It's your interpretation I take issue with. Who is the leader of this . . . this Satanist coven?'

'The new Vicar. He calls himself Magister.'

Unexpectedly, the Doctor laughed. 'The arrogance ! Magister—of course. I should have guessed.'

'Guessed what?' said Jo, quite bewildered.

'Did you fail Latin at school as well as science, Jo?' he asked. ' "Magister" is the Latin word for "Master"!'

.   .   .   .   .

Renegade Time Lord, the Doctor's arch-enemy, instigator of so many evil schemes in the past, the Master's one over-whelming objective always remained the same : Power! The power of the tyrant, to make slaves of all others; the power of the despot, to be ruler, dictator of a country, an empire, a planet; the power of the demi-god, to command a galaxy, a universe; no ambition was too great for the megalomaniac dreams of the Master.

The telephone bell was ringing. The new Vicar of Devil's End picked up the receiver. 'Magister here . . . I see . . . So he has survived, has he? . . . No, no, it doesn't surprise me . . . Nevertheless, I'm grateful to you for letting me know . . . I shall deal with him, never fear. Now get back in there before they begin to suspect—but let me know where he goes the moment he steps outside. You understand . . . ?'

.   .   .   .   .

Bert put down the 'phone, picked up the tray on which the tea for Sergeant Benton stood ready, and returned to the bar. But already the Doctor had left. So had the girl for that matter. But where had they gone? He took the tea over to Benton, who accepted it gratefully, and quietly returned to his task of clearing the mess behind the bar, listening hard.

Mike Yates was talking to the Brigadier on his walkie-talkie.

'. . . and that's about it, sir. Over.'

'I see, Captain Yates.' The Brigadier's voice was crisp and clear. 'So the Doctor was frozen stiff at the barrow, then revived by a freak heatwave. Benton was beaten up by invisible forces, and the local white witch claims she's seen the Devil. Apart from that it's been a quiet night? Over.'

Sergeant Benton grinned. He was obviously feeling better.

'I know it all sounds a bit wild. Over.'

'It does indeed, Yates, it does indeed. Now listen. I'm about five miles away from Devil's End and I seem to have run into some sort of heat barrier. Let me talk to the Doctor.'

Bert, on his hands and knees behind the bar, was at once alert.

'I'm afraid you can't, sir. He's gone up to the dig with Jo Grant. Over.'

So that was it. He must let Mr. Magister know at once. Unnoticed, he delicately moved across the carpet of broken glass and out of the room.

'I see. Well, as soon as he comes back I need to have a word with him. Got it? This heat barrier's quite beyond my ken, I don't mind admitting. Over.'

'Right, sir. Er . . . heat barrier? What kind of heat barrier?'

'No time to stand here nattering, Yates. Too much to do. Out!'

.   .   .   .   .   .

The Brigadier snapped the aerial back and turned to his driver.

'Well, Manders. We'd better have a try at getting in from the south. Let's have a shufti at the map.'

'Sir !'

The Brigadier spread the map out on the bonnet of his staff car and considered. If they circled and came up through Lob's Crick—extraordinary names they gave their villages—they might get round this invisible wall of heat. Might be a hotel there, too. Get some breakfast.

He stood up and looked to the right and to the left. The ten-foot-wide strip of charred earth, like a newly made road, extended both ways cutting across fields, through hedges and through spinneys with no visible end. He turned to his other companion, a worried eighteen-year-old with spots and a brown overall. 'Can't leave you stranded here.'

The young man looked uneasily at the still red hot skeleton of his burnt-out van.

'Lob's Crick would do me fine. I can ring the Guv'nor.'

'Jump in then.'

The powerful car turned carefully, and smoothly accelerated away from the danger area.

'Now then,' said the Brigadier, 'tell me exactly what happened.'

'Well, it were like this. Fine morning, it was, and me singing away like fun—I enjoy these early bread rounds—and the old bus going like a bird and then all of a sudden she started to swerve. I thought I'd got a flat tyre, but no, it were an earthquake, like.'

'We noticed something of the sort ourselves, didn't we, Manders?'

'That's right, sir.'

'Anyway, I was afraid I'd end up in the ditch, so I stopped and jumped out. And that's when I heard this noise.'

'Noise?'

'Like a humming . . . no, a buzzing . . . no . . . I can't describe it really, sir, but it were so loud it got me scared. I just took off. And a good thing I did, because the next moment the old bread van went up like a bomb. Blazing away she were, all in a minute. And that's when you came along, sir.'

The Brigadier surveyed the charred end of his swagger cane, thinking back. The van in flames, the terrified youngster flagging them down, the garbled warning and then, the discovery of the heat barrier itself. Standing a few yards from the burning vehicle, he had used his cane to point at the church tower showing over the trees. 'Is that Devil's End?' he'd asked—and the end of his cane had burst into flames like a Guy Fawkes firework. Good grief, if he'd been eighteen inches nearer, he'd have lost his hand! Next they'd tried throwing in a stick from the hedge; a stone; a steel spanner. All had exploded into flames or turned white with incandescence before being completely vaporised. And yet, inches away from the invisible wall, the temperature of the air was only a few degrees above normal.

'This looks like Lob's Crick, sir,' said Manders.

'If you could drop me at the store . . .' said the roundsman. He grinned ruefully. 'I can just hear my Guv'nor when I tell him his van's gone up in a puff of smoke!'

Some six furlongs beyond the village (which was too small to boast a hotel or even a pub, as the rumblings of the Brigadier's stomach were beginning to testify) Manders brought the car to a stop. Right across the road in front of them and as far as could be seen on either side, extended the same regular strip of burnt earth. A half-brick, lobbed into the air, disintegrated into a thousand burning fragments.

'That settles it,' said the Brigadier. 'We'd better get some of our chaps down. Looks as if it might extend all round Devil's End. Back to the village, Manders. We must get the police in on this before there are any tragedies. And you never know, the village constable of Lob's Crick might even give us a cup of tea!'

.   .   .   .   .

Meanwhile the village constable of Devil's End stared up at the Doctor with dead eyes.

'Poor fellow,' said the Doctor, as he covered P.C. Groom's face with his own waterproof cape.

Jo turned and walked away a few yards. Although, since she joined UNIT, she had experienced the sight of death in many forms, she could never get used to it. 'How did he die?' she said faintly. 'I mean what . . . what killed him?'

'Well, it wasn't the Devil,' replied the Doctor, gravely. 'At least, not exactly.'

Jo looked fearfully at him.

'What do you mean by that?'

But the Doctor did not reply to her question. Moving towards the entrance to the barrow, he tossed over his shoulder: 'I'm going in. Would you prefer to stay outside?'

Jo hurried after him. 'I think I'd rather stick with you— if I'm not in the way.'

The Doctor stopped and looked down into her anxious little face. 'Of course not,' he smiled, 'I'm glad of your company.'

As he started to clear the tunnel mouth of the splintered planks which had proved so ineffective a barrier, Jo glanced timorously around. She had that prickly feeling at the back of the neck which always meant to her that somebody was watching. Or could it be some thing . . . ?

'In we go,' said the Doctor, switching on his torch.

The dank blackness of the earth tunnel was, if that were possible, even less welcoming than when the television lights had guided Jo to the scene of disaster the night before. Soon they were clambering cautiously over the pile of rubble which had buried the Professor and the Doctor. The Doctor turned the beam of his powerful lamp into the black hole beyond. 'What are we looking for?' whispered Jo.

'I'll know when I find it,' replied the Doctor, infuriatingly.

As far as Jo could see the large chamber in the heart of the barrow was completely empty. Here was no treasure, no tomb of a bronze-age chieftain. Professor Horner was again proved wrong.

Inside, they were able to stand upright. The Doctor played his light along the smooth curves of the walls.

'It's enormous,' said Jo, her voice echoing oddly from the depths of the chamber.

The Doctor shone his torch onto the floor and began systematically examining it, foot by foot. 'If my theory's right, Jo, we're all in great danger; mortal danger.'

'You mean . . . everyone in the village?'

'I mean everyone in the whole world . . . Ah!'

The beam of light had fallen on a large bump in the earth floor. The Doctor squatted down by it and produced a little trowel. While Jo held the light, he carefully scraped and dug the hard impacted soil away from a silvery object some fifteen inches long.

'What is it?'

'What does it look like?' returned the Doctor.

'Like . . . like a model spaceship.'

'Full marks! Except that it isn't a model.'

'What is it then?'

The Doctor cleared the last bit of earth. 'Take a look at the shape of this chamber we're in.'

Puzzled, Jo turned the light once more onto the walls—and then back to the tiny spaceship. 'It's the same! I mean, they're the same shape!'

The Doctor nodded. 'Different size, that's all. Try picking it up.'

Jo put out a hand and gave an experimental tug. The metallic object was quite immovable.

'Here, hold this.' She handed the torch to the Doctor and tried with both hands. 'It's fixed down,' she said.

The Doctor shook his head. 'You can't pick it up because it weighs about . . . oh . . . about seven hundred and fifty tons, at a rough guess.'

'Oh, come on! Be serious.'

'I am serious. You see . . .'

There it was again: that prickly feeling. Jo gripped the Doctor's arm. 'Ssh!!!' she breathed. 'Listen . . .' Something was coming down the tunnel: scrape, slither scrape . . .

The Doctor quietly backed against the wall opposite the opening, his arm protectively around Jo's shoulders. He switched off the torch.

Nearer and nearer came the thing in the tunnel: scrape, slither, scrape, slither . . . It stopped. Suddenly two gleaming red eyes were shining out of the darkness and the chamber was filled with a series of uncanny shrieks and roars.

Jo, nearly fainting from fright, still managed to stop herself from screaming as the Doctor turned the full beam of his flashlamp directly onto the thing in the entrance.

There stood the gargoyle from the Cavern. Its misshapen stone body crouching evilly, its claws outstretched, its bat-like wings stretched above its head; it was alive, terrifyingly alive, its blood-red eyes shining from the grotesque face, while from its hideously twisted mouth came roar after unearthly roar.

There stood the gargoyle from the Cavern

6

Meetings

The Vicar was standing at the highest window in the Vicarage—the little window on the top landing—apparently looking across to the treetops at the mighty Goat's Back Ridge. He was watching the Devil's Hump and yet . . . he had his eyes closed. The Master was in full telepathic communication with his faithful servant, the gargoyle, Bok. Through Bok's eyes he could see Jo, shrinking back against the wall of the barrow chamber, and through Bok's eyes, in a moment, he would be witness to the fulfilment of one of his lesser ambitions—the death of his old enemy, the Doctor.

Funnily enough, he was experiencing a twinge of regret. They had not always been enemies. In the early days at school they had been playmates. Even later, though their paths diverged, a friendly rivalry had been as far apart as they would allow themselves to go. If only the Doctor weren't so abominably good! All this claptrap about morality, integrity, compassion and the rest! If only he had seen sense, together they could have ruled the Universe . . . But there it was. The Doctor had chosen. It was his own fault that he had to be killed. The Master came out of his reverie with a start. What in the name of Beelzebub was the stupid creature up to? He concentrated, and a picture formed in his mind's eye : the Doctor advancing on Bok, holding in front of him . . . what was it? Oh yes, a small trowel. Of course, it would be made of steel. Iron had always been a basic magical defence. But Bok had ample power to overcome it. Why didn't he attack?

The Master felt waves of fear flowing from the mind of his creature. 'Attack, Bok! Kill him! You have no reason to be afraid. Kill him!'

Bok raised his hand and pointed it at the Doctor. The moment had come.

Through Bok's ears, the Master heard the Doctor speak. 'Klokleda partha mennin klatch !' he said.

The Master frowned. What was he up to? Those were not the words of power, at least, not ones that he recognised! The effect on Bok, however, was devastating. Recoiling across the smooth earth floor, snarling, he turned and fled down the tunnel. As soon as he was outside, he took to the air and, with his heavy wings beating, flew back towards the Vicarage, whimpering.

His face black with rage, the Master awaited him.

. . . . .

'But you don't believe in magic.' Jo's voice was still trembling.

'I don't, no. But he did, fortunately !'

'So that was some sort of spell that you said?'

'He thought it was. That's why he ran away. Actually it was the first line of a Venusian lullaby. Roughly translated, it goes, "Close your eyes, my darling; well, three of them at least".'

In spite of herself, Jo couldn't help but laugh.

'I must admit that I should have been quite defenceless if he had seen through my little deception,' said the Doctor wryly.

'But what was it?'

'It looked like a gargoyle. Carved out of stone.'

'But it was alive !'

'In a sense,' said the Doctor. 'Come on. Let's get out of here.' Lighting the way for Jo, he led her back down the tunnel into the fine spring morning. It seemed impossible that only a few short minutes ago they should have been in such peril.

'Anyway,' said Jo soberly, as they made their way across the springy turf, 'at least it wasn't the Devil.'

'You mean the creature Miss Hawthorne saw? No, that must have been a hundred times more terrifying.'

70

Jo shivered in the cool breeze. 'If I ever see him, I'll die, I just know I will.'

The Doctor stopped. 'Now listen to me, Jo. You're quite right to be frightened. But not because Miss Hawthorne saw this mythical Devil of yours. She saw something far more real and far more dangerous : an alien being who came here, in that spaceship, from a planet 60,000 light years away.'

'But I don't understand. I mean, why . . . ?'

The Doctor laid a finger on Jo's lips. 'No more questions. Not now.'

With an enormous effort, Jo suppressed her curiosity and followed the tall figure of the Doctor across to Bessie, who was still waiting patiently, where the Doctor had left her in the middle of the night.

.   .   .   .   .

Mike Yates had not been idle while the Doctor and Jo were away. First, he begged from Bert a half-inch paint brush, some ink and a large piece of paper—the back of the poster announcing last year's Garden Fête, so Bert informed him, when the Squire, with a series of chancy bowls, won himself a piglet and insisted on christening it with champagne . . . At last Mike managed to get rid of the garrulous and inquisitive landlord and settle down to his task. Benton, who had flatly refused to go to bed, dozed in the sun, nominally on R.T. watch, listening out for the Brig's next message. Mike had always enjoyed making notices; he took great pride in his skill at lettering. Several times he had to forcibly remind himself of the serious nature of the legend on the poster he was making. Firstly, he referred to the extraordinary events of the night before. These, he informed the village, were being investigated. Secondly, he issued a solemn warning in big black capitals, of the heat barrier. Thirdly, he suggested that all adults (defined as being over eighteen, a perhaps unwarranted assumption) should foregather in the village hall at five o'clock that evening, there to hear some sort of explanation of what was going on, insofar as that were possible, and agree some plan of action. As he was putting a final flourish on the last letter, smiling to himself at Benton's snores, Miss Hawthorne returned.

During the short time she had been away she had contrived to have a bath, change her clothes, re-braid her hair, feed Grimalkin, her familiar tabby cat with a remarkably handsome shirt front, and breakfast sumptuously on muesli and dandelion coffee. As soon as she saw what Mike had been doing, she went off into peals of laughter, braying so heartily that the Sergeant leaped to his feet, ready for instant action. Mike was momentarily cut to the quick, until he realised that it was neither the matter nor the manner of his masterpiece which was the occasion of her merriment, but rather the fact that he contemplated putting it up at all.

'My dear good man,' she gasped, 'it's obvious that you've never lived in a village.'

Mike had to agree that she was right.

'If you had,' she went on, 'you'd never have wasted your time. You're a stranger, you see, a foreigner, and so they'll be suspicious of anything you do, especially anything that smacks of giving orders, dear boy! And how do you suppose Lily Watts is going to react to your playing fast and loose with the village hall like that?'

Benton snorted with suppressed mirth.

'Lily Watts?' Mike said weakly.

'Lily Watts is the letting committee of the hall.'

'The ... er ... chairman?'

'No, no. She *is* the committee. Nobody would dare plan a function without her approval.'

'But surely . . . this is an emergency.'

'You've got to convince *them* of the fact.'

Mike was at a loss. 'All right then, Miss Hawthorne,' he said in desperation. 'You tell me what I should do.'

Miss Hawthorne thought for a moment. 'Well,' she said, 'your only hope of getting that notice accepted would be to get it signed by somebody with a position in the community: the Vicar, say, though that's out of the question, of course, wretched man . . . or Mr. Groom, our village constable . . . or best of all, the chairman of the Parish Council.'

Mike sighed. 'And who's the chairman of the Parish Council?'

'Why the Squire, of course : Mr. Winstanley. Have you any transport? It's quite a walk up Box Hill.'

'Only the helicopter, I'm afraid.'

'Much too ostentatious, Mr. Yates. We'll borrow a bicycle for you.'

And so it turned out. Bert dug out an ancient single-gear sit-up-and-beg machine of uncertain vintage and as Mike wobbled unsteadily off after Miss Hawthorne, Bert set off on foot in the other direction straight to the Vicarage, to report this latest development to Mr. Magister.

.   .   .   .   .

The Squire had a headache. He had noticed before the odd coincidence that these migraines of his often came in the morning after a long evening at 'The Cloven Hoof'. 'All that stimulatin' conversation, too much for the old nerves. Always was a sensitive child . . .' The front door bell rang and jangled furiously between the Squire's ears. As the effect subsided, leaving the normal dull throb, the door opened and his housekeeper appeared.

'It's that Miss Hawthorne, sir. And a Mr. Yates.'

'I'm not in, Mrs. Anstey, I'm out. I'm ill. I'm dying, woman!'

'Ah! There you are, Squire.'

The Squire groaned. Only Miss Hawthorne would barge in like that without so much as a by-your-leave.

'I am not well, madam.'

'Then we shan't detain you long. This is Mr. Yates.'

Mrs. Anstey quietly left. She knew better than to tangle with Miss Hawthorne in this mood.

'Miss Hawthorne, please. I tell you, I'm not well. Please go away.'

'All in good time, Mr. Winstanley,' replied the white

witch. 'We want you to sign something. Where is it, Mr. Yates?'

Mike reluctantly produced his poster. He had an uncomfortable feeling that this interview wasn't going quite right. He'd better try a little diplomacy. 'We were rather hoping, sir, that you might chair the meeting this evening.'

The Squire immediately dug in his heels. Chair a wretched meeting, eh? He would have been prepared to sign anything, just to get rid of this pestilential pair, but not if it meant having to be chairman. Always bein' chairman, dammit! Worst job in the world. And him at death's door, too. 'Let's have a look at the blasted thing.' Taking it from Mike, he puzzled his way through it. 'What's all this about a heat-barrier? What the deuce is a heat-barrier?'

'Well, sir, we don't quite know. But it seems to be extremely dangerous.'

'Have the authorities been told?'

'Er . . . yes. I suppose they have.'

'Then it's up to them to cope. As for the rest of it, let sleeping dogs lie, that's my motto. Sorry about the Professor and all that, but still . . .'

Miss Hawthorne was exasperated. Silly old fool! Hadn't as much intelligence as Grimalkin. She raised her voice. 'Now listen to me, Squire . . .' The Squire winced and put a tender hand to his temple. At once Miss Hawthorne's voice softened. 'Why, Mr. Winstanley, I do believe you have a headache!' The Squire could only nod. 'Why didn't you tell me? I'm not a witch for nothing, you know.' And she started ferreting in her handbag.

Mike Yates watched her, fascinated. Was he really about to witness a demonstration of real witchcraft, albeit white witchcraft?

Miss Hawthorne surfaced, clutching a small glass phial filled with a golden liquid. She removed the stopper and proffered the phial to the somewhat anxious Squire.

'Now, wait a minute . . .'

'A simple potion, nothing more. Knock it back, like a good boy.'

Winstanley suspiciously accepted the potion. He glanced at each of them. 'Well . . . bung ho and all that . . .'

As soon as he had drunk it, Miss Hawthorne jumped to her feet. Placing a bony forefinger on the centre of the Squire's forehead, she started to mutter under her breath. The Squire was quite taken aback. Not daring to move, his eyes darted to and fro as if he were seeking a way of escape. Gradually, however, his face cleared, and by the time Miss Hawthorne had completed her incantation, if such it was, he was actually smiling.

'It's gone!' he said. 'My migraine, my headache, quite gone!'

'Of course,' said Miss Hawthorne. 'Sign here, please,' and she held out the poster and a pen.

'With the greatest of pleasure, dear lady,' beamed the Squire, taking the pen and signing with a firm hand.

Two minutes later, having successfully fended off the celebratory drink the Squire had tried to thrust upon them, Mike and Miss Hawthorne were coasting down the long drive.

'Well,' said Mike, 'I really take my hat off to you. I can't say I ever really believed in magic before but . . .'

'Magic,' said Miss Hawthorne scornfully, 'that wasn't magic. I wouldn't waste good witchcraft on him.'

'What was it, then?'

'An infusion of a herbal analgesic—about as powerful as a couple of aspirin.'

'And the spell?'

'Pure suggestion to increase the placebo effect.'

'I beg your pardon?'

'He believed it was a spell too, you see. As a matter of fact, I was reciting—"Mary Had a Little Lamb". So now you know all my little secrets, don't you?' And smiling archly, she sailed away down Box Hill with Mike desperately pedalling after.

.   .   .   .   .

Sergeant Benton and his partner had just executed a double natural turn into a hesitation running reverse. The applause was deafening. Finishing the quickstep with a ballet lift, the Sergeant tossed Mavis ten feet in the air and caught her neatly on the little finger of his left hand.

'Mr. Benton,' said the judge, as he handed over the Championship Cup, 'I am proud to know you. What is more, I think I can say without fear of contradiction, "Bleep . . . bleep . . . bleep . . . bleep".' Sergeant Benton woke up. 'Bleep . . . bleep . . . bleep . . .' continued his receiver. Hastily he pressed the 'transmit' button.

'Greyhound Three. Over.'

'Is that you, Benton? What's going on? You all asleep or something?' The Brigadier's voice was not friendly.

'Er no, sir . . . that is, not all of us. Over.'

'Mm . . . Captain Yates there?'

'No, sir.'

'The Doctor?'

'No, sir.'

'I see. Well, listen Sergeant, we still can't get through this wretched heat barrier. Incinerates anything we try. Tell the Doctor, will you? Over.'

'Sir, have you . . . I mean, well, can't you go round it, sir? Over.'

'The thought had occurred to me, Sergeant Benton.'

The door of the pub swung open as the Doctor walked in with Jo.

'I've sent out patrols,' continued the Brigadier's voice, *'and as far as I can see . . . what's that, Osgood? Ah, yes . . . yes, the final report has just come through. The perimeter of this thing is an unbroken circle, ten miles in diameter, its centre being the village church. Over.'*

The Doctor walked over and took the walkie-talkie from Benton's hand. 'Lethbridge Stewart? The Doctor here. What about going over the top of it?'

'The R.A.F. are just coming through now. Hang on a minute.' Doubly distorted, the voice of the R.A.F. could be heard faintly—but the message was quite clear : *'Red*

Zero Four to Trap Two. No soap, I say again, no soap. Last test canister exploded at four thousand five hundred feet altitude. Estimate dome-shaped barrier above village approximately one mile high at apogee. Over . . .'

Benton gave Jo a worried look.

'Did you hear that, Doctor?' resumed the Brigadier, *'we're locked out. Over.'*

'Or we're locked in. Thank you, Brigadier. We'll be in touch.' And he switched off, handing the receiver back to Benton.

'You're supposed to say, "Out", Doctor,' said the Sergeant reproachfully.

The Doctor started to unfasten his cloak. 'Well,' he said, 'we would appear to be in the middle of a sort of lethal mushroom, ten miles across and a mile high.'

Sergeant Benton got up from his chair and stretched. 'I dunno,' he said, 'I'm lost. I wish I had a clue what's going on.'

Jo brightened. 'Oh,' she said. 'Well, you see . . .'

'All in good time, Jo,' interrupted the Doctor, 'all in good time. Ah, Miss Hawthorne, the very person I need. And Captain Yates. Good!' And immediately he and the new arrivals plunged into a morass of plans, possibilities, ways and means.

Jo looked at the Sergeant and shrugged.

'Do you know what it's all about?' asked Benton.

'Not really,' she answered, 'just that it's aliens. From outer space.'

Sergeant Benton sighed resignedly. 'It always is,' he said.

.   .   .   .   .

'Come in, Vicar,' cried Montmorency Winstanley, 'the very man. Been wantin' to have a word with you. Sit down, sit down. What'll you have? Scotch?'

Mr. Magister raised a declining hand. 'Thank you, no,' he said, 'why should I put a thief into my mouth to steal away my brains?'

'Eh?'

'Paul.'

'Paul who?'

'Saint Paul, I'm afraid.'

'Ah.' The Squire decided not to have another.

'And what was it you wanted to have a word about, Squire?'

'Oh, yes.' Winstanley sat down in the tapestry armchair opposite the Vicar and leaned forward with an earnest expression. 'It's like this . . .' he said. There was a long pause. 'It's just that . . .' Another long pause.

'Yes?' said Mr. Magister encouragingly.

'Can't remember,' said the Squire, getting up and crossing to the sideboard.

'I'm not at all surprised,' said the Vicar, sympathetically. 'A man in your position, a leader . . . nay, *the* leader of the community, must have so many things on his mind.'

The Squire, with the air of a man carrying the affairs of the world on his shoulders, splashed a little soda into his whisky.

'Indeed,' the Vicar went on, 'that is precisely why I have come to see you. In troubled times like these it behoves us to stick together. Wouldn't you agree?'

'Us?' enquired the Squire, lowering himself into his chair again.

'Of course. The leaders; the front-runners; the . . . er . . . though I hesitate to use an unfashionable word . . . the élite.'

The Squire raised an eyebrow. What was the fellow getting at?

'I feel the people of the village are becoming restive. Since the unfortunate events of last night there has been an ugly smell of panic in the air. I think it's up to us . . . to you, in fact . . . to set an example; to give a lead . . .'

Sounded like sense. Got the root of the matter in him this fellow, even if he was a padre. 'Er . . . what are you suggesting?' asked the Squire.

'Well, that's up to you, of course. After all, you're the Squire.'

Winstanley took an uneasy swig of his drink. 'Open to suggestions, Vicar.'

'Well now, I would suggest that you should call a little meeting. Not too large, you understand, say thirty or forty of the more prominent villagers—why, you could have the meeting in here—and make it clear the attitude they should take. What do you say?'

The Squire was staring at him with glazed eyes.

'What do you say, Squire?' repeated the Vicar.

The Squire seemed to wake up. 'Hens,' he said.

'Hens?'

'What I wanted the word about, Elsie Bates's hens. Bewitched, apparently.'

The Vicar took a deep breath. 'Precisely the sort of thing I meant,' he said, 'such nonsense must be nipped in the bud. These people must be *told* what to think and what to do. They must learn to obey. Now, if we were to hold this meeting . . .'

'Yes, yes, I heard you. It's all fixed up. Chairing the wretched thing myself. Five o'clock in the village hall, if Lilly Watts has no objection.'

The Vicar seemed irritated. 'No, no, no! I'm talking about action, decisive action, action *now*, not a W.I. gossip party.'

'Well, really!'

'It's quite time you started acting like the Squire, Winstanley.'

Winstanley sat up. 'You may be the Vicar, Vicar, but I'll thank you not to take that tone with me.'

'Aha,' cried Mr. Magister, 'a man of spirit! Exactly what's needed at a time like this.'

The Squire was a little mollified. 'Mm . . . be that as it may, I still don't see what you're getting at.'

The Vicar jumped to his feet and started to pace up and down. 'Decadence. That's what I can see on every side. All this talk of democracy, equality, freedom. What this country needs is decision, power, strength. Strong men, men of power, men of decision; men like *you*, Winstanley.'

No getting away from it, he was a sensible chap. 'Go on,' said the Squire.

The Vicar came close to him. 'Listen to me. Listen to my words. I *know*.'

Extraordinary eyes the fellow had. Big and black . . . or no . . . more like a deep purple . . . 'Who . . . who are you?' said the Squire.

'I am the Master,' said the Vicar, softly. 'I control a power which can save the world. And if you choose, you can share my triumph.'

With an effort the Squire tore his eyes from the Master's gaze. 'Power? What power?'

A flicker of anger crossed the Master's face. 'I control the forces which have been unleashed in Devil's End during the last few hours.'

'What?' said Winstanley, 'all that business at the dig? Are you trying to tell me you were behind all that?'

'Exactly,' said the Master.

'Ridiculous,' said the Squire and burst out laughing.

The Master flushed. 'You require proof. Very well, proof you shall have.' Closing his eyes and lifting his head, the Master started to mutter strange words, words compounded of sounds powerful in themselves, words to send a shudder down the spine. At once the room seemed to come alive. The curtains fluttered as if in a strong breeze. The sideboard tilted and fell over, depositing its load of glass on the floor with a crash. The priceless Meissen china figure on the grand piano flew up in the air and hurled itself into the hearth. The portrait of the nineteenth-century Admiral Winstanley over the fireplace split neatly down the middle and fell to the ground. And all the time the door was slamming open and shut and the windows were breaking pane by pane. The very air seemed to quiver, as a whining sound like a thin shriek grew louder and louder until it threatened to split the very fabric of the house.

'Stop it! Stop it!' cried Winstanley.

For a moment, the Master ignored him. Then, as if coming back from far away, he looked up. He snapped his fingers. At once the room was still.

'Well?'

'I'll do anything . . . I'll do anything you say,' gasped the terrified Squire.

'Very well. I shall be back in an hour.' The Master's speech was slurred. 'You understand?'

'Yes, yes, of course.'

The Master turned and walked out of the shattered room. Squire Winstanley sank slowly into the tapestry chair and buried his face in his trembling hands.

His headache was coming back.

7
Explanations

Sitting round the rickety old oak table in the little back room of 'The Cloven Hoof' Jo, Mike and Sergeant Benton were tucking into a traditional 'Ploughman's Lunch'— large slabs of cheese, crusty new bread with farm butter and crunchy pickled onions; all washed down with pints of draught cider or strong ale. Miss Hawthorne had graciously accepted one small apple, stating it as her considered opinion that too much eating in the middle of the day led to sluggish vibrations in the afternoon.

'Do come and eat something, Doctor,' called Jo.

But the Doctor was too far away to think of food. Surrounded by piles of books of every shape, size and age, he was hunting here and there through them, making notes and leaving slips of paper as book marks.

'Well, well, well! The *Grimoire* of Pope Honorius!' The Doctor had seized an ancient leatherbound volume with great excitement. 'A copy I never knew existed . . .'

'You have the pick of the finest collection of occult material in the country there, Doctor,' said Miss Hawthorne proudly, 'though why you wanted me to bring it, I can't think.'

'I hope that will become clear. Apart from anything else, I'm being pestered for an explanation. These books will help me to provide it.'

Miss Hawthorne looked puzzled. 'But Doctor, there is only one possible explanation : this is the supernatural at work.'

The Doctor looked up from his notes. 'Nonsense !' he said.

Benton thoughtfully chumped on a pickled onion. 'What about that thing that got me? That was real enough.'

The Doctor had returned to his books. 'There's nothing more real than a force-field, Sergeant,' he said, marking a large coloured picture of a goat, 'even a psionic force-field.'

Miss Hawthorne bristled. To have her cherished beliefs challenged ! It was unthinkable. 'You're being deliberately obtuse, Doctor. We are dealing with the supernatural, I tell you. The Occult ! Magic !'

The Doctor shook his head. 'Science,' he said.

'Magic !'

'*Science*, Miss Hawthorne.'

Mike Yates finished off his beer. 'Really,' he said, 'what does it matter? There's no point in getting all hot under the collar about words. The important thing is to find a way to stop it, whatever it is.'

'How can you stop it without *knowing* what it is?' said Jo indignantly, leaping to the Doctor's defence as usual.

'Well done, Jo,' said the Doctor, getting up, 'you're being logical at last.'

'Oh, am I? Thanks,' said Jo, doubtfully.

'We'll turn you into a scientist yet. Now then. If you've all finished perhaps we could clear a space.'

One end of the table was quickly cleared of the remains of the meal and the Doctor was able to spread out a number of books. 'Right,' he said, 'here we go,' and he opened the first book. 'Who's that?'

'It's an Egyptian god, isn't it?' said Jo.

'Top of the class. The God Khnum—one of their gods with horns.' He opened the next book. 'A Hindu Demon— with horns.' Another. And another. 'The Ancient Greek god Pan—with horns. A bust of Jupiter—with horns. A statue of Moses—yes, even he's got horns. The Minotaur—the bull-headed monster of Crete. Our old friend the Horned Beast—the Devil with the head of a goat . . .' The Doctor went on opening book after book, until the table was filled with pictures of horned beings.

Miss Hawthorne was not impressed. 'You could go on all day and all night showing us pretty pictures,' she said tartly. 'It proves nothing. Horns have been a symbol of power ever since . . . Oh, ever since . . .'

'Even since man began,' agreed the Doctor. 'Look.' He showed them yet another picture—a photograph of a prehistoric cave-painting which seemed to show a group of a witch doctors dancing, all with horns upon their brows. 'But has it ever struck you to ask yourself why?' the Doctor continued. 'Creatures like that have been seen over and over again throughout the history of man, and man has turned them into myths—into gods or devils.' He gestured towards the pictures. 'But they're neither. They are creatures from another world . . .'

Even Miss Hawthorne was silenced.

'You mean,' said Benton slowly, 'like the Axons, and the Nestenes—and the Cybermen?'

'Precisely,' said the Doctor, 'but far, far older and immeasurably more dangerous.'

'Charming,' murmured Mike Yates.

'Are you suggesting that these creatures came to Earth in spaceships?' said Miss Hawthorne, regaining her composure.

'Yes, I am,' he replied. 'They're Dæmons* from the planet Damos; and that's a long long way from Earth.'

'Sixty thousand light years,' put in Jo, wisely.

'That's right. The other side of the Milky Way; and they first came to Earth nearly one hundred thousand years ago . . .'

'But why? I mean, why should they want to?' asked Benton.

* pronounced *deemons*.

So the Doctor went on to tell them something of the history of these alien beings, the Dæmons, or Demons. He told of their evolution and the development of their culture over long aeons even before life began on Earth. When the first land creatures were crawling out of our oceans, the Dæmons already had a fully developed civilisation with a sophisticated science and technology. By the time man appeared, the Dæmons had been space-travellers for many centuries and had established a tradition of scientific exploration and experiment throughout the Galaxy. They arrived on Earth just in time to help *homo sapiens* kick out Neanderthal Man and they have been appearing on and off ever since, merely observing most of the time but occasionally giving history a push in the right direction . . .

'There you are,' said Miss Hawthorne, triumphantly, 'that proves you're talking nonsense. This . . . thing that Professor Horner loosed on the world is evil. You said so yourself. And now you tell us that they have been helping mankind for a thousand centuries !'

'Yes,' said Jo, 'and you say they're from another planet. Then what's all this jazz about witchcraft and covens and all ?'

'A very good point, Miss Grant,' put in Miss Hawthorne.

'But don't you see,' explained the Doctor, 'all the magical traditions are just the remnants of the Dæmons' advanced science. And that's what the Master is using !'

'Mm . . .' Miss Hawthorne was unconvinced. 'And how do you know all this anyway ?'

'Yes, Doctor,' said Mike, 'you didn't seem to know what was going on at first.'

'I learned it at school,' said the Doctor grumpily, 'chapter thirteen of the Galactic History. Unfortunately, I forgot it all.' He stood up and started to clear away the books.

'You must have gone to a very odd school—and you must have a very peculiar memory,' said Miss Hawthorne.

'That, madam, is my misfortune,' said the Doctor

acidly, for she had touched on a sore point. 'In any case, it's all in these books of yours, if you know how to read them properly.'

'Then these creatures *are* linked with the Black Arts,' she said. 'They *are* evil.'

'Amoral would be a better word, perhaps,' the Doctor replied. 'They help Earth, but on their own terms. It's a scientific experiment to them. We're just a cageful of laboratory rats.'

'Then what's the Master up to?' asked Mike.

'He's established a link with the Dæmon from the barrow. What frightens me is the choice—domination by the Master or total destruction.'

Jo, who had been stacking the books in a neat pile, looked up aghast. 'You mean this Dæmon could destroy the Earth?'

'What does any scientist do with an experiment that fails? He throws it in the rubbish bin. And you must admit that mankind doesn't look a very successful species at the moment.'

'But Doctor . . . you're talking about the end of the world!'

The Doctor looked at her very seriously. 'Yes, Jo,' he said, 'I am.'

.   .   .   .   .   .

The Squire's entrance hall had seen many a Minuet and Quadrille, indeed many a Charleston and Tango, though it was now many years since last a Hunt Ball was held there. Now, thirty-seven men and women, mostly middle-aged, stood in awkward groups, exchanging *sotto voce* trivialities and waiting to be told why they were there. As the big door from the drawing-room opened and the Squire appeared, closely followed by the vicar, there were a few scattered handclaps, an embryonic burst of applause, quickly stillborn as the set faces of their betters told the assembled villagers of the gravity of the occasion. The Squire mounted the short flight of stairs to the first landing, which made a natural platform, with the famous Winstanley stained-glass window as a backing. The groups started to drift together as it became obvious that Mr. Winstanley was about to make a speech.

'Just tell them why you've called them together,' murmured the Master in his ear. 'Leave the rest to me.'

'Of course, of course,' said Winstanley.

Turning to the villagers, he lifted his hand for silence. 'Meeting to order, please! Thank you! Thank you, ladies and gentlemen!' The subdued chatter died away and thirty-seven faces looked expectantly up at the Squire.

'Now then,' he said, 'as you know, my speeches are like me—short, but packed with good solid meat,' and he slapped himself a couple of times on the belly while he waited for the respectful chuckle he knew would greet this terrible joke, which was an old and trusted friend. Laboriously and at some length the Squire started to go through the events since midnight. The announcement of the heat barrier caused a buzz of wonder, quickly stilled as the Squire told them of the death of P.C. Groom and pointed out some of its implications.

Seeing that Winstanley was fairly launched, the Master stepped quietly down to the bottom of the stairs and beckoned to Tom Wilkins, the garage owner, who was standing with one or two more members of the coven. Nodding towards the little study door down the hall, the Master whispered in Wilkins' ear. Tom Wilkins, glancing up at the Squire, who was still going strong, nodded and slipped quietly away.

'So it seemed to me,' the Squire was saying, 'that we ought to get together and have a bit of a chat about the situation. Before it gets out of hand.'

A murmur of approval.

'Now, it appears that Mr. Magister here has had a few thoughts on the subject, so I've asked him to say the odd word . . . Vicar?'

As Tom Wilkins disappeared into the study, he could hear Mr. Magister starting his 'odd word' with the obligatory joke: 'Now, I promise you that this isn't going to be a sermon . . .' followed by the ritual chuckle from his audience. Then he shut the door and could hear no more. Crossing to the untidy desk, he pushed aside a pile of bills and pulled the telephone across. He dialled.

'Yes? Who is it?' an impatient voice answered.

'That you, Bert?'

'Who do you think it is, Tom Wilkins—Old Nick?'

'That's not funny, Bert,' said Wilkins looking over his shoulder. Asking for trouble it were, making stupid cracks like that.

'Well, what do you want, then? I've got a bar full of people . . .'

'Ah, yes. Magister wants to know what that Doctor's up to. He's still there, isn't he? Him and the rest of his lot?'

'Yes, he's still here. In the back.'

'Well, better get in there and find out what's going on. Magister wants to know, like.'

'Does he now? Then he'd better come and mind my bar if he wants me to run errands for him. You go and tell him that.'

'Aw, come on, Bert!'

'I'll be going in to clear the table when things ease off out here. It'll have to wait till then.'

'Okay. Better ring me back on this number,' and he read it out.

When he rejoined the others in the hall, the Vicar had just finished his opening platitudes and was getting down to business. 'Even though I am a newcomer here, already I feel that I know you—indeed, that I know you well. You, Mr. Thorpe . . .' Ron Thorpe, the prosperous owner of the grocery in the High Street, smirked ingratiatingly. 'Are you still padding the bills of the local gentry?' went on the Vicar. Winstanley gave the spluttering Thorpe a sharp look.

'Don't trouble to deny it, Mr. Thorpe,' smiled the Vicar, 'you see, I know. And what about you, Charlie— how's your conscience? Will you get the Post Office books to balance in time? Mr. Greville, has your wife come back from her sister's yet? Will she ever come back, do you suppose? Not while that pretty young Rosie's still about, I'll be bound . . .'

It was so obvious that the Vicar's chosen victims were guilty that the rest of his listeners immediately started to search their own consciences and, with one or two exceptions, began to blush in anticipation and fear of what the next few moments might reveal.

The Master, however, was satisfied with his trivial show of power. 'Please don't be worried, any of you. Your little secrets are quite safe with me. And don't be angry either. You see, I'm on your side.'

His audience eyed him suspiciously.

'If you listen to me and do as I say, you can get exactly what you want, your dearest ambition, your most secret desire. If you listen to me!'

His audience stared at him in hostile silence.

.   .   .   .   .

'A spaceship fifteen inches long?' Mike Yates said with a laugh, 'you buy those from the toyshop.'

'Honestly, Mike, I saw it myself,' said Jo, 'up at the barrow. It's what that creature came in apparently.'

'Then what are we all worrying about?' said Mike, 'he must be only a wee little demon the size of that pepper-pot!'

'Now really,' said Miss Hawthorne, 'you seem to forget that I have seen him. He was getting on for thirty feet tall.'

'But that's exactly what gave me the clue,' said the Doctor. 'You see, the Dæmons can diminish themselves as well as any object they choose. When that spaceship landed it was something like two hundred feet long and thirty feet across. And the Dæmon himself can be anything from thirty feet tall down to the size of the pepper-pot—or a grain of pepper, for that matter.'

'But where's the clue in that?' asked the Sergeant.

'Well, the freeze-up, you see. And the heat wave.'

'Mm?' said Jo, 'say again, Doctor. You've lost me.'

'Oh really, Jo. $E = MC^2$.' The Doctor looked in despair at the group of uncomprehending faces.

'You're the Doctor,' said Jo, shrugging.

'If you lose mass, the energy has to go somewhere. So it's lost as heat.'

'I think I see,' said Mike, slowly. 'It's like the gas in a 'fridge. When it expands, it takes heat from the inside, so the food and stuff gets cold . . .'

'. . . and when the gas is compressed again, it gives heat off, so that radiator thing at the back of the refrigerator gets warm!' Sergeant Benton beamed with pleasure at his own cleverness.

'Well done, Mike. And you, Sergeant,' said the Doctor. 'That's not exactly how it works, but it's a very good comparison.'

Miss Hawthorne was not looking quite so sure of herself as before. 'Well, it all sounds very plausible, I'll admit, but I can't say that you've convinced me. How do you propose dealing with this . . . this Dæmon?'

'Well,' said the Doctor, sitting down and starting to make some calculations on a scruffy piece of paper that had fallen from one of the books, 'well, if it were magic we were facing, it would be a hopeless task. As it is, I think we can attack him through this very physical effect he's produced—the Brigadier's heat-barrier . . .'

The door opened and Bert's cheerful round face appeared. He spoke to Jo. 'Mind if I clear away?'

'No, no, go right ahead.'

'Like anything else?'

'No, thank you. That was delicious.'

In he came to clear the table and do a little spying on behalf of the Master. But to his chagrin, nothing was happening. Nothing at all—except for the Doctor scribbling figures on a scrap of paper. The others were just sitting or standing around, staring into the distance. Oh well, if there was nothing to report, okay, there was nothing to report. At least he could get on with his work . . .

.   .   .   .   .   .

Brigadier Lethbridge Stewart felt considerably less naked. With a squad of troops and a few vehicles, not to mention his Mobile H.Q., he felt ready to tackle anything, even this infernal heat-barrier.

'Osgood!'

'Yessir?' replied his technical Sergeant, who was in charge of all the complicated electronic equipment carried in the Mobile H.Q.

'Anything from Strike Command yet?'

'Not yet, sir.'

'Mm. Very good.' The Brigadier stepped down from the van and raised his binoculars, and stared across the invisible barrier. That must be the church. Looked peaceful enough. He lowered the glasses and pulled out his walkie-talkie.

'Greyhound Two. Over.'

'That you, Yates? Now listen. We're going to blast our way in. I'm in touch with the Artillery and R.A.F. Strike Command. You'd better get everybody evacuated to the cellars. Report when the operation's complete. Right? Over.'

Instead of the formal 'Wilco' from Yates which the Brigadier expected, there was a scuffling noise, followed by the Doctor's voice.

'Lethbridge Stewart, you'll do no such thing! Of all the idiotic plans . . . In the first place, the energy released could only strengthen the barrier. In the second place, you could provoke the most terrible reprisals; and in the third place, I have a better idea. Over.'

The familiar feeling of frustration the Brigadier so often experienced when dealing with the Doctor began to creep over him. 'Well, what is it?' he snapped. 'I'm not going to stand here like a spare lemon waiting for the squeezer. Do you hear? Over.'

'Have you got the Mobile H.Q. there?'

'Of course.'

'With the new Mark IV A condenser unit?'

'Hang on.' The Brigadier turned towards the van. 'Osgood!' he bellowed.

Osgood's worried face appeared at the door.

'Have we got a . . . a Mark IVA condenser unit? It's new apparently.'

'Yessir. Installed last week.'

'Good. Don't go away, Sergeant. *Yes, Doctor we have. Over.*'

'*Excellent,*' replied the Doctor, '*then I can solve your problem—and maybe ours into the bargain. We'll build a diathermic energy exchanger. Is your technical fellow there?*'

'*He's listening.*'

'*Right then. Tell him to build an E.H.F. wide-band-width-variable-phase-oscillator with a negative-feedback circuit, turnable to the frequency of an air-molecule at . . . what IS the temperature of the barrier, Brigadier?*'

The Brigadier looked enquiringly at Sergeant Osgood, who, looking more worried than ever, shrugged helplessly.

'*I'm sorry, Doctor,*' said the Brigadier, '*we've no idea what you're talking about. Over.*'

'*It's a simple enough question, I should have thought. How hot's the barrier? Over.*'

'No, no, no, what you said earlier. The oscillating feedback bit . . .'

The irritation in the Doctor's voice was quite clear even through the distortion of the tiny speaker. '*Oh, very well,*' he said, '*I'll have to come out and explain. Don't do anything until I get there. Understand?*'

The Brigadier sighed. '*All right, Doctor, we'll try it your way. But get a move on, will you?*'

'*I'll be there in ten minutes.*'

'*Make it five. Out.*'

.   .   .   .   .

The Doctor handed the walkie-talkie back to Mike and picked up his cloak.

'Of all the idiotic plans,' said Jo, 'as if blowing things up solves anything.'

The Doctor looked at her severely. 'The Brigadier,' he said, 'is doing his best to cope with an almost impossible situation. And since he is your superior officer, you might show him a little respect. Are you coming?' and he swept out. A slightly rebellious, but definitely subdued Jo Grant followed him.

'Are you sure there's nothing else I can get for you,' said Bert.

'Er . . . no, no thanks,' said Sergeant Benton.

Bert carried the loaded tray back to the kitchen and hurried straight to the telephone.

.   .   .   .   .

'Right, okay, got that,' said Tom Wilkins, slammed down the 'phone and hurried out of the study.

By using every ounce of practised charm, every trick of the demagogue, the Master had at last got the audience on his side. 'Fools! Rabble!' he thought to himself, 'that I, the Master, should demean myself so.' But then, the thought came again, a happy slave is an efficient slave. Of course he could compel them to follow, but how much better for the sheep to run into the pen of their own accord.

'You have chosen wisely,' he was saying . . . 'Everything is possible if you follow me. You can be the rulers! I offer you the world!'

A great round of applause greeted his peroration. At this moment, however, Tom Wilkins pushed his way through to the front.

'Mr. Magister . . .'

'Yes? What is it? Why do you interrupt me?'

'It's that Doctor . . .'

The Master snapped his fingers irritably to stop any further indiscretion. Coming swiftly down to Wilkins, he inclined his head and listened to Tom's whispered report. Then, having murmured a word of two of orders, he stood upright and another snap of his fingers sent Tom scurrying for the door. This little demonstration of power did not go unnoticed by the audience, who found it not at all to their liking. In those few short moments he had lost them.

'Very well then,' he resumed, silencing the angry buzz of chatter, 'the world can be yours. All I ask in return is your submission; your obedience to my will!'

No one spoke for a long moment. It was the Squire who found the voice of the meeting. 'What's all this about submission and obedience? You said we were going to rule ...'

The Master's patience snapped. '*You* rule! You are but dust beneath my feet! You refuse my offer. Very well, I will give you another choice : serve me or I shall destroy you!'

A shock of fear; he meant it.

'Well, if that's your brave new world, you can keep it,' said Winstanley, walking down the stairs. 'I think this meeting is at an end. I should be grateful, Vicar, if you would be so good as to leave.'

The Master smiled. Throwing back his head, he uttered a curious chattering noise from the back of his throat. Almost immediately the immense stained-glass window shattered into a hundred thousand splinters of colour, like a shower of gemstones, and Bok, the stone gargoyle, landed at the Master's side.

The Master snapped his fingers yet once more and pointed at the Squire, in whose face anger, amazement and terror could all be seen. Bok raised a twisted claw. There was a flash of red fire, a puff of smoke—and the Squire had disappeared, vaporised.

The Master spoke into the sudden silence. 'Is there anyone who agrees with the Squire?'

Not surprisingly, nobody did.

'Thank you,' the Master continued. 'It does my heart good to know that I have such a willing band of followers!' He looked round the room and smiled benevolently. 'Today is May Day. Go and enjoy yourselves. Celebrate the festival with your families. When I need you, I shall send for you ...'

And he laid a kindly hand on the head of the faithful Bok, crouching balefully at his side.

8

The Second Appearance

'But are you sure you can manage?' said Miss Hawthorne anxiously, as Sergeant Benton carried the large pile of books through the door, and out onto the green.

'Not the first time I've had a bit of a punch-up, Miss Hawthorne,' said the Sergeant, 'and I don't suppose it'll be the last.'

'You're a very courageous young man,' she said, following him out.

Mike Yates closed the door behind them and watched, smiling through the window, as the big Sergeant and the wiry little spinster crossed the middle of the green, where the UNIT helicopter was standing patiently chewing the cud.

'Well,' he thought, as he turned back into the room, 'what now?' He and the Sergeant had been ordered by the Brigadier to 'stay put and keep your eyes peeled', an order which he had every intention of interpreting very liberally, should the occasion arise. For the moment, however, he seemed to be stuck here with no particular job to do. Right, this was a good chance to have another go at thinking things out—without going to sleep, this time! Jo was quite right. Blowing things up was no way to solve a problem. Brain was the thing, not brawn. So, where had they got to? Where was the enemy? Ah, but first, *who* was the enemy? The Master or the Dæmon? Both of course, but still, even if they managed to sort out the Master—and that was a big enough job in itself—they would still have to face the Dæmon. So, where was he? According to Miss Hawthorne's story, he was almost certainly in the Cavern under the church. Why not go and have a look, then? Well, apart from the danger, there was the added difficulty that at the moment, if the Doctor's theory was correct, the Dæmon was about as big as a grain of sand; for all practical purposes, he was invisible.

Mike walked down to the window and looked out at the church, seeking inspiration. 'Here's a character in a hurry. Still he certainly knows how to handle that motor-bike,' he thought. Mike Yates realised with a sudden start exactly what the character on the bike was up to, riding up onto the grass, coming to a skid stop and running straight towards the UNIT helicopter.

'Hey!' yelled Mike, as he rushed out and ran across the grass to cut him off. The man, a thin wiry individual with a ferrety face, ignored him. Mike put on a spurt and managed to reach the chopper just as the man started to clamber aboard. Mike Yates pulled him out. Wilkins swung round and landed a surprisingly heavy blow. Mike, though a little shaken, fought back. One, two, three, straight at the chin. The fellow ought to have been out for the count. He seemed quite impervious to the heaviest blows Mike could muster up. It was like fighting an automaton, a robot. Wilkins drew back his right hand and swung it like a club. It was a blow quite outside the normal run of boxing and should have been of little or no use. The effect on Mike Yates was devastating. Connecting with the side of his head, the blow sent him flying sideways as if he weighed nothing. He crashed to the ground and for a few vital seconds lay there, senseless. He recovered to hear the roar of the helicopter engine. Staggering to his feet, he stumbled towards it through the gale of wind raised by the flying rotors. Too late. As he reached it, it took off. Mike grabbed for the port landing skid as it rose past his face—and found himself off the ground, suspended ten, fifteen feet in the air. His grip, weakened by the recent blow, faltered and he fell to the ground. The weeks of careful parachute training every UNIT agent had to undergo had taught him how to fall correctly or he would have inevitably have broken a bone. Rolling to his feet, all in a movement, he stared frantically around the green—and espied the motor-cycle, abandoned by Wilkins. In less than half a minute from the time of the helicopter taking off, Captain Yates was on the bike and away on a seemingly impossible chase.

.   .   .   .   .

The beginning of the trip in Bessie was a little icy. Jo still felt hurt at the way the Doctor had spoken to her.

'I should put on your safety-belt, Jo,' he said, as they rattled away over the cobblestones outside 'The Cloven Hoof'.

Jo ignored him. It wasn't as if he'd be going fast and it wasn't far. Only five miles, the Brigadier had said.

Unfortunately, the Brigadier had established himself and his Mobile H.Q., on the road approaching Devil's End from the south-east, over the downs. This meant that although he was only five miles away from the village on the map—the shortest line between the two points—poor Bessie had over ten miles of twisting and turning, upping and downing, even before she got to the comparatively straight road across the downs.

Suddenly Jo realised that the Doctor was singing a jolly little song. She grinned to herself. She could never be cross with him for long. 'You sound happy,' she said. 'You must be very sure this idea of yours will work.'

The Doctor looked surprised. 'I was singing because . . . oh, because the sky is blue, I suppose.'

'But the Dæmon . . . and the end of the world and all?'

'Oh, yes, of course, the end of the world. But that's not now. That would be tomorrow—or this evening—or in five minutes' time. And right now, the sky is blue. Just look at it!'

Jo looked . . . and looked again. It certainly was blue! A deep, almost cobalt blue overhead fading to a pale greeny duck-egg blue near the horizon. She stared round, drinking in the blueness, becoming the blueness—and suddenly found that she was singing too!

'See what I mean,' smiled the Doctor.

Slowly it penetrated her consciousness that when she had looked to the left of the car, the sky hadn't been absolutely clear. She looked again and saw that it was the UNIT helicopter, coming straight towards them. 'Look, Doctor,' she cried.

The Doctor pulled up. 'Something must have happened,' he said. 'Benton and Yates were supposed to stay in Devil's End . . .'

'Well, we'll soon know,' said Jo, 'he's coming in to land.'

But he wasn't. He came down so low that if the Doctor and Jo hadn't ducked, he'd have taken their heads off. Then he swept up in a tight turn, obviously to come in again.

The Doctor started off. 'Who's driving that thing?'

'Well, it certainly isn't Mike. Look, there he is,' and she pointed at Mike on the motor-bike, taking a short cut across the moorland.

The helicopter had positioned itself for another descent. Now it started to swing down towards Bessie once more.

'Hold on, Jo,' shouted the Doctor, 'we're in for a bumpy ride.'

As the helicopter plummeted down on an inevitable collision course, the Doctor pulled on the wheel and swung off onto the grass, bumping and rattling across the moor.

Mike Yates roared up alongside. 'He's handling it like an expert!' he yelled to the Doctor, as the bike ran on a parallel course.

'Like a man possessed, you mean,' countered the Doctor. 'I'll try to draw him off.'

'No, Mike, stay back. He's after me, not you.'

But Mike swerved away from Bessie, pulling out his automatic. Controlling his bike with one hand he started to take highly inaccurate pot-shots at the helicopter as it started its third attack. At first it looked as if the firing might have frightened the helicopter off, but after a few moments it came in again—and again—and again . . .

'What's he trying to do?' screamed Jo, as the car swerved violently to the left and right, with the helicopter relentlessly in pursuit.

'He's trying to drive us into the heat barrier,' shouted the Doctor. 'There it is, dead ahead!'

Jo could see, very clearly, the strip of blackened turf crossing the downs which obviously marked the position of the barrier.

Now the Doctor stopped zig-zagging and was apparently bent on blowing Bessie up, for he was driving straight for the barrier, the helicopter close behind.

'Doctor!'

'Hang on, Jo. Hang on!'

At the last possible moment the Doctor flicked the wheel to the right. Bessie went over onto two wheels with a violent lurch, recovered, and ran neatly parallel to the burnt track of the barrier. The helicopter desperately tried to follow, but in vain. Meeting the barrier at about fifty feet, it exploded in a ball of flame.

'We've done it, Jo!' shouted the Doctor pulling up the car. But Jo was no longer in the passenger seat. That last swerve had been too violent. Jo had been thrown out.

The Doctor reached her at just the same moment as Mike Yates on his bike. She was quite unconscious. The Doctor quickly examined her. If only she had put on her seat-belt!

'Is she all right?' asked Mike anxiously.

'Nasty knock on the head, but that seems to be all. She should be all right,' answered the Doctor. 'Better get her into Bessie and take her back to the pub. She'll need rest and quiet for a bit.'

'Okay,' said Mike. 'How about you?'

'I'd better get across to the Brigadier. He's probably about to burst a blood vessel.' He nodded towards the UNIT vehicles which were visible on the other side of the barrier, about a hundred and fifty yards to the north-east.

As he helped Mike to lift Jo gently into the back of the car, the Doctor said, 'Look, Mike, you and the Sergeant had better stay at the pub. I'm going to need you when I get back.'

'Righto,' said Mike.

Having seen them safely on their way, the Doctor

climbed on the motor-cycle and set off, bumpety-bump, towards the Mobile H.Q.

'Well, Doctor,' said the Brigadier as he arrived, 'twenty thousand pounds of UNIT money gone up in a puff of greasy smoke.'

'You have the mind of an accountant, Lethbridge Stewart,' said the Doctor as he dismounted. 'So, this is your heat barrier, eh?'

'It is,' replied the Brigadier. 'And if you get any nearer, you'll know it. Watch this!' He picked up a large stone and tossed it towards the Doctor standing on the other side of the barrier. As it hit the invisible barrier, it exploded in a flash of fire.

'Even rock,' said the Doctor.

'Wood, rock, four-inch armour-plate; you name it, we've tried it. It's impenetrable.'

'A hasty and probably inaccurate assessment. Now then, I can't stand about gossiping. Have you enough cable to reach those high-tension pylons over there?'

The Brigadier estimated the distance. 'Should have, why?'

'We'll need at least 10,000 volts to get through the barrier. After that the machine will be charged sufficiently for what I have in mind.'

At the Doctor's request, the Brigadier called Sergeant Osgood over to listen to the explanation. He came, all his worries in abeyance, happily clutching a large pad to take down his instructions from the famous Doctor.

'What's the principle of it, sir?'

'Negative diathermy. Buffer the molecular movement of air with reverse-phase short-waves.'

'Beyond me,' said the Brigadier.

'It's just like a large version of those microwave ovens they use to heat up meat pies, Lethbridge Stewart. Difference is, we'll use it to cool the air down. Quite simple, really.'

'Simple,' gasped Osgood, all his worries returning. 'It's impossible!'

'Sergeant Osgood,' replied the Doctor, gently, 'according

to classical aerodynamics, it's impossible for a bumble bee to fly! Let's get on with it, shall we?'

.　　　.　　　.　　　.　　　.

Young Stan Wilkins, unaware of his uncle's death in the helicopter, gritted his teeth. What was he, a baby then, to be afeared of the dark? Moving quickly to the first of the candlesticks, he relit the big black candles with their shrouds of melted wax, trying not to look at the menacing shadows the light conjured from the depths of the Cavern. As he lit more and more candles—about half would do, so Mr. Magister had said—his nerve began to return. Magic! It was difficult to believe that he was mixed up in it. He'd always heard tell of secrets not to be spoken out loud; of the love-spells and recipes for potions, for instance, which the girls whispered to each other when the menfolk weren't around—pretended to laugh at them they did, with their mini-skirts and their perfume, but Stan knew better. Another thing he knew—because Bob Woods had told him and she was Bob's Gran after all—was that when old Mrs. Slenter inherited that £2,000 from her brother Josiah, it was on account of her having got fed-up waiting and made a little doll of candle grease and christened it Josiah, and then shoved a darning needle through its heart. And nobody could deny, could they, that it was his heart killed him? Just stopped. Proof, that was . . . So when his Uncle Tom said to come along to the coven like, well he'd jumped at it. Get anything he wanted, Tom said, when he'd learnt how. Didn't want to kill nobody, though he wouldn't mind making old Prune-face jump a bit, putting up the rent like that. His Mam hadn't cried so much since Dad died. Last straw, like. No, he knew what he wanted. Just enough money to put down on a cottage, and a good job so that his Mam wouldn't have to go out scrubbing no more. What was the good of being an apprentice? Learning a trade! Huh! Cheap labour for Uncle Tom, more like.

He finished lighting the last candle on the Stone of

Sacrifice and arranged the ritual vessels neatly on their black cloth. There. Just about in time, too. He'd better get going, before Mr. Magister showed up. Here, hang on a moment. If he didn't go; if he hid somewhere in the Cavern, then he could watch Mr. Magister. Learn some of his secrets, like!

Hearing a noise outside the door, he quickly slipped into the alcove behind him and hid behind the right-hand pillar.

The door swung open . . .

.   .   .   .   .

The Master, quite pleased with the day so far, walked briskly down the lane leading to the side gate into the churchyard. He smiled. A very fitting end for the Doctor, to be blown up in that stupid car of his. Pity about Miss Grant. She could have been useful in many ways.

A distant explosion. The Master's head swung round. There it was, away to the south-east, an ugly cloud of black smoke rising slowly above the treetops. The Master's smile faded. So. It was done! It had to be done and now it was done. He turned into the churchyard and walked up the path to the vestry door.

Even as he robed himself for the ritual, his mind was full of memories of his sometime friend. The time they played truant together, 'borrowed' the Senior Tutor's skimmer and went on an unauthorised visit to the Paradise Islands; the time he fooled the High Council of the Time Lords into thinking it was the Doctor who had put glue on the President's perigosto stick; the time the Doctor saved his life by . . . He shook his head fiercely. This was no time for weakness. If he was to control his guest, he would need all his strength and power.

Good, he thought, as he went down into the Cavern. The boy had carried out his instructions well. Everything was prepared.

Stan peeped out from behind his pillar. What was Mr. Magister doing? Ah, lighting the charcoal for the incense. Now he was stretching his hands over the Stone of Sacrifice and murmuring in a low voice. Stan strained to hear, his own lips moving in sympathy as he caught a familiar phrase. 'Io Evohe!' Now a flash of flame and a puff of coloured smoke; the Master's voice louder now, and clearer:

> *'By the power of the earth,*
> *By the power of air,*
> *By the power of fire eternal*
> *And the waters of the deep ...'*

Why, it were just the same as last night. What were he up to? The Master's voice became loud and commanding:

> *'... arise at my command!*
> *Azal! Azal!'*

Stan, holding the stone pillar, felt it tremble under his hands. He could hear a low soughing, as of a distant wind. The air was of a sudden surprisingly cold, even for the dank Cavern.

The Master was now reciting an incantation in some foreign tongue ... this was it! This must be the secret. He didn't say this lot last night. Stan desperately tried to seize hold of the strange sounding words and stow them in his memory, but they slipped away and were lost in the echoes of the Cavern. The ground was starting to shake now and the temperature was dropping fast. The Master's voice rose in a crescendo as he reached the climax of his invocation:

> *'... Malelt Tilad Ahyram!'*

An horrendous crack as of the thunder of hell, and the very earth lurched, throwing Stan to the floor. In desperation and despair, clinging with his fingernails to the cracks in the rock floor, he felt a wave of unearthly coldness sweep over into his body and through his bones. A foul animal stench made him retch. Over the sound of weird shrieking that now echoed round the Cavern, Stan again heard the voice of the Master. No longer was it triumphant, self-willed, commanding. Now it was filled with terror and supplication.

'Stop! Go back to the mark! You will destroy me! No! No!'

Stan forced himself to look up. The Master had evidently been thrown to the ground, just as he had himself. Advancing upon him, not ten feet away from Stan himself, were the giant legs of some creature so tall that his head was almost touching the roof of the Cavern. The legs, covered with shaggy hair like that of a goat, ended in a pair of gigantic hooves.

The Master had scrambled to his feet and recovered some of his usual arrogance. 'Go back, I say! Azal! I command you! Back, in the name of the Unspeakable One . . .' And the Master uttered a word of such power that once more the ground shook as if the world would crack.

The creature hesitated, and slowly retreated to the flagstone with the esoteric carving. Stan, as fascinated as he was terrified, tried to see what manner of face it had, but succeeded only in catching a glimpse of an ear; an ear almost human, but pointed and with a thick coating of hair. As the noise and the earthquake subsided, Stan struggled to his feet and squatted by the frost-enrimed pillar.

The Master gazed up, triumph in his face. 'At last,' he breathed.

A great rumble, as the bass tones of the creature's voice were heard for the first time. 'Speak,' it said.

'Azal, I bid you welcome. I am the Master. I brought you here.'

'That I know,' growled Azal. 'Tell me why you now call me.'

The Master drew himself up. 'I charge you . . . and I require of you . . . that you should give me your knowledge and your power.'

'Why should I?'

'So that I can rule these primitives on Earth and help them to fulfil your plan.'

'You are not one of their kind.' It was a statement rather than a question.

The Master showed no sign of surprise that the Dæmon should have recognised that he was not a native of Earth.

'I am superior to them in every possible way. That is why I should be their leader.'

There was a long silence as Azal appeared to digest this proposition. When he spoke at last, it was to demonstrate once more his uncanny power. 'There is another here of your race,' he rumbled.

This was more than the Master expected. 'He has been destroyed,' he said.

'No,' said the Dæmon, unemotionally. 'You are mistaken. He lives.'

The Master frowned.

'If you are superior by virtue of your race,' continued Azal, 'then so is he. I would speak with him.'

The Master was displeased. 'I think not,' he said coldly.

The Cavern shook with the anger of the Dæmon. 'Take care, creature,' he boomed. 'With your few pitiful grains of knowledge you have summoned me here. But I am *not* your slave—nor are you immortal!'

The Master obviously realised that he had gone too far. 'Forgive me, Mighty One,' he said, bowing respectfully. Azal's growls subsided. 'Nevertheless,' continued the Master, 'I claim that which is rightfully mine.'

Again the Dæmon did not answer at once. At length, he spoke slowly and thoughtfully. 'It is true that your mind at least is superior to the mind of man . . . and your will is stronger . . .'

Stan couldn't take his eyes from the Master's face. It was alive with evil glee, a triumphant malice horrible to see.

'Then I am to be your choice?'

Again the silence. 'I shall consider,' he said at last.

The Master's face betrayed his disappointment. 'You will come again?' he asked flatly.

'I shall appear but once more,' replied Azal. 'But be warned . . . there is danger. My race destroys its failures and this planet smells to me of failure. I am the last of the

Dæmons on this world. It may be that I shall destroy it
. . . and you. Do you still wish me to come again?'

The Master took a deep breath. 'I do,' he said.

9
Into Danger

Even five miles away at the heat barrier Azal's arrival made
itself felt. The ground swayed like the deck of a small ship
as it leaves the shelter of harbour. The jangle of the church
bells came faintly across the woods and the downs, as if in
warning.

The Brigadier came out of the Mobile Headquarters, just
at this moment. The Doctor was directing Sergeant Osgood in the construction of a complicated piece of apparatus almost too big to fit onto the back of a Land Rover,
and appeared to be quite oblivious of the shaking of the
ground.

'Doctor!' called the Brigadier. 'What's going on?'

'Mm?' said the Doctor, looking up abstractedly. 'What
do you want now, Lethbridge-Stewart?'

'It seems to have escaped your notice, Doctor, that there
is an earthquake.'

The Doctor stared vaguely over at the church. 'Oh yes,
so there is. The Dæmon must have appeared once more.'
He turned his attention back to Sergeant Osgood's contraption. 'No, man, no! You're trying to channel the entire
output of the National Power Complex through one transistor! Reverse the polarity!'

The Brigadier felt the old feeling of frustration creeping up on him once more. 'But, Doctor, aren't you going to
do anything about it?'

'I *am* doing something about it. I need that machine as
much as you do. In any case, it's quite clear from Miss
Hawthorne's books that the Dæmon always appears three
times. It's the third appearance we have to worry about.

That's when we could find ourselves in real trouble if we haven't finished this wretched machine.'

Sergeant Osgood rightly took this to be a dig at him. 'We'd get along much faster if we knew what we were doing, sir.'

'I couldn't agree with you more, Sergeant,' the Doctor said bitterly. 'Now please do your best to concentrate.'

Osgood, very conscious of the Brigadier's presence, struggled to keep quiet.

A corporal appeared in the doorway of the Mobile H.Q., and handed the Brigadier a signal.

'Excellent,' he said as he read it. 'Right, Osgood, we've fixed it with the electricity wallahs for the power to be off for fifteen minutes. Are you ready to link up?'

'No, sir.'

'Well, *when* will you be ready, for heaven's sake?'

Osgood shrugged. The Doctor answered for him. 'Christmas after next, I should say. A rough estimate, of course.'

Stung by this sarcasm, Osgood could not stop his feelings from spilling over. 'If you push 10,000 volts through this lash-up, you'll blow it, anyway,' he complained.

'Just do what you're told, Sergeant,' said the Brigadier calmly. 'The Doctor knows what he's doing.'

'Yes, sir,' replied the Sergeant, obviously not believing a word of it, and moved away to sort out the junction boxes ready for the link-up to the electricity supply. The Brigadier moved as close to the Doctor as the heat barrier would let him.

'*Do* you know what you're doing?' he asked quietly.

The Doctor smiled charmingly. 'My dear chap,' he said, 'I can't wait to find out!'

.   .   .   .   .   .

That Jo did not sleep right through the earthquake caused by the appearance of Azal was perhaps somewhat surprising, as she only recently had been injected with a powerful sedative by Doctor Reeves. When Mike appeared in the pub carrying the still very woozy Jo, Bert at once helped Mike to take her upstairs, while Miss Hawthorne and the Sergeant went out to find the busy Doctor Reeves. By the time he had been found (visiting Lily Watt's youngest, whose measles turned out to be painted on with a ball-point pen) Jo was apparently quite awake, but obviously suffering the effects of the blow on her head.

'In the Cavern,' she moaned, as he examined her. 'He said the danger was in the Cavern .. !'

Doctor Reeves filled a hypodermic syringe. 'Just lie still, my dear. Try to relax. This won't hurt.'

'But the Doctor . . .' she gasped, trying to sit up. 'I must help him; I must help him to find the Master.'

Mike made her lie down on the bed again, so that Doctor Reeves could give the injection.

'Take it easy, Jo,' said Mike, as she weakly struggled against his firm but gentle grip, 'as soon as the Doctor gets back, we'll all go and sort out the Master. Now, don't worry!'

By this time the injection was beginning to take effect. 'No, no, we must go now . . .' protested Jo, feebly, '. . . there's no . . . time to . . . be . . .' Her voice trailed away and Mike felt her relax. He disengaged himself and looked anxiously at Doctor Reeves.

'That's better,' the physician was saying. 'A few hours' sleep and she'll be as right as rain. How did she come to fall out of the car?'

'Well, you see . . .' began Mike, and stopped as he realised the enormity of the tale he had been about to tell. 'It's a long story, Doctor Reeves,' he said, steering him to the door . . .

The heavy sleep induced by the sedative should have lasted for two or three hours, but when the house began to shake she was instantly awake, sitting up clutching the bed-clothes, with a nightmare fear filling her stupefied mind. As the shaking started to die down, her fears, if not forgotten, were overcome.

'The Cavern . . .' she mumbled to herself, climbing shakily out of bed. 'I must get to the Cavern . . .'

She weaved her way to the door. The 'quake had in fact stopped, but to Jo it seemed that the floor was going up and down like an airliner in bumpy weather. She opened the door but stopped, when she heard Mike Yates's voice.

'I'm going to see what's happening,' he was saying.

'You mustn't. It's too dangerous . . .' That was Miss Hawthorne.

'The Doctor did want us to stay here, sir,' interposed the voice of Sergeant Benton. 'So did the Brigadier for that matter . . .'

Jo gently closed the door. They would stop her! Mike had prevented her from going before; she wasn't going to give him a second chance.

As she opened the window, hanging on to the pretty flowered curtain to help keep her balance, she remembered the first time she met the Master. He had hypnotised her and had nearly succeeded in making her blow the Doctor up, not to mention herself and the UNIT officers. She shuddered and clutched at the curtain as dizziness overtook her. No, she wouldn't let herself remember. She *must* help the Doctor, she must . . . In her confusion she was by now convinced that the Doctor was in the Cavern, menaced by the Dæmon and the Master. She was determined to rescue him.

Climbing laboriously out of the little dormer-window, she slid down the tiles to the flat roof of the garage, which had been built on at the side of the old stone building. From here it was an easy climb, via a drain pipe and a handy pile of beer crates, to the cobbled yard. Grimly holding on to her senses, she made her way out of the yard to the green and set off, steering a somewhat erratic course, on her journey to the churchyard.

.   .   .   .   .

When Azal disappeared again, Stan was hiding his face, waiting in abject fear to be seized by the monster that Mr. Magister had conjured up from nowhere—or from the ground—or, could it be, from the Kingdom of Lucifer himself?

Azal had continued his dreadful warnings. He had talked of his centuries-long sleep in the barrow, awaiting the time when, as the last of his race to be left on Earth, he would awaken and judge the results of their 'experiment'. He told of the dead planets of Talkur and Yind where all life had been dispassionately destroyed by the race of Dæmons. Now perhaps it was to be the turn of Earth to suffer the same fate.

At length, he appeared to become uncomfortable. Charging the Master once more to bring 'the other not of this planet' before him, he started to turn on the spot like a dog about to sleep, the stamping of the great hooves making the echoes of the Cavern ring like bells, with a note so low as to be more felt than heard.

Stan shrank back behind his pillar of stone, convinced that this creature . . . could it be the Old One himself? . . . would see him. What unimaginable punishment would be in store for him then? If Azal was in fact aware of Stan's presence he chose to ignore it. More likely, it was as far beneath his notice as the presence of a cockroach would have been to the terrified Stan. With the bellow of an angry bull, he silenced the Master's protest at his demand to see the Doctor.

'Go now!' he boomed, 'lest the manner of my leaving should strike the very breath from your body. I shall return . . .'

Stan caught a glimpse of Mr. Magister's scarlet robe as it swirled past him. He heard hasty footsteps across the rocky floor. The heavy door creaked open; the slam of its closing echoed through every cell of Stan's quivering body. He was alone with the Creature. He buried his face in his hands and waited, all hope, all courage gone.

The ground began to shake once more as the strange noise started again, that strange shrieking like the thousand discordant voices of an infernal choir. Stan could feel it getting hotter . . . and hotter . . . and hotter. The sweat from his forehead mingled with the cold sweat of his hands and the tears of anguish and terror which forced their way past his clenched eyelids. Soon it was so hot that it hurt to breathe. Stan, gasping for his life, knew why the Master had been sent away. His mind battered by the sound, his body unbearably shaken by the earthquake, his throat and his lungs tortured by the searing heat, Stan at last slipped into merciful oblivion.

.   .   .   .   .

Outside the Cavern, in the churchyard, the heat and the quaking of the earth were by no means so bad. However, the high wind that sprang up at the same time made it impossible for Jo Grant to stay on her feet. Swept bodily sideways against the ivy-covered wall bordering the lane, she clutched at the branches of the creeper in an effort to hold her own against the pressure of the air. Suddenly, she realised that the tendrils of the ivy were squirming under her fingers like a fistful of serpents. Larger ones seemed to be reaching out to clutch her by the throat. 'Elementals!' she thought with terror, remembering Miss Hawthorne's description of the attack on the Sergeant. She pushed herself violently away from the wall. Still bemused by the blow on her head and Doctor Reeves's injection, she had no strength left to resist the hammering of the unnatural wind. Staggering this way and that, her legs buckling beneath her, she soon collapsed, as unconscious as the poor benighted Stan, in the long grass under the old elm in the corner of the churchyard.

.   .   .   .   .

Once more the distant clanging of the bells of the church caught the attention of the group at the heat barrier, where Sergeant Osgood was desperately assembling various pieces of equipment into what seemed to him an electronic hotch-potch. It obviously had no chance at all of being any help in either getting them through the barrier, or in coping with this monster, whatever it was.

Large tendrils of ivy were reaching out to clutch Jo by the throat . . .

'He's going,' said the Doctor, frowning, 'I'd better get back. His next appearance could mean disaster.'

'We'll be after you in two shakes of a billy-goat's tail,' said the Brigadier.

'Hm,' grunted the Doctor, as he crossed to the motorbike, 'that might have been better put. The goat isn't a particularly favourite animal of mine at the best of times, but at the moment . . .' He kicked the engine into roaring life.

Sergeant Osgood stood up. 'Er . . . Doctor . . .' he said, hesitantly.

'Surely you can get the thing working now, Sergeant,' said the Doctor, suppressing his irritation with difficulty.

The Sergeant blinked his eyes, bleary with concentration, and rubbed the back of his aching neck. 'Well . . .' he began.

'You'll just have to,' the Doctor interrupted, 'we may have very little time left.' He revved the engine impatiently.

'Wait, Doctor,' cried Osgood, 'I still don't understand how you lock the pulse-generator to the feed-back circuit. They'll never be in phase !'

'Well, of course they won't, that's the whole point . . .'

'How do you do it, then?'

'Dear, oh dear, oh dear,' sighed the exasperated Doctor. 'You can tell him, can't you, Lethbridge Stewart?' A glance at the blank expression on the Brigadier's face gave him his answer. 'Oh very well then,' he went on resignedly, 'I'll explain once more. And please *listen* this time . . .'

.　　　.　　　.　　　.　　　.

Mike Yates struggled to his feet as the 'quake died away. 'Really,' he said, 'this is getting a bit monotonous.'

'It's no joking matter, Mr. Yates,' said Miss Hawthorne, severely settling her *pince-nez* into their accustomed position.

'Are you all right, ma'am?' asked Sergeant Benton.

Miss Hawthorne's eyes softened as they rested on her

brave rescuer, her gentle knight, her Prince Charming. 'Thank you, yes indeed,' she trilled, 'how too, too sweet of you to ask!'

Benton, blushing, turned to Mike. 'Er . . . do you think we ought to check on Miss Grant, sir?' he suggested.

'According to Doctor Reeves she'd go on sleeping if the house collapsed around her, never mind an itsy-bitsy earthquake,' said Yates. 'Still, I take your point.'

'I'll go,' said Benton eager to escape the embarrassment of Miss Hawthorne's presence.

'No, no, stay where you are.' Mike ran lightly up the stairs, grinned at himself for knocking on the bedroom door —as if she could answer, anyway!—and went in.

'The little idiot,' he said to himself as, at a glance, he took in the empty bed and the curtains flapping gently in the May Day breeze. He hastened to the open window and looked out. It was at once clear how she'd got out of the room and down to the ground. 'But where on earth could she have gone?' he thought, 'she surely wouldn't try to get to the Doctor . . .'

Suddenly he realised. Of course! He turned and ran out of the room and down the rickety stairs. 'Jo's gone,' he quickly informed the others.

'But that's impossible,' said Miss Hawthorne, who was busy combing her even more than usually wild hair, 'we've been here the whole time. We'd have seen her.'

'She's gone out through the window. I'm going after her.'

'But do you know where she is?' asked Benton, puzzled.

'I know all right. She's gone to the Cavern under the church!'

'Oh, no!' gasped Miss Hawthorne, dropping a handful of hairpins.

'As soon as the Doctor gets back,' went on Mike, 'tell him what's happened. Right?'

'Right, sir,' answered the Sergeant. 'But do be careful. Don't go copping it like I did.'

'Not if I can help it,' returned the Captain, and hurried out.

'Well, well, well,' said Miss Hawthorne, firmly subduing

an errant lock of wispy hair, 'there's more to that young man than I thought . . .'

. . . . .

Stan Wilkins woke up. Why was his cheek resting on cold rock instead of on his friendly old pillow, lumpy though it was? He gingerly moved an arm. His hand touched the rough stone pillar and at once memory came flooding back, and with it his fear. All was quiet now and the intolerable heat had died away. Stan carefully sat up and peeped into the Cavern. It was empty. Apart from a lingering smell— an animal smell—there was nothing to indicate that he had been through anything but a hideous dream.

Cautiously he stood up and crept across the Cavern and up the steps to the door. As he put his hand on the great iron handle, he froze. Voices! Mr. Magister was in the vestry, talking to someone.

'And do the job properly. The Doctor's been in my way far too long.'

'But what if I can't find him, Magister?'

That sounded like the landlord of 'The Cloven Hoof', that did, though it was funny to hear the cocky Bert Walker sounding so uncertain of himself.

'Make sure you do.'

'Right, Magister. I'll do my best.'

For a moment, Stan thought that they had both left the vestry, but then he heard the Master's voice once more.

'You know, Walker, I was foolish, very foolish, to speak with Azal alone. It might easily have ended in total disaster. Next time I shall use the full ceremony. If I am to control Azal, I shall need every ounce of power I can summon up. Every possible member of the coven must be present. Pass the word.'

'Very good, Magister.'

So Bert was a member of the coven too! Stan stood for a moment digesting the fact, as he listened to the sound of first the main vestry door and then the back door which opened onto the Vicarage path. If Bert was a member, and he'd never known it, then anybody he met might be. Anybody in the village. It would be very interesting to see who came to the 'full ceremony' whatever that might be. With a shock, Stan realised that he wanted to come himself. Now that his terror was rapidly becoming nothing but a memory, he could recognise the fascination the whole thing held for him. A guilty thrill ran through him as it came to him that he was the only one, bar the Magister himself, to have seen the . . . the Dæmon. Yes, that's what Azal had called himself . . .

It should be safe by now. Cautiously he opened the creaking door, crossed the vestry, and escaped to the churchyard, running down the path and across the green, taking grateful gulps of cool fresh air.

.   .   .   .   .

As Mike Yates came through the side gate of the churchyard he saw the vestry door starting to open. Diving for cover behind the old elm tree, he watched as Bert, with a badly concealed air of urgency, half walked and half ran down the main path to the green, jumped into a scruffy old car and drove away. That gun he'd been carrying. It didn't look like a shotgun. More like a rifle. Now, whatever would the respectable landlord of a village pub be doing with a rifle?

The problem was pushed to the back of Mike's mind as the vestry door swung open yet again and a spotty youth, little more than a boy, shot out and away. After forcing himself to wait a few minutes more, Mike emerged from his hiding place and made his way through the long grass back to the path, and with infinite caution pushed the vestry door open. A moment's pause. Nothing. Mike suppressed the tremors in his stomach. 'Here goes,' he thought, and in he went.

Cradled in the aromatic grass, Jo Grant peacefully dreamed of childhood holidays in the springtime, quite unaware that her would-be rescuer had passed by not three feet away.

.   .   .   .   .

'. . . and it comes out here.' The Doctor pointed to the bottom of the enormously complicated circuit diagram he had scratched in the sandy soil with the point of a stick.

'Thank you, Doctor,' said the Brigadier. 'We'll keep our fingers crossed. Frankly I didn't understand a word of it, but I'm sure the Sergeant has got it straight now. Right, Osgood?'

Osgood gulped. 'Right, sir . . . I think.'

'Good grief, man,' exploded the Doctor, 'it's as simple as Einstein's Special Theory of Relativity!'

'We'll manage somehow,' said the Brigadier hastily.

'Good,' said the Doctor, 'and when you do get the thing finished, bring it through the barrier and down to the village at once,' and away he roared on the powerful bike.

The Brigadier sighed. 'You know, Sergeant,' he said, 'sometimes I wish I worked in a bank.' He turned away and caught sight of a group of soldiers laboriously unrolling a heavy cable. 'At the double there!' he shouted, moving towards them.

Osgood resentfully watched the Doctor vanishing across the downs. All very well for him to be so superior. It was his idea, so of course he understood it. He wouldn't find it so flaming easy to understand Osgood's scheme for breeding racing pigeons using cross-linked characteristics like the shape of the flight feathers and the bird's speed. For a moment the Sergeant felt an overwhelming wave of nostalgia for the warm sweet smell of his pigeon-loft. Shaking himself crossly, he tried once more to concentrate on the faint scratchings ten feet away across the heat barrier. Now, then. What was it about the pulse-generator? Analogous to the principle of the laser, the Doctor had said. How could it be? The two things were entirely different. The man was just a . . . hang on . . . if you took the oscillator signal through a series of tuned circuits . . . Suddenly excited, the Sergeant pulled out his pad and started sketching possible ways of doing it. Of course, of course! Absurdly simple. Why hadn't he seen before? Almost running, he hurried to the Mobile H.Q., nearly knocking over the Brigadier. 'Sorry, sir,' he gasped, 'but I'm on the track of it at last. Just got to get a few more bits and pieces . . .'

'Well done, Sergeant,' beamed the Brigadier, 'knew I could rely on you. I'd better get on to the Electricity fellows, then. Put them on standby.'

It seemed no time at all before the Sergeant had fitted the new components. They just seemed to fall into place. Now for a first test! Not on the heat barrier, of course, too little power for that. But at least it would show if he was on the right lines . . .

'Sergeant!' bellowed the Brigadier from the doorway of the van.

'Sir?'

'Is it you making that horrible racket on the radio? Can't get a thing through. The air's thick with it.'

'Yes! Yes! I'm testing, you see, sir. This is fascinating!' Sergeant Osgood's happy face appeared over the top of his machine. 'It's not quite right yet, but even on the battery it's really pumping it out! It's a sort of controlled resonance principle, you see . . .'

'Never mind the mumbo-jumbo, Osgood. Keep the wretched thing switched off.'

'Sorry, sir, I can't,' replied the Sergeant. 'Must finish the tests!'

'How long are you going to be before you've got it ready?'

'Matter of minutes, sir,' said Osgood, cheerfully, 'I've really got the hang of it now!' His face disappeared behind the odd-looking contraption. Almost at once, there was a loud bang and a puff of smoke. The blackened and disappointed face of the Sergeant slowly reappeared.

'An hour, sir. At least!' he said ruefully.

· · · · · ·

Bert settled himself comfortably into the bracken and checked his gun. Full magazine, one up the spout, safety-catch on. Like being back in the army. Bert cocked his hat over his eyes to keep out the sun and peered along the winding road below him. Bound to come down it, wasn't he? Only way off the downs, like.

The smell of the warm earth took him back even further to soft Wiltshire nights, poaching on the Winstanley Estate when he was a young 'un. Many a pheasant he'd had off the old Squire, let alone rabbit and hare. Went down fine with a bit of red-currant jelly, hare did.

Jolted back to the present moment by the approaching sound of a motor-cycle, Bert stared at the rifle disbelievingly. Going to kill a man? Whatever had come over him that he should even think of such a thing?

Around the corner came the figure of the Doctor, cloak flying, hair streaming in the slipstream, as he leaned from side to side down the bends of the hill.

All scruples forgotten, Bert slipped the safety-catch, raised the rifle to his shoulder and fired. Got him! He'd swerved off the road onto the green. No, must have missed him. Going straight, he was, making for the woods. No fool, this Doctor. Once more Bert took aim but this time he fired at the rear tyre of the bike. Ah! That really was a hit! The Doctor had somersaulted off the bucking bike and had landed on his back. He was up already and running like an Olympic sprinter for the cover of the trees. His broad back filled the sight of the rifle. Like target practice—or shooting a pheasant on the nest. It was almost too easy.

Bert smiled and lovingly squeezed the trigger . . .

10

The Third Appearance

'Missed him? How could you have missed him?' The Master's face, usually so controlled, twisted in anger.

'I'd swear he read my thoughts,' replied Bert, desperately seeking a way to avert the wrath he expected. 'Just as I pulled the trigger, he darted off to the right. When I'd realised what had happened, he'd gone. And by the time I'd got after him . . .'

'Yes, yes, yes. Excuses waste time.' The Master had regained his usual coolness. 'The important thing is : where is he now?'

'Well . . . I lost him in the woods, you see. I expect he's on his way back to the village.'

The Master smiled malevolently. 'I expect he is,' he said. 'Then we must see that he's given a suitable welcome! Mustn't we?'

.   .   .   .   .

Sergeant Benton was not used to feeling helpless and frustrated. In his experience, most worries soon disappeared if you did something about them. Didn't seem to matter much what you did. Move into action and in the long run things would sort themselves out. And here he was, stuck in this blooming pub, under orders not to move except in the direst emergency, with Miss Hawthorne as his only companion. Miss Hawthorne, who seemed to have taken a fancy to him; Miss Hawthorne who treated him with an exasperating mixture of exaggerated deference and the sort of bossy affection you would expect her to lavish on a pet poodle. And to top it all, there seemed to be something wrong with communications. He'd tried to contact the Brigadier to tell him about Miss Grant and the Captain, but there'd been so much interference that he'd given up the attempt.

Pacing up and down the room like a wild animal in a cage, he tried to work out the best thing to do. At least he was free of Miss Hawthorne's chatter for a while. The longer she stayed in the kitchen, the better. Gave him a chance to have a bit of a think. Now then. If he were to go after Captain Yates he might miss the Doctor when he came back. If, on the other hand, he scrounged some transport and went to the heat barrier, he might be letting the Captain down. Angrily he pulled out his walkie-talkie. Maybe the dratted thing would have cleared itself by now.

'Hello, Trap Two, hello Trap two. Do you read? Over?'

'Trap Two', the call-sign for the Mobile H.Q., remained obstinately silent. Or if it was replying it was drowned in the heavy static. Better try the Brig's personal call-sign.

'Hello, Greyhound. Hello, Greyhound. This is Greyhound Three. Do you read. Over?'

Again, nothing could be heard above the interference. No, wait! Wasn't that a voice? The Sergeant strained to catch it. Was it or wasn't it? Ah! There it was again . . .

'I've brought you a nice cup of tea, Sergeant. I do hope you like China.'

Benton was jerked out of his concentration with an almost physical jolt. Miss Hawthorne, smiling archly, was standing in the doorway with a tray in her hands.

'There seemed to be nobody about,' she went on, 'so I took the liberty of boiling a kettle myself.'

'Oh, for Pete's sake,' snapped Benton, shaken out of his usual courtesy. Miss Hawthorne's eyes widened.

'What's the matter? Don't you like tea?'

'Look, Miss Hawthorne. Something's gone badly wrong. We've no idea what's happening to Miss Grant or the Captain; the Doctor should be back here by now; I can't get through to the Brigadier—and you're nattering on about tea!'

Miss Hawthorne smiled placatingly. 'You must learn the art of waiting, Sergeant,' she said as she carried the tray carefully across the room and set it on the table. 'The Doctor will come. Or else he won't. And that's all that can be said. Now then, milk or lemon? I shan't let you have any sugar. It's bad for the teeth—not to mention the nerves!'

Benton suddenly grinned. She was right, of course. 'Okay, Miss Hawthorne,' he said, 'you win.'

Giving an approving nod, she started to pour the tea.

'Greyhound Three. Greyhound Three. Come in please. Over.' The unmistakable tones of Brigadier Lethbridge

Stewart filled the room. Benton grabbed his walkie-talkie.

'Hello, Greyhound. This is Greyhound Three, receiving you loud and clear. I've been trying to raise you, sir. Terrible interference. Over.'

'Yes, well, the less said about that the better. I'm seizing the opportunity of a lull to have a quick word with the Doctor. Over.'

'Sorry, sir. I don't quite understand. Over.'

'What's the matter with you, Benton? I want to speak to the Doctor. Will you put him on please? Over.'

'But . . . I thought he was still with you, sir. Over.'

'No, he left here . . . oh, a good forty minutes ago. Hasn't he turned up yet? Over.'

Sergeant Benton suddenly felt very worried. It was all very well to be philosophical, but anything could have happened.

'No, sir,' he replied. 'Not a sign of him. Do you suppose he's all right, sir? Over.'

The Brigadier sounded equally concerned. 'Maybe he's piled up that wretched motor-bike . . .'

'Want me to go and look for him, sir? Over.'

There was a long silence. Benton spoke once more. 'I say again, shall I have a shufti round, sir? Over.'

'Yes, yes, I heard you, Sergeant. I was thinking. Better give him a bit longer. And if he does turn up, tell him we're running into a bit of trouble with our . . . our feed-back phasing . . . is that right, Osgood? Yes, that's it, Benton. Tell him will you? Greyhound out.'

Before Benton could speak, the air was filled with the same impenetrable interference as before.

'I didn't tell him about the others,' he said, 'I mean, let's face it, Captain Yates should have been back with Miss Grant ages ago—and now the Doctor seems to have disappeared as well.'

'More waiting, I'm afraid, Sergeant,' said Miss Hawthorne, sipping her tea.

'Not on your life, Miss Hawthorne,' said Benton, decisively. 'I'm going to have a nose around that Cavern.'

'Look what happened last time,' said the white witch,

putting down her cup. 'It would be much better if you were to stay here and wait for the Doctor. I'll go and look for the others. After all, I can claim a modicum of experience in such matters.'

'I'm sorry, ma'am. No offence, but you'll do as you're told.' He crossed to the window and looked out.

'Anyone in sight, Sergeant?'

'Not a soul. They're keeping under cover, and I can't say I blame them. Tell the Doctor where I've gone, will you?'

As he moved to the door, Miss Hawthorne held up her hand. 'Wait ... listen ...' she said.

Sergeant Benton stopped. Carried on the May Day breeze, the tinkling of fairylike bells, the thin piping of a tin whistle, the clack-clack-clack of wooden staves ...

'What is it?' breathed the Sergeant, prepared by now to believe anything. If this was Titania, Queen of the Fairies, come to pay her respects to the awakened Dæmon, okay, let her come. Just as long as she kept out of his way. He'd got quite enough on his plate, thank you.

'It's the Morris dancers,' said Miss Hawthorne.

'Morris dancers!' exclaimed the Sergeant, joining her at the window.

'It's May Day. We always have the Morris dancers on May Day.'

Round the far corner a little procession appeared, headed by the traditional dancers of the Morris, with their hats and ribbons, their bells and their staffs. Leading them was the piper and a squat raggedy character apparently made of bits of torn paper. Equipped with the ancient jester's bladder on a short stick this Paper-Man capered round, his unruliness contrasting with the formality of the figures traced by the dancers themselves. Behind the performers a band of villagers both young and old straggled unevenly.

'Charming,' said Miss Hawthorne. 'Don't you think so?'

'Round the twist, if you ask me,' answered Benson.

Now a group of villagers had formed a circle round the Maypole in the middle of the green. Taking hold of a ribbon each they awaited their moment. The Morris dancers finished their dance and there was a moment of absolute stillness.

'One! Two! Three!' A distant voice floated across the green. Everybody in sight sprang into violent action. The Morris men, to the frenetic wail of the pipe, danced the dance of the quarter-staff, their ribbons flying, their bells a-tinkle. Round and round went the Maypole dancers, weaving their ribbons into an intricate lace of colours. Even the spectators, urged on by the ubiquitous Paper-Man and his bladder, jigged and jogged in time to the irresistible lilt of the whistle.

'Hey, look! There's the Doctor!' exclaimed the Sergeant with relief.

Struggling through the swirling bodies, the tall figure of the Doctor was instantly recognisable. Soon he was near to the Morris dancers themselves. Smiling genially at the Paper-Man, who was jumping round him, like a gleeful chimp, belabouring him with his jester's bladder, he seemed to find himself by accident in the middle of the Morris ring —and each time he moved to escape, a staff just happened to be in his path.

'What's going on?' said Benton. 'Here, I'm going out to him.'

'Wait!' The peremptory tone of the white witch was so full of authority that Benton automatically obeyed.

The music had died away. The dancing stopped. All eyes turned to look at the Doctor, imprisoned in a ring of quarter-staffs. In the silence, the Doctor's voice could be clearly heard. 'Now really! Please get out of my way. I'm in a great hurry.'

It was the Paper-Man who answered, in the unmistakable tones of Bert Walker. 'You're being invited to join our May Day revels, Doctor. I'm sure you don't want to disappoint us—or Mr. Magister.' And from inside his ragged paper coat he produced a small but dangerous looking automatic.

'All part of the tradition, I suppose,' said Benton grimly, bringing out his own gun.

'No!' said Miss Hawthorne, clutching his arm.

From inside his ragged paper coat he produced a small but dangerous looking automatic.

'The Doctor needs help,' said Benton, wrenching himself free and making for the door.

'There are too many of them,' cried Miss Hawthorne.

The Sergeant took no notice but threw open the door. There stood one of the larger Morris dancers. With a swift sidestep, he brought his staff crashing down onto Benton's wrist, sending the gun flying from his hand.

From his years of training, the Sergeant's reaction was instant. His other hand grasped the staff and with a mighty pull overbalanced the burly Morris dancer so that he staggered through the door. The Sergeant went for his gun but the man had recovered himself and with the precise toe of the practised dancer he sent it sliding out of reach.

The fight that followed was very nearly as one-sided as Mike Yates's battle with Wilkins on the village green. Although Benton managed to hold him off for a while, the man moved with the agile ferocity of a wildcat, in spite of his size. Blow after stinging blow found its mark, while Benton's ripostes time and again connected with empty air. Even the occasional blow that landed seemed to have no effect.

Miss Hawthorne hovered on the fringe of the combat uttering shrill cries of distress. But her air of helplessness was deceptive. Seeing that her dear Sergeant was weakening, she seized her handbag and leapt to his aid, swinging it in a wide arc to meet the Morris man's head with a curiously heavy thud. Her method of fighting proved considerably more effective than Benton's. Without even a groan, the man crumpled at the knees and limply slid to the floor. Benton looked down at him in astonishment. 'What happened?' he asked.

Miss Hawthorne displayed the handbag dangling from her wrist. 'I hit him with my reticule,' she said.

'Your *what*?'

'That's right,' she said, diving into the handbag and producing a large crystal ball. 'In such situations, the outcome's a certainty !'

'Very handy. I'm much obliged to you,' said Benton, picking up his automatic and going towards the door again.

Miss Hawthorne stopped him once more. 'Please, Sergeant, I know those people well. They're not really wicked. Most of them, anyway.'

'So? They've still got the Doctor, haven't they?'

'You can't take them all on.'

'What are you suggesting?'

Miss Hawthorne stared earnestly up at him. 'It's up to us to show them how mistaken they are. Now listen carefully...'

.   .   .   .   .   .

It was useless for the Doctor to struggle as he was bound to the Maypole. Held firmly by four of the largest of the locals and with Bert's gun held within inches of his face, he had no chance of a surprise escape. His best hope, perhaps, was to talk them out of it...

'You're all making a very grave mistake,' he said, raising his voice so that as many as possible could hear his words. 'Mr. Magister is planning to make you all his slaves,' he went on. 'I am the only one who has a chance of stopping him.' The Doctor looked around to see the effect of his words. Several of the villagers were obviously ready to hear more.

'He's lying. He is your enemy,' Bert said angrily. 'Slaves! He must be crazed to think you'd believe that. Why, you know that Mr. Magister will protect you, care for you—aye, and give you everything you've ever wanted.' A murmur of approval came from his listeners.

'This foolishness must stop!' cried the Doctor urgently. 'Mr. Magister will bring disaster on us all...'

'Don't listen to him. He's the enemy, I tell you. He's a black witch!'

Quite taken aback at this, the assembly stared at him blankly. The Doctor was quick to seize the advantage.

'That's nonsense and he knows it,' he said loudly. 'I'm no witch. It's Mr. Magister who...' He stopped abruptly as one of his guards gave him a hefty backhander across the mouth.

126

'A witch. Do you understand?' continued Bert as if the Doctor hadn't spoken. 'A witch! And you've always known what you should do with a witch, haven't you? "Thou shalt not suffer a witch to live!"'

The crowd stirred uneasily. Their old folk still handed down stories, some three hundred years old or more they must have been, dark tales of witch hunts, tales of neighbour denouncing neighbour, tales of old women taken by night, tales of torture and death.

'Are you out of your mind?' gasped the Doctor and was again silenced by a heavy hand.

'That's right, friends. "Thou shalt not suffer a witch to live."' Bert looked round his audience as a shudder of delighted fear ran through them. 'Burn him . . .' he said.

There was a moment of stupefied silence. Then, from the back came a voice. 'Aye. Burn him!' it cried. Then another. And another. And from all sides came an ever increasing chorus, 'Burn him! Burn him! Burn him!'

Bert smiled with satisfaction. Things were going well.

.   .   .   .   .

Jo Grant opened her eyes. She was looking into the depths of a cool green forest. She could hear the distant hum of a bumble bee in the warm silence. How peaceful it was . . .

Suddenly she sat up, the forest dwindling to a patch of long grass. Her fear came back with a rush, making her head swim. She must get away . . . Struggling to her feet she stumbled on still wobbly legs to the churchyard gate. There she stopped. No. The Doctor was in danger. She must go to him. Resolutely turning, she made her way to the vestry door, went straight in without a pause, crossed to the Cavern entrance and walked down the steps. But then her resolution faltered. She looked round the Cavern with its flickering shadows. Where was he, this creature from another world, this Dæmon? Or was Miss Hawthorne right? Was he really the King of Hell himself, conjured from his fiery realm by the secret arts of the Master? Almost she turned to run away, but her still confused mind insisted that somewhere here, in this disquieting place, the Doctor needed her. She walked timidly forward; where could he be? She rounded a pillar—and started back with a barely stifled scream. Squatting on his pedestal, Bok, the gargoyle figure, stared at her evilly. But now, she realised, he was stone once more, a grotesque inanimate carving.

Moving forward again, she spoke in a tremulous whisper: 'Doctor! Are you there?' Her heart leapt as a hand was clamped over her mouth and she was pulled back into the darkness of one of the alcoves cut into the cave wall.

'Ssh!' a voice breathed. 'They're in and out all the time.' It was Mike Yates.

'Why didn't you stay in bed?' he went on, taking his hand away.

'I had to find out what's going on. The Doctor needs me,' she whispered.

'The Doctor's not here. He's still with the Brig.'

Jo's mind was becoming clearer every second. 'I'm an idiot,' she said.

'You can say that again,' said Mike. 'As idiots go, you'd win a prize, coming here. The whole place is alive with booby-traps.'

'Booby-traps? You mean, bombs?'

'I mean spells; elementals; the Doctor's psionic force fields . . .'

Jo shivered. She said, 'Where . . . where are they?'

'All over,' answered Yates. 'Here, I'll show you. Pass me one of those books.'

Jo looked around her. On a table nearby, a small pile of cheap paperbacked guides awaited the coins of the summer visitors. She picked one up and passed it to Mike.

'Thanks. Now watch this.'

Gauging the distance carefully, he tossed the book onto the marked flagstone. Instantly there came the sound of a fierce rushing wind and the book was viciously torn into a hundred fluttering pieces. As abruptly as it came, the wind died.

Jo watched, round-eyed. 'It's a trick! It's a horrible conjuring trick,' she breathed at last.

'Do you think so?' said Mike grimly. 'Remember Benton and what happened to him?'

Jo was silent.

'Come on,' continued Mike. 'Let's get out of here before they . . . ssh!' Pulling her back into the sheltering darkness of the alcove once more, Mike laid a finger on Jo's lips.

Into the Cavern came a procession of robed and hooded figures. Forming a circle around the Stone of Sacrifice, they began a low chanting, repeating 'Io Evohe! Io Evohe!' over and over until, echoing and re-echoing around the reverberant cavern, it became an unbroken background of hypnotic noise.

The door flew open. The noise ceased on the instant. In the more than silent stillness, the Master, once more enrobed in scarlet, descended the steps, bearing before him a large and wicked knife with a handle of carved black ebony and a razor-sharp blade of the finest steel. This he placed on the Stone of Sacrifice by the ritual vessels. Moving the chalice to one side, he tossed a pinch of incense onto the still glowing charcoal in the thurible. A flash of red flame sent a puff of smoke sailing up into the shadows of the high roof. As if this was the signal, the chanting began once again : 'Io Evohe! Io Evohe . . .'

'Mike, I'm scared,' said Jo, her voice little more than an exhalation.

'Don't worry,' replied Mike in the same tone. 'The Doc'll soon be back—and Benton knows where we are.'

'As my will, so mote it be,' intoned the Master.

'Nema,' responded the coven.

> 'Hearken to my voice, oh dark one;
> Ancient and awful; Supreme in artifice;
> Bearer of power . . .'

As the sonorous voice rolled round the Cavern, Jo's hand tremblingly looked for Mike's and gripped it hard. It responded with a reassuring squeeze.

Now the Master picked up the ritual knife from the Stone of Sacrifice and held it high in the air.

'Behold this blade, Athame; the knife of power, the blade of power; the knife of blood. Know it as my will; as sharp, as cruel and as ruthless. Know the blade of blood, the blade of sacrifice . . .'

Jo clutched Mike's hand even harder. 'What does he mean?' she whispered. 'Sacrifice? Mike! What does he mean?'

The panic in her voice would have made it sound throughout the Cavern, but that the coven had started to chant once more, 'Io Evohe . . .' as the Master intoned the secret words of the Great Conjuration.

'What's he saying? What language is that?'

'Ssh!' replied Mike, 'I don't recognise it any more than you do.'

'It's evil. It sounds all wrong; all upside down . . .'

The Master was nearing the end of his incantation '. . . DNAW ONSSA ETIHW SAWECE ELFSTIB! MALELT TILAD AHYRAM!'

A hooded figure struck a large gong. As the booming clang resounded through the distant corners of the Cavern, the dust of centuries floated down like smoke into the light of the candles. The Master turned to the figure behind him who, diving a hand beneath his black robe, produced a feebly flapping white hen. Squawking an ineffectual protest, it was laid out on the black cloth before the Master.

'Azal!' he cried, 'we have power over life, thou and I. Accept this life, which I dedicate to thee . . .'

Jo started forward. 'No!' hissed Mike, grabbing her arm.

The Master raised the knife high above his head while two of his acolytes stretched the neck of the chicken, which was now lying quite still as if resigned to its fate.

'EKO, EKO, AZAL!' cried the Master, exultantly.

'EKO, EKO, AZAL!' responded the coven.

The knife started to descend, its blade flashing in the light of the multitude of candles.

It was too much for Jo to bear. Wrenching herself free from Mike's grasp, she rushed through the circle of chanting figures and thrust herself between the Master and the Stone of Sacrifice.

'No! No, stop it!' she sobbed. 'It's evil! Can't you see that? It's evil!' Seizing the hapless bird from the hands of its guardians she held it in her arms as if to protect it from the knife, but it struggled free and ran clucking to safety.

'How very touching,' said the Master, 'but you see, my dear, you're too late . . .' He raised his arms once more and stared into the darkness behind Jo.

'Azal!' he cried in triumph, 'I welcome thee!'

Jo spun round. She could feel the unearthly cold, the shaking of the ground and hear the weird howling which she had experienced the night before. And now she saw the cause. Growing rapidly to a height of over twenty feet, a figure with the legs of a great animal was stamping the rocky floor with its cloven hooves; its face, with its hooked nose, its cruel eyes, its fanged teeth, was the face of a devil; while from its brow swept two magnificent goat horns.

The Dæmon had appeared for the last time . . .

I I

The Rescue

'Are you sure you know what you're up to?' asked the desperately worried Sergeant Benton, as he watched the last few bundles of wood being added to the pile which buried the Doctor's feet.

'Of course I do,' replied Miss Hawthorne, a trifle aggrieved. 'The working of the human soul is my subject, after all. As a witch, I am an expert.'

'That's all very well, ma'am,' replied Benton, 'but if we wait much longer, the Doc won't care very much either way.'

'There *is* such a thing as the Psychological Moment, Sergeant,' answered Miss Hawthorne, leaving him at the window and crossing to the door of the pub. 'If our plan is to work . . .'

'Hang on,' broke in the Sergeant, 'I think your Psychological Moment's arrived . . .' One of the villagers who was standing around the pinioned Doctor, had picked up a stick with a bundle of rags tied to the top. Bert Walker, still incongruously dressed in his costume of torn paper, was pouring something out of a can onto the rags. Then, striking a match, he lit the rags, which flared up into a smoky torch.

'That's it,' snapped the Sergeant. 'For Pete's sake get a move on !'

'Good luck,' said Miss Hawthorne, and opened the door.

'Right, Mr. Thorpe,' said Bert. Followed by the fascinated but horrified eyes of the silent people, Thorpe walked towards the pyre, where the Doctor awaited his fate, his chin held defiantly high.

'Now,' said Bert.

Thorpe stretched out his arm, but before he could actually set alight the pile of wood, a shout from the direction of 'The Cloven Hoof' made his and every other head swing round.

'Stop ! Stop, I say !'

It was Miss Hawthorne, her cloak flying out behind her, her arms waving frantically as she ran surprisingly fast across the green. 'Stop ! Or you will bring a terrible retribution upon yourself !'

Thorpe stood up, nervously awaiting the arrival of the eccentric figure. Her hair, so recently disciplined, was asserting its freedom and shedding hairpins around her as she panted to a standstill. She fumbled desperately for her *pince-nez* and fastened them precariously back in place. She fixed a birdlike eye on Thorpe.

'You would dare to harm the great white wizard, Quiquaequod ?' she enquired.

'Wizard ?' he said uncertainly.

'Take no notice of the old fool,' barked Bert.

'You mean . . . he's a wizard ?' said Thorpe, looking at the Doctor.

'You wouldn't listen to me before—and now you're in the power of Mr. Magister. I was proved right, wasn't I?'

A murmur from the villagers, almost of agreement. Thorpe looked wildly around for guidance.

A voice came from the back of the crowd : 'What are we waiting for? I thought we were going to burn him!'

'Quite right, friend,' said Bert, 'get on with it, man.'

Thorpe lifted the torch.

'Wait! Listen to me!' Miss Hawthorne's voice trembled with urgency. 'Under Mr. Magister, you have been frightened, injured, your property has been destroyed. Serve the great Quiquaequod! There lies peace and great joy . . .'

'Here, give it to me.' Bert grabbed the flaming torch from Thorpe's hand and made to light the fire. But he was prevented by a powerful hand on his shoulder, the hand of Wally Stead, the cowman.

'Hang on, Bert,' said Wally, mildly. 'Just suppose the lady's speaking the truth? We're going to look a right parcel of fools if we burn the wrong one, aren't we now?'

Bert looked at the irresolute faces surrounding him. 'Very well,' he sneered, 'if he's such a great wizard, let's see him untie himself.'

The faces cleared and turned with relief to the Doctor, awaiting a miracle. 'You choose to mock Quiquaequod,' the Doctor said haughtily. 'I will not. I do not choose to loosen my bonds.'

'No, because you can't, that's why,' said Bert triumphantly.

'But you will give a sign of your power, won't you, oh mighty one?' said Miss Hawthorne, her left eyelid twitching with the ghost of a wink.

'Of course,' agreed the Doctor. 'Er . . . what had you in mind?'

Miss Hawthorne looked around the village green as if seeking inspiration. 'I know,' she cried, 'that street lamp! Shatter the glass.'

The Doctor looked puzzled. Miss Hawthorne nodded at

him meaningly. 'Er . . . that one by the churchyard gate?' asked the Doctor.

'Considering that it's the only one in sight, it's quite probable that she does mean that one,' said Bert, sarcastically.

'Shatter it. Yes. Yes, of course. Let's see now . . .' The Doctor caught sight of Miss Hawthorne nodding even more vigorously.

'Oh, very well,' he said. 'Lamp! I order you to shatter!'

And shatter it did. As the fragments of glass tinkled onto the cobblestones, a gasp of amazement came from the crowd. Sergeant Benton, watching covertly from the pub window, grinned with satisfaction. Quite a tricky shot that, at such long range and with an automatic—especially an automatic with a silencer . . . It was to be hoped the old boy would guess what was going on. Yes, he obviously had.

'You see?' he was saying, 'I should hate to have to harm anybody, but honesty compels me to point out that the lamp could have been you. Any of you.'

The crowd shrank back.

'Now then,' went on the Doctor, 'watch the weathercock on the church tower.'

'Blimey,' thought Benton. 'He must think I've got a rifle.' The weathercock was at least half as far again as the broken streetlamp. The Sergeant raised his gun, squinted along the sights and pulled the trigger. The weathercock remained unmoved. The people of Devil's End went on watching expectantly

'Well?' Bert said hastily.

The Doctor glanced at Miss Hawthorne, but she was too busy short-sightedly trying to locate the weathercock to notice his desperation. The Doctor took a deep breath and called, 'Now!'

Sergeant Benton aimed once more; there it was, the wretched bird, full in the sights. The gun coughed apologetically as he fired. The weathercock spun violently as the bullet hit its tail. The exclamations from the green were almost a cheer and one simple soul tried to start a round of applause. For a moment Bert was nonplussed. It seemed that he was in danger of losing all his followers.

'Drop that torch,' said the Doctor. 'You're beaten and you know it.'

'Am I?' snarled Bert and lifted the torch. But before he had a chance to thrust it into the heart of the pyre he gave a sharp cry of alarm as it flew from his fingers as if by magic, landing on the ground a good twelve feet away.

'That was a near one,' thought Sergeant Benton. 'If I'd missed that time, the Doctor would have had it.'

This last demonstration of the power of the mighty Quiquaequod had quite convinced the last doubters.

'Daughter of Light,' said the great wizard, 'would you be so good as to untie me?' Blushing with pleasure and relief, Miss Hawthorne stepped forward. Seeing that the bundles of wood were in her way, Wally Stead started to clear them.

Bert frowned. 'You won't scare me with a lot of daft tricks. Mr. Magister has the real power.'

'In comparison he is worth nothing,' Miss Hawthorne said scornfully. 'Quiquaequod has twice his power.'

'Of course I have,' said the Doctor, trying to intimidate Bert with an arrogant wizard-like stare.

'Right then,' said Bert, not in the least dismayed, 'let's see if you can turn aside a bullet!' and from under his coat of paper scraps he drew his gun.

'Ooops!' thought Sergeant Benton, 'I'd forgotten that,' and he took careful aim at Bert's hand, only to find his view completely blocked by Miss Hawthorne, as she instinctively stepped back.

The Doctor was apparently quite unconcerned. 'I'll give you one more chance, you foolish man. Look behind you.'

'I'm not an idiot,' said Bert, 'that's the oldest trick in the book; you can't fool me.' But his hand was shaking.

The Doctor raised his voice. 'You see that car, everybody? The little yellow car.'

All heads swung round; all, that is, save Bert's.

'Let my familiar spirit bring that car to me,' went on the Doctor in a loud and confident tone.

Miss Hawthorne looked at the Doctor, appalled. Was the man mad? She tried to attract his attention with a hiss and a surreptitious shake of the head.

'Honk honk!'

Miss Hawthorne turned back as a gasp of amazement came from the watching crowd. Giving another cheerful honk on her horn, Bessie started trundling across the green, her headlights flashing.

Bert said unsurely, still refusing to look, 'You won't frighten me. Do you think I'm as stupid as this lot?'

All attempts at concealment abandoned, Sergeant Benton stepped out of the door of 'The Cloven Hoof', his mouth dropping open as he watched the little old car going to the rescue of her beloved Doctor. As she approached, faster and faster, the crowd scattered, leaving Bert standing right in her path.

'Honk, honk!'

Bert spun round with a yell of fear and fired at her. By this time, however, she was right on top of him. Before he could dodge, he was knocked flat, the gun flying from his grasp. As Bessie stopped, with Bert lying between her front wheels shaking with fear, a sigh of wonder escaped from the crowd. Miss Hawthorne ran to the Doctor and started to untie his bonds.

'You really are a magician!' she said quietly, breathless with admiration. The Doctor shook his head.

'Sorry to disappoint you, madam, but I'm not.'

Sergeant Benton came running up. 'How on earth did you do it, Doctor?' he said, making sure that no one could hear him.

'Elemental, my dear Benton,' smiled the Doctor wickedly.

Before the Sergeant could react to the Doctor's excruciating joke, a commotion amongst the people caught his attention. Bert Walker had pulled himself free of the car and was making a dash for it.

'Oh no you don't, mate,' said Benton and with a low tackle which would have done credit to any Rugby international, he brought the fleeing man to the ground. Pulling out his gun, he aimed it at the now terrified Bert.

'You're not going anywhere, chum,' he said. 'We've all got a date with the Master. Haven't we?'

.　　　.　　　.　　　.　　　.

It was when the chicken was produced and stretched out for the Master's knife, that Stan Wilkins finally decided that he wanted no more part of this 'magic'. Chanting a few nonsense words was one thing, blood sacrifice was quite another. All very well twisting a bird's neck for the pot, but this was just plain nasty. He was trying to gather his fast disappearing stock of courage and call a halt to the proceedings, when the girl made her spectacular intervention.

And then Azal appeared once more. In spite of his earlier experience, Stan was at least as frightened as the other members of the coven. Cowering on the floor by the feet of the elated Master, he could hardly bring himself to look up into the great lowering visage of the Dæmon.

'Azal! Once again I bid thee welcome!' The Master's voice rang through the Cavern. Stan could see the girl—Miss Grant, Mr. Magister had called her—shrinking back against the Stone of Sacrifice, her face twisted in a soundless scream.

'On your feet, you worms,' said the Master contemptuously.

Slowly, one by one, the coven stood up.

'That's better,' said the Master. 'And now, Miss Grant, what are we to do with you? Have you any suggestions?'

Jo tore her gaze away from the awesome figure looming over them and looked at the Master. His face, as evil in its way as the face of the unearthly creature he had conjured up, wore a sardonic smile.

Nobody moved. Then, in a moment, Jo made a frantic bid to get away and two coven members went to seize her, only to be bowled over by the eruption of Mike Yates from his hiding place. So taken by surprise were the Master and all his followers that Mike might very well have made good his escape, pulling the almost fainting Jo Grant after him.

The Master, however, snapped his fingers and pointed at the gargoyle figure of stone.

'Bok! Stop them!'

Mike whirled and pulled out his gun, firing round after round at the imp as it leapt from its pedestal. Round after round hit it fair and square and bounced off its scaly stone body, to ricochet dangerously around the Cavern.

Bok snarled and raised a twisted claw.

'Not yet!' cried the Master.

Once again Mike fired. A ball of fire streaked from Bok's pointing finger to strike the automatic like a bolt of lightning. As the gun jumped from his fingers, he quickly raised his hands in token of surrender.

Azal looked down, dispassionately watching the earth creatures at their puny quarrels. The outcome was of little or no concern to him.

'You are very wise, Captain Yates,' said the Master. He raised the ritual knife which he still held in his left hand and pointed it at Jo.

'Take the girl and robe her in the ceremonial tabard,' he ordered those nearest to her. 'She will make a very welcome addition to the Sabbat.' He laid the knife on the Stone of Sacrifice.

'No! No!' screamed Jo as they started to drag her away. With a cry of fury, Mike Yates tore himself free from his own captors and leapt to her rescue. But he had no chance: struck sharply with the butt of his own gun a moment later, he lay senseless on the cold stone floor, unable even to hear Jo's cries of distress as she was hauled up the steps and out through the door.

Stan was shaking; a cold white rage filled his body at the thought of the pretty young girl stretched on the Stone of Sacrifice, as the chicken had been, at the mercy of the Master's knife. And yet, what could he do? To get himself killed was no way to help her.

'Two of you. Take *this* out of here.' The Master's foot disdainfully indicated Mike's unconscious body. 'Make certain he is secure. He may be useful later, as a hostage. Return as soon as you can. When they bring the girl back we shall resume the ritual.

Stan started forward before anybody else could offer himself and with the help of Arthur Sidgwick, the retired sailor who mended the village shoes, he lugged Mike up the steps into the vestry. Finding a length of tasselled cord (remnant of some long forgotten curtains) Stan and Arthur tied the senseless Captain by the hands and feet. Neatly, efficiently, all ship-shape and Bristol fashion, Petty Officer Sidgwick R.N. (Ret.) made quite sure that when Mike Yates came to his senses, he would find himself quite helpless. One advantage of a sailor's knot, however, is that they can be easily untied when necessary. After Arthur had turned away with a grunt of satisfaction at a good job well done, it was the work of a moment for Stan to pull loose his seamanlike bowlines and reef-knots.

Arthur turned back. 'What are you up to?' he demanded.

'Just checking,' said Stan.

Arthur grunted again and disappeared through the door. Stan leant close to Mike's ear.

'Wake up,' he hissed urgently. 'You've got to get help!'

But Mike didn't stir a muscle.

Stan shook his head despairingly. He'd have to go back or the Master would miss him. He turned and miserably went back to the candle-lit Cavern . . .

. . . . .

In spite of the shaking of the ground, Benton kept Bert covered. As slippery as an eel, the fellow looked.

Most of the villagers fell over. Miss Hawthorne sat down with an ungraceful thump.

'Another earthquake!' she gasped. 'That can mean only one thing; the third appearance!'

'In the Cavern?' asked Benton as the movement of the ground died away.

'Where else?' said the Doctor, grimly.

'Right then. Better get over there, hadn't we, Doc?'

'No, no, no. We must wait. And don't call me, "Doc"!'

'Sorry, Doc, I mean, Doctor. Wait? What for?'

'The right moment.'

Benton groaned. Another of them!

'You see,' cried Bert to the crowd of villagers who were anxiously waiting for someone to tell them what to do. 'You see! I told you. This chap's frightened!'

'Of course I am,' returned the Doctor, 'and so should you be . . . and your friend Mr. Magister. We're facing the greatest danger the world has ever known!' He turned to the people standing around him, and raised his voice. 'I'm going to tell you the truth . . .'

'No, Doctor,' gasped Miss Hawthorne, 'you'll lose all the advantage we've gained.'

'I've got to risk it.'

Thorpe came over, straightening his tie. 'What truth? What are you talking about?'

The Doctor looked this way and that at the puzzled faces. 'I'm not a magician or a wizard or anything of the sort,' he said.

Bert was being firmly held captive by Wally Stead and the equally large Fred Treglowne, the Cornishman who lived down by the bridge, growing potatoes and minding his own business. Now bewildered, Fred loosened his grasp. Bert seized the opportunity to pull himself free. 'You see! I told you!' he cried to the Doctor's thoroughly confused listeners.

'And neither is the Master,' went on the Doctor.

'You tricked us!' said Bert.

'Yes I did. But only to save you from him.'

'To save your own life, you mean.'

'Of course, that too.'

Bert swung round triumphantly. 'There you are, do you hear him? He admits it!'

But Bert wasn't to have it all his own way. Thorpe ran his fingers nervously through his thinning grey hair. 'Just pipe down a couple of minutes, will you, Bert?'

'But you heard him . . .' protested Bert.

'Just shut up. We want to hear what he's got to say.'

Seeing that the others largely agreed with Thorpe, Bert reluctantly subsided.

Miss Hawthorne was perhaps the most confused person present. Knowing the trickery involved in the Doctor's display of magic, she nevertheless was quite nonplussed by the behaviour of Bessie. Surely this strange man must have power. He certainly looked like a magician! She could contain herself no longer. 'But what about your car? How did you make it move by itself?'

'Science, not sorcery, Miss Hawthorne. Look!'

The Doctor took out his little black box and twiddled the knob. 'Honk honk!' said Bessie, coyly blinking her headlights.

'Well, I'll be . . . blowed,' said Sergeant Benton hastily editing his exclamation in deference to the presence of Miss Hawthorne.

'And your Mr. Magister uses no more magic than that.'

Bert's expression betrayed his fear—his fear of losing his most cherished belief. 'You're talking rubbish,' he said, without much conviction. 'Mr. Magister's a magician, I tell you. The things I've seen him do . . . impossible things! He must be a magician.'

'You're wrong,' replied the Doctor calmly. 'All his feats are based on science—ours or the science of the Dæmons.'

'Tell me this then, if you're so clever. How could he call him up in the first place except by sorcery?'

'How indeed,' thought Miss Hawthorne finding herself a temporary ally of the abominable Bert Walker.

'He uses violent emotions—greed; hatred; fear; the emotions of a group of ordinary human beings, whipped up to an extraordinarily high level. They generate a tremendous charge of psycho-kinetic energy, which the Master channels for his own purposes.'

Miss Hawthorne pushed a straying lock of hair from her eyes. 'But that *is* magic,' she said, 'that's precisely what black magic *is*!'

'No, Miss Hawthorne. It's science. The secret science of the Dæmons!'

'Are you trying to tell me that the rituals, the invocations—indeed the Sabbat itself—are just so much window-dressing?' She was trembling all over with frustration and indignation.

The Doctor put a calming hand on her arm. 'No, no. They're essential—to generate and control the psionic forces—and thereby control the Dæmon himself.'

Miss Hawthorne digested this. For the life of her, she couldn't see where the difference lay...

As far as Sergeant Benton was concerned all this chat was just a waste of time. Surely there was something they could do instead of just standing around nattering...

'Doctor,' he said, 'Captain Yates said to tell you. He went off to find Miss Grant. Thought she'd gone to the Cavern.'

'Jo? But I thought she was in the pub.'

'She climbed out of the window.'

'I see.' The Doctor rubbed his chin thoughtfully. 'Well,' he said, 'the Captain is pretty efficient. He should be capable of looking after the pair of them.'

Benton was shocked. 'But shouldn't we get over there, Doctor?' he said. 'Get into the Cavern, I mean, and sort out this Dæmon thing?'

'And how do you propose to do that, Sergeant Benton?'

'Well...er...'

'Exactly. We must wait.'

'What for?'

'The energy-exchanger—this machine the Brigadier's building for me. With that, I shall be able to drain off our visitor's energy. Then perhaps we can "sort him out"!'

.   .   .   .   .   .

'That's it, sir! We're ready to have a go...' Sergeant Osgood shakily took off his spectacles and wiped them with a grimy handkerchief.

'And about time, Sergeant,' said the Brigadier. 'Right, into your vehicles everybody.'

As the UNIT troops piled into their Land Rovers, the Brigadier strode over to Osgood. 'Well,' he said, 'what are you waiting for?'

'I suppose I'm a bit nervous. I mean . . . what if it doesn't work?'

'Only one way to find out.'

'Yes, sir.'

Osgood closed the power switch. The odd-looking machine started to hum. In sequence, Osgood closed three more smaller switches, carefully monitoring the results on a bank of dials and adjusting the output.

'Can't see anything,' grumbled the Brigadier.

'It's got to build up power, you see, sir. Keep watching. You should see something any minute.'

And sure enough, he did. A small circle of flame—or so it seemed—appeared in the middle of the heat barrier, about six feet off the ground.

'Good grief, it's working,' said the Brigadier, who had very little faith in the wonders of modern technology.

As the note of the machine's hum steadily rose both in pitch and volume, the flame began to spread; to become a circle; to grow until it touched the ground. At last it settled into a tunnel of flame about twelve foot high extending right through the barrier.

The Brigadier stepped forward and held out his cane. This time it did not burst into flames. He withdrew it and held it close to his face; then cautiously applied a finger. 'Hot,' he said, 'but passable, if we go through at speed.' Running to his own vehicle he jumped in. 'Right,' he called out, 'if I get through safely, the rest of you follow.' Giving a nod to his driver, the Brigadier pulled his cap down low and hunched down into his seat. The Land Rover turned away from the heat barrier in a wide arc, to gain speed.

Osgood anxiously watched the wavering needles on his dials. Didn't look too stable. They'd better get a shift on.

The Brigadier's vehicle turned and started its run for the tunnel.

'Stop! Stop!' shouted Osgood, as the tell-tale needles sank towards zero. The tunnel of flame collapsed; disappeared; vanished. The Brigadier's driver, foot hard on the brake, struggled for control as the vehicle skidded and slithered through the mud towards the heat barrier—and certain death for its occupants. At last he managed to get it under control, and the Land Rover came to a shuddering halt approximately two and a half feet from the edge of the barrier. The Brigadier unfolded himself. He climbed out of the vehicle and walked over to the Sergeant.

'What's the matter, Osgood?' he enquired gently. 'Want to get rid of me, do you? Fancy having a new Commanding Officer?'

'I'm sorry, sir,' gasped the poor Sergeant. 'It was the power, you see. The reaction was using it faster than it could build up.'

'I see. Can you do anything about it?'

'I'll try, sir.'

The Brigadier noticed an extra large switch on the back of the machine which Osgood so far hadn't used. 'What's that for?' he asked.

'It's a booster switch,' answered Osgood.

'A power booster?'

'Yes, sir.'

'Use that then.'

'But, sir, the Doctor said we weren't to—or rather, only in an emergency. He said it was too dangerous.'

'Mm. I see.'

'Give me a few more minutes. I'm sure I can do something.'

'Very well. But for Pete's sake be sure this time. I don't fancy being roasted alive ...'

Sergeant Osgood gulped and turned back to the machine. Now then, it was a matter of balancing the input and the output. Some sort of homeostatic control; a negative feed back ... He plunged back into his circuits desperately working out the figures in his head as his fingers fumbled with the wiring.

.   .   .   .   .

Mike Yates had a headache; his arms were twisted uncomfortably behind his back and he didn't know where he was.

What was that chanting? Was he in church? Then why was he lying on the floor? With a shock like a blow to the heart, he remembered. Jo! They'd got Jo!

He rolled into a better position and started pulling frantically at the rope round his wrists. Hullo, it was loose! In a few moments he had managed to slip his hands free. Struggling into a sitting position he untied the knots at his ankles.

Now then, back to the Cavern. Hurring to the door, he gently opened it a few inches, hoping that the noise of chanting would drown its creaking. He peeped through.

Yes, there she was : a pathetic little figure in a long white robe. But she was still safe, thank Heaven. Then he realised with a pang of horror that he had no chance of getting to her. Not only was she standing right by the Master at the Stone of Sacrifice, surrounded by the coven, but Bok was crouching not ten feet away from the door, eyes darting to and fro, obviously on guard. It was no good. He must get help. Closing the door quietly, he ran across the vestry and out of the door. Praise be, there was the Doctor!

'Doctor. Doctor! you must come. They've got Jo!'

'What?'

'They've got her in the Cavern, and Heaven knows what they're going to do to her. That creature's in there; the Master calls him Azal.'

'Azal!' said Miss Hawthorne in an awestruck voice. 'That's almost the same as Azael—and he was one of the fallen angels!'

Sergeant Benton already had his walkie-talkie out and was calling up the Brigadier.

'Give that to me, Sergeant,' snapped the Doctor. '*Hello, Brigadier? Are you there?*'

'*That you, Doctor? Over.*'

'*They've got Jo. That machine must come through now. NOW, do you understand? At once. There's no more time.*'

'*Wilco, Doctor. We're on our way. Out.*'

The Doctor handed the radio back to Benton. 'Right,' he said, 'some of you round to the side of the church. The rest of you come with me. Nobody's to do anything until I give the word. Understand?'

The villagers started to spread out, Bert Walker amongst them, hoping to slip away unobserved. But the giant hand of Wally Stead took hold of his arm. 'We'll stick together, shall we?' he said quietly.

At this moment however, the vestry door burst open and there, like a wicked toy, stood the little figure of Bok. The villagers recoiled in terror as the stone imp half flew, half hopped down the churchyard path and perched on the stone wall. Everybody's attention was riveted on the gargoyle. It was Bert's opportunity. Wrenching himself free from Wally, he ran forward towards the master's faithful servant. Too late he realised the stupidity of his action. Lifting his grotesque twisted claw Bok pointed it at Bert, who stopped in sudden terror.

'No, no,' he shrieked. 'Friend! I'm a friend!'

But Bok was unmoved. A flash of fire came from his outstretched claw; a puff of smoke and Bert disappeared, vaporised by the monster's evil power.

12

Into the Cavern

'For Heaven's sake, Sergeant Osgood, let's get going!'

The energy exchanger was crackling and humming; sparks flew from it and a thin stream of smoke rose from its innards.

'We're up to the maximum, sir, and it's still no good,' said Sergeant Osgood.

The Brigadier looked at the heat barrier, where the tunnel of flame was wavering on the point of collapse, as it vainly tried to stabilise itself.

'You'll have to use the booster,' said the Brigadier.

'If we do, sir, she'll blow us all sky high.'

'We're going through, Osgood. Booster on.'

'But, sir . . . !'

'Dammit, man, get out of the way . . . !' The Brigadier stepped forward and slammed home the large booster switch. At once the noise of the machine grew louder, the crackling and the sparks even more alarming. Osgood peered through the smoke at the dials, not daring to believe what they were telling him.

'Look, it's working!' said the Brigadier with all the satisfaction of the man who has completed a long a difficult task.

'Yes, but sir . . . !' protested Osgood.

'Proof of the pudding, Sergeant,' said the Brigadier briskly and strode to his Land Rover.

The tunnel of fire now stood rock steady, making an obviously safe passage through the heat barrier. And so it proved. The Brigadier's Land Rover roared through at some forty miles an hour, showing no more signs of damage than a slight smell of scorched rubber. He was quickly followed by the rest of the vehicles—all but Osgood's.

'Come on, man,' shouted Lethbridge Stewart.

'Yes, sir, just coming. Disconnecting the power cables, sir. Shan't be a jiff.'

The Brigadier's walkie-talkie crackled. *'Hello, Brigadier,'* said the Doctor's voice. *'What's going on?'*

'We're through, Doctor. I say again, we're through. Over.'

'And the machine?'

'Not yet. Over.'

'Lethbridge Stewart, I can't trust you to do the simplest job! The machine should have come through first. I need it desperately.'

'Not to worry, Doctor,' said the Brigadier impassively, *'it's on its way. Over.'*

There followed a strange noise as of distant shouting and cheering. The Doctor came through again, very excited.

'The exchanger's working! It's bleeding off the energy. This gargoyle creature is staggering about as if some-somebody's put some knock-out drops in its hell-juice. Bring the machine through, Brigadier!'

'Wilco, Doctor. Out.' The Brigadier raised his voice : 'Get

a move on, Sergeant !'

'Right, sir,' said Osgood as he climbed into the back of the Land Rover where the spluttering machine was smoking furiously. Its hum had risen to an ominous shriek and it was visibly shaking. In a moment, it was through the tunnel and pulling up safely clear of the heat barrier. The noise was by now quite deafening and Osgood could hardly see the machine, let alone the dials, for the thick wreath of smoke enveloping it. Brigadier Lethbridge Stewart beamed with delight. Things were going right at last. He spoke into the walkie-talkie.

'*You can stop worrying, Doctor. It's through. Over.*'

'*And about time,*' the Doctor's voice answered, irascibly. '*Get it over here fast.*'

The Brigadier's triumph had a very short life. A shout from Sergeant Osgood killed it.

'Sir ! Sir ! It's running away !' He could hardly make himself heard above the indescribable noise coming from the machine.

'Switch it off, man.'

'I can't, sir; I can't stop it !'

'Right, out of it, Osgood. Get down, the lot of you.'

Osgood and his driver jumped from the truck and sprinted to cover. All the rest of the UNIT troops hit the deck. Battle veterans to a man, they knew an explosion was coming just as well as the Brigadier did. And come it did. With an ear-splitting roar the Doctor's precious energy excharger blew up, shattering into a thousand pieces any hope of using it against the Dæmon.

'The tunnel's gone, sir,' said Osgood, mournfully, in the ensuing silence.

'*Brigadier! Are you all right?*' It was the Doctor's voice again '*What was that noise?*'

'The machine. It's gone west. Blown itself up. Still, at last we're the other side of the barrier. Be with you right away. Out.'

* * * * * *

'And a fat lot of good that'll do,' said the Doctor as he handed the walkie-talkie back to Benton.

On the churchyard wall Bok, who had come to the point of collapse while the energy exchanger was working, now was slowly recovering.

The Doctor eyed him and said, 'I'm going in, before that creature recovers.'

'But you can't go in now,' protested Miss Hawthorne, 'not without some sort of protection. Why, you said yourself it would be suicide.'

'Keep the rest back,' said the Doctor to Mike Yates, as if Miss Hawthorne had said nothing.

'But, Doctor, don't you think . . .' began Yates. But the Doctor had gone, sprinting past the still bemused Bok towards the church. As he reached the vestry door, the stone imp whirled and pointed. The ball of flame flew through the air to end as a spectacular Guy Fawkes explosion against the door as it closed behind the Doctor.

Miss Hawthorne gazed after him. Her eyes filled with tears. 'Good-bye, Doctor . . .' she murmured.

．　　　．　　　．　　　．　　　．

When Jo Grant was brought back into the Cavern by the two men who had dragged her screaming away, Stan Wilkins knew at once that the young man addressed as 'Captain Yates' by the Master had not yet managed to make his escape. If he had, it could not fail to have been noticed by the guardians of the girl. They would have raised an immediate alarm. He must be still unconscious. Or perhaps those knots weren't loose enough . . . Stan's attention was caught by the sight of the poor girl's stricken face, eyes big with fear, her cheeks as white as the ceremonial robe she was wearing over her own clothes. No longer struggling, she dumbly allowed herself to be led forward and be presented to the Master, who stood waiting for her by the Stone of Sacrifice.

'Why, Miss Grant,' he said, giving a courteous bow. 'How very good of you to join our little ceremony.'

Jo looked at him with as much defiance as she could muster. 'The Doctor will come. You'll see,' she said.

'I hope he will. I shall be able to . . . ah . . . kill two birds with one stone.'

Jo shuddered.

'Not a very happy metaphor, I agree. But appropriate, you must admit.'

'Why don't you just get on with it?'

'What a very good suggestion. Thank you, my dear.' The Master turned back to the Stone of Sacrifice, looked up at the cruel unfeeling face of Azal and spoke in the ceremonial tones of invocation. 'As my will, so mote it be.'

'As thy will, so mote it be,' echoed the coven, continuing, 'Io Evohe . . . Io Evohe . . .'

'Psst . . .' hissed Stan to his next door neighbour in the circle. It happened to be Mr. Ashby, who kept the shop.

'What is it?' he answered, out of the corner of his mouth.

'He's not really going to . . . to sacrifice her, is he?' Stan asked under cover of the general chanting.

'Looks like it.'

'But why?'

'To get power, of course; power to control . . . him,' and Mr. Ashby nodded towards the Dæmon.

'We've got to stop it,' said Stan, his fear lending urgency to his voice.

'Yes? You feel like trying?'

'But—'

'Shut up, boy, or you'll have the both of us going the same way.' Mr. Ashby resumed chanting along with the others and wouldn't even let Stan catch his eye.

While the rest of the coven had been keeping up the monotonous repetition of 'Io Evohe' the Master had recited a Litany of Hate and of Power directed at the Dæmon.

> '. . . Prince of Evil; Prince of Fire;
> Keeper of the Keys of Hell; Bearer of the Sword;
> Hearken to my voice;
> Hearken to my will.'

Turning to his chanting acolytes, he raised a hand. They fell silent.

'To do my will shall be the whole of the Law,' he intoned.

'To do thy will shall be the whole of the Law,' they repeated. 'Io Evohe! Io Evohe!'

'Bring the girl,' ordered the Master, pointing to the Stone of Sacrifice. The two who were holding her by the arms started to lead her forward.

'No, no, no! You can't mean it. Please! Please!' Her terror reduced her voice almost to a whisper. Again the Master lifted a restraining hand. Jo's captors stopped.

'You beg so prettily, my dear. But you see, I am so near to attaining one of my greatest ambitions : power to control, to rule, an entire planet—this planet, Earth. Nothing and nobody can be allowed to stand in my way.'

'You're mad . . . insane,' she breathed.

'I suppose I am, from your point of view,' said the Master. 'You can hardly be expected to view the matter objectively. But I do want you to understand that it would give me no pleasure to kill you.'

A gleam of hope came into Jo's eyes. 'You mean . . . ?'

'Oh, don't mistake me,' said the Master hastily, 'if it is necessary to sacrifice you, then sacrificed you shall be. However . . .'

He turned and looked up into the leathery face of the Dæmon, time-weathered by the centuries.

'Azal!' he called. 'The moment for the decision draws near. Once more, I demand the power that . . .'

Azal's great rumbling tones filled the Cavern. 'You demand!'

'And why not? Who in the whole galaxy is not my inferior? There is not one creature !'

'Not . . . even . . . one?' It was like being in the middle of a thundercloud, thought the terrified Stan.

The Master obviously decided that he had gone quite far enough for the moment. He bowed to Azal. 'None save the last of the Dæmons,' he said.

Azal's wrath was appeased. The Master turned to Jo.

'You see?' he said regretfully.

Jo could hardly grasp his meaning.

'I'm sorry, my dear. I really am,' said the Master, 'but you will at least have the satisfaction of knowing that you will be sacrificed in a worthy cause.'

'He means it. He really means it,' thought Stan desperately, looking at Jo, whose struggles were becoming so feeble that her captors were almost having to hold her up.

The Master looked up once more at the Dæmon. 'Oh mighty Azal, accept thou this offering as token of our fealty . . .' He picked up the ceremonial knife and touched its razor edge with a delicate thumb as though testing its sharpness. Nodding to Jo's two supporters to bring her to the Stone, he raised the knife high in the air.

'This is it,' thought Stan, 'it's the last chance to save her . . .'

'In the name of Athame . . .'

Stan took a deep breath.

'Hold!' The gargantuan voice of the Dæmon rang once more through the Cavern. The Master, plainly disconcerted by this unrehearsed turn of events, lowered the knife and looked up at Azal, hardly bothering to hide his arrogant impatience.

'Well?' he said, sourly.

'You tell me that you are strong enough to bear the Dæmon's burden of knowledge and power; that you . . .'

'I tell you . . .'

'BE SILENT! You tell me that you are superior to mankind in all respects; that you should lead them, rule them, be Master of their world. All this you would have me believe. Is that not so?'

'It is so, oh mighty one,' said the Master, a puzzled expression on his deceptively noble face.

'Then tell me also, oh Master of the Earth, how is it that one of these Earthlings you despise so much has made so much of a fool of you.'

The Master was even more puzzled. 'I . . . I'm afraid I don't understand,' he said, his arrogance visibly crumbling.

'Indeed?' rumbled Azal. 'Then I shall explain. Your prisoner has escaped to his friends . . .'

Had Stan not already been quaking with fright, the Master's face would have set his knees knocking.

'Go,' snarled the Master to Ashby, who happened to be nearest the door. Ashby rushed away. The door creaked open and slammed behind him. Then there was silence, broken only by Jo's attempts to control her sobs of fear. None of the coven dared to move. The Master was so still that he might have been carved from the same block of stone as his servant Bok.

In a few moments the door flew open. 'It's true, Magister,' Ashby gasped, 'he's gone. And, Magister, they're coming. All of them. They're coming across the green . . . !'

The Master snapped his fingers. Bok jumped up with glee, hobbled over to the steps and scuttled through the door, casually brushing aside the quivering Ashby.

It was plain that the Master was now very angry indeed. The black determination on his face was terrible to see as once more he started the ritual of sacrifice, while the colossus at the end of the Cavern gazed with pitiless eyes. Once again the dreadful ceremony approached its climax. Once again the Master, holding the knife in his left hand, raised it on high.

'In the name of Athame, I dedicate this offering to thee, Azal, in exaltation of thy mighty power!'

This time Stan had no time to think, no time to be afraid. Stepping forward as quickly and as naturally as one might reach out to prevent a child from falling, he placed himself between Jo and the Stone of Sacrifice.

'No, Magister,' he said, with passionate conviction. 'It's not right.'

The Master's eyes flashed. 'To do my will shall be the whole of the law.'

'To do thy will shall be the whole of the law.' The coven, whipped up into a fearful excitement, responded with total sincerity. Stan was on his own.

'It's not right, I tell you. Listen to me, all of you . . .'

153

'Out of the way, son, or you're liable to get hurt,' growled one of Jo's guards.

'Can't you see? It's wrong! It's evil!'

The Master stepped forward. 'Obey me! You will obey me!' he thundered.

Stan still would not budge. 'I'm not going to let you do it . . .' His small voice echoed ridiculously, mocking his puny defiance.

The Master gave a snarl of rage, raised his right hand and smote Stan such a mighty blow that he staggered at least fifteen feet across the uncertain rock floor before he toppled senseless to the ground.

'Obey me!' said the Master to Jo's captors.

This time nothing stopped them. Her feet dragging, Jo was taken to the Stone of Sacrifice, and laid upon its stained surface in a state of stupefied shock.

A ghastly hush descended on the Cavern. The Master closed his eyes and started to mutter the final words of the rite, the secret words, words too terrible to be spoken aloud.

Suddenly, the stillness turned into uproar. A great animal bellow of anguish came from the Dæmon; the coven uttered cries of fear as Azal, until now so motionless, began to stamp his hooves and to sway his mighty body as if a pain too great to be borne was draining all his strength. Even the Master was forced out of the intense concentration with which he had been reciting the words of power. Thwarted once again, his fury turned on the coven. Cursing them for a craven pack of cowardly fools, by the sheer force of his will he quietened them. By the time Azal had begun to recover, by the time his groans had ceased to deafen and his stamping had ceased to shake the very earth, the Master was in control again.

'Nothing shall hinder me!' he raged. 'This girl's life is my way to power. It is mine. Mine to take, mine to give. The waiting is over. She shall die! Now!'

He raised the knife. But this time it was no ritualistic gesture, but a movement full of evil purpose. 'Azal!' he cried. 'This life I give thee. Accept it, and in return, render me thy power . . .'

'Azal!' the Master cried. 'This life I give thee . . .'

As the knife started to descend, the heavy door to the Cavern crashed open. Interrupted yet again, the Master swung round. There stood the Doctor, the light of day behind his head turning his shock of hair into a halo of silver. He slowly walked down the steps and across to the Stone of Sacrifice, the coven falling back in superstitious dread.

With a lightning change of mood, the Master smiled. He laid down the knife and spoke quietly and courteously.

'I've been expecting you, Doctor,' he said. 'You've saved me so much trouble by coming here. I really am most grateful.'

The Doctor ignored him. 'Hello,' he said to Jo, who was still stretched out on the Stone of Sacrifice. 'I can't tell you how glad I am to see you.'

'Oh, Doctor, Doctor,' she replied, finding no words to express her feelings: her relief merely to see him; her fear for his safety; her certainty that this time their old enemy really had the whip hand.

The Master looked from one to the other. 'How touching,' he said.

The Master's sarcasm was wasted on the Doctor. Having assured himself of Jo's safety, he was now utterly absorbed in contemplation of the Dæmon. That such a creature could exist in all his savage beauty was wonder enough, but here, it would seem, staring back at him with his gleaming red eyes, was the living symbol of all the mysteries of evil, the Devil himself.

The Master tried again. 'You realise that you're a doomed man, Doctor,' he said conversationally.

The Doctor forced himself to tear his gaze away from Azal.

'Oh, I'm a dead man. I was dead as soon as I came through that door,' he replied, and it was plain that he meant it. 'So you'd better take care,' he went on, 'you see, I have nothing to lose, have I?'

This thought obviously did not please the Master at all. A man with nothing to lose had nothing to fear. If you could not make a man afraid, how could you control him?

'Enough,' the Master snapped. Then he turned to Azal. 'Destroy him, oh great Dæmon,' he said.

But Azal did not move. There was a moment of silence as he stared at the Doctor.

'Who is this?' he boomed.

'My enemy and yours, Azal. Destroy him!'

Azal still did not comply. 'This is the one of whom we spoke. He too is not of this planet.'

'He is a meddler and a fool.'

'He is not a fool—yet he has done a foolish thing in coming here. Tell me, oh Doctor, why did you come?'

The Doctor stared into the callous uncaring eyes. How could he hope to get through to such a being?

'Why did I come? Why, I came to talk to you.'

'Talk then.'

'First, let her go,' said the Doctor, pointing to Jo.

Azal raised his hand.

'No!' cried the Master, 'I forbid it!'

There was a crackle of fire and Jo's guards fell back with cries of pain. Jo scrambled from the Stone of Sacrifice and ran to the Doctor's side.

'Are you all right?' he asked her.

'I think so,' she replied, though her hands were shaking like the hands of an old woman. 'Yes, yes, of course I'm all right.'

The Doctor looked back to Azal. 'Thank you,' he said.

'You wish to talk.'

'Yes. I came to warn you.'

'Warn me?'

'I came to tell you to leave this planet, while you still can,' said the Doctor firmly.

It almost seemed that Azal was amused; as amused as a man warned to leave his own home by a kitchen mouse. A deep rumbling noise came from the Dæmon's chest which could have been a gigantic chuckle. 'You are bold,' he said at last. 'What could happen to *me*? There is no creature in this Galaxy—nay, in the Universe—that is feared by the Dæmons. Am I to fear you?'

'It may be wise,' answered the Doctor. 'You see, I have a

machine outside that can annihilate you.'

Azal threw his head back as if he was sniffing the air, like a hound seeking a scent. After a moment, he again regarded the Doctor. 'You lie,' he said, with no apparent concern.

'You've already felt its power, I know.' The Doctor's air of confidence was becoming a little forced.

'I have. But the machine is destroyed.'

Jo glanced at the Doctor in sudden trepidation. If this were true, they were lost.

'One of them, yes,' replied the Doctor, after a fractional pause. 'The other is outside the church at this moment. I have only to give the signal . . .'

Again the furious movement of the Dæmon's head. 'You lie,' he said again. 'There was but one machine. It no longer exists.'

'Oh, Doctor,' breathed Jo.

The Dæmon's eyes seemed to look into the depth of the Doctor's mind. 'You have a regard for the truth,' he boomed. 'Why do you lie?'

The Doctor shrugged. 'To try to make you listen to me.'

'Why should I? I have listened and you have lied to me. Why should I listen further? I see no consequence of value.'

The Master seized his opportunity. 'Then kill him! Kill him now!'

Azal gave him an indifferent glance.

'Very well,' he said and lifting his great hand he pointed straight at the Doctor.

13

The Sacrifice

The little caravan of army vehicles came swinging round the corner of the road leading to the village green of Devil's End, completely disregarding the speed limit. The

Brigadier's Land Rover skidded to a stop opposite the knot of people near the churchyard. The Brigadier jumped out and strode across the green to meet Yates and Benton, who were hurrying to meet him.

'Where's the Doctor?' he said briskly, giving the impression that now he had arrived, their troubles were over.

'Gone into the Cavern. Through the vestry,' said Mike Yates.

'Then why are we hanging about as if we were a bunch of schoolgirls at a picnic?' the Brigadier said. 'We'd better get after him.' He turned to give an order to his waiting troops.

'Hang on, sir,' said Yates. 'I shouldn't be too hasty if I were you. Look,' and he pointed to the stone image of Bok immobile by the churchyard gate.

'What, that statue? Horrible looking thing. Never seen anything like that in a churchyard before. Usually get angels. What about it?'

'Watch.'

Mike Yates picked up a large stone and lobbed it into the air in the general direction of the gargoyle. At once it whirled and pointed. The flying stone vanished in a stab of flame.

'Mm. I take your point,' said Lethbridge Stewart, visibly impressed.

'There's been one fatality already. The landlord of the pub. Vaporised, I should think. There was nothing left of him but a puff of smoke.'

The Brigadier looked at the stone imp once more sitting on the wall, its head malevolently swinging from side to side.

'Never mind,' said the Brigadier. 'We'll soon fix him. Corporal!'

Corporal Nevin, the crack shot of UNIT, twice runner up at Bisley, came over to his Commanding Officer at the double. 'Sir?' he said.

'That fellow over there,' said the Brigadier. 'The chap with wings. Five rounds rapid.'

Nevin unslung his rifle and took careful aim. The rifle

159

cracked five times in quick succession. Five times the bullets found their target and bounced off the hard stone with a ricochet whine. Bok was obviously quite unharmed. Snarling, he stared round as if he were trying to trace the source of these pin-prick irritations.

'I could have saved you the trouble, Mr. Yates.' It was Miss Hawthorne, who had joined then unnoticed. 'He has a magical defence. Only a magical attack could succeed.'

The Brigadier looked at her incredulously. 'Magic, madam?' he said. 'What the deuce are you talking about?'

'Oh, this is Miss Hawthorne,' intervened Mike Yates hurriedly, 'you remember, I mentioned her when I first reported on the situation. Miss Hawthorne has . . . er . . .' Mike's mind boggled at the thought of attempting to explain Miss Hawthorne's part in the whole affair . . . 'Miss Hawthorne has been a great help to the Doctor,' he finished lamely.

'I see,' grunted the Brigadier. 'Well, Miss Hawthorne, my name is Lethbridge Stewart. I'm in command here . . .'

Miss Hawthorne's eyebrows rose a little.

'. . . and I think I'm quite capable of coping with what seems to me to be a relatively simple military matter. Now then, Benton!'

The Sergeant sprang to attention, appearing rather incongruous in his sports jacket and flannel trousers. 'Yessir!' he said.

'Machine guns, that's the answer,' went on the Brigadier. 'Armour piercing shells. The thing appears to be made of stone. Very well then we'll break it up. Right?'

'Right, sir,' and Benton hurried away to get the guns set up.

'But don't you see . . .' began Miss Hawthorne.

'Please, madam,' said the Brigadier, impatiently.

'But you haven't a hope of breaking him up with ordinary bullets. Now, if you were to try silver ones, cast in a mould made by a seventh son, at midnight—during the full moon, of course . . .'

The Brigadier snorted and turned a rich shade of brick-red. 'Now, look here . . .' he began. Mike hastily cleared his throat and the Brigadier remembered the courtesy due to a lady.

'Forgive me, Miss Hawthorne. At any other time I should be glad to listen to your fantasies. At the moment I'm too busy. Captain Yates, you'd better fill me in on the situation,' and the two officers walked away, talking hard.

Miss Hawthorne, bridling, pursed her lips. The wretched man obviously had a totally closed mind. Fantasies indeed! She'd show him. Yes, but would she? It was all very well being angry with the Brigadier. He was a soldier after all, so naturally he looked at the situation with the eye of a soldier. Whereas she, Olive Hawthorne, made claim to some little knowledge of the secret arts . . . 'Come along, my girl,' she said to herself, 'face the facts. You're plumb scared, aren't you? Not without justification. I'll admit . . .' and she shuddered as she remembered the face of the Dæmon. 'All the same, if the Doctor was right and this is the end of the world, and you've done nothing to stop it, you'll never be able to look yourself in the eye again . . .' She laughed in spite of herself and set off with a determined air towards her cottage.

'Open fire!'

As soon as two machine guns were in position, Mike Yates gave the order. As the shells slammed into the body of the gargoyle, he staggered under the weight of the blows, recovered and began to move forward like a Polar explorer breasting a blizzard. Supporting himself against the left-hand gate-post, he raised his hand. A flash of unearthly brightness and one of the machine guns disappeared, together with both its crew.

'Cease fire,' yelled the Brigadier above the chatter of the remaining gun. He looked with horror at the wisp of smoke, which was all that was left of two of his men, not to mention the weapon. Ordering an immediate withdrawal to a safe distance, so far as that could be judged, he held a quick council-of-war with Mike Yates and Sergeant Benton.

'Might as well use a peashooter on four-inch armour,' said Mike, gloomily.

'Get the bazooka set up, Sergeant,' ordered the Brigadier.

'Yessir,' answered Benton.

In double-quick time the bazooka was loaded with a high explosive missile. From the partial cover of one of the churchyard's side walls, Benton aimed it at Bok, who was now patrolling to and fro among the tombstones.

'Fire in your own time, Sergeant,' said Yates. Benton nodded, waiting for the opportunity for a perfect shot. It seemed like long minutes rather than a few seconds, before he pulled the trigger. The projectile hit the grotesque stone creature fair and square, blew up and shattered him into hundreds of pieces no bigger than a fist.

'You've done it! Well done, Sergeant!' cried the Brigadier.

Benton's slightly complacent grin turned to a look of consternation. All the pieces of stone were rising from the ground, in complete defiance of the Laws of Physics, and coming together like an oversized three-dimensional jigsaw puzzle; and there sat Bok, as good as new, as ready as ever to annihilate anybody incautious enough to walk into his view.

'I told you so!'

The Brigadier turned. Miss Hawthorne had been watching the whole fiasco.

'And now perhaps,' she went on infuriatingly, 'you'll be ready to listen to reason. How about letting *me* have a go?'

.   .   .   .   .   .

By the time Stan Wilkins had recovered his senses he had remembered everything up to the moment of his own intervention. But what had happened after that? The girl! Was she safe? With a surge of relief, he saw her standing by a tall figure with white hair, wearing a cloak. Whoever this might be, he seemed to have no fear of Azal. Looking steadily up at the Dæmon, who had his enormous hand outstretched with clawed forefinger pointing menacingly, the stranger was speaking in a clear firm voice.

'If you kill me now, you will wonder through all eternity

whether you should have listened to my words . . .'

For a while nobody moved and nobody spoke. Then the Master burst out. 'Well? Why do you wait?' Again a long silence. Again the Master spoke. 'You waste time, Azal. I order you to destroy him.'

This was a tactical error. Azal dropped his arm and looked down at the Master with hooded eyes. 'I command,' he said, 'I do not obey.'

The Master was not one to give up easily. 'But when I called you . . . you came.'

The Dæmon's inscrutable stare did not change. 'I answered your call because the time had come for my awakening. It was my will that someone should awaken me. It chanced to be you.'

The Master scowled. 'Without me . . .' he began.

'Without you, I should still sleep as I have slept these many centuries. But you were the mere instrument of my will. The time had come.'

'The time for the completion of the experiment?' asked the Doctor.

'Or its destruction . . .' agreed Azal, looking at the Doctor as if he were seeing him properly for the first time.

The Master leaned across the Stone of Sacrifice towards the Dæmon. 'Then fulfil your mission by granting the ultimate power to me,' he said eagerly. 'Who else can give these humans the strong leadership they need?'

'I seem to remember hearing someone else talking like that,' said the Doctor, rubbing his chin. 'Now, who was it . . ? Oh yes, of course, that bounder Hitler, Adolf Hitler . . . Or was it Genghis Khan?'

'I have the will,' went on the Master, ignoring the Doctor's interruption, 'you yourself have said it.'

'I am still not convinced.'

'I'm very pleased to hear it,' said the Doctor. Again Azal looked at the Doctor with interest.

'Why?' he boomed, 'do you wish to see this planet destroyed? That is the only possible alternative.'

'I don't agree,' answered the Doctor. 'I have yet another choice to suggest.'

'State it.'

'Leave humanity alone. Just go. You have done enough harm.'

'Harm?' said Azal. 'The Dæmons gave knowledge to man.'

'You certainly did,' said the Doctor, scornfully.

Azal looked puzzled. 'Without the gifts of the Dæmons, man would have remained an animal, living in caves, scavenging all day for enough food to stay alive in misery. Is this what you would desire?'

'Without the gifts of the Dæmons,' retorted the Doctor, 'man would have had a chance to develop at his own pace; a chance to develop the wisdom to control his knowledge. But thanks to you, he can now blow up the world; and he probably will. He can poison his rivers, his land and the very air he breathes with the filthy by-products of this "knowledge". He's started already . . . he can—'

'Enough!' The Dæmon's voice, like a great organ, reverberated round the Cavern. 'Is man such a failure then? Shall I destroy him?'

Before the Doctor could reply, the Master jumped in. 'No!' he said passionately. 'The right leader can force him to learn.'

The Dæmon closed his eyes. His head was thrown back and he was still. Nobody moved. At length, he gave a great sigh, like the wind off the sea blowing through a forest. 'You are right,' he said. 'I have decided. I shall pass on my power.'

The Master stood upright, seeming to grow twice the size. 'Mighty Azal, I thank you.'

'But not to you,' continued the Dæmon dispassionately. 'To him . . .' and he nodded towards the Doctor.

Jo Grant gasped and looked at the Doctor. He was so taken aback by this unexpected turn of events that for a moment he was quite speechless. At last he found his voice.

'No! No! I don't want it!'

Astonishment at the Doctor's reaction lent uncertainty to Azal's voice. 'You refuse my gift? I offer you the world and you refuse it?'

'Of course I do.'

'But . . . why?'

'Don't you understand? I want you to leave. I want you to go away and give man a chance to grow up.'

'If man is a failure, he must be destroyed.'

'No, no, no,' said the Doctor, intensely willing the Dæmon to understand. 'At last it looks as if the people of Earth are beginning to see that they have come very near to killing their own planet. But there can't be a magical solution. They've got to find the answer for themselves.'

'And you would have me leave, my mission uncompleted?'

'Yes. Please go. Back to your own world.'

Azal considered in silence. Then he spoke once more, as coldly and unemotionally as ever.

'I cannot agree. My instructions are precise. I bequeath my power or I destroy all.'

Jo held her breath and clutched the Doctor's arm. Was this to be the end of the world? Here and now?

'So,' said the Master softly, fearful of provoking Azal's wrath. 'You will give your power to me, after all.'

The Dæmon looked at him with something like distaste. 'I shall,' he said after a reluctant pause. 'My time is short.'

The Master struggled to suppress his glee. 'And . . . what about *him*?'

Once more the note of astonishment and incredulity crept back into Azal's voice. 'He is not rational,' he said, 'he is disruptive. He must be eliminated.' He raised his hand and pointed at the Doctor. Flashes of fire began to flicker round the fingertips. The Doctor reeled in pain.

Without a second's thought, as inevitably as if her whole life had been leading to this moment, Jo threw herself in front of the Doctor, shielding him from the attack of the Dæmon.

'No! He is a good man,' she cried. 'If you must kill somebody, kill me, not him!' She stood there, eyes closed, head thrown back, awaiting the bolt of fire which would mean annihilation. But nothing happened. She opened her eyes and looked up.

Azal was behaving very strangely. Clutching his head, he was swaying back and forth as though in pain. His great cloven hooves rang on the rocky floor as he stamped to and fro. His whole body was starting to glow as if lighted up by internal flames and smoke was drifting from him as from a smouldering firework about to explode. His groans of anguish were horrendous to the ear.

'This action does not relate,' he was crying. 'There is no meaning. It does not relate.'

He lifted his head. The great voice was cracked and strained. 'A Dæmon must die alone. Go! Leave me. All of you!'

It was very apparent that this was a good idea. The ground was beginning to shake, a deep rumbling to be heard and the rock surrounding the Dæmon to turn red hot.

Struggling to get through the door they could all hear the cries of pain becoming shrieks of inhuman agony. The last of the Dæmons was dying . . .

.   .   .   .   .   .

Miss Hawthorne was chattering almost gaily as she completed her preparations for coping with Bok. It helped her to put out of her mind a dreadful thought. If she managed to get past the gargoyle, how was she going to deal with Azal? One thing at a time, she thought and concentrated on the task in hand, the drawing in the roadway outside the churchyard of a magic circle containing a five-pointed star.

'It's the Great Pentagram of Solomon, you see, Sergeant. It's the greatest magical defence there is.'

Sergeant Benton had been detailed off to look after the white witch, while the rest of the UNIT troops continued their attempts to get into the Cavern, all of which had failed. An elaborate plan, formulated by the Brigadier and put into operation by Mike Yates, to keep Bok occupied by the vestry door while a covert approach was made on the Church's main door was foiled by Bok's taking to the air. Swooping and turning, hovering and diving, he appeared to be in every place at once. After several more soldiers had nearly been vaporised, the Brigadier had ordered a strategic withdrawal to the green, where he and the rest were now licking the wounds to their professional pride.

'But surely, we don't want a defence?' said Benton, as Miss Hawthorne drew a strange symbol in each point of the star. 'It's an attack we're after.'

'I would never be able to raise enough power for a direct attack. Certainly not by myself. No. It's like judo. We use the enemy's own power against himself.'

'I still don't get it,' said Benton, looking yearningly towards the group of khaki-clad figures on the green.

'It's quite simple,' she replied, as she placed various objects taken from a paper carrier-bag onto the pentagram. 'It's an old occult principle. A magic attack which fails to find its mark recoils on the attacker.'

'I see,' said Benton, becoming interested in spite of himself. 'So you'll stand in the middle of that and call the gargoyle thing a few dirty names. He'll attack you, the fire will bounce back off you and, bingo! He'll vaporise himself.'

'That's more or less the idea,' she agreed, as she sprinkled salt on the articles in the star—some iron nails, a garlic flower, some twigs, a strangely shaped root, and a pile of stones.

'But isn't that rather dangerous?' said Benton.

'Of course it is. Now, be quiet, there's a good boy.' Miss Hawthorne produced what Benton could only suppose was a magic wand. Holding it in her right hand, she traced the outline of the circle and star with it, muttering under her breath. Benton could only catch a few words.

'. . . bound and sealed be all demons and powers of adversity . . . to be a fortress against all foes, visible and invisible . . . in the name of Hertha, blessed be . . .'

She stood up. 'There we are,' she said briskly. 'We've put our shoulders to the wheel and we're nearly at the top of the hill . . . Er . . . I think perhaps, you should get in here with me, Sergeant.'

'Thank you, ma'am, but I'd feel daft standing in that thing.'

'You'll feel very much dafter if our stone friend should hit you by mistake—or on purpose, for the matter of that.'

The Sergeant looked vainly around for help. The Brigadier was apparently involved in a vigorous argument with Captain Yates and Sergeant Osgood.

'Right, Miss Hawthorne. Very thoughtful of you,' he said, and gingerly stepped into the middle of the magic circle.

'Oh, it's not entirely unselfish, Sergeant,' said Miss Hawthrone coyly. 'You see, I need your help.'

'My help? I don't know anything about magic.'

'No, but you play cricket, I'm sure.'

'Well, yes.'

Miss Hawthorne pointed at the heap of stones. 'Do you think,' she said, 'that a good cricketer could hit a wicket at . . . let's see . . .' She gauged her distance between the circle and Bok with a countrywoman's eye. 'Oh . . . about thirty yards, I'd say.'

Benton grinned. 'I can have a go,' he said, and picking up one of the stones, hefted it in his hand to get the weight 'Ready, ma'am?' he said.

'Ready,' she said, holding the amulet which hung on her chest between finger and thumb.

Sergeant Benton threw the first stone. It narrowly missed the imp, but the noise of its bouncing off a headstone served to warn Bok that he was once more being attacked. He turned sharply, a claw half raised, gleaming eyes darting this way and that.

Miss Hawthorne could hardly breathe for suffocating excitement. This was the real thing! Her forays into the actual practice of her craft had been few and simple, mainly concerned with the bringing of good fortune to her friends. But this . . . Now she could find out the extent of her powers for certain. Though of course, should she fail, she wouldn't know anything about it. She smiled wryly at the thought.

'Here we go again,' Benton was saying. He had selected the smoothest and roundest stone from the pile. With a practised flick of the wrist, he sent it flying accurately to its target. It struck Bok a sharp blow on the side of the head. The ugly creature leapt up with an evil snarl. Spotting Benton and Miss Hawthorne and, at once guessing that they were the source of the attack, he raised himself some seven feet into the air with a couple of powerful strokes of his bat-like wings and pointed his claw straight at them.

And then the incredible happened. All at once his eyes turned blank and he seemed to be frozen solid. Falling heavily to the ground, he cracked into three or four pieces, which lay unmoving, the fragments of an inanimate stone carving.

'It worked!' said Benton. But Miss Hawthorne knew better.

'He hadn't even attacked,' she said, sounding almost disappointed.

At that moment, however, the vestry door was flung open and a flock of hooded figures came streaming out. Among them could be seen the scarlet robe of the Master, the distinctive Edwardian clothes of the Doctor and the white tabard which Jo was wearing.

'Get down!' the Doctor was shouting. 'The whole thing's going up at any second.'

Benton seized Miss Hawthorne and pulled her down to the shaking ground. The windows of the church were glowing red with heat and there was a roaring like a furnace at full blast.

The Doctor and the others ran past the remnants of the gargoyle and onto the green, where they flung themselves down with the rest. There was a long moment of suspense.

Then the church blew up.

.   .   .   .   .

The Master stood glowering at Sergeant Benton, who was covering him with a gun, while straining his ears to listen in to the Doctor's conversation with the Brigadier, a little way across the green.

'What happened?' Lethbridge Stewart was saying.

'Jo saved us all,' said the Doctor, smiling down at her.

'I did?' Jo looked up from pulling off the tabard.

'Yes, my dear. By that ridiculous and foolhardy act of self-sacrifice. You see, Azal couldn't handle a fact as illogical and irrational as your being prepared to give up your life for me.'

Mike Yates looked a little bewildered. 'So? I mean, why did that destroy him?'

'All his power was turned back against himself,' said the Doctor. 'You might say he blew a fuse!'

'There you are, you see. Exactly the same magic principle I was trying to use against that stone creature,' said Miss Hawthorne.

'Not magic, Miss Hawthorne, science.'

'Magic, Doctor.'

'Science.'

'Magic,' she said firmly. 'And I shall never know now whether my plan would have worked,' she added wistfully.

'So that would seem to be that,' said the Brigadier. 'Will that heat barrier have cleared itself?'

'Of course.'

'Good. Get ready to move out, Yates.'

'Sir. Benton?'

'Yes, sir.' Benton raised his voice. 'Right, you lot, you heard the man! The picnic's over!'

The UNIT troops pulled themselves reluctantly to their feet and sloped off towards the vehicles.

'And get a move on!' barked Benton.

Unfortunately, his attention had wandered for a moment. Seizing his opportunity, the Master, with a balletic twist, flung his scarlet robe over Benton and made a run for Bessie. Before anybody could stop him, he had jumped in and was rolling away across the green. The Brigadier and Mike pulled out their guns and started firing.

'No! Stop shooting!' cried the Doctor. 'You'll damage Bessie.'

'You want him to get away, man?' snapped the Brigadier.

'Don't worry, Lethbridge Stewart,' the Doctor said and called across the green: 'Bessie! Bring him back!'

The little yellow car obediently swung round and, despite all the Master's efforts, brought him back, straight into the muzzles of the UNIT guns.

The Brigadier looked at the Doctor. 'You want me to ask you how you did that. Well, I won't.'

The Doctor laughed and so did the Brigadier. 'How on earth did you do it, anyway?'

The Doctor winked at Jo. 'Well, it wasn't magic,' he said.

Epilogue

Young Stan Wilkins surveyed the busy village green with mixed feelings. Curious how things worked out. Everybody seemed happy now, and yet, just think, the Squire was dead. Old Josh too, P.C. Groom, the UNIT soldiers and, of course, poor Tom. Yet again, his uncle's death meant that the garage would now be his own. He knew enough about cars to make a go of it—and Mam would have somewhere to live! Aye, it was a funny old world, right enough. Stan took a deep breath of the clean spring air and walked towards the Maypole.

'Listen,' said Miss Hawthorne. 'The birds are singing. And smell the flowers! The May Day miracle has happened again. The earth is born anew.'

Sergeant Benton reported to the Brigadier. 'All under way, sir. The Master's under constant guard.'

'Sergeant,' cried Miss Hawthorne with delight. 'You and I must do the fertility dance to celebrate the deliverance of Devil's End—nay, the deliverance of the world!' And taking his hand, she started to pull him over to the Maypole.

'Sorry, ma'am,' said the blushing Benton. 'I'm rather busy at the moment. Thanks just the same.'

'Nonsense,' she answered gaily. 'Come along at once.'

Watching the suffering Benton, Jo giggled. 'Come on, Doctor,' she said, 'let's give him some moral support.'

The Doctor laughing, allowed himself to be dragged off. Mike Yates turned to Brigadier Lethbridge Stewart.

'Fancy a dance, sir?' he said, straight-faced.

'No, thank you, Captain Yates,' he replied. 'I'd rather have a pint...'

As the two officers walked towards the pub, the piper started to play a lilting tune. The Morrismen began their intricate figures, while around the Maypole the people of Devil's End danced a dance of thanksgiving, a dance of liberation, a dance of joy.

CONTENTS

1

The Nightmare

The tall, thin man with the young-old face and the mane of prematurely white hair was sleeping uneasily. Suddenly he awoke – to a nightmare.

He was still on the battered leather chaise-longue upon which he had dropped off to sleep – but instead of being in his laboratory he was at the centre of a barren, burning landscape.

All around him volcanoes erupted, sending out streams of burning lava. Lurid jets of flame flared up in smoky dust-laden air.

He sat up – and found himself staring at . . . at what?

A row of strange symbols, looking rather like double headed axes. Suspended before them was a huge, glowing crystal, pulsing with light, shaped like the head of a three-pronged spear, or like Neptune's trident.

Suddenly a sinister black-clad figure loomed up before him.

'Welcome! Welcome to your new Master!'

Volcanoes rumbled, lightning flashed and the figure gave a peal of mocking, triumphant laughter.

More strange and threatening shapes swam up before the dreamer's eyes. Strangely carved statues, demonic face-masks with long, slanting eyes . . .

Suddenly everything erupted in flame. Somewhere, someone was calling him. '*Doctor*! *Doctor*!'

The Doctor awoke, really awoke this time, and found himself back in his laboratory at UNIT HQ. A very small, very pretty fair-haired girl in high boots and a striped woollen mini-dress was shaking his shoulder.

For a moment the Doctor stared at his assistant as if he had no idea who she was. Then he said delightedly, 'Jo! Jo Grant!'

'Are you all right, Doctor?'

'Yes, I think so. I must have been having a nightmare.'

'I'll say you were – a real pippin. Here, I've brought you a cup of tea. Do you want it?'

The Doctor took the cup and saucer. 'Volcanoes . . . earthquakes . . .' Suddenly he leaped up. He handed Jo the untouched cup of tea. 'Thank you, I enjoyed that.'

He wandered over to a lab bench, picked up a small but complicated piece of electronic circuitry and stared absorbedly at it.

'Doctor, have you been working on that thing *all* night again?' asked Jo accusingly. 'What is it anyway – a super dematerialisation circuit?'

(At this time in his lives, the Doctor, now in his third incarnation, had been exiled to Earth by his Time Lord superiors. The TARDIS, his space-time machine, no longer worked properly. Much of his time was spent in an attempt to get it working again, and resume his wanderings through time and space.)

'No, no, the dematerialisation circuit will have to wait. This is something far more imporant. It might make all the difference the next time *he* turns up.'

'The next time who turns up?'

2

'The Master, of course.'

The Master, like the Doctor, was a sort of renegade Time Lord, though of a very different kind. The Doctor's wanderings through the cosmos were a result of simple curiosity. Such interventions as he made in the affairs of the planets he visited were motivated always by his concern to defeat evil and assist good.

The Master, on the other hand, was dedicated to evil; *his* schemes had always had conquest and self-aggrandisement as their goals.

Once good friends, the Doctor and the Master had long been deadly enemies. The Master's sudden arrival on the planet Earth had led to a resumption of the long-standing feud between them.

The Master's desire to defeat and destroy the Doctor, preferably in the most agonising and humiliating fashion possible, was quite as strong as his desire to rule the Universe.

And the Master had been part of the Doctor's nightmare . . . Perhaps the Doctor's subconscious mind, or that now-dormant telepathic facility that was part of his Time Lord make-up, was attempting to deliver some kind of warning. Perhaps he had somehow picked up a hint of the Master's latest, and no doubt diabolical, scheme . . .

The Doctor swung round. 'Now Jo, listen carefully. I want you to go and find out, as quickly as you can, if there have been any volcanic eruptions or severe earthquakes recently – anywhere in the world.'

'You're joking of course!'

'Believe me, Jo, this is no joking matter.'

'But I read it all out to you last night,' said Jo indignantly. 'It just shows, you never listen to a word

3

I say.' She went over to a side table, picked up a folded copy of *The Times* and perched on the edge of the Doctor's desk. 'Here we are. New eruptions in the Thera group of islands, somewhere off Greece.'

'Does it say anything about a crystal?'

'What crystal? Look, Doctor, I know I'm exceedingly dim, but please explain.'

'It was in my dream,' said the Doctor slowly. 'A big crystal, shaped something like a trident . . .'

Not far away, in his attic laboratory at the Newton Institute, Professor Thascalos held a trident-shaped crystal aloft. 'Observe – a simple piece of quartz, nothing more.'

Carefully he fitted the crystal into the centre of a cabinet packed with electronic equipment. He placed a transparent protective cover over the apparatus and stepped back.

He was a medium-sized, compactly but powerfully built man, this Professor Thascalos, with sallow skin and a neatly-trimmed pointed beard. His dark burning eyes radiated energy and power.

Beside him stood his assistant, Doctor Ruth Ingram, an attractive looking woman with short fair hair and an air of brisk no-nonsense efficiency about her. Like the Professor, she wore a crisp white lab coat.

She looked exasperatedly at her superior. 'But that's ridiculous!'

'Of course it is, Doctor Ingram,' agreed the Professor. His deep voice had just the faintest tinge of a Greek accent. 'Of course it is. There is no way for me to prove to you that this crystal is different from any other piece of quartz, yet it is unique. As you say, ridiculous!'

4

They were standing in the small inner section of the lab, divided from the rest of the lab by a protective wall of specially strengthened glass.

Slipping off his lab coat to reveal a beautifully tailored dark suit, the Professor moved through into the main laboratory. Like the smaller one, it held an astonishing variety of electronic equipment, crammed into what had once been servants' quarters in a great country house.

Ruth Ingram followed him. 'And this crystal is the missing piece of equipment we've been waiting for?'

'Exactly!'

Suddenly the door burst open and a tall, gangling young man rushed in, managing in the process to fall over his own feet.

'I swear I switch that alarm off in my sleep!' He had a shock of untidy brown hair and a long straggly moustache – intended to make him look more mature – gave him instead a faintly comic air.

At the sight of the Professor he skidded to a halt. 'Oops! Sorry, Prof.'

Stuart Hyde was the third member of the Professor's little research team, a post-graduate student working for a higher degree.

'Simmer down, Stu, for Pete's sake,' said Ruth. But she couldn't help smiling. There was something endearingly puppyish about Stuart Hyde.

The Professor however was not amused. 'Don't call me Prof!'

Stuart groaned. 'In the dog house again!'

The Professor glanced at his watch. 'Be quiet and listen to me. I have been summoned to a meeting with our new Director in exactly two and a half minutes. I shall have to leave the final checks for the demonstration to the pair of you.'

Ruth was both astonished and alarmed. 'Aren't we going to have a trial run first?'

The experimental apparatus on which they had all been working was due to be demonstrated to one of the Institute's directors that very morning – a director who also happened to be Chairman of the Grants Committee.

The Professor shook his head decisively. 'A trial run? It's not necessary, my dear.'

'That's marvellous,' said Stuart gloomily. 'We're going to look a right bunch of Charlies if something goes wrong when this fellow from the Grants Committee turns up. We'll be left there with egg on our faces.'

'Surely, Professor –' began Ruth.

'Now, now, my dear, there's no need for you to worry your pretty little head.'

He could scarcely have said anything calculated to annoy Ruth Ingram more. 'And there's no need for you to be so insufferably patronising, Professor. Just because I'm a woman . . .'

Stuart sighed. 'Here we go again!'

The Professor said instantly, 'You're quite right, Doctor Ingram. Please, forgive me.' He paused in the doorway. 'Now, will you be so good as to run those checks?'

The door closed behind him.

Ruth stood staring furiously at it. 'That man! I don't know which infuriates me more, his dictatorial attitude or that infernal courtesy of his!' She sighed. 'It's all the same really – a bland assumption of male superiority!'

Stuart grinned. 'May God bless the good ship Women's Lib and all who sail in her.'

Privately however, Stuart was thinking that Ruth

had got it wrong. The Professor didn't assume that he was superior just to women.

He was superior to everybody.

Mike Yates spread out the map of the Mediterranean on the Doctor's table and pointed. 'There you are, Jo, the Thera group. Those little islands there.'

Jo looked up at the Doctor who was busy at his lab bench. 'Doctor, come and look!'

'Not now, Jo, I'm busy.'

'But it's that map you asked for.'

A little grumpily the Doctor put down his circuit. 'Oh, I see!' He wandered over and looked at the map. 'Mmm, Thera . . .'

Jo waited expectantly.

'Doesn't mean a thing to me!' The Doctor returned to his bench.

Jo peered at the map. 'It says "Santorini" in brackets. Must be another name for it. What about that?'

The Doctor was immersed in his work. 'Forget it, Jo. I had a nightmare, that's all.'

Jo gave Mike Yates an apologetic look. 'Sorry, Mike.'

He began rolling up the map. 'Not to worry! Better than hanging about the Duty Room. If nothing turns up soon I'll go round the twist.'

'That makes two of us. And here I was thinking we were going off on a trip to Atlantis.'

The Doctor swung round. '*What*?'

'I was just saying to Mike.'

'You said *Atlantis*,' interrupted the Doctor. 'Why Atlantis?'

'Well, it said so in the paper, didn't it?'

7

The Doctor strode over to them. 'The map, Captain Yates, the map!'

Hurriedly Mike began unrolling the map again.

Jo picked up the newspaper. 'Here it is . . . "Believed by many modern historians to be all that remains of Plato's Metropolis of Atlantis".'

The Doctor brooded over the map. 'Of course, of course . . .'

Mike looked puzzled. 'Atlantis? I thought it was supposed to be in the middle of the Atlantic Ocean?'

Jo was studying the article. 'You're out of date. Apparently it was part of the Minoan civilisation – you know, the Minotaur and all that.'

'It's only legends though, isn't it?'

The Doctor straightened up. 'Get me the Brigadier on the telephone, will you Jo?'

'What, now?'

'Yes, *now*,' snapped the Doctor.

Jo leaped up. 'Sorry!' She reached for the phone.

Mike watched her dial. 'The Brig? Why the Brig, for heaven's sake?'

'Search me!' Jo listened for a second, then handed the phone to the Doctor. 'The Brigadier!'

The Doctor snatched the receiver. 'Brigadier? Now listen to me! I want you to put out a world-wide warning. Alert all your precious UNIT HQs. Not that it'll do any good!'

On the other end of the line, Brigadier Alastair Lethbridge-Stewart, Commanding Officer of the British section of the United Nations Intelligence Taskforce, stroked his neatly-trimmed military moustache. 'Thank you very much, Doctor. And against what, precisely, am I supposed to be warning the world?'

'The Master. I've just seen him.'

8

'You've seen him? Where? When?' The Brigadier leaped to his feet. 'Never mind. Stay right where you are Doctor. I'll be with you in a jiffy.'

A few minutes later, the Brigadier was bursting into the Doctor's laboratory. 'Now then, Doctor, you said you'd seen the Master? Where? When?'

The Doctor looked a little sheepish. 'In a dream. Not half an hour ago.'

The Brigadier sank down onto a stool. 'I can hardly put UNIT on full alert on the strength of your dreams, Doctor. In any case, *every* section of UNIT now has the search for the Master written into its standing orders.'

'Priority Z-44, I suppose.'

'Priority A-1, actually.'

'I tell you Brigadier, there is grave danger.'

'Danger of what for heaven's sake?'

'I'm not sure,' said the Doctor tetchily. 'But I tell you I saw danger quite clearly in my dream.'

'A *dream*! If that got out I'd be the laughing-stock of UNIT. Really, Doctor, you'll be consulting the entrails of a sheep next.'

Jo giggled.

The Brigadier glared reprovingly at her and went on, 'Right now, we'd better be on our way to the Newton Institute. Are you ready, Doctor?'

'Certainly not, Brigadier. I'm far too busy to go anywhere.'

'But I told them you'd go. They're expecting two observers from UNIT.'

The Doctor picked up his circuit and went on with his work.

'Shall I go?' asked Jo brightly.

'Certainly not,' snapped the Doctor. 'I need you here.'

Jo turned to the Brigadier. 'What's it all about anyway?'

'TOMTIT, that's what it's about, Miss Grant. A demonstration of TOMTIT.'

'TOMTIT? What on earth does that stand for?' asked Mike.

The Brigadier cleared his throat. 'Well, er . . .'

The Doctor spoke without looking up. 'Transmission Of Matter Through Interstitial Time.'

'Exactly,' said the Brigadier. 'TOMTIT.'

Jo was none the wiser. 'But what does it *do*?'

Here the Brigadier was on firmer ground. 'Brilliant idea. It can actually break down solid objects into light waves or whatever, and transmit them from one place to another.'

'And it *works*?' asked Yates incredulously.

The Brigadier shrugged. 'Apparently. Well, Yates, you'd better come with me, I suppose.'

'Sorry sir,' said Mike a little smugly. 'I'm Duty Officer.'

Unable to contravene his own orders, the Brigadier looked round helplessly. 'Well, someone's got to come with me . . .'

The door opened and a brawny young man in civvies marched in, carrying a weekend bag. 'Just off, sir.'

The Brigadier beamed. 'Sergeant Benton. The very man!'

Sergeant Benton saw trouble coming, and tried vainly to dodge. 'I was just leaving, sir. 48 hour pass.'

'Oh no you're not, Sergeant. You're coming with me on a little trip to the Newton Institute.'

10

'Yessir,' said Benton resignedly. 'The what, sir?'

'The Newton Institute. Research establishment at Wootton, just outside Cambridge . . .'

'Charlatan?' snarled Professor Thascalos. 'How dare you call *me* a charlatan, Doctor Perceval!' His dark eyes seemed to blaze with fury.

The portly silver-haired man on the other side of the desk winced before the Professor's fury, but he stood his ground. 'Doctor Cook is not only Chairman of the Grants Committee, but a colleague and a personal friend of mine. Am I to tell him this afternoon that I am as gullible as that drunkard I have replaced?'

The Professor smiled grimly and made no reply. Doctor Perceval's predecessor had indeed been over-fond of the bottle, an easy man to impress and to deceive.

Doctor Perceval however was a far more sceptical character. 'How is it that I can find no trace of your academic career, *before* your brief visit to Athens University? How is it that you have published nothing, that you refuse even to discuss the hypothesis behind your so-called experiments, that the very name of your project is arrant nonsense? TOMTIT! What, pray, is Interstitial Time?'

The one who called himself Professor Thascalos leaned forward, hands on the desk, staring into the new director's eyes. 'You're a very clever man, Director. I can see that I shall have to tell you everything. You're quite right of course, I am no Professor.'

'Ah!' said the Director triumphantly.

The mellow voice said soothingly. 'I can see that you are disturbed but you have nothing to worry

11

about. You must believe me . . . you *must* believe me . . .'

The dark eyes seemed to burn into the Director's brain, the deep voice vibrated inside his skull. He swayed a little on his feet.

'Must believe you,' he muttered. 'I must believe you.'

The deep voice rose to a triumphant crescendo. 'I am the Master. You will listen to me – and you will obey me. *You will obey me!*'

2

The Test

Suddenly the Director found that everything had become very clear. There was no problem, no reason for concern. It was very simple. All he needed to do was to obey. Indeed the very word vibrated inside his brain. '*Obey . . . obey . . . obey . . .* '

'That's better,' said the Master gently. 'Now, you just sit there quietly and await the arrival of this wretched man from London. And remember – you are perfectly satisfied as to the integrity of my work here and the authenticity of my credentials. You understand?'

The Director sank slowly back into his chair. 'Yes . . . I understand.'

In the laboratory, now filled with the high pitched oscillating whine of the TOMTIT apparatus, Ruth was checking readings on an instrument console. She was using an intercom to call the results through to Stuart, who was crouched over a complex piece of apparatus in the inner lab.

'One point three five nine,' she called.

Stuart's voice came faintly back. 'One point three five nine – check.'

'Two point zero four five.'

'Two point zero four five – check.'

13

'Three point zero six two.'

'Three point zero six two. Check.'

'Fifty-nine and steady.'

'Fifty nine and steady – check.'

Ruth flicked switches and the noise died away. 'And that's the lot.'

'And that's the lot – check, check, check!' parroted Stuart. He came through from the inner laboratory.

'And now we just sit and wait,' said Ruth disgustedly. 'I still think it's just plain stupid not to have a trial run. Ludicrous!'

'Ludicrous, check!'

'Oh, grow up, Stu!'

'No, but I mean it, love, it *is* ludicrous. Just suppose this thing won't wag its tail when we tell it to?'

'They'd withdraw the grant.'

'As sure as God made little green apples. And bang goes my fellowship.'

'Bang goes my job,' said Ruth. '*And* my scientific reputation for that matter.' She snorted. 'Men! It's their conceit that bugs me.'

'Hey, hey, hey,' protested Stuart. 'I'm on your side, remember?'

'Oh well, you don't count!'

'Oh, do't I?'

'Don't bully me, Stu, or I think I'll burst into tears.'

There was a moment of gloomy silence. Then Stuart looked up. 'Let's do it!'

'What?'

'Have a run-through.'

Ruth looked instinctively at the door. 'Without – *him*?'

'Why not?'

'Well, it's the Professor's project after all,' said Ruth doubtfully. 'He *is* the boss.'

'Nominally, perhaps. But when you think how much you've put into it, Ruth, it becomes a joint affair. You've as much right to take that sort of decision as he has.'

Ruth was tempted but uncertain. 'Well . . .'

Stuart played his ace. 'Of course, if you feel you *need* to have a man in charge . . .'

'That does it. We go ahead.'

'That's my girl!'

Ruth gave him an exasperated look and went over to the controls.

Jo Grant looked furiously at the Doctor who was still hard at work on his complex piece of circuitry. He was fitting it into a carrying case which was shaped rather like a table tennis bat. The rounded end held dials and a little rotating aerial.

'You know, Doctor,' said Jo conversationally, 'you're quite the most annoying person I've ever met. I've asked you at least a million times. What *is* that thing?'

The Doctor looked absently at her. 'Extraordinary. I could have sworn I'd told you . . . It's a time sensor, Jo.'

'I see.'

'Do you? What does it do then?'

'Well, it . . . it's a . . . Obviously it detects disturbances in the Time Field.'

The Doctor gave her an admiring look. 'Very good. You're learning, Jo. Yes, this is just what you need if you happen to be looking for a TARDIS.'

'It's a TARDIS sniffer-outer!'

15

'Precisely. Or any other time-machine for that matter. So, if the Master does turn up . . .'

'Bingo!'

'As you so rightly say, Jo – Bingo!'

Stuart was laboriously climbing into an all-enveloping protective suit which made him look like a rather comic astronaut. 'I feel like the back end of a pantomime horse.'

'Very suitable for a keen young man like you,' said Ruth briskly.

'Come again?'

'Starting at the bottom!'

Stuart groaned. 'Anyway, it's all a waste of time. Why should there be any radiation danger at the receiver? We're only going to use about ten degrees.'

'Are you willing to take the risk?'

Stuart thought for a moment. 'No!'

'Then stop beefing and get on with it!'

Fitting the visored helmet over his head, Stuart went through into the inner section of the laboratory – the receiving area.

Ruth operated controls and the TOMTIT noise began, rising steadily in pitch and volume . . .

(Blissfully unaware of all this scientific activity, the Institute's regular window cleaner was setting his ladder up against the laboratory window. He peered curiously at the radiation suited figure in the lab, then reached for his wash-leather.)

Ruth went to a shelf and took down a white marble vase. It had curved sides and a domed lid, and looked rather like a giant chess pawn.

She put the case on a flat surface beneath a complex looking focussing device, then returned to her control panel.

16

Stuart's voice came from the intercom. 'Interstitial activity – nil.'

Ruth checked the dial on her console. 'Molecular structure, stable. Increasing power.'

The oscillating whine of TOMTIT rose higher. In the inner lab the crystal began to glow.

With the Doctor's time sensor in her hand, Jo stood looking apprehensively at the open door of the TARDIS, which was making a strange wheezing, groaning sound. 'I say, Doctor, you're not going to disappear to Venus or somewhere?'

The Doctor's voice came through the TARDIS door. 'No, of course not. Just keep your eyes on those dials!'

Suddenly the dials began flickering wildly, the aerial spun frantically, and the device gave out a high pitched bleeping sound.

'It's working!' said Jo excitedly.

'Of course it is. Make a note of the readings will you?'

Jo grabbed a note pad and pencil.

Ruth was still calling out the readings. 'Thirty-five . . . forty . . . forty-five . . .'

Stuart's voice came back. 'Check, check, check.'

'Increasing power . . .'

The circular aerial on top of the Doctor's device was revolving wildly. It slowed and stopped as the TARDIS noise died away.

The Doctor came marching out, took the note pad with the readings from Jo's hand and began studying it absorbedly.

'Well done,' said Jo.

17

'Thank you,' said the Doctor modestly.

'It's a bit out on distance though. Says the TARDIS is only three feet away.'

'Those are Venusian feet,' said the Doctor solemnly.

'I see. They're larger than ours?'

'Oh yes, much larger, Jo. The Venusians are always tripping over themselves.'

Suddenly the time sensor came to life again. Jo jumped, 'You must have left something switched on in the TARDIS, Doctor.'

'I most certainly did not. Why?'

Jo handed him the sensor. 'Look, it's working again. And the readings are different.'

The Doctor stared indignantly at the sensor. 'That's impossible – unless . . .'

'Unless what?'

The Doctor said slowly, 'Unless someone's operating another TARDIS.'

In the inner laboratory Ruth's voice came to Stuart over the intercom. 'Isolate matrix scanner.'

Stuart reached for a control with his gloved hand. 'Check.' In front of Stuart there was a square metal platform with a focussing device suspended over it – the exact duplicate of the one before Ruth in the outer lab.

Suddenly on that platform there appeared the ghostly outline of a vase.

'It's going to work!' shouted Stuart excitedly.

Ruth's calm voice came back. 'Pipe down and concentrate. Stand by. Initiating transfer.'

Stuart began the countdown. 'Ten . . . nine . . . eight . . .'

The crystal glowed brighter.

In the Director's study the Master had installed himself at the Director's desk, calmly drafting a proposal to double his own grant for the Director to sign. The clock of what had once been the old stables began to chime. Suddenly the Master frowned and looked up. The chiming was slow, dragging, slurred, as if the old clock was somehow running down. But the Master knew better. It wasn't the clock that was slowing down – it was time itself.

'*The fools*!' he snarled, and hurried from the room.

'Four . . . three . . . two . . . one!' chanted Stuart.

In the outer lab the vase became transparent, then faded slowly away . . .

. . . to re-appear, solid and real on the receiving plate in front of Stuart.

Rapidly he operated controls. 'Transfer stabilising. Okay Ruth, switch off. We've done it!'

He expected the noise of TOMTIT to die away, but it didn't. The oscilliating whine rose higher.

He heard Ruth's voice over the intercom. 'Stuart, come here. There's a positive feedback. She's overloading!'

Pulling off his helmet, Stuart rushed back to the outer lab where he found Ruth busy at her console.

Without looking up she said, 'You'll have to bring the surge down as I reduce the power or she'll blow.'

Stuart ran to the console. 'Right.'

The astonished window cleaner was still perched at the top of his ladder, staring at the glowing crystal as if hypnotised. Suddenly a giant surge of power struck him, like a push from an invisible hand.

He flew backwards off his ladder, and *floated* rather than fell to the ground below.

The Master, crossing the courtyard observed this phenomenon without surprise. He hurried towards the door that led to the laboratory.

As he came closer, he leaned forward against the thrust of some invisible resistance, like a man walking against a high wind.

The stable clock was still giving out its low, dragging chime.

In the laboratory itself, the calm centre of this localised temporal storm, things seemed normal enough.

Ruth and Stuart were in the inner lab examining the vase on its metal platform. The crystal was still glowing brightly.

Carefully, Stuart lifted the vase from its platform. 'It looks fine!'

Ruth nodded. 'Be careful. Bring it through here.' She led the way back into the main lab.

Carefully, Stuart stood the vase on a bench. 'I don't believe it. We've really done it!'

'It'll have to be checked for any structural changes,' said Ruth cautiously.

'OH, FOR Pete's sake,' said Stuart explosively, 'it's as good as new, you can see it is.' He grabbed her by the shoulders and began waltzing her round the room to a triumphant chant of 'We've done it, we've done it, we've done it!'

The dance stopped abruptly as they waltzed straight into the Master. He was standing in the doorway, an angry scowl on his face.

The Doctor was studying a map. 'I'd place it in that

segment there, Jo. Anything from fifty to a hundred miles from here.'

'Not much to go on.'

'Not unless he switches his TARDIS on again . . .'

Jo looked hopefully at him. 'Well, you never know. He might.'

'And in that case Jo, if we were a bit nearer, and in Bessie . . .'

'Right,' said Jo. 'Come on then, Doctor, let's go. You bring the map.'

The Master was in a towering rage. 'You are a fool, Doctor Ingram.'

Ruth felt herself quailing beneath the sheer force of his anger, which made her all the more determined to stand up for herself. 'You have no right to talk to me like that, Professor.'

'Be silent! You might have caused irreparable damage.'

'I was in full control the whole time. If you have no confidence in me –'

The Master cut across her. 'That is quite irrelevant. Mr Hyde, why did *you* allow this stupidity?'

'Hang about,' protested Stuart. 'I'm not my sister's keeper, you know. She's the boss.' He hesitated and then admitted, 'In any case, I was the one who suggested it.'

The Master turned away. 'I might have known. Just like an irresponsible schoolboy. You'll pay for this!'

Ruth came to the defence of her colleague. 'The decision was entirely mine, Professor. I take full responsibility for testing the apparatus, and I'm prepared to justify my action at the highest level.

21

Perhaps we had better go and see the Director and sort all this out before the demonstration.'

With a mighty effort the Master controlled himself. When he spoke, his voice was once again calm and reasonable. 'I'm sorry Doctor Ingram, you must excuse me. It will not be necessary to take this matter any further.'

But now Ruth was angry in her turn. 'That's all very well, Professor. After the things you've been saying –'

'Please,' said the Master forcefully. 'Accept my apologies.'

Ruth drew a deep breath. 'Well, perhaps it was a bit unethical of me not to have told you.'

'Come off it, Ruth,' said Stuart. 'He's only climbing down because he needs you for the demonstration.'

'How very clever of you, Mr Hyde,' said the Master smoothly. 'Of course I need you, both of you.'

Stuart couldn't help feeling mollified. 'After all Prof, let's face it, we couldn't risk a foul-up this afternoon, could we?'

'Say no more,' said the Master magnanimously. 'The matter is closed.'

'Well, not quite,' said Ruth a little guiltily. 'You see, it wasn't all plain sailing. We had some sort of positive feedback. There was an overload.'

'But that's impossible.'

'See for yourself.' She tore off the print-out from the computer and handed it to him.

The Master studied it thoughtfully. 'I see . . . Of course, how foolish of me.'

They heard Stuart calling from the inner lab. 'Hey, Ruth, Professor. The crystal – it's still glowing!'

The Master snapped his fingers. 'Of course it is! I see . . .'

Ruth looked dubiously at him. 'You know what caused the overload then?'

'Of course. You must have been drawing some kind of power from outside time itself. We must build a time vector filter into the transmitter.' The Master snatched up a pencil from the bench, and began drawing on the computer read-out paper. 'Here, let me show you.' With amazing speed, he sketched an elaborate circuit diagram. 'You see? In effect, it's a sort of paracybernetic control circuit.'

Ruth studied the diagram. 'Yes, I see. But won't this take some time to line up? The demonstration is at two.'

'Indeed it will – and I'm afraid I must leave the task to you. I am expected to eat a pretentious lunch and exchange banalities with our guests.'

Stuart Hyde was an amiable soul and he was happy that a semblance of good feeling had been restored. 'Don't worry, Prof, you go off and enjoy your nosh. Leave it to the toiling masses.'

'I have every confidence in you, Mr Hyde.' said the Master smoothly. 'And of course, in you, Doctor Ingram.'

Stuart had wandered over to the window. 'Hey, you'd better get your skates on, Professor. The VIPs are arriving . . . escorted by UNIT no less.'

The Master hurried to the window.

An enormous black limousine was gliding up the drive, with an Army landrover close behind it. Gold letters were painted on the side panel of the jeep.

'UNIT,' muttered the Master. 'What are *they* doing here?'

Stuart shrugged. 'Military observers, I suppose.

23

Happens all the time. The Government are the only people with the money for our sort of nonsense these days.'

The Master turned away from the window. 'Doctor Ingram I have changed my mind. *I* shall stay here and set up the time vector filter myself – with the assistance of Mr Hyde, of course.'

Ruth gave him an offended look. 'I assure you I am perfectly capable of constructing the circuit –'

'And I am sure you are equally capable of eating a tough pheasant on my behalf.'

'But why don't you want to go suddenly?'

The Master's voice was throbbing with sincerity. 'I am a life-long pacifist, Doctor Ingram. The association of the military, with violence, with killing . . .'He shuddered delicately. 'Please bear with me.'

Ruth thought the Professor made a most unlikely pacifist, but she had no alternative but to agree. 'Very well. I'll get them to send you some sandwiches across.'

'Good thinking, Batman,' said Stuart. As he helped her off with her lab coat he whispered, 'We've got a right nutcase on our hands!'

3

The Summoning

The occupants of the two vehicles parked outside the Institute were staring in astonishment at what looked like a freak accident. They stood in a little semi-circle around the window cleaner who was laying sprawled out and motionless on the gravel drive.

There were four of them in the group: Doctor Cook, chairman of the Grants Committee, a serious, indeed pompous man in his middle fifties; Proctor his assistant, younger, and nervously deferential; Sergeant Benton, back in uniform and still sighing for his vanished leave; and finally, there was the immaculate figure of Brigadier Lethbridge-Stewart, who was kneeling beside the body and taking its pulse.

'He's not dead, is he?' asked Doctor Cook nervously.

The Brigadier stood up. 'No, he's still breathing.'

'Well – who is he?'

The Brigadier glanced at the ladder still propped up against the building. 'A window cleaner, I presume. Must have fallen off his ladder.' He studied the unconscious but apparently uninjured form. 'It's a miracle he's still alive.'

'Poor fellow,' said Cook indifferently. 'Come

along, Proctor. I trust you'll make the necessary arrangements to get the man to hospital, Brigadier?'

The Brigadier too knew all about the advantages of delegation. 'Yes, of course sir, leave it to me.' He raised his voice. 'Sergeant Benton! See to it will you?'

Bessie, the Doctor's little yellow roadster, shot along the narrow country lane with the Doctor at the wheel. He cut a colourful figure in his elegant burgundy smoking jacket, ruffled shirt and flowing cloak. Beside him sat Jo Grant, a map spread out on her lap, the time sensor resting on top of it. She was wearing a warm fluffy coat over her mini-dress.

She glanced up at the sky which was dull and overcast. 'Isn't it a doomy day? I mean, look at that sky. Just *look* at it!'

The Doctor was concentrating on his driving. 'My dear girl, stop whiffling. We're not out on a pleasure jaunt.'

'Sorry, Doctor.'

What they were out on, thought Jo, was more of a wild goose chase. The plan was to drive about in a more or less random search pattern, covering the general area from which the mysterious time signal had originated.

The Doctor said, 'If it is the Master, we can't run the risk of losing him. So you just keep your eye on the sensor.'

Obediently Jo glanced at the sensor on her lap and found to her astonishment that its little scanner aerial was whirling frantically.

'Doctor, it's working again!'

The Doctor stopped the car. 'What's the bearing?'

Jo made a rapid calculation. 'Zero seven four. And it's . . . sixteen point thirty-nine miles away.'

'That's Venusian miles. That'd be seventy-two point seventy-eight miles . . .' He studied the map. 'Which puts it about – *here*. A village called Wootton.'

'Wootton? But that's where the Brigadier and Sergeant Benton went to.'

'TOMTIT!' said the Doctor. 'If the Master's behind that . . . What time's the demonstration, Jo?'

'Two o'clock, I think.'

'We've got to stop it!'

The Doctor started the car, and flicked the super-drive switch. Bessie streaked away at an impossibly high speed.

Ruth Ingram was thoroughly relieved when lunch was over at last. It *had* been pheasant – tough pheasant – just as the Professor had predicted.

Socially speaking, it had not been the most enjoy-able of occasions. Throughout the meal, Doctor Cook had whinged on about the need for stringent economies. Indeed, he was still doing so now as the little group made its way into the TOMTIT laboratory.

'Well, that's how it is, Charles. It may seem churlish of me after eating your excellent lunch – though how the Institute can afford pheasant I really don't know . . .'

'We *are* in the depths of the country,' protested the Director feebly. He had been silent and abstracted throughout the meal as if part of his mind wasn't really with them at all.

Cook strode on into the laboratory. 'Be that as it may, we are responsible for international funds, public money. I doubt very much whether we should allow ourselves the luxury of either pheasants *or* TOMTITs.' He laughed loudly at his own laborious joke, and Proctor tittered obsequiously.

Ruth looked round the empty laboratory. 'Well,' she said awkwardly, 'the Professor doesn't seem to be here.'

'Obviously,' said the Director pettishly.

Stuart came from the inner laboratory, suited up except for his helmet, which he carried under one arm.

Ruth greeted him with relief. 'There you are, Stuart. Where's the Professor?'

'Search me. He was here a couple of minutes ago.'

'Who is this fellow Thascalos, anyway?' demanded Cook. 'I've never heard of him.'

The Director seemed to come to life. 'Oh, an excellent background, excellent,' he said enthusiastically. 'Surely you've read his paper on the granular structure of time?'

'It's all I can do to keep up with my Departmental papers,' said Cook loftily. 'I leave all the rest to Proctor here.'

He glanced sharply at his assistant, who shook his head apologetically. 'New one on me, sir, I'm afraid.'

The Brigadier was gazing around the laboratory which was cluttered with equipment. 'Fearsome looking load of electronic nonsense you've got here, Doctor Ingram,' he said briskly. 'How does it work – and what does it do?'

Ruth drew a deep breath. 'Well . . .'

'In words of one syllable, please,' said the Brigadier hurriedly.

Ruth smiled. 'I'll do my best. Now, according to

Professor Thascalos's theory, time isn't smooth. It's made up of bits.'

'A series of minute present-moments,' said Stuart helpfully.

Ruth nodded. 'That's it. Temporal atoms, so to speak. So, if one could push something through the interstices between them, it would be outside our space-time continuum altogether.'

The Brigadier gave her a baffled look. 'Where would it be, then?'

'Nowhere at all, in ordinary terms.'

'You've lost me, Doctor Ingram.'

'And me,' said Humphrey Cook emphatically. 'Never heard such a farrago of unscientific rubbish in my life. It's an impossible concept.'

'But we've done it,' said Stuart triumphantly. 'We shoved a vase through here –' He indicated the transmission platform – 'and brought it back in there.' And he pointed to the inner laboratory.

'Shoved it through where?' asked the Brigadier exasperatedly.

Benton, who had been standing silent and a little overawed at the back of the group said unexpectedly, 'Through the crack between now and now, sir.'

The Brigadier shook his head. Where was the Doctor when he needed him? 'I give up. It's beyond me.'

A deep, foreign-accented voice said, 'Then you must see for yourselves!'

In the doorway stood a figure in a radiation suit, features obscured by the visored helmet. 'I must apologise for keeping you all waiting. Shall we begin?'

29

Jo clutched the edge of her seat as Bessie sped along the lanes at a speed, she was sure, of several hundred miles an hour. 'Please slow down, Doctor. It's not safe to drive so quickly.' They were moving so fast that the countryside around them was no more than a blur.

'It's perfectly safe,' shouted the Doctor cheerfully. 'My reactions are ten times as fast as yours, remember. And Bessie's no ordinary car.'

They were streaking along a comparatively straight stretch of road when, to her horror, Jo saw that a main highway was cutting across it at right angles.

They swept up to the junction, the Doctor's foot pressed steadily on the brake, and Bessie stopped – instantly.

Jo gulped. 'Why didn't I go through the windscreen?'

'Because Bessie's brakes work by the absorption of inertia – including yours.'

Suddenly Jo's attention was caught by the whirring of the time sensor. 'It's starting again!'

'Come on, Bessie, old girl,' said the Doctor. 'It's up to you!'

Checking that the junction was clear, the Doctor started Bessie up again and shot off even faster than before.

Unfortunately it was a case of more haste, less speed. Just beyond the junction was the notice board signalling the way to the Newton Institute. The Doctor and Jo shot straight past without even seeing it . . .

In the TOMTIT laboratory, the Master switched on the power. The experiment was about to begin.

'Surely you don't need to wear radiation gear out here, Professor?' asked Ruth.

'A precaution in case of emergency, my dear. I may have to join Mr Hyde in the inner laboratory in a hurry.' He leaned over the intercom. 'Report!'

Stuart's voice came from the speaker. 'Interstitial activity, nil.'

Ruth was placing a rather handsome cup and saucer on the metal transmitting platform. She checked a dial. 'Molecular structure stable.'

'Increasing power,' snapped the Master.

The oscillating whine of TOMTIT rose higher.

Ruth's voice was tense. 'Isolate matrix scanner.'

'Check'

'Increasing power,' said the Master again.

Ruth gave him a worried look. 'But you're into the second quadrant already, Professor.'

'*I know what I'm doing.*' The Master spoke more calmly. 'Initiating transfer!'

He threw a switch and to the astonishment of the Brigadier and the other onlookers, the cup and saucer faded slowly away.

'Good heavens,' said the Brigadier. He looked through the partition and saw the cup and saucer standing on the receiving platform in the inner laboratory, the radiation-suited figure of Stuart Hyde hovering over it.

Suddenly Stuart's voice crackled frantically from the intercom. 'I'm getting too much power again. I can't hold it. Switch off. Switch off!'

Ruth turned to the Professor, and was horrified to see that he was actually increasing the power. 'Turn it off!' she shouted.

But the figure at the controls seemed rapt, enchanted.

31

Throwing back his head the Master roared, 'Come, Kronos – *come*! I summon you!'

4

The Ageing

In the inner laboratory the crystal glowed with a fierce, almost unbearable brightness.

Even through the darkened vision-plate of Stuart's helmet it's intensity was dazzling. He staggered back . . .

Suddenly the transferred cup and saucer glowed brightly, then shattered.

In their place Stuart sensed rather than saw something else beginning to form.

A winged shape . . .

A tendril of fire snaked out, groping aimlessly. It touched Stuart, and his whole body glowed brightly for a second.

He staggered back, clawed at his helmet and collapsed. Beneath the helmet, his face began to change . . .

Ruth saw him fall, and ran to the partition door. She was about to go to his assistance then stopped herself. The radiation level in the inner lab was still dangerously high. But Professor Thascalos was already suited up.

She swung round and called 'Professor!' To her horror, she saw that the Professor had disappeared.

Ruth ran back to the main control console. Stuart

would have to wait. The essential thing now was to turn off the power – if she could . . .

It didn't take the Doctor long to realise that he had overshot his destination. He stopped the car, studied the map and swung the car in a U-turn. Minutes later he was streaking up the drive of the Newton Institute and making one of his amazing stops before the main door.

The Doctor jumped out of the car. 'Right, Jo . . . Oh, good grief!'

Jo Grant didn't move or speak. She was sitting quite still, staring straight ahead of her.

For a moment the Doctor thought she must be stunned by the speed of the journey. The he realised that it was something else entirely that was happening – something that confirmed his worst fears. Someone was interfering with time.

As he turned away from the car, he felt the resistance of the temporal disturbance. Forcing his way through it, the Doctor used the resistance as a guide, letting it lead him to its source. He ran through the archway at the side of the main building, across the courtyard beyond, through the white-painted door on the other side.

In his haste, the Doctor failed to notice a radiation-suited figure, flattened against the wall on the other side of the arch.

As the Doctor vanished through the door the figure snatched off its helmet. His face a picture of frustrated evil, the Master turned and hurried away.

After climbing endless flights of stairs the Doctor dashed into the attic laboratory.

He summed up the situation at a glance. 'Cut the power!'

'I can't,' shouted Ruth frantically. 'The controls won't budge!'

The Doctor studied the console. 'Reverse the polarity'.

'What?'

'Reverse the temporal polarity!'

Ruth snatched an inspection hatch from the top of the console, extracted a circuit, reversed it, and fitted it back into place.

Immediately the whine of the apparatus began dying down. In a few moments it had stopped altogether.

The Brigadier began moving towards the connecting door. 'Is it safe to go in there?'

Ruth shook her head. 'No, wait . . .'

'But what about that poor chap in there?'

Ruth held up her hand for silence, studying a rapidly falling dial. 'Right, the level should be safe now.'

The Doctor and the Brigadier hurried through into the inner lab. Kneeling by the unconscious body, the Doctor lifted the loosened helmet from its head.

The face beneath the helmet was lined and wrinkled, with the pouched and sagging skin of the very old. Above it was a shock of snow-white hair.

Ruth gave a gasp of horror. 'Stuart!'

The Doctor looked curiously at her. 'Who is this man?'

'Stuart Hyde – my assistant.'

'Your *assistant* – at his age?'

'Stuart's only twenty-five!'

'And this man's eighty or more.' The Doctor stared thoughtfully at the ancient face.

Jo Grant came hurrying in, released from her strange paralysis in the car. 'What's happening, Doctor? Were we too late?'

'On the contrary, Jo. I think we were just in time.'

It was some time later and Stuart Hyde was resting uneasily in his own little bedroom in the Institute's residential wing. The Doctor was taking his temperature watched by Ruth Ingram, Jo Grant and the Brigadier.

'How is he?' asked the Brigadier.

The Doctor studied the thermometer for a moment and handed it back to Ruth. 'We must get him to hospital soon, but for the moment he just needs rest. He must have been a pretty tough youngster.'

Ruth sighed, remembering Stuart as he used to be, with all the vitality and bounce of an exuberant puppy. 'He was.'

'Lucky for him. Otherwise the shock of the change would have finished him off.'

'He will be all right, won't he?' asked Jo.

The Doctor nodded. 'He'll survive.'

'Like that?' said Ruth unhappily. 'And for how long? He's an old man!'

As usual the Brigadier was still struggling to understand what was going on. 'But what caused it? Some sort of radioactivity?'

'No, it's more than that.'

'A change in the metabolism?' suggested Jo.

The Doctor rubbed his chin. 'That's more like it, but it still can't be the whole answer. Even if the metabolic rate had increased a hundredfold, the change in him would have taken seven or eight months, not seconds.'

The Brigadier gave up. 'Well, there's only one thing I know that makes people grow old.'

The Doctor raised an eyebrow. 'Yes?'

'Anno Domini, Doctor. The passing of time.'

'We all know that,' said Ruth impatiently.

But the Doctor said, 'Congratulations, Brigadier. You've provided the explanation.'

'Glad to be of service, Doctor. Er – what did I say?'

'Time,' said the Doctor impressively. 'That's the answer. The only possible answer. Stuart Hyde's own personal time was speeded up so enormously that his whole physiological life passed by in a moment. But why? How did it happen?'

Ruth shrugged. 'The Professor might know. But he seems to have disappeared.'

Jo looked puzzled. 'What Professor?'

'Professor Thascalos. TOMTIT's his baby.'

'*What*?' yelled the Doctor indignantly. 'The arrogance of that man is beyond belief!'

'Whose arrogance?' asked the Brigadier wearily. 'I do wish you wouldn't speak in riddles, Doctor.'

'A more classical education might have helped, Brigadier, "Thascalos" is a Greek word –'

'I get it,' interrupted Jo. 'I bet "Thascalos" is the Greek for "Master".'

Stuart moaned and stirred.

Ruth leaned over him. 'He's coming round.'

'Help . . .' muttered Stuart. 'Help me . . .'

'It's all right,' said Jo soothingly. 'You're safe now.'

The old man glared wildly at her. 'Safe? No-one's safe. He's here . . . he's here. *I saw him.*'

Ruth tried to settle him back on his pillows. 'The

37

poor boy's delirious,' she said. 'Don't try to speak, Stu. Just rest.'

'No, wait,' snapped the Doctor. 'Let him talk. What did you see?' He leaned over the terrified old man. 'Answer me!'

'Danger!' muttered Stuart. 'The crystal . . . *the crystal.*'

His body arched and he flung his head from side to side.

Ruth tried to push the Doctor aside. 'You must stop this!'

The Doctor ignored her, leaning over Stuart. 'Speak up, man! What was it you saw?'

'I say, steady on, Doctor,' said the Brigadier.

'Doctor, *please*,' pleaded Jo.

But the Doctor was not to be distracted. 'Be quiet all of you.' He leaned over Stuart. 'Stuart, answer me! *What was it*?'

Suddenly Stuart sat bolt upright. '*Kronos*!' he screamed hoarsely. 'It was Kronos!' He fell back unconscious.

'I should have known!' said the Doctor softly. 'Doctor Ingram, I want you to come with me. You must tell me everything you know about Professor Thascalos and about this machine of his.'

'Shall I come too?' asked Jo.

'No, you'd better stay here with this poor fellow. If he starts talking again, call me at once.' The Doctor headed for the door and with a helpless look at the others, Ruth followed him.

'Better lock the door behind us, Miss Grant,' advised the Brigadier.

The Doctor paused. 'Don't hang about, Brigadier, I've got a job for you too, you know!'

38

In the duty room at UNIT HQ Captain Yates was noting his superior's requirements on a message pad.

'Newton Institute, Wootton. Yes sir, got that, sir. Over.'

The Brigadier's voice crackled from the RT. Unfortunately, there was rather more crackle than message. Mike Yates flicked the switch. 'Say again, sir, I didn't quite get that. Over.'

The Brigadier was standing by his land rover which was still parked outside the Newton Institute. He raised his voice. 'I said, bring some men down with you, Captain Yates, I feel as naked as a baby in its bath. Light and heavy machine guns . . . oh, and shove a couple of anti-tank guns in the boot, will you?'

Mike's voice was puzzled. 'You've got tanks there, sir?'

'You never know,' said the Brigadier ominously. 'Over.' Although the Brigadier didn't really know what he was up against, he did know that the average alien menace seemed distressingly immune to rifle bullets. Maybe something heavier would do the trick.

Mike Yates said, 'Right, sir, I've got all that. And when, sir? I mean how soon?'

'Oh, the usual,' said the Brigadier calmly. 'About ten minutes ago! Oh, and Captain Yates, the Doctor wants you to bring his TARDIS with you. Over.'

'Right, sir. Over and out.'

'Over and out.'

The Brigadier turned as he heard voices behind him. Humphrey Cook and his assistant Proctor were marching out of the Institute, followed by a protesting Director.

'I'm sorry, Charles,' Cook was saying. 'The whole things smells of bad fish. You'll be well out of it.'

The Director seemed compelled to argue a hopeless case. 'But I would stake my reputation on the integrity of Professor Thascalos.'

'You already have, Charles. A foolish gamble at very long odds. It is scarcely surprising that you lost.'

'Humphrey, please . . .'

'I'm sorry, Charles. I see no alternative to a full Whitehall enquiry. One can only hope we shan't have to parade our dirty linen at Westminster.'

The Brigadier stepped forward. 'Forgive me, Mr Cook.'

'Doctor Cook, actually.'

'I beg your pardon, *Doctor* Cook. I couldn't help over-hearing what you were saying.'

'Well?'

'This affair is no longer in your hands, sir. It is now a security matter and I have taken over.'

'You have no right, Brigadier.'

'I'm sorry, sir, I have every right. Subsection three of the preamble to the seventh enabling act, sir. Paragraph twenty-four G, if I remember rightly.'

'Oh,' said Cook completely deflated.

'So, bearing in mind the Official Secrets Act, you will please say nothing to anyone about today's events.' He glared fiercely at Proctor. 'Either of you.'

Proctor opened his mouth to protest, but Humphrey Cook snapped. 'Oh, be quiet, Proctor.' He turned back to the Brigadier. 'You can't possibly have grounds for such high-handed –'

'This man Thascalos is known to me,' interrupted the Brigadier. 'He is a dangerous criminal and an escaped prisoner. Sufficient grounds, I think?'

Cook rounded on the defenceless Proctor. 'Oh, come along, Proctor. Don't stand about.'

They both got into the car, and Cook leaned out of the window to fire a parting shot at the Director. 'You will be hearing from me, Charles.'

The limousine swept away down the drive and disappeared from view.

The Brigadier watched it go with the satisfaction of one who has thoroughly routed the enemy. He turned back to the Director, who was walking back into the main building with slow, almost stumbling steps. 'Excuse me, sir!'

The Director didn't seem to hear him.

'Doctor Perceval!'

Slowly the Director turned, his expression vague, almost blank. The poor old boy was still reeling under the shock, thought the Brigadier. 'Are you feeling quite well, sir?'

'What? Yes, of course I am. This whole matter has been a great shock of course . . . What did you want?'

'I should like this place evacuated of all but essential personnel at once.'

'But that's nonsense,' spluttered Perceval. 'I can hardly think, Brigadier, that you have the remotest idea what you are asking. There are projects in train here which –'

'I'm sorry, sir, but it's absolutely necessary. Sergeant Benton is keeping an eye on that infernal machine of yours until the troops arrive, but I cannot be responsible for the consequences unless you do what I ask.'

The Director attempted a last protest. 'Brigadier, you may enjoy playing soldiers, but –'

The Brigadier said crisply, 'By three o'clock

41

please, Doctor Perceval.' He turned to go, then paused. 'By the way, if the Master should contact you, don't try to hold him. Just let me know at once.'

'Who?'

The Brigadier smiled wryly. 'I'm sorry. I meant the Professor of course. Professor Thascalos.'

The Director looked worried. 'But surely he'll be miles away by now?'

'I doubt it. Why should he have any idea that we're on to him? Believe me, he'll be back!'

5

The Legend

Sergeant Benton sat in the inner lab, staring unblinkingly at the TOMTIT machine. So far, no-one had tried to run away with it.

There was a tap on the outer door. 'Who is it?'

'Me! Ruth Ingram. The Doctor's with me.'

Benton got up went through the outer lab and opened the door, admitting Ruth Ingram and the Doctor, who looked quizzically at him. 'Any trouble?'

'I've been a bit lonely, that's all.'

'Good, good,' said the Doctor absently. He stared thoughtfully at the TOMTIT machine.

'But *why* won't you explain, Doctor?' asked Ruth, obviously continuing an unfinished conversation.

'Because I have to be sure that I'm right. Now, where's this crystal?'

'Through here.'

Ruth led the way to the inner lab and lifted off the transparent cover, revealing the crystal socketted into its place in the machine. 'There.'

The Doctor stared at the crystal in fascination. 'The Crystal of Kronos. Then I am right.'

Ruth frowned. 'Kronos? That's what Stuart said. *Please* explain, Doctor – that's if you really do know what it's all about.'

'You'll find some of it difficult to accept, I warn you.'

'Try me.'

'Well – luckily you're at least familiar with the idea of stepping outside space-time.'

'I've lived with the concept for months.'

The Doctor said solemnly, 'And I've lived with it for – for many long years. I've been there, and a strange place it is too.'

He paused staring thoughtfully into space – or perhaps into space-time. 'A place that is no place, where creatures live, creatures beyond your imagination. Chronivores – time-eaters – who can swallow a life as a boa constrictor can swallow a rabbit, fur and all.'

'And this Kronos is one of these creatures?'

'That's right. The most fearsome of the lot.'

When the Director finally reached his office, he found the Master sitting in the big armchair beside his desk, drinking his brandy and smoking one of his best cigars.

'You!' gasped the Director. 'What are you doing here?'

'Don't panic. Close the door and come here.'

'But they'll find you!'

'Not if you keep your head. Why should they look in here? Now calm down and tell me what's been happening – and don't fidget, please!'

Ruth Ingram said, 'But surely, Doctor, Kronos was just a Greek legend, wasn't he? He was the Titan who ate his children.'

'Exactly. And what's more, one of the children in the legend was Poseidon, the God of Atlantis.'

'Are you trying to tell me that the classical gods were real?'

'Well, yes and no. Extraordinary people the Atlanteans, you know, even more extraordinary than their cousins in Athens. If reality became unbearable, they would invent a legend to tame it.'

'Like the legend of Kronos?'

'Exactly! Kronos, a living creature, was drawn into time by the priests of Atlantis, using that crystal.'

'You mean that crystal is the original? The actual crystal from Atlantis?'

'It is. And your friend the Professor is trying to use the crystal exactly as it was used four thousand years ago – to capture the Chronivore.'

'And that's what you meant when you talked of the most terrible danger just now?'

'Do you mean danger to us?' asked Benton. 'Or to the world?'

The Doctor said gravely, 'The danger is not just to us, or our world, or even our galaxy, but to the entire created Universe.'

Puffing peacefully on his cigar, the Master listened to the Director's stammered tale of recent events.

'And now here you are,' moaned the Director. 'Suppose somebody should walk in here now and find me talking to you?'

The Master sighed. 'My word, you are a worrier, aren't you? Come here.'

Reluctantly the Director obeyed.

'Closer,' orderd the Master. 'Now, look into my eyes. There is nothing to worry about. Nothing. Just obey me and everything will be all right. Just . . . obey . . . me!'

'Obey,' said the Director dully. 'I must obey, and everything will be all right.'

'That's better. Now go and arrange for the evacuation like a good boy, and let me get on with my sums.'

The Master took pad and pencil from a table beside the armchair and began a series of complex and abstruse calculations. 'You know Director, it's some time since I found such a good subject for hypnosis as you've turned out to be. It's quite like old times . . .'

Calmed and reassured, the Director sat down at his desk and began a series of telephone calls.

The time sensor in his hand, the Doctor was examining the TOMTIT apparatus with the sceptical expression of a garage mechanic checking over a very old car.

'There are two things I don't understand. One is the unexplained power build-up you had. The other is the strength of the signal I picked up on my time sensor.'

'You said yourself,' Ruth pointed out, 'the time sensor picks up *all* time field disturbances.'

'Indeed it does.' The Doctor began wandering about the lab. 'But the signal was far too strong for a crude apparatus such as this.' Suddenly the Doctor stopped in front of a tall green computer cabinet, the needle on the sensor flickering wildly. 'Aha!'

Benton came over to him. 'What is it, Doctor?'

'I knew it had to be around here somewhere. This, Sergeant Benton, is the Master's TARDIS!'

'I'm sorry, but you *must* leave. At once, please,' said the Director and put down the phone.

He heard the Master muttering, ' . . . now, if E equals mc cubed . . .'

'Squared, surely?'

'What?' The Master looked up.

'E equals mc squared – not cubed.'

'Not in the extra-temporal physics of the time vortex,' said the Master irritably. 'Now you've made me lose my place. You're an interfering dolt, Perceval.'

'I'm sorry. What are you doing?'

'Trying to find the reason for that massive power build-up we experienced. It makes the experiment uncontrollable. Even the filter didn't prevent it.' The Master frowned. 'Logically, it just shouldn't happen.'

'Logically, it just shouldn't happen,' said the Doctor.

'But it did.' Ruth pointed out.

'It did indeed. So, logically there's only one thing to do. Wouldn't you agree, Sergeant?'

'Oh yes, sure, Doctor. Er – what, for instance?'

'Switch on the power and see for ourselves.'

Ruth Ingram drew in a deep breath. 'Right!'

She switched on the power.

The machine began its low whine.

The Doctor studied a dial. 'It's reading ten – already.'

'That's impossible,' gasped Ruth.

Benton was looking through the open door to the inner laboratory. 'Doctor! Doctor, the crystal's glowing!'

The Doctor came to join him. 'Sergeant Benton, you're a strong man. Go in there and pick up that crystal.'

'After what happened to that chap Stuart?'

47

'It's perfectly safe at this low level.'

'If you say so, Doctor.'

Sergeant Benton's faith in the Doctor was limitless. He went to the crystal and tried to lift it from its resting place.

It refused to budge.

'It's fastened down,' he grunted.

'It isn't, you know,' said the Doctor. 'you can see it isn't.'

Benton heaved until his muscles cracked. 'I can't shift it.'

'No, of course you can't – because it isn't really here at all. It made the jump through interstitial time. It must still be linked to the original crystal all those thousands of years ago.'

Ruth gave him a baffled look. 'Then where is this original crystal?'

'Where do you think? In Atlantis, of course.'

Lightning streaked across the night sky of Atlantis, followed by a great rumble of thunder. In the Temple, a neophyte shuddered with fear. The gods were abroad tonight. He was little more than a child, olive skinned and curly haired, a priest's servant and apprentice. He glanced at the glowing crystal on the sacred altar and braced himself to do his duty.

His bare feet pattering on the marble floors of the temple, he ran to where Krasis, the High Priest, stood watching the lightning flare across the night sky.

The terrified neophyte threw himself to the ground at Krasis's feet. 'Holiness! Holiness, come quickly. The Crystal is afire.'

Tall and gaunt, an impressive figure in his priestly

robes, Krasis strode across the temple to where the crystal rested upon the altar. It was glowing fiercely.

Krasis lifted his hands in a gesture of worship. 'At last, Kronos, at last! The time is come, and I await your call.'

From behind a pillar a tall young man stood watching, a look of fascinated interest on his darkly handsome face. His name was Hippias, one of the High Council of Atlantis. He had long been fascinated by anything to do with Kronos.

The phone in the TOMTIT lab rang, and Benton snatched it up. 'Sergeant Benton . . . Oh, hello, Miss Grant . . . Yes, he's here. I see . . . Yes, hang on . . .' He turned to the Doctor. 'It's Miss Grant. She says Stuart Hyde is coming round. He's in a bit of a state it seems.'

The Doctor was already heading for the door. 'Tell her I'm on my way, Sergeant. You'd better stay here on guard. Coming, Ruth . . . Doctor Ingram?'

'Ruth will do. Yes, of course I'm coming.'

They hurried from the room.

In the sick bay, Jo was still chatting to Sergeant Benton on the phone. 'Yes, I'm all right, honestly. No, not scared exactly, just a bit . . . well, you know, churned up. And a merry Michaelmas to you too . . .'

She heard a groan from the bed. 'Oh lor, I'm neglecting my patient!'

Putting down the phone, she hurried back to the bed, where Stuart Hyde was writhing uneasily. 'Kronos . . .' he muttered. 'Kronos!'

Jo leaned over him. 'Are you all right?'

Suddenly he opened his eyes and stared wildly at her. 'I felt him coming back!'

'Kronos!' He clutched her arm. 'Don't let him touch me. The fire ... I'm burning. I'm burning ...'

Jo pushed him gently back on the pillows. 'It's all right, you're safe now. It's all right, honestly it is.'

Stuart stared at her as if seeing her for the first time. 'Who are you?'

'Jo – Jo Grant.'

'Where am I?'

'You're in your own room.'

Stuart groaned. 'I've got the granddaddy of all hangovers.' He rubbed his forehead and suddenly caught sight of his hands – the wrinkled hands of a very old man. 'My hands. What's happened to my hands?'

'It's all right,' said Jo soothingly. 'It's difficult to explain.'

'Give me a mirror. *A mirror*. Where's my shaving mirror?'

'There isn't one,' said Jo desperately. 'I'll get you one later. Now, just lie down ...'

But Stuart had spotted his shaving mirror on the bed-side table. Before Jo could stop him he lunged for it, snatched it up – and gazed in the mirror at his own eighty-year old face.

'No ... no ...' he groaned. Tossing the mirror aside, he buried his face in his hands.

6

The Ambush

'Point zero zero three five seven,' said the Master thoughtfully. 'Good!'

The Director asked timidly, 'You've finished?'

'Yes, at last. So, it's back to the lab.'

'But they've got someone on guard.'

'Yes, I suppose they have. You don't happen to know who it is, do you?'

'A Sergeant Benton, I think.'

The Master smiled. 'I see. Well, I think I know how to deal with him.'

By now the Doctor and Ruth Ingram had arrived.

Stuart, a little calmer now, was trying to give some account of what had happened to him. 'It was just after the cup and saucer appeared . . . I was about to switch off when it . . . happened . . .' His voice broke and faded away.

'Go on, old chap,' said the Doctor encouragingly. 'You're doing fine.'

With an effort, Stuart continued. 'It was like a tongue of flame. Like all my body was on fire. All my life, my energy, was being sucked out of me.'

The Doctor leaned forward. 'Why did you say "Kronos"?'

'Because that's who it was.'

51

'But how did you know?' asked Ruth.

'I just knew, that's all.'

'You mean you heard a voice or something?'

'No, I just knew.'

'A race memory,' explained the Doctor. 'We all have them.'

'What *is* Kronos?' asked Jo. 'Or should I say who?'

'Later, Jo, later.' The Doctor turned back to Stuart. 'Go on, what else?'

'Nothing else . . . till I woke up like this.' There was anguish in Stuart's voice. 'Doc, am I really an old man now? Is there anything you can do – or am I stuck like this?'

The Doctor hesitated. 'I don't know. But I promise you – we'll do everything we can.'

The phone rang in the TOMTIT laboratory. Sergeant Benton snatched it up, hoping it would be news of his relief. 'Hullo?'

He heard the quavering tones of the Director. 'Is that Sergeant Benton?'

'Yes.'

'This is the Director. The Brigadier wants you to meet him at once – here, back at the main house.'

'But I don't get it. Back at the house?'

'At once.'

'But that means leaving the lab unguarded.'

'Ah . . . well, he said to be sure to lock up. Those were his very words.'

'I don't know, Doctor Perceval,' said Benton worriedly. 'You put me in a bit of a spot. The Brig told me to stay here, no matter what. He'll have my stripes if I don't.'

In the Director's study the Master hissed, 'What's the matter?'

The Director said, 'Hold the line a moment please, Sergeant,' and put his hand over the mouthpiece. 'I don't think he believes me.'

'I'm not surprised, I've seldom heard a more inept performance. Tell him to ring the Brigadier for confirmation.'

'But you can't –'

'Do as I tell you.'

The Director took his hand from the mouthpiece. 'Sergeant Benton? I suggest you check with the Brigadier personally.' He paused. 'Oh, you want his number?' The Director looked helplessly at the Master who pointed wearily to the other telephone on the desk. The Director swallowed. 'I think you can get him on five-three-four. Yes, that is correct. Goodbye.'

A minute later the other phone rang. To the Director's amazement the Master picked it up and spoke, not in his own voice but that of the Brigadier. 'Lethbridge-Stewart. That you, Benton?'

In the lab Benton said, 'Yes sir. I've just had rather a peculiar phone call.'

'Nothing peculiar about it, my dear fellow,' said the familiar voice. 'Perfectly simple. I need you over here at the gate house. On the double.'

'Yessir,' said Benton woodenly. 'I quite understand, sir. Right away.'

He put down the phone and stood considering for a moment. He went to the window and opened it wide from the bottom and left the laboratory by the main door, locking it behind him.

The Director stood staring anxiously out of his study window while the Master stood idly leafing through a sheaf of calculations.

Without looking up the Master said, 'Well?'

The Director shook his head. 'No sign of him. Do you really think he'll – Ah, just a moment. There he is!'

The tall figure of Sergeant Benton came through the arch and rounded the corner of the gate house. 'It worked! It really worked!'

'Of course it worked,' said the Master sharply. 'Now see if the corridor's clear.'

The Director went to the study door and peered out. 'Not a soul, Professor.'

Tucking his notebook in his pocket, the Master led the way from the room.

Sergeant Benton meanwhile was clambering across the roof of an outbuilding just beneath the laboratory. He climbed a fire escape ladder bolted to the wall, swung agilely across to a nearby drainpipe and climbed through the window that he himself had left open. Back in the lab he closed the window and stood just to one side of it, looking out.

A few minutes later he saw the Master and the Director come out of a side door and hurry across the courtyard towards him. Drawing his service revolver, Benton ducked out of sight behind the TOMTIT machine and waited.

Before long he heard a key turn in the lock – naturally, the Director would have keys, he thought – and the lab door opened. He heard voices. First the Director. ·

'But Professor, you haven't much time.'

Then the Master. 'Time? Soon I shall have all the time in the world – literally!'

'In an hour or so the place will be swarming with soldiers.'

'Perceval, you irritate me. Be quiet! I tell you, nothing and nobody can stop me now.'

Sergeant Benton couldn't help feeling that this was his cue. He rose slowly from behind his hiding place, revolver levelled. 'Put your hands in the air, both of you.' The two men obeyed. 'Now, turn round – slowly!'

The Master swung round, an expression of sheer astonishment on his face. 'Well, well, well. The resourceful Sergeant Benton.'

'You didn't really think you could fool me with a fake telephone call, did you? It's the oldest trick in the book.'

'I underestimated you, Sergeant. How did you know?'

'Simple. The Brigadier's not in the habit of calling Sergeants "my dear fellow".'

'Ah, the tribal taboos of Army etiquette,' sneered the Master. 'I find it difficult to identify with such primitive absurdities.'

Benton grinned with savage enjoyment. 'Primitive or not, mate, you're still in the soup without a ladle – aren't you?'

The Master came forward. 'You must let me explain . . .'

Benton raised the revolver. 'Keep back.'

The Master stopped his advance, hands raised. 'Of course, of course. You see, Sergeant, the whole point is . . .'

Suddenly his eyes widened as he looked over

Benton's shoulder. 'Doctor, what a very timely arrival!'

Benton's eyes only flickered for a fraction of a second, but it was enough.

The Master sprang forward with tigerish speed, wrenched the gun from his hand and threw him against the wall with such force that he slid stunned to the ground. The Master looked down at him. 'You were wrong, Sergeant Benton. *That* is the oldest trick in the book!'

Turning away, the Master hurried to the TOMTIT apparatus and switched it on.

'What are you doing?' quavered the Director.

'I am going to bring someone here who will help me to find the power I need. Without it I am helpless.'

'I don't understand . . .'

'Of course you don't understand. How could you understand? Only one thing stands between me and total power over the Earth – over the Universe itself. He who I am calling here will show me how to harness that power. Now – you watch that crystal!'

The whine of the apparatus rose to a sort of triumphant howl. The crystal glowed brighter and brighter, till the whole room was filled with its blazing light.

Sergeant Benton, slowly recovering consciousness, opened his eyes and found himself staring straight into the glowing heart of the crystal.

And there, in the centre of that radiance, a shape was beginning to form . . .

7

The High Priest

To Benton's unbelieving astonishment the shape grew larger, became solid and real.

Suddenly an extraordinary figure was standing beside the crystal – a tall gaunt old man, in flowing white robes, a short red cloak and a jewelled breastplate. His long grey hair was bound with a circlet of silver and his haggard, lined face was filled with power and authority. A gold medallion hung about his neck. He was Krasis, High Priest of Atlantis.

Since the crystal in the temple had begun to glow, Krasis had kept ceaseless vigil by the altar, purifying himself by prayer and fasting.

At last the summons had come. The fire of the crystal had reached out, enveloped him, and transported him to this strange place.

The Master strode into the inner lab and spread out his hands in greeting. 'Welcome! Welcome!'

The old man drew himself up proudly. 'I am Krasis, High Priest of the Temple of Poseidon in Atlantis.'

'Of *Poseidon*? Surely Kronos is your Lord?'

'You would dare to profane with your impious tongue the great secret, the mystery no man dare speak? Who are you?'

The Master's eloquence was more than a match

57

for that of the old priest. 'I am the Master, Lord of Time, and Ruler of Kronos.'

'You lie! No-one rules Kronos!'

'I shall – with your help,' said the Master arrogantly. 'Together we shall become Masters of the Universe.'

Astonished as he was by these strange events, Sergeant Benton wasn't too astonished to gather his strength and choose his moment. The Master, the Director and the strange new arrival were all in the inner lab. Scrambling to his feet, Benton ran for the main door.

The Director saw him go and called, 'Professor!'

The Master swung round, but Benton was already disappearing through the door. 'Oh, let him go, he can do us no harm now.'

The Master turned to Krasis. 'Come with me!'

He led him through to the main laboratory.

Krasis gazed about him in wonder. 'Is this the abode of Lord Kronos?'

'No. But with you to assist me, I shall bring him here.'

Krasis fixed him with a reproving glare. 'I exist only to do the will of Kronos – and he is not to be commanded.'

'Ah, but surely Kronos obeyed the Priest of Poseidon as a pet dog obeys his master?' His voice hardened. 'The truth now, Krasis!'

Reluctantly Krasis said, 'So it is written.'

'Then you must have the formula – the secret of how to control him.'

'It is lost,' said Krasis sadly. 'For five centuries it has been lost to Atlantis.'

'And was nothing handed down?'

'Nothing save the Great Crystal – and the seal of

the High Priest.' Detatching it from its chain, Krasis held out the gold medallion.

The Master took it and studied it eagerly. The flat golden disc was carved with elaborate symbols. The Master studied them eagerly. 'But that's it. From this seal I can learn the correct mathematical constants. Kronos is in my power at last!'

Stuart Hyde had been carefully loaded into a wheelchair, and Ruth Ingram, escorted by Jo Grant, the Doctor and the Brigadier, was wheeling him out of the front door of the Institute towards a waiting ambulance.

Understandably, Stuart wasn't in the best of moods.

'Rest, that's what you need,' said the Doctor rather more cheerfully than was really tactful. 'That's all you can do at the moment – rest until your body recovers from the shock.'

'A charming prospect I must say,' grumbled Stuart. 'You'd better find out about my old age pension, Ruth. After all, I'll be twenty-six in seven weeks' time.'

'Try not to be too bitter, Stu,' said Ruth gently.

Suddenly Sergeant Benton came pounding towards them. 'Doctor! The Master's in the lab!'

The Master was carefully transcribing the mathematical symbols carved into the great seal. The Director watch him in puzzlement. 'But how can Atlantean symbols mean anything to you?'

'Comparative ratios remain constant throughout time,' said the Master confidently. 'If you have nothing intelligent to say, Perceval, keep quiet!' He punched a complicated set of co-ordinates into the TOMTIT console. 'And now – we switch on!'

He turned on the power, and the rising whine of the apparatus filled the room.

In the inner lab the crystal began to glow. Krasis raised his arms in worship.

Sergeant Benton meanwhile was concluding what he himself felt was an extremely unlikely story.

The Doctor frowned. 'Are you sure he said he was from Atlantis?'

'Yes,' said Benton simply. 'He just appeared, from nowhere.'

The Brigadier wasn't interested in apparitions. He was only interested in the Master. 'Right, what are we waiting for? On the double, Sergeant Benton – Doctor! Females stay under cover, all right, Miss Grant?'

The Brigadier dashed off towards the laboratory. Benton at his heels.

'Brigadier, wait!' shouted the Doctor.

'And wait for me!' called Ruth Ingram. 'Females under cover indeed!' She ran after Benton and the Brigadier.

Jo felt suddenly strange and shivery. She heard a strangled cry from behind her and turned. 'Doctor, look!'

Stuart Hyde was recovering his youth at amazing speed. Grey hair turned to brown, the skin became firm and youthful, the eyes clear and bright – and suddenly there was a puzzled-looking twenty-six year old Stuart sitting in the wheelchair.

The Doctor studied the phenomenom thoughtfully. 'A massive feedback of time . . . We're too late, Jo. Kronos is coming!'

In the laboratory the crystal was pulsating, blazing with light. The Master stared into the heart of the fiery glow, raising his arms in a gesture of welcome. 'Come, Kronos, come!'

Krasis, the High Priest, stared enraptured at the crystal. Doctor Perceval, the Director, looked on in horrified fascination.

In the heart of the crystal a shape was beginning to appear. Perceval peered into the fiery glow, trying to make it out. At first it seemed like a giant bird, then like a man, finally more like a man with wings, though the head was still birdlike . . . He heard the steady beat of mighty wings. The winged shape grew bigger and bigger emerging from the crystal until it was somehow *there* in the laboratory, a shape of blazing white light thrashing about in the confined space like some great eagle in a too small cage.

Krasis prostrated himself in worship, but the terrified Director screamed and turned to run. The noise and movement seemed to attract the winged creature's attention, and it swooped down on him like a great bird of prey. Fiery wings enfolded him, swallowed him up and Humphrey Perceval ceased to exist, his very being absorbed by Kronos, so that not an atom of him remained.

As the Director disappeared, Kronos resumed the terrifying swirl of activity. The fiery wings thrashed about frantically, sending whole shelves of equipment smashing to the ground.

The Master was beginning to fear that he had raised a monster he could not control. 'Kronos! Be at peace!' he roared. 'I am your friend.'

Krasis raised his head, gazing worshippingly at the restless fiery form. 'You will never control Kronos.

He is the ruler of time. He is the destroyer. We are doomed!'

'Rubbish!' said the Master. A sudden idea came to him and he snatched up the Great Seal of Atlantis and held it out before him. 'Kronos, hear me! I order you to be at peace and obey!'

Kronos recoiled, and the beating of the wings lessened in intensity.

The Master laughed. 'Well, well, well! So, the pet dog does obey his Master!' He advanced upon Kronos, driving the fiery being back into the inner lab and slamming the door. 'Now, stay in your kennel till I have need of you!'

The Doctor and Jo watched as the retreating figures of the Brigadier, Sergeant Benton and Ruth Ingram suddenly ceased to retreat and became motionless.

Still striving to move forward, their bodies were frozen, like running figures when the film is stopped.

'What's the matter with them?' asked Jo.

The Doctor said, 'You stay back.'

He began running towards Ruth Ingram, the nearest of the group. As he approached her he felt the resistance of the temporal distortion. Forcing his way through it, the Doctor grabbed Ruth's arm and yanked her back towards Jo. As he retreated, movement became easier. By the time they reached Jo, Ruth was back to normal. She blinked and looked around. 'What happened?'

'That's it,' said the Doctor. 'She's outside the limit of the effect now.'

He ran forward and repeated the rescue operation with Benton.

Ruth looked on in astonishment. 'What happened to me? What's going on?'

'Don't worry,' said Jo reassuringly. 'The Doctor will explain – I hope!'

While Kronos thrashed about the inner lab like an angry eagle, the Master was working busily at the TOMTIT controls.

'What are you doing?' asked Krasis.

'Reducing the interstitial flow rate. Now don't interrupt me, I must concentrate.'

'You do not have the power to control him,' screamed Krasis.

'I shall have, never fear. Just give me time!' He made a final adjustment. 'Now – I must put him back where he belongs!'

The hum of power rose higher and, as it did so, Kronos began to dwindle and fade.

The Doctor led the astonished Brigadier back to the others. Since the Brigadier's own subjective time had been slowed down, it seemed to him as if he had been running normally when the Doctor appeared from nowhere, and hustled him back to his starting point at impossible speed. Not unnaturally, the Brigadier was both astonished and indignant. 'Doctor! Will you kindly explain . . .'

'There's no time to explain now. Benton, take the wheelchair, everybody inside, quickly!'

The Brigadier was still spluttering. 'What? What?'

'Come along, man,' said the Doctor impatiently, and bustled everybody away.

Kronos seemed to be rushing away, becoming both fainter and smaller at the same time. Finally the winged shape seemed to disappear into the heart of the crystal.

The Master mopped his brow, and said sarcastically, 'It's safe to go in now, most noble High Priest. Thank you for your help.'

Krasis followed him into the inner lab. 'I am no slave that I should serve you, I serve only the gods.'

'You will serve me, Krasis, and like it!'

'You dare to mock the High Priest?'

The Master stretched out a hand to the controls. 'Take care, Krasis! I can always bring Kronos back!'

Instinctively Krasis recoiled. 'No! No, I beseech you . . . What is your will?'

'Knowledge!' said the Master simply. 'Your knowledge of the ancient mysteries.' His voice rose in anger. '*Why* could I not control him?'

Krasis said scornfully, 'For all your sorcery, you are as a child trying to control a wild elephant. A puny child!'

'But I have the crystal!'

'That crystal is but a part of the true Crystal of Kronos.'

The Master was furious. '*A part!*'

'Only a small fraction,' said Krasis loftily.

'A fraction – and the rest is in Atlantis?'

'Deep in the vaults of the Temple of Poseidon. Guarded night and day from such thieves as you. You may command the slave but never shall you control the Mighty One himself!'

The Master had already recovered from his setback, and his deep voice was filled with arrogant confidence. 'You think not? We shall see.'

He reached out and grasped the crystal.

8

The Secret

In the Great Temple of Atlantis, Hippias held high a blazing torch and pointed dramatically at the empty altar. He was a tall, exceptionally handsome young man with glossy black hair that fell to his shoulders in shining ringlets in the Atlantean style. Wearing only the brief Atlantean kilt, he was a noble and impressive figure. 'You see, most venerable King – the crystal is gone!'

Beside him, King Dalios was, at first sight, almost comically unimpressive. Just a little old man with long flowing white hair and a jutting beard, clutching his night-robe around him.

And yet there *was* something impressive about Dalios, the calm and wisdom that come only with great age. He looked thoughtfully at his excited young councillor. 'And Krasis?'

Hippias spoke in a deep thrilling voice. 'I was there, O King! The sky opened and a spear of fire was hurled by the hand of Zeus . . .'

'Yes, yes, yes,' said Dalios impatiently. 'I saw the thunderstorm myself. What next?'

'They disappeared,' said Hippias simply. 'Krasis and the Crystal together – like smoke! What does it mean, Lord Dalios? Are the gods angry? Has the time come at last?'

Dalios looked pityingly at him. 'You are young, Hippias, as young in years as in the Sacred Mysteries. What do you know of Kronos?'

Hippias gasped, at the sound of a name almost too holy to speak. As if reciting some lesson learned by heart, he said, 'The years of Kronos were the great years of Atlantis. Perhaps some day he will return to us.'

'That is my fear,' said Dalios solemnly. 'Our world is in great danger. Come.' He led the young man through a secret door, and down endless winding stairways, until they were deep in the heart of the catacombs beneath the Temple.

As they descended the final flight Dalios turned and glanced over his shoulder at the young councillor. 'How old would you think me, boy?'

'A great age, Lord Dalios,' said Hippias respectfully.

'*How* great?'

Hippias hesitated. 'Four score years – more perhaps . . .'

Dalios smiled a little sadly. 'A stripling of eighty summers . . . No, Hippias, when these eyes were clear like yours, I saw the building of the Temple. I was a witness to the enthronement of the image of the great god, Poseidon himself.'

'But that was – it must have been five hundred years ago.'

Dalios nodded. 'Five hundred and thirty-seven.'

Hippias gazed wonderingly at him. 'Lord Dalios, would you have me believe that you are of such an age?'

'I am,' said Dalios quietly, and led the way on down the stairway.

The stairs led to a short passage. At the end of it

there was a great bronze door set into a wall of solid rock. Dalios produced a massive key, and after a moment the door creaked open.

It was as if he had opened the door to a furnace. A fierce white light blazed forth from the doorway. Hippias staggered back, his hands over his eyes. 'What is the light?'

'It is the true Crystal of Kronos,' said Dalios solemnly. '*This* is the great secret, the veritable mystery. Now that Krasis has gone no-one but you shares that secret. You must guard it with your life!'

Hippias bowed his head. 'I shall, my Lord.'

Suddenly a shattering bellow came from the doorway.

Hippias looked at Dalios in alarm. 'Do not fear,' said the old man calmly. 'It is the Guardian.' He called through the doorway. 'Return to your rest. It is I, Dalios.'

The bellowing died away. 'Who was it?' whispered Hippias. 'You said that no other person shares the mystery.'

'The Guardian is a person no longer,' said Dalios sadly. 'A thing, a creature too horrible to imagine, half-man, half-beast. Come.'

Stuart Hyde's wing room was a sprawling untidy sort of place. A row of home-made shelves divided the living from the kitchen area and there were clothes, books and records everywhere.

Stuart, who now seemed fully recovered from his sudden rejuvenation, opened the door and gestured everyone inside. 'Make yourself comfortable – if you can!'

The Brigadier was still in a state of some indignation. 'All right. Doctor, what next? Having picked us up by the scruff of the neck and bundled us in here, what do you propose to do with us?'

'Nothing at all,' said the Doctor cheerfully. 'There's nothing to be done at the moment – except wait.'

Jo giggled. 'I seem to have heard that before.'

'Speaking personally,' the Doctor went on calmly, 'I'd love a nice cup of tea. How about it, Stuart?'

'I'll put the kettle on,' said Stuart amiably. 'Get the mugs out, will you, Ruth? How about a sandwich anyone? Only marmalade, I'm afraid.'

'I'd love one,' said Benton unwisely.

'This isn't a picnic,' exploded the Brigadier. 'One moment you're talking about the entire Universe blowing up and the next you're going on about tea. What's happening, Doctor?'

'A great deal, Brigadier. For instance, you were caught in a hiatus in time. Being without becoming, an ontological absurdity.'

'I don't understand a word you're saying!'

'It's true,' said Jo. 'I saw it. You and Benton and Doctor Ingram were stuck.'

'Nothing of the sort, Miss Grant.'

'Oh, you wouldn't be aware of it,' said the Doctor. 'Your time had slowed to a standstill too.'

'And all this is because of that TOMTIT gadget?' asked Benton.

'So it would seem. After all it did make a crack in time, didn't it?'

Jo blinked. 'A what?'

The Brigadier said wearily. 'Oh, a "gap between the now and the now", as Sergeant Benton would no doubt put it.'

Benton looked embarrassed.

The Doctor patted him on the back. 'Exactly, very

68

well put. So we're bound to experience all sorts of freak side-effects.'

'You mean, even leaving Kronos and the crystal right out of it?' said Ruth, coming out of the kitchen section. 'Marmalade sandwich?'

'Correct.' The Doctor began wandering round the room, collecting odds and ends.

She looked puzzled. 'But why weren't we affected ourselves, when we were working on the thing? *We* didn't get slowed down.'

'If you stand right under a fountain you don't necessarily get wet, do you?'

'I see,' said Ruth. She didn't, of course, but it seemed to be all the answer she was going to get.

'Well, I'm dashed if I do,' said the Brigadier. He noticed the Doctor's strange activity. 'Doctor, what are you doing?'

'Me?' said the Doctor blandly. 'Collecting!'

The Master completed the last of a long series of adjustments to the TOMTIT apparatus, switched on and stepped back.

In the inner lab the crystal began pulsing with light once more. With each pulsation the intensity of light seemed to fade a little.

The Master rubbed his hands. 'Right! Now we shall soon be ready to move.'

'But, Master,' said Krasis nervously. 'The Mighty One. He may return.'

The Master laughed. 'Fortunate Atlantis to be blessed with such a courageous High Priest. Never fear, Kronos will only return if I desire it.'

'But the crystal . . . what are you doing?'

'I am draining the time energy from the crystal. Otherwise we could scarcely take it with us.'

69

'We? Where are we going?'

The Master looked surprised. 'Where? Why, to Atlantis, of course!'

The Doctor was still gathering up his collection of odds and ends. By now he had accumulated a wire coat hanger, a set of keys, some kitchen weights and the top part of a broken coffee maker. As he continued his prowling round the room the Doctor muttered, 'He must be stopped!'

'Fair enough,' said the Brigadier hopefully. 'Why don't we get on with it?'

'Because without the TARDIS we can't even begin to find out what he's up to.' The Doctor peered round the room. 'I need a bottle.'

'How about this?' Stuart held up a milk bottle.

'No, no, one with a narrow neck. A wine bottle would do.'

'Moroccan Burgundy, for instance?' Stuart fished a bottle from underneath the bed.

'Yes, that'll do nicely. And the cork?'

Stuart scratched his head. 'You've got me there.'

Ruth came out of the kitchen. 'Will this do, Stu?'

Stuart grinned. 'Remarkable efficiency, the cork's still on the corkscrew. There you are, Doc.'

'Well done!'

The Doctor sat down at Stuart's battered table and began sorting through his strange assortment of objects.

The Brigadier was losing patience. 'Doctor, I must insist – what are you up to?'

'Delaying tactics, Brigadier! A small fly in the Master's methaphorical ointment.' With that the Doctor set to work.

As far as the Brigadier could make out, he was building some sort of a tower . . .

The glow of the crystal became fainter and fainter still, until at last it died away.

Krasis gave the Master a look of awe. 'The fire is dying. You are indeed the Master.'

Working in absorbed silence, the Doctor was happily fitting his strange assortment of oddments into a sort of ramshackle structure.

Jo and the others watched in fascination as he sliced the cork neatly in half, jammed one half back in the neck of the bottle, fixed a needle into the half-cork and fixed the other half of the cork on the other end of the needle thus creating a sort of pivot or axis. He took two forks and fixed them by the spikes into the upper cork so they projected like arms, one on each side.

Stuart leaned over to Ruth and whispered, 'Another nutcase!'

She nodded and whispered. 'Fruit-cake standard!'

Jo overheard them. 'You just wait and see,' she said loyally. But even Jo was beginning to wonder exactly what the Doctor was up to this time.

The crystal was completely inert now, and the Master switched off the apparatus. 'There, it is finished. You must help me to carry the crystal, Krasis.'

Krasis shrank back. 'No, no . . . I dare not.'

'There is nothing to fear,' said the Master impatiently. 'You will do as I tell you.'

Krasis gave him a look of sheer terror. 'Do not compel me, I beseech you.'

71

Somehow, heaven knows how, the Doctor succeeded in balancing the top of the coffee maker on top of the cork. With the two forks projecting like out-stretched arms, the whole thing resembled a kind of mobile, or one of those balancing toys which can be bought in novelty shops.

'But what is it meant to be?' asked the Brigadier irritably.

The Doctor laughed. 'You're a Philistine, Brigadier. It isn't meant to be anything it just *is*.' The rickety structure started toppling and the Doctor corrected its balance. 'I hope.'

'You mean it's just a ridiculous piece of modern art?' asked Ruth.

The Doctor looked hurt. 'No, no, my dear, it's a Time Flow Analogue.'

Stuart gave her a reproachful glance. 'Of course it is, Ruth. You ought to have seen that at a glance!'

The Doctor went on making adjustments to the nonsensical tower. 'The relationships between the different molecular bonds form a crystalline structure of ratios.'

The Brigadier sighed. 'Does that make any sort of sense, Doctor Ingram?'

'None whatsoever!'

'I thought as much,' the Brigadier said determinedly. 'Doctor, please stop this silly game at once!'

The Doctor was infuriatingly calm. 'Patience, Brigadier, patience!' He tapped one of the projecting forks and the whole contraption began revolving like some lunatic roundabout. It wobbled alarmingly, but by some miracle it didn't collapse. However, the Doctor clearly wasn't satisfied. 'Oh dear!'

'What's up?' asked Jo.

'It doesn't work!'

'You astound me,' said the Brigadier acidly.

'Bad luck, Doctor!' Stuart handed the Doctor a mug. 'Here, have a cuppa and drown your sorrows!'

'A cup of tea!' said the Doctor joyfully. 'Of course! Tea leaves!' Swigging down the tea in one long swallow, he began balancing the empty mug on the top of his tower.

The Master was still trying to calm Krasis's fears. 'I give you my solemn pledge, Krasis, the crystal is still totally inactive.'

Krasis stared fearfully at the inert crystal. 'It looks dead . . .'

'Of course it is, I promise you . . .'

Cautiously Krasis stretched out his hand towards the crystal.

'Right,' said the Doctor. 'Here we go!'

He tapped the projecting fork again. The whole contraption began to revolve. It spun faster, faster, faster, until suddenly it was glowing with a weird unearthly light . . .

The crystal was glowing too and Krasis snatched back his hand with a yell of fear. 'The crystal is afire. The Great One comes again!'

'The meddling fool!' snarled the Master, and rushed to the control console.

The Doctor's strange contraption was spinning faster and faster, glowing ever more brightly.

Jo stared at it as if hypnotised. 'But what does it do, Doctor? I mean, how does it affect the Master's plans?'

'It's just like jamming a radio signal, Jo. We used to make them at school to spoil each other's time experiments.'

Ruth stared at the strange contraption which continued to glow and revolve in defiance of all the laws of physics. 'I don't believe it. I just don't believe it.'

The Master adjusted controls in rapid succession, slammed home the power switch . . .

. . . and the Doctor's contraption exploded with a bang and a shower of sparks.

The Doctor stared philosophically at the smoking ruins. 'Ah well! It was fun while it lasted!'

A UNIT convoy was speeding through country lanes towards the Newton Institute. In the lead was a UNIT land rover, behind it a canvas-hooded army lorry filled with troops, and behind that an open truck, in the back of which was a blue police box.

The Master was carrying the crystal, still mounted in a section of TOMTIT equipment, towards the laboratory door. It was a considerable task and since Krasis was now too terrified to touch the crystal, he had to perform it alone.

Suddenly the static-distorted voice of Mike Yates crackled through the lab. 'This is Greyhound Three. Over.'

The Brigadier's voice came in reply. 'This is Greyhound, Greyhound Three. And where have you been, Captain Yates? Over.'

'Won't be long now, sir. We're about ten miles away. Over.'

'Well, get your skates on will you? We need the Doctor's TARDIS here double quick. Out.'

'Greyhound Three. Wilco. Out.'

The Master replaced the crystal and its TOMTIT mounting, and studied a watch-sized mini-screen strapped to his wrist. He had left the audio-scanner switched to the UNIT frequency and now the vision scanner had homed in on the signal. To Krasis's astonishment the little screen now showed the UNIT convoy going on its way.

He shook his head in wonderment. 'Images that move and speak, wagons with no oxen to draw them . . . this is indeed a time of wonders.'

'I will show you greater wonders than either,' said the Master savagely. Still studying the screen he began operating controls with his other hand.

Krasis looked on fearfully. 'Master . . . Lord . . . you are not bringing the Mighty One here once more?'

'Certainly not. Just a little demonstration of my power over time. Watch carefully.'

Mike Yates was at the wheel of the land rover, leading the little convoy. They were on a long straight stretch of road, completely empty.

Then, all at once, it wasn't empty any longer. A knight in full armour, lance levelled, was galloping straight towards them.

9

Time Attack

'Look out,' yelled Mike and swerved off the road to his right, jamming on the brakes. The two vehicles behind him swerved off to left and right in turn and the armoured knight clattered through the gap and galloped on down the road.

Mike jumped out of the land rover, now slewed off the road at an angle and snatched up his RT. 'Greyhound? This is Greyhound Three. We're stuck in the mud. Forced off the road by some goon in fancy dress, I think. Over.'

On the other end of the radio link, the Brigadier stared disbelievingly at his RT. 'Are you suffering from hallucinations, Captain Yates? Or have you been drinking? Over.'

'No sir, but I could do with one, I don't mind telling you,' said Mike Yates frankly. 'This character in armour just galloped straight at us. You know, sir, the King Arthur bit. And then he vanished.'

'In a puff of blue smoke, I suppose,' came the Brigadier's sarcastic voice. 'Really, Yates, you have been drinking!'

In the lab, the Master looked at the stranded convoy on his mini-screen and smiled evilly.

'And that, Captain Yates, was just a sample.'

He busied himself at the controls. Amongst its other functions, the TOMTIT apparatus recreated the powers of the legendary Timescoop of the Time Lords, forbidden by Rassilon in the Dark Time. The Master was enjoying this opportunity to try it out . . .

Captain Yates raised his voice and bellowed, 'Righto, lads, out of the lorry and get these vehicles out of the mud. Get a move on, I want to get out of here.'

There was a flat crack, and something spanged off the side of the land rover.

Mike Yates whirled round, and opened his eyes in astonishment. On a little hill not far away a handful of men had appeared from nowhere, grouped around a cannon. They wore old fashioned doublets and breastplates and round helmets, and they carried long muskets. Roundheads!

'Take cover!' yelled Yates – just in time, as a ragged volley of musket balls hummed overhead like angry bees. 'Hey, what do you think you're up to?' he yelled indignantly.

The cannon boomed and a cannon ball whistled overhead.

'Keep down,' shouted Yates. 'They mean it!'

Yates and his men peered from behind the flimsy shelter of their vehicles, and the Captain reached for his RT. Heaven knows what the Brigadier was going to make of this one . . .

'I'm listening, Captain Yates,' said the Brigadier impassively. 'Over.'

'Another hallucination, sir. Roundhead troops,

attacking us with ball ammunition. Cannon balls, in fact. Over.'

'Captain Yates, if this is some sort of joke –'

The Doctor interrupted him. 'Believe me Brigadier, this is no kind of a joke. This is deadly serious.'

'All right, Doctor, you tell me what's going on.'

'Don't you see? A horseman in armour – roundheads – the Master's using that crystal to bring them forward in time.'

'So why don't we get over there and stop him?'

'It would be suicide without the protection of the TARDIS.'

'Which is stuck in the mud being battered by roundheads,' said Sergeant Benton.

'We'd better go and fetch it then,' said the Doctor cheerfully. 'Come along, Jo. Coming, Brigadier?'

'Benton, you stay here,' ordered the Brigadier. 'If the Master pokes his nose out you know what to do.'

'Yessir.' Benton was determined that the Master wouldn't escape him a second time.

'Can I come?' asked Ruth.

'And me?' said Stuart hopefully. 'I've always fancied myself as a cavalier.'

The Brigadier shook his head. 'Sorry, you'd better stay here with the Sergeant. You're the only ones who can handle that infernal machine apart from the Doctor. I must ask you to place yourself under Sergeant Benton's command. Both of you, right?'

'Full of old world charm, isn't he?' said Ruth resignedly. She reached for her lukewarm cup of tea.

The Doctor and Jo were already sitting in Bessie when the Brigadier hurried out of the building. 'Do

78

buck up, Lethbridge-Stewart,' urged the Doctor. 'Get in!'

The Brigadier headed for his land rover, a powerful new model of which he was very proud. 'Sorry, Doctor, matter of some urgency, better go under my own steam.' He got behind the wheel. 'Try not to be too far behind!'

The Brigadier started the engine and roared away.

The Doctor grinned wickedly at Jo and started the engine, and flicked the Superdrive switch.

The Brigadier wasn't yet fully aware of the Doctor's latest modifications to Bessie. He was considerably surprised when just as he was gathering speed on a straight stretch of road, Bessie flashed past him effortlessly and vanished into the distance . . .

The Master and Krasis were watching the battle on the Master's mini-screen.

It was still inconclusive. The roundheads' weapons took some time to reload, and their fire was far from accurate. The Master grimaced in frustration.

Krasis stared at him. 'But why? Why do you do all this? Do you fear this TARDIS so much?'

'I fear nothing,' snapped the Master. 'But I intend to go to Atlantis and I don't want my enemy to follow me.' He glared at the screen. 'Get on with it, you useless seventeenth-century poltroons!' Shaking his head, he reached for the controls.

So far Mike Yates had ordered his men to fire over their attackers' heads. But the roundhead muskets, although primitive, were still deadly, and when another of his men fell wounded, Mike Yates decided that enough was enough. He took a grenade from the arms locker in his land rover, sprinted forwards to a point of vantage, pulled the pin and hurled the grenade in the classic overarm throw, dropping to the ground as he did so. The grenade arced through the air and exploded . . . just after both roundheads and cannon disappeared.

Mike Yates raised his head and saw to his astonishment that his attackers had completely vanished . . .

The Master laughed. 'I could have told you that wouldn't work, Captain Yates.' He adjusted the controls yet again. 'Now, stand by to duck. Here comes the grand finale.'

The picture on the Master's mini-screen changed. Now it showed a tiny stubby-winged plane droning across the sky . . .

Ruth Ingram cocked her head at the strange putt-putting noise. 'What's that?'

Stuart shrugged. 'Sounds like a motor-bike.'

Sergeant Benton was peering out of the window. 'It seems to be coming from the sky . . .'

The Doctor and Jo were zooming towards the ambush site in Bessie.

'Something wrong with the engine, Doctor?' shouted Jo.

'Never! Why?'

'I can hear a funny noise.'

The Doctor made one of his astonishingly smooth stops. 'So can I. But it's not the engine.'

Jo listened. 'It's coming from over there . . .'

The Brigadier screeched to a halt beside them. 'What's up?'

'Listen!' ordered the Doctor.

The Brigadier listened to the strange putt-putting sound from overhead and looked unbelievingly at the Doctor. 'It can't be!'

'Oh yes it can,' said the Doctor. 'Displaced in time, but real enough. It's a V.1.'

'A what?' asked Jo.

'A buzz-bomb. A doodlebug. A kind of robot plane – a flying bomb! The Germans used them against England at the end of the Hitler war.'

'What did they do?'

'Blew up sizeable chunks of London,' said the Brigadier. 'If that engine sound cuts out, fall flat on your face. It means the bomb is on its way down!'

Jo pointed off into the distance. 'Look, there's the convoy!'

And there it was, just disappearing into a little wood that spanned the road some way ahead.

The Brigadier grabbed his RT. 'Greyhound Three, Greyhound Three, can you hear me Yates? Over.'

Yates's voice came back, badly distorted. 'Greyhound Three . . . only just . . . Over.'

'Yates, that thing is a flying bomb, and it's headed your way. Over!'

'Say . . . again . . .' crackled the voice. 'Must be . . . trees . . . cannot read you . . . Over.'

(The Master made a final adjustment and waited, smiling.)

The puttering of the engine stopped, leaving a sinister silence. The Doctor grabbed Jo's arm. 'Out of the car. Get down!'

The Brigadier was still yelling into the RT. 'Yates, it's a bomb! It's a bomb! Get out of it, Yates!'

To his relief he heard Mike Yates's voice coming

81

back over the air. 'All out, lads. It's a bomb. Dive for cover!'

There was an ear-splitting crash and a column of flame and smoke shot up from inside the wood.

As the echoes of the explosion died away, the Brigadier tried the RT again. 'Yates? Captain Yates? Can you hear me?'

There was no reply.

10

Take-Off

In Stuart's room Sergeant Benton was trying frantically to raise someone – anyone – on the RT. 'Brigadier, come in please. Greyhound Three, come in
. . . Captain Yates, can *you* hear me, sir?'

Silence.

Benton gave the others a stunned look. 'It's no
good, I can't raise them. They must have copped it.'

Inside the little wood there was a scene of devastation. The truck containing the Doctor's TARDIS
had been blown clear off the road, and the TARDIS
lay on its side in a little hollow. The other vehicles
were slewed at an angle amongst the trees. Several
of the trees had caught fire and there was smoke
and flame everywhere.

A solitary farm labourer rumbled up on his tractor
and stared at the chaotic scene in amazement. 'What
happened then?'

A dazed UNIT sergeant was staggering to his feet.
'Dunno. Some sort of explosion.'

'I know, I heard it,' said the labourer simply. He
pushed his cap to the back of his head. 'Funny that!
It were just about here one of them doodlebugs
come down. Back in 1944 that was . . .'

83

The Master flicked off his mini-screen. 'You know, I thoroughly enjoyed that.'

'You have destroyed this TARDIS?' asked Krasis in awe.

'Unfortunately it cannot be destroyed. But people can. We'll have no more trouble from them for a while.'

By the time the Doctor, Jo and the Brigadier arrived, UNIT discipline was asserting itself and things were sorting themselves out. The UNIT sergeant had taken command, and those who had escaped unhurt were caring for the wounded and checking the damage to the vehicles.

They found Mike Yates leaning against a scorched land rover. His face was blackened, his clothes were charred and he was bleeding from an ugly scalp-wound. 'Now you keep still, Mike, and take it easy,' said the Brigadier. 'You've finished work for the day.'

Mike managed a feeble grin. 'Sorry about the TARDIS, Doctor.'

'Don't worry, Mike. We'll soon have her on her feet again.'

Already a team of UNIT soldiers with ropes was busily hauling the TARDIS into an upright position.

The Doctor drew Jo aside, took the time sensor from Bessie and handed it to her. 'Now, Jo, I want you to keep a close eye on this. As soon as you see the slightest reaction, you let me know.'

'Right, Doctor.'

The UNIT soldiers had fixed their ropes to the labourer's tractor. At a signal from the sergeant, he began driving forwards. With the unwieldy dignity of a drunken dowager, the TARDIS was straightened into an upright position.

Much to his relief, Sergeant Benton had finally managed to raise the Brigadier on his RT. 'Very good, sir, I'll stand by. Glad you're all okay, sir. We really thought you'd copped it! Benton out.'

He put down the RT and turned to Ruth and Stuart, who appeared to be in the middle of a blazing row.

'It's a daft idea anyway,' Stuart was saying. 'I've had one basinful, I don't feel much like another. You heard what the Doctor said.'

'For a member of the so-called dominant sex, Stu, you're being remarkably feeble.'

Benton looked amusedly at their angry faces. 'Is this a private fight, or can anyone join in?'

Stuart turned to him as an ally. 'Boadicea here only wants to creep over to the lab and nobble the Master.'

'And supposing the time field is still working?'

'We shan't know that till we try, shall we?' said Ruth crisply.

To Stuart's horror, Benton headed for the door. 'Right then, what are we waiting for?'

'You're worse than she is!' moaned Stuart.

The Master's escape was still very fresh in Benton's mind. 'So you're suggesting we just sit here and let the Master treat us like a load of twits?'

'Look mate, you're paid to play James Bond games. I'm a scientist.'

'Oh, Stu!' said Ruth reproachfully.

He swung round on her. 'And don't *you* start! You'd be the first to clobber me if I mucked it up.'

'Well, you could at least have a go,' she said indignantly. 'Oh, why are men so spineless?'

'Look lovey, I'm not *men*. I'm Stuart Hyde, registered card-carrying fully paid-up coward!'

Benton and Ruth didn't answer. They just looked at him.

'Don't look at me like that! For Pete's sake!' Still no-one spoke. 'Oh, all right,' said Stuart wearily. 'I'll come.'

'Thanks, Stu,' said Benton solemnly. 'I knew you wouldn't let us down.'

Stuart grunted. 'Just give me time, that's all.' He grabbed a giant spanner from a shelf by the door and waved it martially. 'Well, come on then, what are we waiting for?'

The Master opened the front of the tall green computer cabinet like a door, heaved up the section of TOMTIT equipment in which the crystal was set, and led the way inside. 'Come, Krasis, we have work to do.'

Nervously Krasis followed.

He was astonished to find himself in a large and well-lit chamber – in the centre stood a complex many-sided shape. An altar perhaps, thought Krasis. He looked about him in awe. 'Master, what is this place? Is it a temple?'

The Master put down the equipment and the crystal on a specially prepared table next to the control console. 'Do not let it concern you, Krasis.'

'So vast a space inside so small a box,' said Krasis wonderingly.

The Master seized his opportunity to keep Krasis thoroughly overawed. 'My power is greater than your imagination can encompass. You just remember that. Your only interest at the moment is to realise that Atlantis awaits us.' His hands moved over the controls. 'First I must test the power levels.' The console of the Master's TARDIS began throbbing with power. He studied the instruments and nodded in satisfaction. 'Good. A few more minutes recycling and we shall be ready to leave!'

By now the Doctor's TARDIS was standing upright again.

Jo came running up to the Doctor who was standing at the roadside supervising preparations to get his TARDIS back on the road, and then onto the now-repaired truck.

'Doctor, quickly! I'm getting a reading!'

He took the time sensor from her and studied it. 'It's very low,' muttered the Doctor. 'And it's fading again. He must be testing before take-off, the power drain would have been enormous . . .' He raised his voice. 'Brigadier, the Master's on the move again.'

The Brigadier came hurrying up. 'Right, Sergeant, get the Doctor's machine loaded up!'

'There's no time for that! I'll have to take-off from down there.'

'I thought your TARDIS still wasn't working?' said Jo.

'It isn't, not properly. I intend to use the time sensor as a homing device, and put my TARDIS inside his. Then wherever he goes I'll go with him.'

The Doctor made his way down to the TARDIS with Jo and the Brigadier close behind him. He paused by the TARDIS door. 'Well, goodbye, Lethbridge-Stewart. I'll make contact as soon as possible.'

'*We'll* make contact as soon as possible,' corrected Jo.

The Doctor raised his eyebrows. 'We, Jo?'

'We!'

'Nothing I can say will dissuade you?'

'No.'

'Oh! Well, you'd better come along then!'

The Doctor went inside the TARDIS and Jo followed.

Even when you knew the TARDIS was bigger on the inside than on the outside, thought Jo, the actual experience still continued to be something of a shock.

She looked around her. Something had altered, something about the circular configuration of the walls. 'Doctor, the TARDIS looks different.'

'Oh, just a spot of re-decoration, that's all.' From time to time, the Doctor altered some detail of the TARDIS interior. More often than not he decided he didn't like what he'd done and reverted to the original. Dismissing the subject, the Doctor said seriously, 'Jo, you do realise that what I'm about to do is appallingly dangerous?'

'I've been in the TARDIS with you before.'

'Very well. You've been warned.'

Jo watched while the Doctor studied the still faintly registering time sensor, and made a number of minute adjustments to the controls.

The TARDIS console began humming gently, and the Doctor straightened up. 'The two TARDISes are now operating on the same frequency. Now for the tricky part . . . This is the time setting. It's critical to the billionth part of a nanosecond. Do you see?'

'No.'

The Doctor sighed. 'If it's infinitesimally low, we'll miss entirely and go whistling off to Heaven-knows-where. If it's too high, by even the tiniest fraction of a moment . . .'

The Doctor slapped his hands together. 'Whoomph! Time Ram! The atoms making up this TARDIS would occupy precisely the same space and time of those of the Master's TARDIS.'

'But that's impossible!'

'Of course it is. So, what do you think would happen?'

'Whoomph?'

'Exactly. Extinction. Utter annihilation. Still want to come?'

'It's my job, remember?'

'Glad to have you aboard, Miss Grant,' said the Doctor solemnly.

Jo gave him a mock salute. 'Glad to be aboard, Doctor!'

The Doctor grinned and operated the controls, and the TARDIS vanished with its usual wheezing, groaning sound. At the wheel of his tractor, the farm worker watched it dispassionately. 'Londoners!' he muttered disapprovingly.

Taking a circuitous route through the shrubbery, Benton, Stuart and Ruth worked their way round the building, and then dashed through the arch that led to the Master's lab . . .

In the TARDIS, the centre column of the control console was rising and falling steadily. 'Mmm, yes . . .' said the Doctor thoughtfully. 'Well, so far, so good!'

'How long will it take us to get there?' asked Jo.

The Doctor rubbed his chin. 'Well, that's the curious thing. No time at all, really. We're outside time. But, of course, it always seems to take a certain amount of time. Depends on the mood, I suppose.'

'What, your mood?'

'No, the TARDIS's.'

'You talk as if she was alive, Doctor!'

'Depends what you mean by alive, doesn't it? Take old Bessie, for instance . . .'

The centre column began slowing perceptibly, and the Doctor broke off. 'We're coming in to land already Jo.'

Suddenly a curiously familiar wheezing, groaning sound filled the air – and a large computer cabinet appeared on the other side of the control room.

The Doctor stared at it in dismay. 'Oh dear, oh dear! Well, it was always on the cards, I suppose.'

Suddenly Jo realised what had happened. 'The Master's TARDIS is inside ours, instead of the other way round!'

'Quite! Very curious effect, that. I don't quite understand how it happened.'

The Doctor switched on the scanner and found himself gazing into the swirling patterns of the time vortex. 'That's strange . . . Oh no, of course. We're seeing through the TOMTIT gap into the time vortex. Wait there, Jo.'

The Doctor strode determinedly through the TARDIS door.

After a moment Jo heard him exclaim, 'Good grief!' Then he called, 'Jo, come out here a moment will you?'

Jo followed him, and found herself standing in a control room like, and yet curiously unlike, the Doctor's own. She glanced over her shoulder – and there was the square blue shape of the TARDIS she had just left. 'I don't get it!'

'Don't you? Follow me.'

The Doctor led the way across the strange control room and out of the door on the other side.

Jo found herself back in the more familiar control room of the Doctor's TARDIS – with the computer cabinet that disguised the Master's TARDIS behind her.

'I still don't get it!'

'Oh really, Jo, it's quite simple. My TARDIS is inside the Master's.'

'But his is inside yours!'

'Exactly! They're both inside each other. I should have expected that.'

'So what can we do now?'

The Doctor smiled. 'I'll give you three guesses.'

Jo pretended to consider. 'Wait?'

The Doctor snapped his fingers. 'Right first time.'

The Master and Krasis were back in the laboratory and the Master was making a few final adjustments to the main TOMTIT controls.

Krasis was looking out of the window. 'Master, look! Men in wagons!'

The Master hurried to the window. Coming up the drive of the Institute was the UNIT convoy, arriving at last. He hurried back to the controls. 'I'll soon deal with *them* . . .'

The Brigadier was leading the convoy in his land rover. He came to a halt and the other vehicles drew up in line behind him.

The Brigadier leaped over the side of the land rover and began barking orders. 'Right, A squad here, B squad round the back. Keep your eyes open. At the double no-oo-oo . . .'

Time suddenly slowed. To the Brigadier, everything felt normal but, as the time field took effect, Krasis and the Master saw the Brigadier and his men freeze like statues. 'That'll keep them nicely unoccupied for the time being. In you go, Krasis!'

Krasis recoiled. 'Where?'

The Master flung open the front of the computer cabinet. 'Into my TARDIS, man, and be quick about it!' Reluctantly Krasis obeyed.

The Master made a last adjustment to the TOMTIT console. 'They won't stop me now!'

The lab door was flung open and Ruth Ingram appeared. 'Sorry, Professor, that's where you're wrong!' Behind her was Stuart Hyde, nervously brandishing his enormous spanner.

The Master took a step forward. For all his moderate size he was enormously strong, and he knew full well that he could brush these two aside like cobwebs. 'Well, well, well, my devoted assistants! And are you going to stop me?'

'Not by ourselves, no,' said Ruth steadily. 'Take a look behind you.'

The Master's lip curled in scorn. 'Oh, really! You don't expect me to believe . . .'

From behind him Benton's voice said, 'Suit yourself mate. But you'd better get those hands up!'

The Master whirled round. Benton had just finished clambering through the window and was covering him with the big service revolver. Slowly the Master raised his hands. 'I should have finished you off when I had the chance.'

'You'll never get another one. Stuart, see if he's got a gun.'

Stuart moved to search the Master – and made the elementary mistake of coming between the Master and Benton's gun. It was only for a second, but for the Master it was long enough.

With one savage sweep of his arm, he sent Stuart spinning across the room. Then he dashed into his TARDIS, closing the door in Ruth's face as she tried to follow him. Seconds later, the computer cabinet disappeared before her astonished eyes.

In the Master's TARDIS, Krasis was pointing to a square blue shape by the far wall. 'Master, look! The other one. Your enemy is here!'

The Master gave an exultant laugh. 'Good! Now I've got him really trapped!'

11

The Time-Eater

Inside *his* TARDIS, the Doctor was being pitched about like a passenger in a small boat on a stormy sea. Jo was sent flying across the control room. She picked herself up and clung to the console. 'Doctor what's happening?'

'We're on our way, Jo. The Master's taken off for Atlantis!'

'But the TARDIS has never behaved like this before!'

The Doctor was struggling frantically with the controls. 'The two TARDISes are operating out of phase, that's why.'

Suddenly the TARDIS seemed to settle down a little. 'There,' gasped the Doctor. 'That's better. I've managed to calm her down. She has a very nasty temper when she's roused.'

'I never know if you're joking or not,' said Jo, rubbing an ache at the base of her spine. 'I think I've bruised my tailbone.'

'I'm sorry about your coccyx Jo, but these little things are sent to try us.'

'My what?'

'Your coccyx – your tailbone!'

Another voice said, 'I'm sorry about your coccyx too, Miss Grant.' The Master's face had appeared

in the scanner screen set into the TARDIS wall.
'How very sociable of you both to drop in!'

Ruth Ingram was staring at the still gently throbbing
TOMTIT apparatus. 'I think we ought to turn it off.'

Benton disagreed. 'I don't think we should touch
it.'

'Why ever not?'

'The Doctor was going after his TARDIS – and
that thing's some sort of time-machine, isn't it?'

'So?'

'So we'd better leave well alone, Miss.' Benton
couldn't help feeling that interfering with TOMTIT
might somehow foul things up for the Doctor.

'Very well. You're in command, Sergeant
Benton.'

'And a right muck-up I've made of it,' said Benton
bitterly.

'Come on, it's not exactly *your* fault.'

'Don't look at me,' said Stuart hurriedly. 'You
can't say I didn't warn you, now can you, Sergeant?'

'I'll listen to you next time. That was the nearest
I'll ever come to capturing the Master, that was.'

'Oh, come on, it isn't the end of the world after
all.'

'Isn't it? The Doctor seemed to think it might be.
No telling where the Master is by now – or *when* he
is for that matter!'

Ruth gave a sigh of exasperation. 'Honestly, you
two make me sick. Standing about moaning like a
couple of old women.'

Stuart was indignant. 'Old women?'

'Look, I mean it, Stu. Okay, so the Master's gone
off somewhere. And whether he's gone into the
future or the past – well, frankly I don't know and

I don't care. The point is, we're still here and now, and the first thing we've got to do is to define the problem.'

Stu had wandered over to the window during this little speech. At this point he turned and said, 'You can stop right there, Ruth, the problem is defined. Come and look.'

They joined him at the window and looked down at the Brigadier and his men, still frozen in their temporal stasis.

'It's the Brig,' said Benton wonderingly.

Ruth said, 'Exactly the same as before.'

'But how can it be the same as before,' said Stuart, 'now that the crystal's gone?'

'Don't you remember? The Doctor said TOMTIT works quite independently, even without the crystal.'

Benton looked alarmed. 'Do you realise this means we're trapped?'

'Now will you let me turn off the transmitter?'

They wrangled for a few minutes longer but at last Benton said 'All right, turn it off.'

'Ah, a man of decision!' Ruth hurried to the controls. The TOMTIT noise began to die away.

'Go on then,' said Benton. 'Turn it off!'

'I have.'

'But – they're still stuck!'

'That's impossible!'

Stuart turned from the window. 'Well, you'd better go and explain it to them, love. *They* still think they're stuck, apparently.'

'And we're still trapped,' said Benton. 'In here!'

'Now, Doctor, what can I do for you?' said the Master smoothly. 'Or is your visit purely social?'

'Oh, I thought we might have a little chat.'

'What an excellent idea. Why not join me out here?'

'Because one step outside my TARDIS and that would be the end of me!'

The Master looked hurt. 'You have a very low opinion of me!'

'You've noticed that, have you? Well, well, well!'

'It may interest you to know, Doctor, that I've put a time lock on your TARDIS. You cannot leave – unless I lift it, of course.'

'Do you think I haven't thought of that too? You're as trapped as I am. You can't even open your door unless I wish it.'

'Alternatively, I could fling you out into the time vortex,' the Master continued. 'I very much doubt if you could do that to me. So, do be very careful.'

'Do you really think I care what happens to me at the moment? Don't you realise that your plans could bring disaster to the entire Universe?'

The Master yawned and flicked a switch on his console. The Doctor's voice faded, leaving his silently mouthing face on the screen.

The Master turned to Krasis. 'An excellent brain, I must admit, if a little pedestrian. But what a bore the fellow is!'

'Is he dangerous?'

'Dangerous enough. But don't worry, I can deal with him.'

'In there?' asked Krasis. 'Surely, he is safe in there?'

The Master chuckled. 'As soon as he realises he's talking to himself, he'll be out in a flash.' He glanced at the scanner and saw the Doctor suddenly stop talking, his face indignant. 'Ah, he's realised at last.

That took a long time, the slow-witted fool. Now you watch. He cannot bear not to have the last word!'

The Doctor saw the Master wave mockingly and turn away from the screen. 'He's not even listening. He's turned down the sound!'

'Well, that's not very nice!'

'I've *got* to make him listen, Jo. It's our only chance of stopping him!'

'You're not thinking of going out there, are you?'

'Not if I can possibly help it!'

'What are you going to do then?'

'He's turned off his sound receiver, so I must make myself heard without it. "If the Thraskin puts his fingers in his ears it's polite to shout." Old Venusian proverb.' The Doctor reached into a storage locker beneath the console and pulled out a tangled mass of circuitry.

'Ah!' said Jo, wondering, as usual, what the Doctor was on about. 'What's a Thraskin?'

The Doctor was dismantling the assembled circuits. 'Archaic word,' he said absently, 'seldom used since the twenty-fifth dynasty. The modern equivalent is Plinge.'

'And what does Plinge mean?'

The Doctor was busily reassembling the circuits in a different sequence. 'Oh for heaven's sake, Jo, I just told you. It means Thraskin.'

Ruth Ingram meanwhile was carrying out a very similar operation on the inner circuitry of the TOMTIT machine.

'But why?' Benton was asking. 'I mean, when you

turned it off, the Brig and Co. should have speeded up again. Why didn't they?'

'Well, I'm not sure, but it looks as if TOMTIT has made a permanent gap in the structure of time. Our only hope is to close it up again.'

'And how are you going to do that?' asked Stuart.

'I'm turning the circuits upside down, so to speak. It's a bit empirical, but you never know.'

Benton looked baffled. 'Empirical?'

'That, Sergeant Benton, means I haven't a clue what I'm doing.'

'Join the club,' said Stuart cheerfully.

Benton scratched his head. 'So, it's just trial and error? Have a go and see what happens?'

'More or less!' She fitted the circuitry back into TOMTIT and switched on. 'Right, Stu, you monitor the interstitial activity. If it goes over sixty, give us a shout.'

'What's the upper limit?'

'If it goes over seventy, say a prayer and duck.'

'What do I do?' asked Benton.

'Just stay out of the way and look pretty. Right, Stu, are you happy?'

'Ecstatic.'

'Then let's have a stab at it.' She switched on, and the TOMTIT sound began.

'Interstitial activity, nil.' reported Stuart.

'Molecular structure, stable. Increasing power.'

Stuart began calling out readings. 'Three five. Four zero.'

'How's the time wedge?'

'Steady on zero zero four.'

'Right. Isolate matrix scanner.'

'Check! Four, five, five zero . . .'

'Interstitial activity?'

99

Stuart's voice was tense. 'Shooting up. Five five, six zero . . . It's running away again.' Ruth worked frantically at the controls. 'Decreasing power.'

Stuart's voice went on in a kind of chant. 'Seven five, seven zero, six five, six zero . . .'

Benton was leaning forward over the console trying to make sense of what was going on. Without realising it, he was resting one hand on the transmission platform.

'Five five, five zero, four five, four zero, three five, three zero . . .'

Benton felt a strange tingle running through him. He tried to snatch his hand away and found he couldn't move . . .

Suddenly he felt himself *dwindling* . . .

'Okay, that's enough,' said Ruth. She switched off and the power hum faded away. She hurried to the window and Stuart joined her.

The Brigadier and his men were still frozen in time. Despairingly Ruth said, 'It's made no difference. They're still stuck.'

Stuart turned back to the console. 'There we were the skin of a gnat's whisker from the big bang and —'

'Nothing happened at all,' concluded Ruth.

There was a strange wailing cry.

Stuart was staring in astonishment at the other side of the console. 'Nothing? Come and see!'

Ruth came over to look.

On the floor a baby was squalling indignantly as it tried to free itself from a tangle of army uniform. Benton, like Stuart before him, had been a victim of the TOMTIT's temporal interference, but in the opposite chronological direction.

Sergeant Benton was now just over one year old.

The Master waited patiently, eyes fixed on his monitor screen.

'Master, what is he doing?' asked Krasis.

'Exactly what I would do in his position.'

'And what is that?'

'Wait and see, Krasis, wait and see!'

Suddenly the screen lit up, showing the Doctor's face. The Doctor's voice rang loud and clear through the Master's control room. 'Testing, testing, testing! One, two, three, four, five!'

The Master laughed. 'I thought as much!'

'I've boosted my audio and over-ridden your sound circuits,' announced the Doctor, cheerfully. 'You can't turn me off now, can you? You've got to listen to me!'

'Have I, Doctor? Have I really?'

The Master's hands flicked over the controls.

The Doctor settled down to lecture the Master on the evil of his ways. 'Obviously you've not been able to bring Kronos through yet, or you wouldn't be going to Atlantis, so there may yet be time to make you realise your folly.' Suddenly the Doctor's words became twisted, garbled . . .

In his TARDIS, the Doctor listened in amazement to the sound of his own voice. What he had actually said was, 'Surely you must see the dangers you risk?' But somehow what came out was, 'Illursh ooee tsum ees uth serjnade eeoo ksirr?'

On the screen the Master leaned forward. 'I'm so sorry, Doctor. What was that again?'

The Doctor glared indignantly at him and shouted, 'I said, surely you must see the dangers you risk?'

But what he heard himself saying was, 'Eea dess, illursh ooee tsum ees uth serjnade eeoo ksirr . . .'

Angrily the Doctor switched off the scanner. 'Of all the low underhand tricks!'

'What happened? What language was that?'

'English,' said the Doctor indignantly. 'Backwards! He's picking up my words even before I say them, and feeding them back to me through the TARDISes' telepathic circuits, so that they come out backwards.'

Jo realised that the Master was reversing not the letters but the actual syllables of the Doctor's words. It was exactly like hearing a tape played backwards, but at normal speed.

'Did you say the TARDISes were *telepathic*?'

'Of course,' said the Doctor matter-of-factly. 'How else do you suppose they would communicate? Well, that settles it. I have no choice. Now listen, Jo, when I go out there –'

'You're not going out there!'

'What else can I do?'

'You said yourself it would be suicide to go out there without the protection of the TARDIS.'

'I've got to risk it, Jo. He's got to be stopped. But that's no reason to put you into any danger. As soon as I go through that door you must close it after me.'

'But then you'll be shut out.'

'And you'll be safely shut in. And you mustn't open up to anybody or anyone until I say.'

'I won't do it,' sobbed Jo. 'I won't.'

Gently the Doctor touched her cheek. 'You'll do as you're told, Jo. It's your job, remember?'

'But Doctor, if anything happens to you –'

'I know, Jo, I know. Now, go and open that door.'

The Master smiled triumphantly as the door of the

police box opened and the Doctor emerged. 'There, Krasis! What did I tell you?'

'Won't you introduce me?' said the Doctor.

The Master nodded to Krasis, who said proudly, 'I am Krasis, High Priest of the Temple of Poseidon.'

'Greetings to you, Krasis,' said the Doctor politely. 'Any friend of the Master's is an enemy of mine.'

'Oh come, Doctor,' said the Master wearily. 'Must we play games? I take it you have something to say to me before I destroy you?'

'Yes, I most certainly have!'

'The usual song of death and disaster? I do wish you'd learn a new tune, Doctor.'

The Doctor drew a deep breath. 'Now, just you listen to me for once. If you try to take control of the Universe through Kronos, you risk total destruction of the entire cosmos.'

'Of course!' said the Master arrogantly. 'All or nothing – literally! What a glorious alternative!'

'You're mad! Paranoid!

'Of course, Doctor,' said the Master. 'Who isn't? I'm just a little more honest than the rest, that's all. Goodbye, Doctor.'

The Master threw the switch on the TOMTIT machine.

The crystal began to glow.

'No, Master, no!' shrieked Krasis.

But it was too late. The winged form of Kronos was emerging from the fiery heart of the glowing crystal, and the beating of his mighty wings filled the Master's control room. Holding up the Seal of Atlantis for protection, the Master shouted, 'Behold, Kronos, a rare, a delicate feast for you. A Time Lord! Devour him! *Devour him*!'

Kronos swooped down, wrapped his fiery wings about the Doctor and engulfed him.

In the Doctor's TARDIS, Jo Grant had seen everything on the scanner. She gave an anguished cry of 'Doctor!' and fainted dead away.

12

Atlantis

When Kronos unfolded his wings the Doctor was
gone, vanished leaving no trace behind.

His appetite unsated, Kronos bore down on the
Master and Krasis, filling the air with the terrifying
beating of his wings.

Krasis cowered away with a scream of terror, but
the Master stood his ground, holding up the Great
Seal of Atlantis. 'Kronos, be at peace – I command
you! *Be at peace!*'

For a moment nothing happened. Then, with
astonishing suddenness, Kronos began to shrink, to
dwindle, and vanished into the heart of the glowing
crystal.

The Master laughed exultantly. 'You see, Krasis?
Kronos is my slave!'

Suddenly Jo's face appeared on the scanner. Her
faint had lasted only a few moments, and she was
desperate to discover the Doctor's fate.

The Master looked up. 'Miss Grant?'

'What's happened to the Doctor? You must help
him!'

'Ah, he's beyond my help, my dear. He's beyond
anybody's help!'

'That thing – that creature – really swallowed him
up?'

'Now that's a nice point,' said the Master judicially. 'Yes – and no! Yes, it engulfed him, no it didn't actually eat him up. He's out there in the time vortex, and there he's going to stay.'

'Then he is alive?'

'Well, if you can call it that. Alive forever, in an eternity of nothingness.' The Master chuckled. 'To coin a phrase – a living death!'

'That's the most cruel, the most wicked thing I ever heard.'

'Thank you, my dear,' said the Master, modestly accepting what he saw as a compliment. 'Now, what about you, Miss Grant? You're an embarassment to me . . . as indeed is that antiquated piece of junk of the Doctor's.'

Jo was close to tears. 'I don't really care any more. Do what you like – just get it over with!'

'Your wish is my command,' said the Master courteously. His hands moved over the controls, and the picture of Jo on the scanner began to rock and spin as she, and the TARDIS, were hurled out into the time vortex.

The Master touched another control and the picture on the screen showed the TARDIS spinning away into the infinite nothingness of the vortex. 'Goodbye, Miss Grant!'

The sudden, whirling acceleration caused Jo to lose consciousness yet again. She awoke stretched out on the control room floor, with a strange sense of peace. The TARDIS seemed to be poised, at rest. Dozens of voices were whispering gently in her ear. *Jo . . . Jo . . . Jo . . .*

Somehow one voice seemed to dominate the rest. 'Doctor?' she said feebly.

Thank heavens you're alive, Jo!

'Doctor! It *is* you!' She sat up, looked round, and found she was still alone. 'Doctor – where are you?'

I'm nowhere, Jo. Still in the time vortex. The TARDIS is relaying my thoughts to you.

'What are all those other voices I can hear?'

Those are my subconscious thoughts. I shouldn't listen too hard if I were you – I'm not all that proud of some of them.

Resisting the temptation to eavesdrop on the Doctor's subconscious, Jo said, 'I still don't understand, you must be *somewhere*. Tell me how I can get you back.'

You can't Jo – but luckily the TARDIS can. That's why she's put us in touch.

'What do you – I mean, what does *she* want me to do?'

Go to control panel number three.

Jo obeyed. 'Okay. Now what?'

Lift the little lid marked 'Extreme Emergency'.

'Right.'

There's a red handle inside. Got it?

Jo lifted the lid and saw the handle beneath. 'Yes.'

Then pull it!

Jo grabbed the handle and tugged hard.

Nothing happened – until a voice behind her said quietly, 'Hello, Jo.'

She spun round and saw the Doctor sitting cross-legged on the floor, a little dishevelled, but very much alive. 'Doctor!' she cried joyfully and ran to hug him.

In the outer hall of the Great Temple of Poseidon, a royal council was about to begin.

The chamber was enormous, dominated at one

end by the huge statue of the god Poseidon. In front of the statue was a raised stone dais upon which were set two carved thrones.

The trumpeters at the great main doors raised their long curved horns and blew a fanfare. Immediately a richly-dressed procession of priests and nobles, the High Council of Atlantis, filed into the temple, taking their places before the dais.

Crito, the Elder of the Council, rapped on the marble floor with his staff of office. 'Open the doors!'

The doors to the inner temple opened and a smaller procession appeared. In the lead was King Dalios, his ornate robes contrasting with his unimpressive stature.

The woman who came behind him, borne in a litter by four giant Nubian slaves, more than made up for Dalios's unimpressive appearance. Tall and imposing, red-haired and voluptuously beautiful, gorgeously robed and with an elaborate jewelled head-dress, she looked every inch the queen that she was. This was Galleia, Queen of Atlantis, Consort of King Dalios.

Priests, slaves and temple guards flanked the royal couple as they took their places on the twin thrones. The assembled Councillors bowed their heads and once again Crito rapped on the marble floor with his staff. 'Peace, my brothers! His Holiness, the Most Venerable Priest of Poseidon, King of the Ten Kings will hear his Council.'

Before anyone else could move, the handsome figure of young Hippias stepped forward and bowed low. His voice rang clearly through the temple. 'Your Holiness, Most Venerable Priest of Poseidon . . .'

Nearly five hundred years of public life had made

King Dalios somewhat impatient of official ceremony. He leaned forward, cutting off the string of complimentary titles. 'Yes, yes, yes, I hear you, friend Hippias.'

Hippias bowed again. 'My Lord, may I speak plainly?'

'It would grieve me to think you would ever speak otherwise. Speak as a friend should speak.'

Hippias tossed back his long coiled ringlets in an orator's gesture. 'You are popular, Dalios, and the people love you. Will their love fill their bellies in the winter when the granaries are empty?'

There was a shocked silence. This was close to treason. Then Dalios spoke. 'Your words are plain indeed, Hippias. What would you have me do? Would you have me order the rain to fall?'

'Yes, Dalios, I would!'

'Have a care, Hippias.'

But Hippias was not to be deterred. His eloquent words rang like a trumpet-call through the temple. 'Indeed, I *shall* have a care. A care for the peace of Atlantis. A care that foolish superstition, old wives' tales, and the fear of old men shall not prevent our caring for them as our rank demands.'

Myseus, another young Councillor, stepped forward. 'He speaks the truth, Lord King. Many think as we do.'

'You know not what you ask,' said Dalios wearily.

'Must I be plainer still?' cried Hippias. 'I know quite well. I ask for the blessings our forefathers once enjoyed. I ask for the divine Power to be given back to the land from which it was so cruelly stolen!'

Now Hippias was adding blasphemy to treason, and the temple exploded in uproar.

109

Krasis re-appeared as the Master returned to the control room, looking sinisterly elegant in a black, high-collared coat.

'Master, why are we not yet in Atlantis?'

The Master was busy at the console. 'My dear Krasis, I must work out the landing co-ordinates as accurately as possible. Your people must realise immediately that I am the Master, that I come from the gods, and that I am bringing Kronos back to them.'

'Where in Atlantis will you arrive?'

The Master gave him a look of surprise. 'Why, smack in the middle of the temple of course!'

It took the intervention of King Dalios himself to quell the near-riot. He rose from the throne, stretching out his hands, his voice surprisingly deep and strong for such a frail old man, and called out, 'Brothers, peace, peace, I say. Be silent!'

And all at once there was silence.

Dalios spoke again. 'I shall speak plainly too. You ask for the blessings of the Golden Years. I tell you plainly, there came a time when Atlantis grew to hate them. What would you have, Hippias, if you were Master of Kronos, Ruler of Time?'

There was a shocked murmur. To speak the name of Kronos was near-blasphemy, even for the king.

'Would you have ten crops in one season?' Dalios went on. 'A surfeit of fishes, an ocean of wine? Then take the barren soil as well, the stinking piles of rotting meat, an idle, drunken, cruel people. I tell you plainly, the gifts of Kronos were a curse. That is why we, of our own choice, banished him and renounced them.'

'But Dalios –' protested Hippias.

Shocked, Crito intervened. 'Be silent, Hippias! The King speaks!'

Sulkily Hippias subsided and Dalios went on. 'I have seen a temple, twice the size of this in which we stand, fall through a crack into the fiery bedrock of the earth. I have seen a city drowned, a land laid waste by fire. So listen to an old man's fears. If Kronos should come again, I tell you plainly – Atlantis would be doomed. You hear me, Hippias? Doomed, destroyed, never to rise again!'

Hippias seemed about to reply, thought better of it and turned angrily away.

Dalios sat brooding on his throne for a moment. He knew, because he had seen it, that interference with the true course of time produced short term benefits and eventual disasters. The physical catastrophes were bad enough, the fires, the earthquakes, the floods. Far worse was the moral and spiritual corruption brought by too much ease and wealth. The gifts of Kronos had been given up just in time. They had come very near to destroying Atlantis.

Now Hippias was clamouring for their return. And he was not alone. There had been as many Atlanteans shouting in support of Hippias as against him – perhaps more.

The voice of Queen Galleia broke in on his thoughts. 'Listen – I heard strange music. There it is once more . . .'

An unearthly sound shattered the silence of the temple, and a strange shape appeared in the centre of the temple – a tall green box. It was, in fact, the computer cabinet from the TOMTIT laboratory; in his haste the Master had forgotten to reprogram his chameleon circuit.

The overawed Atlanteans drew back. Dalios raised his voice. 'Guards!'

Nervous but determined, the temple guards came forward, ringing the box with their three-pronged spears. The door opened and a black-bearded, black-clad man stepped out.

Finding a razor-sharp trident inches from his face, the Master brushed it casually aside.

Dalios stepped forward to confront him. 'Who are you?'

'I am the Master. I am an emissary from the gods.'

The newcomer's voice was deep and compelling and there was a murmur of awe from the crowd. Dalios however was not so easily impressed. 'Indeed? Any god in particular?'

The Master studied Dalios for a moment, realising that here was no primitive to be impressed with tricks and mystic talk. 'Of course . . . Why should you trust me?'

He snapped his fingers and Krasis appeared from the doorway behind him. Since everyone knew that Krasis had been snatched up by the gods on the night of the great storm, the crowd was more over-awed than ever. Even Dalios was shaken. 'Krasis!'

The Master said, 'Now do you believe me?'

'What do you want?' whispered Dalios.

'To speak of the ancient mysteries. The secrets of the mighty Kronos.'

There was a terrified gasp from the crowd.

'You are brave indeed, O Master,' said Dalios. 'An emissary of the gods.' He raised his voice. 'Brothers, should I listen to this man?'

Queen Galleia had been staring in fascination at the newcomer since his arrival. 'He has the very bearing of a god himself.'

'He appeared from the heavens, like Zeus,' muttered Myseus.

'I know of many such tricks,' said Dalios dismissively. 'Krasis?'

The eyes of the High Priest glittered fanatically. 'Most Venerable, I have seen – *him*.'

Dalios lowered his voice. 'You have seen Kronos?'

Krasis nodded eagerly.

'We must speak privately,' said Dalios. 'Crito, the Council is at an end. Come, Lady.'

Crito rapped on the floor with his staff. 'The Council is at an end. The King departs. Sound trumpets!'

The fanfare rang through the temple and the King and his entourage moved towards the inner door.

Galleia rose to follow and stood for a moment, eyes fixed on the Master. As he moved past her, he paused, his dark eyes burning into her own. He inclined his head, very slightly, not in the salute of a courtier to a queen, but as a greeting between equals.

The Master went on his way, and Galleia stood staring after him. 'The bearing of a god,' she said, almost to herself, and moved away.

But Hippias heard, and stood staring angrily after her. In his gaze there was all the bitterness of an established favourite who has been suddenly replaced.

The Doctor finished his calculations and looked up. 'There we are, Jo. On our way to Atlantis.'

'But I thought you couldn't just take the TARDIS where you wanted to. I mean you haven't managed to fix it yet, have you? Or have you?'

'Not entirely,' admitted the Doctor. I'm relying on the time sensor to lead us to the Master's TARDIS.'

'But not inside it?'

'I hope not, not this time. We'll soon find out!'

He operated the landing controls.

Krasis and Hippias, both awaiting the result of the Master's audience with the King, found themselves confronted by a second miracle, as a tall blue box appeared beside the Master's TARDIS. The Doctor and Jo stepped out. Jo looked round in astonishment at the massive temple, with its great statue, the robed priests and Councillors and the Greek-looking guards.

The Doctor beamed amiably at Krasis. 'Well, well, well, small world, isn't it?'

Krasis stared unbelievingly at him. 'You are still alive!'

'So it would seem.'

Krasis soon recovered from his astonishment. 'But not for long! Guards, slay them!'

13

The Guardian

Hippias stepped forward, raising his hand. 'No! I forbid it!' He turned to Krasis. 'Are you mad? Who are these strangers? Why should they be slain on sight?'

'They are the enemies of the Master – and therefore the enemies of our people and our land.'

The Doctor said, 'We have come to warn you –'

'Silence!' screamed Krasis. 'You will regret this interference, Lord Hippias!'

Hippias ignored him. 'Guards, take them to the King.'

In the King's simply furnished private chambers, Galleia stood quietly by the door, a silent witness to the interview between the Master and her husband. Her eyes never left the Master, who stood dominating the seated figure of the King.

But despite appearances, Dalios was proving difficult to impress. 'If the High Priest saw fit to break a sacred trust, is that good reason for the King to follow him?'

Once more, the Master's voice was deep and compelling. 'Krasis saw the crystal in my hand, saw Kronos himself, saw him dominated by me. Krasis knows that I am the Master of Kronos.'

'Krasis is but a slave at heart,' said Dalios dismissively.

The Master leaned forward, staring hard at the unimpressive little figure seated before him. 'Maybe. But Krasis has learned that it is well to obey me.'

Dalios looked at him, with a mild, amused curiosity. 'You seek to make me fear you?'

The Master sat on the couch, close to Dalios, staring deep into his eyes. 'Not at all,' he said, his voice deep and soothing. 'But if you will only see, with Krasis, that I am the Master, then naturally you will obey me.' His voice deepened, became more urgent. 'You will obey me. *You will obey me!*'

To the Master's astonished fury, Dalios shook his head and laughed. 'A very elementary technique of fascination. I am too old a fish – too old in years and in the sacred mysteries – to be caught in such a net. You are no messenger from the gods.'

'But you saw me descend from the skies!' protested the Master.

Dalios chuckled. 'Tell me then, what of great Poseidon? What did he have for breakfast? Fish, I suppose! And what of Zeus and Hera? Tell me of the latest gossip from Olympus. Do tell me!'

It was a new experience for the Master to be mocked and not one he cared for, but he controlled his anger. 'I underestimated you, Dalios.'

'I am no child to play with such painted dolls. Kronos is no god, no Titan. I know that, and so do you.'

The Master bowed his head. 'The King is old in wisdom.'

Once again Dalios laughed at him. 'Now you try to flatter me. You pull a string and wish to see me

116

dance.' Dalios's voice hardened. 'You shall not have the Great Crystal!'

The Master rose with as much dignity as he could muster. 'I shall go now, Dalios. I have nothing more to say to you.'

Even now Dalios had the last word. 'You have said nothing to me yet. When you find the true word to speak, I shall listen!'

Humiliated and dismissed, the Master left the chamber.

There was worse to come. Outside, he met the Doctor and Jo Grant, being escorted by Hippias to an audience with the King. Astounded the Master stared at them, literally speechless with fury.

'Can't think of a thing to say?' asked the Doctor. 'How very embarrassing!'

'How about, "Curses, foiled again"?' suggested Jo helpfully.

The Master turned and stalked away furiously.

'Come,' said Hippias, and led them into the royal chamber.

As they entered, Queen Galleia slipped away by the door that led to her own quarters. She had listened angrily to the debate between the Master and the King. It seemed wrong to her that the fascinating stranger had been sent away, unhappy and rejected.

It was a situation that could be remedied.

As Jo and the Doctor were shown in, King Dalios rose courteously to greet them. 'Strangers are uncommon in our land – though not this day, it seems. Who are you?'

The Doctor bowed. 'This, your Majesty, is Jo – Jo Grant.'

'Welcome, Jojogrant,' said the King solemnly.

'Surely, as in ancient times, a goddess has descended from Olympus!'

Jo was taken aback. 'But I'm not a goddess, honestly I'm not.'

Dalios chuckled. 'Of course you're not, my child. Forgive the clumsy gallantry of an old man. I fear I'm sadly out of practice. Hippias!'

'My Lord?'

'Take the Lady Jojogrant to the Queen while I talk with . . .'

'Oh, this is the Doctor,' said Jo hurriedly.

'With this learned man,' said Dalios.

'This way, Lady,' said Hippias.

Jo hesitated, looking worriedly at the Doctor. He smiled reassuringly. 'You'll be all right, Jo.'

Jo followed Hippias from the room.

Left alone, the Doctor and Dalios stood silent for a moment, summing each other up.

Dalios was a priest as well as a King, and, as he had demonstrated to the Master, an adept in ancient knowledge. He had the ability to see the essential nature of a man. Just as he had sensed evil in the Master, he saw the goodness of the Doctor and the honesty of his intentions.

'Forgive the roughness of your welcome,' said Dalios. 'Hippias has all the delicacy of a red-necked fisherman.'

'Nevertheless, he did save our lives.'

'Indeed,' said Dalios thoughtfully. 'He kept that to himself! Now Doctor, why have you come to Atlantis?'

In her private chamber, a room rich with tapestries and jewelled ornaments, Queen Galleia sat nibbling grapes while Lakis, her favourite slave girl, dressed

118

her hair. Lakis was an unobtrusively pretty brown-haired girl, quite eclipsed by the more flamboyant beauty of her mistress.

'Tell me,' asked Galleia, 'what did you think of this Master, Lakis?'

'He had the bearing of a god, Lady.'

'My very thought. In fact my very words. Are you mocking me, Lakis? Would you dare? No, I hardly think you would. Are you frightened, then? I shall not be angered by your reply if it is an honest one.'

'I like the Lord Hippias better,' whispered Lakis shyly.

Galleia tossed her head. 'A sweetmeat! A confection for a child's taste. This Master would not cloy on the tongue, as Hippias does!'

Lakis bowed her head. 'He is very handsome.'

Galleia stared into the distance. 'Handsome? Aye, he looked well enough, I suppose. But it was a face of *power*, Lakis. A man with such a face would dare to risk a world to win his desire.' She laughed. 'Hippias is but a petulant boy.'

'And a foolish one, no doubt, to trust a queen,' said Hippias from the doorway.

Galleia rose angrily. 'Foolish, certainly, to think himself man enough to love one.' She turned to Lakis who was fleeing from the room. 'No, Lakis, come back. The Lord Hippias is not staying.'

Hippias bowed. 'The Lord Hippias would not be here at all but that he has been sent on an errand by the King.'

'Then give me your message, boy – and go!'

Hippias turned and called, 'Lady!'

Jo Grant came into the room.

Hippias said curtly, 'Lady Galleia, may I present

119

to you the Lady Jojogrant. The King would have you treat her as an honoured guest.'

'How do you do?' said Jo. She held out her hand, then hurriedly withdrew it under Galleia's icy stare. With vague memories of old historical movies, Jo did a sort of improvised curtsey and said, 'Greetings!' This seemed to go down rather better.

Galleia inclined her head. 'Greetings Lady.' She looked at Jo's striped mini-dress and fluffy coat. 'You come from a far land?'

'Couldn't be much farther.'

'She fell from the skies,' said Hippias. 'Like the Master.'

'A day of wonders,' said Galleia.

'You can say that again.'

Galleia looked at her in surprise. 'Why should I wish to? Lakis, take the Lady – Jojogrant –'

'It's just Jo actually,' interrupted Jo.

'Your pardon. Take the Lady Jo to my maids and see that she is given attire more fitting for a lady of the court.'

'Yes, Lady,' said Lakis obediently.

'And hurry back, Lakis, I have an errand for you.'

'Yes, Lady.' Lakis led Jo from the room.

Hippias said mockingly. 'Are there no errands for me to run? A flower, perhaps, a token of undying love for some lordling of the Court? But no, it would be dead before it was delivered.'

'You are impertinent, Hippias. Remember, I am Galleia, Queen of Atlantis, daughter of Kings and wife to King Dalios. Have a care!'

Hippias bowed his head. 'Your pardon, I took you for another. I knew a Galleia once, you see, a woman not the Queen. A sweet and loving lady, I took you for her. Please, do forgive me.'

Galleia bit her lip in anger, then turned and sat down, her back to Hippias. 'You may leave me now.'

Hippias bowed. 'I thank you, Lady.'

He strode from the room just as Lakis reappeared.

Galleia summoned her. 'Lakis, come here at once. Come closer.'

'Lady?'

'Go to the Master. Go to him quietly when no-one is near and say to him one word.'

'What word, Lady?'

'Kronos.'

'Kronos!' said Dalios unhappily. 'Kronos . . . Kronos . . . Kronos . . . I am the last alive who *knows,* who remembers with a fear to twist the guts. And these fools would have me bring him back.'

The Doctor said, 'But why didn't you destroy the Crystal?'

'We tried,' said Dalios sadly. 'We merely split the smaller crystal from it. It cannot be destroyed.'

'Of course, just like the TARDIS,' muttered the Doctor. He looked up. 'The Great Crystal has its being outside time. Only its appearance is here.'

'You are a philosopher, friend Doctor.'

'If wisdom is to seek the truth, I am.'

'Then help me, Doctor,' pleaded Dalios. 'Help me to find a way to stop this evil man. Help me to save Atlantis from destruction.'

The Master marched arrogantly into the Queen's chamber and stared about him. 'Where is she?'

'If you will please wait, Lord,' begged Lakis.

He was already turning away. 'The Master waits

for no-one. I shall return when the Queen is ready to speak to me.'

Galleia appeared in the inner doorway. She looked at the Master with the sleepy, wide-eyed stare of the cat in her arms. 'Please stay,' she said calmly. She put down the cat, which strolled lazily from the room, and sat on the couch. 'Lakis, serve wine for this Lord – and then go. See to the needs of our other guest.'

With trembling hands, Lakis poured wine and hurried thankfully away.

The Master sat on the couch, close to the Queen, and gazed in her eyes. In his deep, mellow voice he said, 'You are beautiful, O Queen!'

Galleia purred, like one of her own cats.

Lakis reached the next room just as Jo appeared in her new court dress, a simple Grecian-style gown. With her hair redressed in Atlantean-style ringlets, Jo looked even more attractive, and certainly more sophisticated, than usual.

She surveyed herself in the mirror with approval. 'Wow, what a fantastic dress! Do you reckon it'll get mum's approval?'

Lakis stared at her. 'Mum? Do you mean Queen Galleia?'

'That's right. Let's go and give her a preview.'

Lakis held her back. 'No, I'm sorry. She does not wish to be disturbed, The Lord Master is with her. They speak of the sacred mysteries.'

'Kronos and all that?'

'It is forbidden –' began Lakis.

'But that *is* what they're on about?'

'Yes.'

'Right,' said Jo determinedly, and headed for the connecting door.

Again Lakis stopped her. 'No! You mustn't go in. You mustn't!'

'Listen,' said Jo reassuringly. 'I'll be as quiet as – do you have mice here?'

Lakis nodded.

'I'll be as quiet as an Atlantean mouse!'

Gently she opened the door, and stood listening to the low voices that came from the couch in the centre of the room.

The Master and Queen Galleia were rapidly coming to an understanding.

'You are a man who knows what he wants, Lord Master.'

'And takes it,' said the Master arrogantly.

'You want the Crystal.'

'And I am going to have it.'

'Not without my consent.' There was an edge to Galleia's voice.

The Master said smoothly. 'Of course not. Yet I am confident that you will give it.'

It would have been simple enough for the Master to hypnotise Queen Galleia. Already under his influence she would have shown none of the resistance of Dalios. But somehow it was more amusing, and more satisfying to his enormous vanity, to dominate her by the sheer power of his personality.

'Why should I help you?' asked Galleia.

'For the sake of Atlantis, Lady. Would you not see her restored to her former glory – rich, powerful, mighty amongst the nations of the world? Who would not wish to be ruler of such a mighty country?'

Galleia considered this alluring prospect – and

went straight to the point. 'No harm must come to Dalios.' In her way she loved the old man, though more as a father than a husband.

'Why should it? He will reign for many long years, the beloved ruler of a happy and prosperous people.'

'And you –'

The Master sighed theatrically. 'Purely because of Lord Dalios's great age, it might be well if he were relieved of the more onerous burdens of kingship. The reins of power should be in stronger hands – such as yours, Lady Queen.'

He placed a black gloved hand over Galleia's jewelled fingers. After a moment, she covered his hand with her other one. 'And yours?'

'It would be my pleasure to serve you . . . Of course, when the end comes for Lord Dalios, as it must come for all men, then perhaps . . .' Again the Master sighed.

The conquest of Galleia was complete. 'The Crystal shall be yours,' she breathed . . .

. . . but not so quietly that the listening Jo didn't hear. She strained her ears to catch the Master's next words. 'And where is the Great Crystal?'

'Deep in the earth, beneath the temple. Dalios has a key – and so has Krasis.'

'Then Krasis shall take me there!'

'I wish it were as simple as that. No-one can get near, save Dalios himself. It is certain death, even to try.'

'But what is the danger?'

'The Guardian!'

'Yes, but who is this Guardian?' asked the Doctor.

King Dalios sighed. 'A beast, a man, you may take your choice. Once he was my good friend, a fellow Councillor. He was a great athlete, and just as I longed for the wisdom the years alone can bring, he craved great strength, the strength of the bull, and a long life in which to use it.'

'A harmless enough ambition, I would have thought!'

'And so should I,' said Dalios sadly. 'And Kronos granted his wish, as he granted mine. But in his sport, Kronos gave my friend not only the strength but the head of a bull. And so he has remained, these past five hundred years and more.'

The Doctor recognised the origin of an old legend. 'The Minotaur,' he whispered. 'I'm sorry, go on!'

'There is little more to tell. He determined that no-one else should suffer as he has suffered. Until the last day of his life, for which he longs so ardently, he will guard the Crystal. No-one can approach it. Even to try is certain death!'

'Well, Krasis,' said the Master mockingly. 'Would you like to volunteer?'

'No, Lord no!' sobbed Krasis. He had been summoned by the Queen for an urgent conference.

Queen Galleia said thoughtfully, 'Then perhaps we should send someone down who is skilled with the sword. One who longs with all his heart to seize the Crystal – and whose death would be of little account.'

'Who, Lady?' asked Krasis.

'One who will listen to you, Krasis. The Lord Hippias of course.'

Jo, who was still eavesdropping on the conversation, heard a horrified gasp from behind her and slipped back into the anteroom.

Lakis was frantic with fear. 'What can we do? What can we do?'

'Tell the Doctor, that's what. Take me to the King!'

'I dare not, Lady Jo.'

'Would you rather let this Hippias face the creature?'

Lakis shook her head. 'Quickly then.'

They slipped away.

Lakis led Jo down endless corridors until they came to the entrance to the King's quarters. A trident-bearing guard barred their way. 'Halt!'

'Take us to the King,' demanded Jo.

Crito, the Chief Councillor, stepped from the shadows 'The King is not to be disturbed.'

'But it's a matter of life and death,' protested Jo.

Crito smiled. 'It could be indeed – yours!'

Jo was about to argue further, when Lakis pulled her aside.

'Be careful – the Lord Crito is no friend to Hippias.'

'Oh, for Pete's sake,' said Jo impatiently. These palace politics were a great nuisance, she thought. Suddenly Lakis pulled her deeper into the shadows.

Hippias and Krasis were coming along the corridor, deep in conversation. Hippias was carrying a sword.

'They must be going for the Crystal,' whispered Jo. 'I'll follow them. You try to get in to tell the Doctor and the King what's happening.' Gathering up her long skirts, Jo hurried away.

She followed the two men along the gloomy torch-lit corridors of the palace, and across to the adjoining temple. She followed them through the secret door

126

behind the altar of Poseidon, and through the maze of tunnels below the temple. The winding steps and tunnels led lower, lower, until the two men rounded a bend and disappeared from view.

Jo hurried on, rounded the bend herself, and found herself at the top of a steep flight of steps. At the bottom she saw Hippias, sword in hand, stepping through a door set into the rock wall. She heard an angry bellow.

'No, Hippias!' called Jo. She rushed down the steps to call him back. But as she reached the bottom, Krasis appeared from the shadows and thrust her through the still-open door, slamming it closed behind her.

She found herself in a great stone cavern, dimly lit by a flickering torch set into a wall bracket, its roof supported by many huge pillars. Hippias was nowhere in sight, although his abandoned sword lay close to the door. She turned back and hammered on the door.

'Let me out,' she screamed. 'Let me out!'

A shattering roar came from behind her.

Jo turned and saw a terrifying creature stalking towards her out of the shadows. The body was that of a huge, immensely muscular man, wearing a leather loin-cloth.

The head was that of a bull.

The creature threw back its head, gave a savage roar, and charged towards her.

14

The Captives

Lakis was by nature a timid girl, but in this emergency she found unexpected reserves of courage. Waiting for a moment when Crito was talking to the guards, she dodged around them and dashed into the royal chamber.

Dalios was still talking to the tall white-haired stranger. The two men looked up surprised as she skidded to a halt. 'Lord King, forgive me! Lord Hippias and the High Priest have gone to the lair of the Guardian, followed by the Lady Jo.'

The Doctor leaped to his feet. 'What? Lord King, tell me how to reach them!'

The many pillars supporting the chamber roof were what saved Jo's life. The Minotaur moved quickly, but it was relatively clumsy, and the smaller Jo was much more agile.

Time after time, the creature charged with a savage roar. Time after time it was left baffled, swinging its great head to and fro as Jo ducked into hiding behind a pillar.

Unfortunately the space before the door was clear. Even if the door hadn't been locked, there was no chance of reaching it without being seen.

Jo flattened herself behind a pillar, gasping for

breath. She was getting very tired. The Minotaur however, seemed as fresh as ever. And if Jo once started to slow down . . .

It was searching behind the pillars now, looking for her. As the snuffling of its breath came closer, Jo prepared for another spring – and wondered how many more she could manage . . .

The Doctor came haring into the temple – and found his way barred by Krasis and a temple guard.

'Seize this intruder,' screamed Krasis.

The guard raised his trident-spear, but the Doctor was in no mood for interruptions.

Wrenching the spear from the guard's grip he swung it round horizontally and thrust it forward under the chins of both Krasis and the guard, so that they were held back against the wall on tiptoe. Maintaining his grip with one hand, the Doctor snatched the key from Krasis's belt with the other.

'Sorry to hold you up like this, Krasis, but I need that key!'

Snapping the trident across his knee the Doctor disappeared through the secret door, leaving Krasis and the guard gasping for breath behind him.

Somehow Jo had been driven away from the main door, into a network of tunnels and passages on the far side of the hall. All the time she could hear the bellowing of the Minotaur as it pounded after her. The creature was hunting her, she realised, driving her towards the heart of its maze.

The Doctor came through the door and looked around the underground hall.

'Jo!' he called. 'Jo, where are you?'

From the far side of the hall he heard a faint cry of, 'Doctor!' It was followed by a distant bellow.

The Doctor began running towards the sound.

The Minotaur's plan had succeeded at last.

Jo was trapped in a blind alley at the end of which was a shining mirror set into the wall. The Minotaur lowered its head and bellowed, ready to charge.

Exhausted, Jo awaited her fate.

Suddenly Hippias appeared behind the Minotaur. He had been lost in the maze all this time, tracking Jo and the Minotaur by the sound of the creature's bellowing.

Faced by the terrifying sight of the Minotaur when he had first come through the door, Hippias's nerve had broken. Throwing down his sword, he had fled into the darkness of the maze.

Now, seeing Jo in danger, his courage returned. 'Stay back!' he shouted. The creature whirled round. Snatching a blazing torch from its bracket on the wall, Hippias hurled it at the creature's head – and missed.

The crushing force of the Minotaur's charge sent him to the ground. Scrambling to his feet, Hippias dodged behind the monster, leaping upon its back in a vain attempt to throttle it . . .

Reaching up and seizing him in its great hands, the Minotaur held Hippias high above its head. It stalked towards the cowering Jo at the end of the cul-de-sac and hurled the struggling body of Hippias at her. Jo leaped aside. Hippias crashed into the mirror, shattering it into fragments and exposing the wall beyond. He fell to the ground and lay still.

Swinging round on Jo, the Minotaur prepared to

charge again – when there came another distraction. This time it was a shout of 'Toro! Ah, Toro!'

It was the Doctor. He had slipped off his cloak and now he was holding it so the red silk lining faced the Minotaur, and he was giving the traditional cry of the Spanish bullfighter: 'Toro! Hey, Toro!'

The Minotaur charged. The Doctor flicked the cape aside and the Minotaur shot past, missing him by inches.

As quick as any fighting bull in the arena, the Minotaur spun round and charged again. Once again the Doctor flicked the cape, and this time as the creature charged past he dealt it a savage chopping blow with his fist on the back of its bull-neck. The Minotaur stumbled and fell to its knees. It shook its head and bellowed dismally.

The Doctor turned and ran to Jo, who was watching terrified, pressed against a stone wall. 'Are you all right, Jo?'

'Just about! Are you all –' Jo broke off to shout a warning: 'Look out, Doctor!'

The Minotaur had lumbered to its feet and was charging straight towards him. The Doctor leaped aside, taking Jo with him.

The Minotaur slammed into the stone wall with such incredible force that it smashed a hole in the wall's centre section, bringing down not only the wall but part of the ceiling as well. There was a rumble of falling stone and the monster vanished beneath a pile of shattered masonry.

Jo turned and saw the shattered body of Hippias. 'He saved my life, Doctor.'

The Doctor made a quick examination. 'I'm afraid he's dead, Jo.'

The Doctor saw a gleam of light beyond the shattered wall and peered into the chamber beyond. 'It's the Crystal Jo. The Crystal of Kronos!'

They clambered through the gap, and seconds later they were standing before a circular stone altar on top of which reposed a huge glowing crystal, a larger version of the one used in the TOMTIT machine.

The Doctor pointed. 'There you are, Jo, that's what all the fuss is about.'

'It's beautiful – but at the same time it's horrible. It gives me a funny feeling.'

'Cheer up, Jo. Now we've got the Crystal, the Master's little game is at an end.

'Not quite,' said a voice behind them.

They turned and saw Krasis and several temple guards. They must have reached the chamber by its proper entrance, thought the Doctor.

'The game is just beginning,' said Krasis triumphantly. 'A pity that you will not live to see the end.'

'That's where you're mistaken, Krasis,' said the Doctor firmly. 'And if you value your own life you will take me to see the King!'

The Doctor stared indignantly at the black clad-figure in Dalios's chair. 'I asked to see the King!'

The Master smiled and spread his hands. 'But I *am* the King, Doctor – for all practical purposes. Didn't Krasis tell you? A jolly fellow, our Krasis. He loves a joke!'

The Doctor glared at Krasis's malignant face. 'Does he really?'

The Master settled himself comfortably in Dalios's chair. 'A complete success, our little palace revolution.'

'What's happened to King Dalios?'

'Why, nothing, Doctor.'

Queen Galleia entered. The Master rose and bowed.

The Doctor gave her a quick glance. 'So Dalios is still alive?'

'Of course,' said the Master. 'Alive and treated honourably.'

Galleia came majestically towards them. 'Even though Dalios is an old man, the King is still the King.'

The Master gestured towards the Doctor and Jo. 'And now it seems I must thank you both!'

'What for?' asked Jo.

'Why for giving me the Great Crystal, Miss Grant.'

The Doctor glared indignantly at him. 'You don't mean to say you still intend to go ahead with this stupid plan?'

'I most certainly do, Doctor. And tomorrow, you will both receive a suitable reward – an introduction to the mighty Kronos. This time there will be no mistakes!'

'I wouldn't count on that,' said the Doctor angrily.

The Master snapped his fingers. 'Take them away!'

The Doctor and Jo were led away.

The Master turned to Galleia. 'You seem discontented, my love. You would question my decision?'

'Perhaps. It depends what you mean to do.'

'You must learn to obey, my love. To do my will. To carry out my commands like a soldier.'

Galleia's eyes blazed angrily. 'Or like a servant girl? You must learn, *my love,* that Galleia is a Queen.' She strode disdainfully away.

The Master stroked his beard and sighed. It looked as if their association was to be a short-lived one after all.

The Doctor and Jo were both chained to the wall in the same bare stone cell. They were reacting to imprisonment very differently.

The Doctor was leaning against the wall in the most comfortable position he could manage – which wasn't very comfortable at all. Jo, meanwhile, was wrestling frantically with her chains.

'Any luck?' asked the Doctor.

She shook her head. 'They didn't include Atlantean chains in my UNIT escapology lessons. It's no good.'

The Doctor nodded consolingly. He had given their chains a thorough inspection on their arrival, and decided that, since he had left his sonic screwdriver in the laboratory, there was nothing to be done.

Moreover, he was in a strangely philosophical mood, as if he had only to bide his time and somehow things would work out. A strange feeling for someone chained to a dungeon wall and condemned to annihilation . . .

Jo felt no such optimism. 'Doctor, what are we going to do?'

'We'll just have to play it by ear.'

'What will happen if the Master wins?'

'The whole of creation is very delicately balanced in cosmic terms, Jo,' said the Doctor thoughtfully. 'If the Master opens the floodgates of Kronos's power, all order and all structure will be swept away and nothing will be left but chaos.'

'It makes everything seem so – pointless.'

The Doctor smiled at her. 'I felt like that once, when I was young. It was the blackest day of my life.'

Jo looked curiously at him. It was very seldom that the Doctor embarked upon any kind of personal reminiscence. 'Why was that?'

'Ah well, that's another story. I'll tell you about it one day. The point is, that day was not only my blackest, it was also my best.'

'What do you mean?'

His eyes gazing into the past, the Doctor began to speak. 'When I was a little boy we used to live in a house that was perched halfway up the top of a mountain. Above our house near the mountain peak, there sat under a tree an old man. A hermit, a monk . . . He'd lived under this tree for half his lifetime, so they said, and had learnt the secret of life. So, when my black day came, I went and asked him to help me.'

'And he told you the secret?'

The Doctor nodded.

'Well, what was it?'

'I'm coming to that, Jo, in my own time. I'll never forget what it was like up there . . . All bleak and cold, just a few bare rocks with some weeds sprouting from them and some pathetic little patches of sludgy snow. It was just grey. Grey, grey, grey . . . The tree the old man sat under was ancient and twisted, and the old man himself – he was as brittle and as dry as a leaf in the Autumn.'

'But what did he *say*?'

'Nothing,' said the Doctor simply. 'Not a word. He just sat there, expressionless, while I poured out my troubles. I was too unhappy even for tears, I remember. When I'd finished, he lifted a skeleton hand and he pointed. Do you know what he pointed at?'

Jo shook her head.

'A flower,' said the Doctor softly. 'One of those little weeds. Just like a daisy it was. I looked at it for a moment, and suddenly I saw it through his eyes. It was simply glowing with life like a perfectly cut jewel, and the colours were deeper and richer than you could possibly imagine. It was the *daisiest* daisy I'd ever seen.'

'And that was the secret of life? A daisy?' She laughed. 'Honestly, Doctor!'

The Doctor smiled. 'Yes, I laughed too! Later, I got up and ran down that mountain and I found that the rocks weren't grey at all. They were red and brown and purple and gold. And those pathetic little patches of sludgy snow were shining white in the sunlight!'

The Doctor was silent for a moment or two. Then he said, 'Are you still frightened, Jo?'

'Not as much as I was.'

'I'm sorry I brought you here.'

'I'm not.'

'Thank you,' said the Doctor quietly.

Suddenly the cell door crashed open and a guard thrust Dalios into the cell. 'Inside, old man.'

Dalios made a quavering attempt to assert his dignity. 'I demand to be taken to the Queen.'

'You'll do as you're told,' said the guard indifferently, shoving him back.

Dalios was outraged. 'How dare you lay your hands on me? I *shall* see the Queen. Out of my way, slave.'

He tried to thrust the guard aside, and the guard, almost by reflex, swung the butt of his trident. Dalios staggered back beneath the blow and collapsed close to the Doctor and Jo. The guard moved away, slamming and locking the cell door.

By stretching their chains, the Doctor and Jo could just reach Dalios. The Doctor lifted the old man's head. 'Dalios!'

The old man had been badly beaten. The guard's blow was the last of many. His eyes fluttered. 'Who would have thought it – my sweet Queen . . .'

'Is the Master responsible for this?'

'Aye. He sought to bend me to his will . . . But it is no matter. Come closer . . . I have so little time . . .'

'What is it?' asked the Doctor gently.

Dalios's voice was faint. 'Atlantis is doomed. I tell you the vision of a dying man. You are a true philosopher, friend Doctor. The world must be saved . . . and you are the one to save it.' Dalios's head fell back, and his eyes closed.

'Don't worry, Dalios. We shan't fail you,' said the Doctor fiercely.

But Dalios could no longer hear him.

15

The Return of Kronos

Once again the Council of Atlantis was assembled in the great hall of the temple.

Once again, two figures sat on the throne-like seats on the raised stone. Just as before, one was Queen Galleia. But this time, the other was the Master.

Crito rapped on the floor with his staff of office. 'Silence. The Lady Galleia, Queen of Atlantis, speaks!'

Galleia rose. 'Brethren of the Council – my faithful few.' (This was a reference to the fact that over half the council had mysteriously disappeared.) In a ringing voice she continued: 'Our troubles are now at an end. No longer shall we fret beneath an old, defeated King. I present to you his Holiness, the Most Venerable Lord Master.'

The Master rose, looking about him with arrogant self-satisfaction. Everything was prepared.

In front of his own TARDIS stood the TOMTIT apparatus on a specially prepared altar, this time with the large crystal attached. Nearby sat the Doctor, a bound and guarded prisoner, with Jo at his side, unbound, and Krasis standing guard over her.

The Doctor looked up at the Master, standing on

the dais beside Galleia. 'Getting a bit above yourself, aren't you?'

'Silence!' screamed Krasis.

The Master began to speak. 'Greetings to you, my brothers. I grieve to see the Council so small. Yes I rejoice that you, the few who put me here have come to claim your just reward. You shall see the Mighty One himself, Kronos the Most Terrible.'

There was a murmur of awe from the little crowd.

The Master held up his hand, 'Krasis, the High Priest, will assist me. Krasis, beware!'

Krasis went to the TOMTIT console and operated the few simple controls that the Master had shown him the night before. There was a hum of power and the crowd drew back.

The Doctor raised his voice. 'What's happened to the rest of the Council? Are they alive?'

The Master looked down. 'The point is academic, Doctor. In another minute or so it will be of no further interest to you.'

'Satisfy my curiosity then. Are they indeed alive? Or are they dead – like King Dalios?'

'Dalios is unharmed,' said Galleia quickly.

'The King is dead, Madam,' said the Doctor.

'It's true,' said Jo. 'We were there in the cell with him when he died.'

Galleia stared at her. 'You were there? You saw him die?' She turned to the Master. 'Is this true?'

The Master made no answer.

Galleia rose and approached him. 'Is this true? Is the Lord Dalios, the King, no longer alive? *Answer me*!'

'He is dead,' said the Master indifferently.

'You were responsible for his death,' shouted the Doctor.

139

Galleia looked accusingly at the Master. 'But you promised me . . .'

'I promised you power,' said the Master impatiently. 'And you shall have it. Power to realise your most ambitious dreams.'

Galleia was not listening. 'You promised he should not be harmed.'

The Master shrugged. 'He was an old man – and stubborn.'

Galleia aimed a savage blow at his face, but he swept her hand aside and she fell back. She turned to the temple guards. 'Seize this man!'

As the guards began closing in on the Master, he called out: 'Krasis! The switch!'

'No! Stop him!' shouted the Doctor.

But it was too late.

Krasis threw the power switch and the Crystal blazed into fiery life.

The towering winged figure of Kronos seemed to burst from the heart of the Great Crystal, filling the temple with the beat of his mighty wings.

To his horror, the Doctor saw that in this manifestation Kronos was larger and more uncontrollable than ever – a fact that the Master failed to realise.

'I, the Master, welcome you Kronos,' he bellowed. 'I bid you to do my will.'

Kronos began swirling to and fro, swinging back and forth across the temple, sending the crowd fleeing in terror.

'Do you hear me, Kronos?' shouted the Master. He pointed to the Doctor. 'I command you to destroy that man!'

Kronos ignored him. Already the temple was beginning to shake, great stone blocks falling from the walls and ceiling. The air was filled with dust and the screams of the wounded and dying. There would be death and destruction in plenty in Atlantis that day, but it would be at the whim of Kronos alone.

'He'll never obey you,' shouted the Doctor. 'Don't you understand what you've done? He's uncontrollable.'

Even now the Master refused to admit defeat. 'I need more power,' he muttered. 'All the power in the Universe is waiting for me – in another time, another place.'

He ran to the TOMTIT apparatus and wrenched free the Great Crystal.

'Stop him,' shouted the Doctor. 'He mustn't get away!'

But no-one dared approach the Master or the Crystal.

No-one but Jo Grant.

Darting from her place at the Doctor's side Jo ran to the Master, reaching him just as the Crystal came free. In a desperate attempt to slow the Master down, she leaped upon his back.

It had not the slightest effect. The Master ran for his TARDIS clutching the Crystal, and carrying Jo Grant, who hung on like a child playing piggy-back.

To the Doctor's dismay, Jo, the Master and the Crystal all disappeared inside the Master's TARDIS – which promptly dematerialised.

The Doctor called to Galleia. 'Your Majesty, set me free!'

Galleia snatched a sword from the body of a fallen guard and began severing the Doctor's bonds. 'You and Dalios were right, Doctor,' she sobbed. 'I was wrong. Go quickly! It is too late now to save my people.'

The Doctor sprinted to his TARDIS and vanished inside. Moments later, the TARDIS too disappeared.

Queen Galleia stood alone in the centre of the temple. Above her Kronos roared to and fro, bringing down the roof and walls with his fiery passage, in an orgy of destruction.

The destruction would not come to an end until the entire city of Atlantis had been destroyed.

The Master was handcuffing Jo to the console of his TARDIS. (Just like the Master to have built-in fittings for prisoners, thought Jo.)

'There, Miss Grant. I think we've seen the last of the Doctor. Buried for all time under the ruins of Atlantis. You know, I'm going to miss him!'

'He's not finished,' said Jo stubbornly. 'I know it.'

'Nonsense, my dear. Of course he is.'

'You're the one who's finished,' said Jo. 'Do you really think that – thing out there will ever let you control it?'

'I do so already. He came at my call. You saw that for yourself.'

'Like a tiger comes when it hears a lamb bleating,' said Jo scornfully.

The Master smiled. 'Nicely put, my dear. Worthy of the late lamented Doctor himself.' He laughed exultantly. 'You know, I could kick myself for not having polished him off long ago.' He strolled over to the Great Crystal, which rested on a table by the console. 'Just think of the future. Dominion over all time and all space. Absolute power forever, and no Doctor to ruin things for me.'

'Don't worry, Jo,' said the Doctor's cheerful voice. 'I'll soon sort him out for you.'

Jo looked up and saw the Doctor's face beaming at her from the scanner screen. 'Doctor!'

The Master laughed, slightly bitterly this time. 'Really, Doctor, you must be as indestructible as that wretched TARDIS of yours! And how exactly do you propose to sort me out?'

'By making you see reason – and by making you destroy that Crystal.'

'And why should I do that? I have my TARDIS, I have Kronos, and I have Miss Grant. Now, my reason tells me that I hold all the cards.'

'But there's one you've forgotten,' said the Doctor calmly. 'I hold the trump card. I can stop you whenever I please.'

For a moment the Master looked worried, then he laughed. 'You're bluffing, Doctor.'

'Am I? What about Time Ram?'

'Time Ram,' said the Master uneasily. 'You couldn't do it in that pathetic old crock of yours. You'd never be able to lock on to my TARDIS.'

'I've already done it. The two TARDISes are operating on the same frequency, and our controls are locked together. See for yourself.'

To his horror the Master saw the needle on a particular dial creeping remorselessly towards the danger zone. 'You know what'll happen if that control goes over the safety limit, don't you? Tell him, Jo.'

A little unsteadily Jo said, 'The two TARDISes will occupy precisely the same space and the same time and that means –'

The Master slammed a fist down on the console. 'I know what it means!'

'Do you?' said the Doctor remorselessly.

The word seemed forced from the Master's lips. 'Oblivion.'

'Top of the class,' said the Doctor. 'Utter destruction. For you, the TARDIS, the Crystal.'

'And for you and your TARDIS and Miss Grant, Doctor,' snarled the Master.

'Of course. But Kronos will be free again, and the Universe saved.'

Defiantly the Master straightened up. 'Very well. Go ahead. Time Ram!'

'You don't mean it,' whispered Jo.

'Why should I dance to the Doctor's tune like a performing poodle. If you want to stop me, Doctor – *try*!'

'Very well,' said the Doctor quietly. 'Goodbye, Jo.'

'Goodbye, Doctor.'

The needle on the Master's dial crept closer and closer to the danger zone. It was hovering on the edge of it when it quivered and stopped.

The Master looked up at the screen. 'Well, Doctor, why have you stopped?'

'To give you one last chance.'

'Rubbish. You can't bring yourself to destroy Miss Grant. Admit it. It's that fatal weakness of yours, Doctor. Pity. Compassion.'

The Master pronounced the words like curses. 'For a moment, you almost had me believing you.'

'Don't think about me, Doctor,' called Jo. 'Think about the millions who will die. The millions who will never be born. Do it, Doctor, quickly!'

The Doctor hesitated. 'There may be another way, Jo.'

'Of course there is,' shouted the Master. 'The way to unimaginable glory.'

Jo saw that she could just reach the control on the Master's console – the equivalent control to the one the Doctor was using on his own. If she pulled that lever, it would mean Time Ram. Suddenly Jo Grant saw that she had to make the sacrifice that the Doctor would never make himself.

'Goodbye, Doctor!' She lunged forward and pulled the lever.

The needle slipped into the red zone.

Somewhere in space-time two TARDISes merged and disappeared. And for Jo Grant everything vanished in a ball of fiery white light.

Jo awoke to find herself, lying on the floor of the Master's TARDIS. Mysteriously, she had been freed from her handcuffs. Close by was the Master, stretched out unconscious.

Jo cautiously got to her feet, and made for the door. She opened it upon nothingness. Not land or sea or space – just nothingness.

Suspended in the nothingness, quite close, was the Doctor's TARDIS.

Jo stepped out into the void, walked carefully across to the police box and went inside.

The Doctor lay unconscious on the floor of the control room. Jo knelt beside him and shook him gently. 'Doctor. Wake up!'

He opened his eyes and blinked at her. 'Jo! Are you all right?'

'Oh yes,' said Jo, matter of factly. 'I'm dead, of course, but I'm all right.'

The Doctor got up. 'What on Earth are you talking about, Jo? You're no more dead than I am.'

'Yes, but that's it. I mean, that's what I *mean*. You're dead too – and so's the Master.'

'And I suppose we're in Heaven?'

Jo shrugged. 'Must be. Or somewhere. Come and have a look.'

She led the way to the still open door, and stepped out into the void. Cautiously the Doctor followed.

She turned to him, gesturing around the vast nothingness. 'Fantastic, isn't it?'

'Fascinating,' said the Doctor dryly. 'Though somehow I don't think we're in Heaven.'

'Well, where are we then?'

'That's just it,' admitted the Doctor. 'I don't know myself. You shouldn't have put us into Time Ram, Jo. Besides, I was just on the point of doing it myself.'

'Really?'

'Now look here, Jo –' He broke off, and smiled ruefully. 'No, not really.'

A sort of vast throat-clearing took place behind them and they turned to see a colossal face. It was a female face, beautiful and exotic, so large that they could have crawled upon the shapely nose like flies.

The Doctor was in a state where he felt nothing could surprise him. 'Greetings,' he said calmly.

The face spoke in a clear bell-like voice that reverberated everywhere. 'Your courtesy is always so punctilious, Doctor!'

'You know me?'

'Of old.'

'Do please forgive me, but I can't seem to place you.'

'I am Kronos,' said the face.

'You!' said Jo in amazement. 'But – you're a girl.'

'Shapes mean nothing.'

'But you were a raging monster before,' persisted Jo. 'An evil destroyer.'

'I can be all things,' said the voice. 'A destroyer, a healer, a creator. I am beyond good and evil as you know it.'

'Where exactly are we?' asked the Doctor.

'On the boundary of your reality and mine. You brought yourselves here.'

'With the Time Ram?'

'At the moment of impact I was released. That saved you . . . and took you here, to the threshold of being.'

The Doctor nodded. 'I see. So what happens now?'

'I owe you a debt of gratitude that nothing could repay. What would you wish?'

It was Jo who answered. 'To go back home.'

'In the TARDIS,' added the Doctor.

'You shall.'

'What about the Master?' asked Jo curiously.

'He will stay here.'

'What will happen to him?'

'Torment,' said the face sweetly. 'The pain he has given so freely shall be returned to him in full.'

The Master staggered out from his TARDIS and fell to his knees. 'No,' he screamed. 'Please Doctor, help me. I can't bear it. Please, Doctor, please!'

The Doctor turned back to the great face. 'O mighty Kronos, I ask one more favour of you.'

'Name it.'

'The Master's freedom.'

'He made a prisoner of me!' said the voice angrily.

'I know. But will you allow us to deal with him in our way?'

147

'I do not understand you. But if that is your desire, so let it be.'

The Master rose from his knees and stood facing the Doctor. 'Thank you, Doctor,' he said humbly.

'Don't thank me,' said the Doctor brusquely. 'You're coming back to Earth with us.'

The Master bowed his head, clearly a broken man. 'Yes, of course,' he whispered.

The Doctor stepped back and motioned the Master to enter the TARDIS. The Master walked slowly forward, gave the Doctor a shove that sent him staggering against Jo, spun round and vanished inside his own TARDIS.

'Stop him,' yelled the Doctor, but it was too late.

The Master's TARDIS promptly dematerialised.

'You asked for him to be given his freedom,' said the voice amusedly. 'He has it!'

'Here we go again,' said Jo.

She followed the Doctor into his TARDIS.

Stuart Hyde held out a spoonful of mush to the baby on the laboratory floor. It stared disapprovingly at the spoon and said distinctly, 'No!'

'Come on, Baby Benton,' coaxed Stuart. 'Come on, get it down you!'

Ruth looked up from her work at the console. 'What are you feeding him on now?'

'The remains of my lunchtime sandwiches, mashed up with some cold tea.'

'Well, stop playing mothers and fathers and come and give me a hand here. I think I'm nearly there.'

'What are you trying to do?'

'Well, if I'm on the beam, I should be able to close up the gap in time for good,' She made a last adjustment. 'Right, switch on, Stu.'

'Okay!' Putting down his saucer of improvised baby food, Stuart switched on.

Inside the TARDIS, Jo was saying, 'But why, Doctor? Why did you even ask?'

The Doctor adjusted the controls, and studied the rise and fall of the central column.

'Would you condemn anybody to an eternity of torment, Jo – even the Master?'

'No, I suppose I wouldn't.'

'Well, neither would I – even if he was responsible for the destruction of Atlantis.'

'It's terrible when you think of it,' said Jo suddenly. 'All those people . . .'

The central column was slowing its rise and fall.

'Jo,' said the Doctor gently, 'we're about to land in England – in your time. That all happened three thousand five hundred years ago . . .'

Once again Stuart was calling out the readings, 'Three five, four zero . . .'

'Increasing power,' said Ruth.

Suddenly another sound drowned out the TOMTIT noise, and a blue police box appeared in a corner of the lab. The Doctor and Jo Grant stepped out.

'Suffering monkeys!' said Stuart faintly.

Ruth was too absorbed in her experiment to notice. 'Now concentrate, Stu!' she called. 'Isolate matrix scanner.'

'Check!' He returned to the power readings. 'Six zero, six five, seven zero . . .'

'See if it's working, Stu!'

Stuart ran to the window and saw that the Brigadier and his men were back to normal. He could hear the Brigadier shouting orders.

Stuart turned back from the window. 'Yes, it is!'

'Good!'

The Doctor studied the power readings. 'It seems to be working a bit too well.'

'It's running away,' shouted Ruth.

'Everybody get down!' shouted Stu. 'It's going to go up!'

They all took cover as the TOMTIT console overloaded and blew up.

In the absence of the crystal however, the result was nothing more serious than a loud bang, a shower of sparks and a lot of smoke.

Ruth got to her feet and studied the shattered console.

'You'll have to start all over again,' said Jo.

Ruth shook her head. 'I couldn't, not without the Professor. Just as well I suppose.'

'Well, it's done its job, thanks to you,' said the Doctor. 'Everything's back to normal.'

As if to prove the Doctor's point, the Brigadier burst into the room, revolver in hand. 'Stand quite still everyone.' He broke off, staring round the somewhat unexpected group. 'Er – where's the Master?'

'A very good question, Brigadier,' said the Doctor.

'Ah, Doctor, glad to see you're back. And you, Miss Grant . . .'

The Brigadier suddenly registered Jo's Atlantean costume. 'Miss Grant, what are you doing in that extraordinary get-up?' Without waiting for a reply the Brigadier went on, 'And where, for heaven's sake, is Sergeant Benton?'

150

Stuart clutched Ruth's arm. 'The baby! We forgot the baby!'

Sergeant Benton arose from behind the TOMTIT console. He had been restored to his full age and size, and he was wearing nothing but a very inadequate improvised nappy, and an embarrassed smile.

He looked around the circle of smiling faces, and said plaintively. 'Would someone please tell me exactly what's been happening around here?'

And that too, thought the Doctor, was a very good question!

DOCTOR WHO

0426114558	**TERRANCE DICKS** **Doctor Who and The** **Abominable Snowmen**	**£1.35**
0426200373	**Doctor Who and The** **Android Invasion**	**£1.25**
0426201086	**Doctor Who and The** **Androids of Tara**	**£1.35**
0426116313	**IAN MARTER** **Doctor Who and The** **Ark in Space**	**£1.35**
0426201043	**TERRANCE DICKS** **Doctor Who and The** **Armageddon Factor**	**£1.50**
0426112954	**Doctor Who and The** **Auton Invasion**	**£1.50**
0426116747	**Doctor Who and The** **Brain of Morbius**	**£1.35**
0426110250	**Doctor Who and The** **Carnival of Monsters**	**£1.35**
042611471X	**MALCOLM HULKE** **Doctor Who and** **The Cave Monsters**	**£1.50**
0426117034	**TERRANCE DICKS** **Doctor Who and The** **Claws of Axos**	**£1.35**
042620123X	**DAVID FISHER** **Doctor Who and The** **Creature from the Pit**	**£1.35**
0426113160	**DAVID WHITAKER** **Doctor Who and The Crusaders**	**£1.50**
0426200616	**BRIAN HAYLES** **Doctor Who and The Curse** **of Peladon**	**£1.50**
0426114639	**GERRY DAVIS** **Doctor Who and The Cybermen**	**£1.50**
0426113322	**BARRY LETTS** **Doctor Who and The Daemons**	**£1.50**

Prices are subject to alteration